F

THE LIO

"*The Lion of Senet* is one of those rare hybrids, an SF plot
compounded with the in-depth characterization of
a good fantasy tale. It is a book that recognizes the old
saw, any sufficiently advanced science is
indistinguishable from magic, and makes good use of
the premise. Jennifer Fallon mines the rich
borderland between fantasy and SF to produce a tale of
deception and ambition in a battle between science and
religion. Well-rounded characters and conflicts that
are ethical as well as adventurous make for
an intriguing read."
—Robin Hobb

"In *The Lion of Senet* Jennifer Fallon has created
a fast-moving and exciting fantasy saga of betrayal and
deceit, peopled by an engaging cast of characters. I
can't wait to see what new twists she will bring
to the plot in Book Two!"
—Sarah Ash, author of *Lord of Snow and Shadows*
and *Prisoner of the Iron Tower*

ALSO BY JENNIFER FALLON
The Lion of Senet

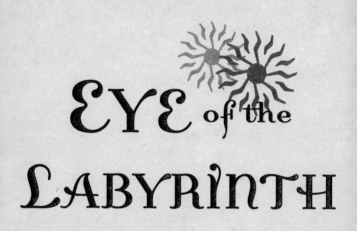

EYE of the
LABYRINTH

BOOK 2
OF THE SECOND SONS TRILOGY

JENNIFER FALLON

BANTAM BOOKS

EYE OF THE LABYRINTH

A Bantam Spectra Book / May 2004

Published by
Bantam Dell
A Division of Random House, Inc.
New York, New York

ISBN 0-553-58669-6

Manufactured in the United States of America
Published simultaneously in Canada

OPM   10   9   8   7   6   5   4

For Amanda,
and as always, Adele Robinson

Acknowledgments

We have some interesting discussions in my house, usually late at night and frequently incomprehensible to the casual observer. We talk, argue and agonize over worlds that don't exist and the people who populate them as if they are real. It is not possible to quantify the value of these discussions when it comes to populating the world of Ranadon.

I wish to thank my son David for the idea of diamond blades and for reminding me that sometimes you have to take a risk to change the world you live in. I cannot thank my daughters enough: Amanda, for being my sounding board and for providing so many bright ideas that it would be impossible to list them all; and TJ, for her constant reading of draft after draft of this series and for reminding me that some stories are too big to tell in a single volume.

I must also thank Peter Jackson for his help in defining the world of Ranadon, and Doug Standish for working out the physics of Ranadon's solar system. If there are mistakes or inconsistencies, they are totally mine, because I kept rearranging the universe to suit my imagination instead of the other way round.

Special thanks must go to the gang from Kabana Kids Klub, especially Ella Sullivan for keeping me on the straight and narrow regarding the geology of Ranadon, and Erika Rockstorm, for her assistance in ironing out some details of this world. I must also thank Ryan Kelly for his advice, his mathematical prowess, and for helping Dirk appear so clever, and Stephanie Sullivan, Analee (Woodie) Wood, Fi Simpson and Alison Dijs for being such economically viable (it sounded better than cheap) proof-readers.

Once again, I have Dave English to thank for helping me look like I know something about ships and sailing, and my good friends John and Toni-Maree Elferink for knowing way too much about the human body and what happens when you do terrible things to it.

I would also like to acknowledge Fiona McLennan and the Phantophiles from the Voyager Online community for their enthusiasm and support, for keeping my spirits up and for providing quite a few of the names that crop up throughout the series.

Last but not least, I wish to thank Lyn Tranter for her help and support, and the staff at ALM for being so wonderfully patient with my eccentricities and Stephanie Smith for giving me so much leeway with the story, when all she wanted was for me to "tidy up the last chapter a bit…"

There was a door to which I found no key:
There was a veil past which I could not see:

THE RUBAIYAT OF OMAR KHAYYÁM
(translation by Edward J. Fitzgerald, 1859)

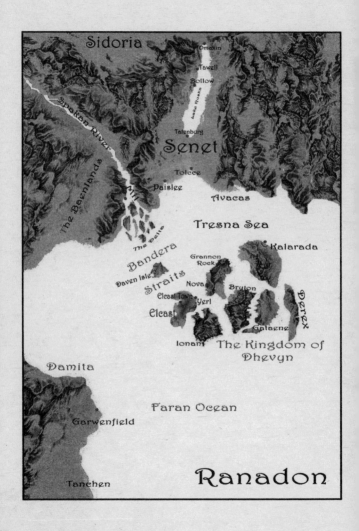

EYE of the
LABYRINTH

PART ONE

A CHANGE OF SEASONS

Chapter 1

The worst thing about funerals was the smiles, Morna Provin thought. The wary, tremulous, uncertain smiles that never reached the eyes. The hesitant, insincere, I-don't-know-what-to-say-to-you smiles that everyone wore when attempting to express their sympathy, while inside they recoiled from this blatant reminder of their own mortality.

Morna walked behind the carriage bearing Wallin's body down toward Elcast harbor feeling numb. The first sun was high in the red-tinted sky. Perspiration stained her black silk gown in dark, unsightly patches under her arms and across her back.

Why do we wear black in this heat? she wondered idly. *Or clothes with so many layers?*

What half-witted fool invented the petticoat?

The Duchess of Elcast wore a dark veil over her face, which provided her with some small measure of privacy, but she knew every eye was on her. Did the onlookers think her dignified in her dry-eyed composure—or cold and unfeeling? She had not allowed herself to cry or even grieve yet; had not allowed herself to contemplate the future. Morna simply refused to think about it.

Rees Provin, her eldest son and the new Duke of Elcast, walked in front of her. Beside him was his bride of three months, Faralan. Rees had assumed his duties as duke with a competence that made her feel proud—and more than a little obsolete. He had organized the funeral, seen to it that his father's bequests were distributed in accordance with his wishes, done everything that needed to be done, efficiently and gracefully, without once asking for her advice or counsel.

Of Morna's missing youngest son, Dirk, there was no sign; no news for the past two years. Morna grieved the loss of her second son more than she could describe. *To lose a child was a pain no parent should bear,* she thought. To lose the son she had borne to Johan Thorn had been exquisitely painful, a fact that undoubtedly gave the Lion of Senet and the High Priestess no end of amusement.

There had been no word of Dirk for so long. There were rumors, of course. Rumors that he had fled to Sidoria or Galina; rumors that he was in the Baenlands. The only thing she knew for certain was that Dirk had supposedly raped a Shadow-dancer, killed Johan Thorn and then fled Avacas a wanted man.

She could not imagine what had driven him to do such terrible things. Antonov had written to her after it happened, positively gloating as he described the events that had forced Dirk to flee.

What did you do to him, Anton? What evil did you infect my son with that he would turn from the intelligent, thoughtful boy I loved into a murderer and rapist in a few short months? She had thought about trying to get a message to Dirk, but she had no idea where to find him. Even if she did, the risk was too great. Dirk would come home one day, she was certain.

Morna ran her eyes over the crowds that lined the streets, half-hoping to see him. She had delayed the funeral for as long as she could, in the hopes that word would reach Dirk, wherever he was. He would not be able to appear openly, she knew, but surely he would not miss this day. Dirk had loved Wallin like a father. For most of his life, he was the only father Dirk had known. Dear, patient, understanding, forgiving Wallin. It was Wallin who had tried to comfort her when she learned about what happened in Avacas. It was Wallin who reminded her that things were not always as they seemed.

And now he was gone, struck down by the very thing that made him what he was—his heart. One minute he was sitting at the High Table, sharing a joke with Rees; the next he could not breathe. He had died in her arms on the floor of the Great Hall of Elcast Keep, and taken a part of her with him when he left.

Morna Provin had not merely lost a husband. Wallin's death meant she no longer enjoyed the protection he provided. She had lived these past twenty years because Wallin had begged for her life, and now he was no longer here to shield her. She glanced over her shoulder as the funeral procession wound down the steep road toward the town. Tovin Rill walked behind them with his youngest son, Lanon. His expression was grave. The Senetian governor had done nothing but express his sympathy so far, but Morna knew she was living on borrowed time. Her fate was inevitable and, in some ways, she thought, not undeserved.

If she felt anything, it was a deep sense of disappointment, mostly in herself.

She had promised to do so much. *But in the end I was no better than you, Johan,* she admitted silently. *For all my noise about freeing Dhevyn, about carrying on the fight, what did I end up doing? Exactly what you did, my love. I hunkered down somewhere safe and let the world pass me by, fooling myself into believing that I was just waiting for the right time, the right circumstances, before I acted.*

Even worse, I gave birth to the son you never knew you had, and then raised him so well, he killed you...

The procession reached Elcast Town, wending its way through streets lined with mourners. Wallin had been a good man, a good duke, and his people genuinely grieved his passing. Some of them threw petals on the carriage as they passed; a few smiled those uncomfortable smiles Morna had come to loathe. She kept her eyes fixed on the back of the carriage. It was easier not to look them in the eye.

When they reached the harbor, the procession came to a halt and the Guard of Honor stepped forward. They lifted Wallin's body from the carriage and bore it down to the water to the mournful beat of a lone drummer. The guard placed Wallin's body on the floating bier that was anchored near the beach. Rees stepped forward, accepting a flaming torch from the Sundancer Brahm Halyn, who waited by the bier. Her son waded into the shallows, hesitated for a moment as he said a silent farewell to his father, and then touched the flame to the pyre.

The wood had been drenched with oil so it caught immediately. Rees waited, to make certain the flames had taken hold, and then, with the help of two of the guard, pushed the bier out into the water. The silence would have been complete, but for the monotonous drumbeat, the distant squawking of gulls and the crackle and hiss of the flames as they consumed Wallin's body.

Morna wished she could cry. She wished her numbness would go away and leave her free to feel the pain. Wallin was a good man. He deserved to be mourned properly.

They watched the bier floating on the harbor, the tall column of thick smoke pouring from the oil-soaked wood. Morna found herself fascinated by the smoke. It was an allegory for her whole life. An angry fire that had burned so brightly for such a short time until eventually, like her dreams and ambitions, her whole existence ended up as nothing more than a smoky haze that dissipated into the red sunlight, gone and forgotten.

"My lady?"

Morna looked down at the beach. Rees was wading back to shore, his expression grim, his shoulders stiffly set.

"My lady?" Tovin Rill repeated from behind her.

So soon, she thought. *They're not even going to wait until the fire is out?*

Rees walked up the beach and stopped in front of her. He was so like Wallin to look at—solid, stocky and dependable—but he did not have Wallin's heart. Or his compassion.

"I'm sorry, Mother."

So Rees had known about this in advance. She heard Tovin Rill snap his fingers behind her, heard the guards moving to surround her.

"Please go quietly, Mother," Rees begged. "Don't make a scene."

Morna lifted the veil and looked around. There were a dozen or more Senetian soldiers waiting to take her into custody. Tovin Rill was looking at her expectantly.

What does he think I'm going to do? Whip out a sword from underneath my skirts and fight my way to freedom?

Young Lanon Rill refused to meet her gaze, obviously uncomfortable with his father's role in this. Faralan was crying silently. The townsfolk looked on in wordless dread, too afraid to object. *Or maybe they don't want to object. Maybe they feel I am finally getting what I deserve.*

"Where are you taking me?"

"To the garrison in town, my lady," Tovin informed her. "You'll be held there until Landfall."

Landfall. *They're going to burn me alive.*

Faralan bit back a sob. "I'll have your things brought down to you, my lady," she promised, as if having her own hairbrush handy would somehow ease the terror of knowing she was to be executed.

"Thank you, Faralan," she replied graciously, and then turned to the captain of Tovin's guard. "Captain Ateway? Could I lean on your arm? I seem to be a little unsteady this evening."

Why aren't I screaming? Why am I not afraid?

Ateway glanced at Tovin Rill, who nodded his permission, and then stepped forward to offer the dowager Duchess of El-cast his arm. "This way, my lady."

She didn't know what to say to him. *What* does *one say when they are being led away to die? Why don't I feel anything?*

So she smiled at him.

She smiled at them all. She smiled at Tovin Rill, who had sat like a vulture for the past three years, waiting for an opportunity like this. She smiled at her son, Rees, who wore Wallin's face, but had inherited nothing of the man. She smiled at her daughter-in-law, Faralan, who was just eighteen and far too inexperienced to assume the responsibilities of a duchess. She smiled at Lanon Rill, who had once been Dirk's friend. She smiled at the townsfolk, who did nothing but stand and watch her being led away.

It was one of those I-don't-know-what-to-say-to-you smiles.

Chapter 2

Kirshov Latanya turned on his bunk with a muffled groan as the Kalarada trumpets announced rising of the second sun. Every muscle he owned was aching, and he was sure his body must be a mass of black and purple bruises. He pulled the pillow over his head, wishing for just a few more moments of blessed sleep before his day began again.

All his life, Kirsh had been looking forward to joining the Queen's Guard. He had dreamed about how proud he would be as he rode at the side of his queen, ready to give his life for her in some noble and glorious cause. Of course, in his dreams, the queen had been some faceless, vague and regal figure—nothing like bossy little Alenor. And he had never had to deal with *politics*. The dream had been his driving force for as long as he could remember.

Reality was proving to be vastly different.

Kirsh had always reasoned that if he kept out of the political games his father delighted in, he could somehow escape their consequences. He didn't really care about the High Priestess Belagren, or the fact that she and the Queen of Dhevyn were frequently at odds. It made no difference to him at all that his father was admired and despised in almost equal measure. The power struggles between the islands of Dhevyn and the mainland kingdom of Senet held no interest for him. What had happened in the past had happened, and there was not a damn thing he could do about it. Kirshov wanted to be a soldier. He wanted to make a name for himself so that he would be something more than a superfluous second son.

Dirk had tried to warn him, on more than one occasion, that he could not maintain such a position for long. He'd had several heated arguments with him when they were both in Avacas, as his cousin from Elcast had tried to awaken his political conscience. Kirsh would have none of it. He was going to join the Queen's Guard. He was not going to be a ruling prince, so it didn't matter what he did. Dirk had called him a fool. He had tried using Alenor as an excuse. Dirk had even given him several very eloquent and logical reasons why, as prince consort, he would at least need to make an effort to understand what was going on around him.

Dirk had been ignorant of the true role of a consort, Kirsh reflected bitterly. As he was frequently reminded by his brothers-in-arms in the Queen's Guard, his role was to stand at stud, nothing more.

It was obvious that they considered him barely up to even that task.

It was two years since Kirsh had presented himself to the Lord Marshal the day he arrived on Kalarada after an awkward reception held in the palace, to (supposedly) welcome him to Dhevyn. The Lord Marshal had droned on, explaining his duties in the Queen's Guard and the training regime he would undergo before formally being given a commission as an officer.

"You'll find things a little different here on Kalarada, your highness," Rove Elan had explained to him. "You'll be just another soldier, I'm afraid. Rank is earned on merit in the Queen's Guard. Your civilian rank, that of the Princess Alenor's consort, or even our future regent, counts for nothing here."

"I know that, my lord. I expect no special consideration because of who I am or who my father is."

Rove Elan smiled faintly. "Oh, you'll find yourself judged on who your father is, your highness, but it may not be the reaction you imagine. This is the *Queen's* Guard. The Queen of Dhevyn, not Senet, and you would do well to remember that."

"I'm not ignorant of the political situation, my lord," he said, which was not entirely accurate, but neither was it actually a lie.

"You're likely to be sorely tested here, until the others have accepted you. You will be judged on how you react to that testing."

"I believe I can look after myself, my lord."

Rove nodded. "From what I hear, you're more than capable of taking care of yourself, but we're not like your father's Palace Guard, full of mercenaries and men seeking fortune and position. Here, you are expected to put your comrades and the protection of the queen above personal glorification."

"And you think I can't do that, sir?" he asked, a little offended.

"I've no idea if you can do it or not, your highness," Rove said with a shrug. "But it will be up to you to prove that you can."

The training grounds of the Queen's Guard were located inside the small keep that guarded the steep access road to the palace. The shadow of Kalarada Palace loomed over the keep, its bulk concealing the sun for a good part of the day and most of the night. Kirsh had found the gloom a little disconcerting at first. He still remembered the first time Rove Elan had led him toward the high paling fence that surrounded the fighting arena in the shadow of the gray stone outer wall.

There were two hundred or more men present, training in pairs with blunted practice swords, thick quarterstaves or short, broad-bladed spears. Kirsh looked around with interest and the professional eye of a man who had been trained to handle weapons as soon as he was old enough to pick up a blade. The men of the Queen's Guard were competent, he decided, but not outstanding. There was not a man he could see that he did not feel he could best.

"So this is Antonov's cub."

They stopped and turned toward the voice. The man who had spoken was about the same height as Kirsh, but of a much heavier build. He had tossed his shirt aside to train, and his well-developed muscles glistened with sweat. He had a head of thick dark hair and a scowl that made Kirsh wonder if he practiced it in the mirror each morning when he shaved. He glanced around to find all activity in the yard had come to a halt. Everyone was staring at him.

"This is our master-at-arms, Dargin Otmar," the Lord

Marshal explained with a nod to the other man. "He's all yours, Dargin. Try not to break him. Or damage that pretty face of his. I believe the Princess Alenor may have a use for him someday."

Kirsh stared after the Lord Marshal as he turned and headed back to the barracks.

"I hear you think you're pretty good," Dargin remarked, wiping his hands on his discarded shirt and throwing it aside.

"I never claimed to be anything of the kind," Kirsh answered, glancing around warily. The other men had abandoned their training and were leaning on the railing of the yard, watching him with interest. He smiled disarmingly. "Perhaps my reputation has preceded me."

"Oh, your reputation has preceded you, Latanya, I can promise you that."

Kirsh grinned and flexed his fingers in anticipation. "What's this then? The traditional let's-beat-the-crap-out-of-the-new-boy ceremony?"

"No," Dargin replied, "it's more along the lines of a let's-make-certain-the-Lion-of-Senet's-cub-knows-his-place ceremony. We've no room in the Queen's Guard for cowards, boy. It's time to see if you're a better man than your father."

Kirsh's grin faded. "I may be sworn to serve the Queen of Dhevyn, sir, but I'll not allow you to insult my father."

"You're not sworn to the queen, boy. That's a privilege you've yet to earn. All you're sworn to do is stand at stud for the crown princess."

The rest of the guard roared with laughter. Kirshov looked around him, hoping to see even the slightest hint that one of these men was on his side. It was an idle hope. Kirsh looked back at Dargin and then nodded and began to unbutton his coat. "Very well. Which one of you is it to be?"

Dargin laughed harshly. "Either you really are as good as you think, or you're a damn fool, boy."

Kirsh threw his jacket over the railing and shrugged his shoulders a few times to loosen them up, before smiling coldly at the master-at-arms. "Let's find out, shall we?"

Dargin's fist was like a sledgehammer. It took Kirsh completely by surprise. He staggered backward, blinking back the

white spots that danced before his eyes, derisive laughter ring-
ing in his ears. His jaw felt as if it had been relocated on the
other side of his head. Kirsh shook his head groggily, quashing
the anger that threatened to make him lose his temper, and
turned to face Dargin. The metallic tang of blood filled his
mouth.

"That wasn't fair. I wasn't ready."

The master-at-arms was standing with his arms crossed,
grinning broadly. "It's fair you want, is it? Is that how they fight
in Senet?"

Dargin moved again, faster than Kirsh would have believed possible for such a big man, although this time Kirsh was
ready for him. He blocked the blow with his right arm and
struck back with his left, scoring a hit in the older man's gut,
hard enough to make him grunt. That small sound was enough
to satisfy Kirsh. Dargin could be hurt. It was just going to take
an awful lot to do it.

"So, the cub has teeth," Dargin laughed, dodging away
from Kirsh's next blow.

Kirsh did not rise to the bait. He was not that easily pro-
voked. Anger led to foolish mistakes, and one mistake with
Dargin could prove fatal. He stood his ground, consciously con-
trolling his breathing, balanced on the balls of his feet, waiting
for Dargin to move again.

The master-at-arms came at him, this time a little more
cautiously. The one hit that Kirsh had managed to land was apparently enough to convince Dargin that he would be in trouble
if he let his guard down. But with that cautious respect came the
knowledge that if he really meant to prove his point, he had to
win, and that the young man he faced was unused to defeat.
Not because he was arrogant or cocky, but because Antonov
had made damn sure his son was more than capable of taking
care of himself.

Dargin feinted to the left and caught Kirsh with a glancing
blow to the side of his head, which he dodged at the last moment. Kirsh struck back, landing a solid punch under Dargin's
jaw, then, with his right leg, he swept the bigger man's feet out
from under him. Dargin landed heavily on his back, but rolled

clear before Kirsh could press home his advantage. He gained his feet quickly, slamming his fist into Kirsh's chest so hard Kirsh could hear his ribs breaking. He staggered backward, but Dargin gave him no respite. He hammered the younger man mercilessly. Kirsh managed to land a few more blows, some of them even making an impression, but every time he breathed in a sharp pain stabbed at his left side. Relentlessly, Dargin pushed him back until he struck Kirsh's broken ribs again. With a cry of sudden pain, Kirsh dropped to his knees. Dargin immediately stepped back, panting heavily. "You're hurt."

Kirsh bit back the sarcastic urge to say: "No? *Really?*" He looked up at the master-at-arms through pain-filled eyes, breathing as shallowly as possible.

"I can keep fighting," he gasped.

Dargin smiled. Kirsh was rather pleased to notice blood dripping from a cut over his eye and a large bruise beginning to manifest itself on his jaw. At least he'd given a good account of himself.

"It's not my intention to kill you, boy."

"You could have fooled me," Kirsh muttered, grimacing as he took a breath that sent a sharp spear of pain through his side.

"You're too used to fighting men who pull their punches. That'll not happen here." Dargin turned to one of the men who had been watching the fight. The spectators' reaction disturbed Kirsh almost as much as Dargin's obvious desire to beat him to a pulp. They had not cheered and chanted the way men did, watching a fracas. They had stayed silent and observed the entire exchange with the detached interest of men watching some sort of scientific experiment. "Alexin, get him to the physician. He'll need to bind up those ribs of his if he's to be of any use to anyone."

Dargin stepped forward and offered Kirsh his hand. Kirsh studied it for a moment warily, before accepting it and letting Dargin pull him to his feet. "You've got guts, boy, I'll grant you that."

Kirsh didn't answer. It hurt too much to speak. He eyed the men surrounding him with caution, but there was no malice in their expressions. They simply thought he needed taking down a peg or two. The realization was something of a shock to him.

"Come on," said Alexin. Kirshov accepted his assistance reluctantly and let himself be led away. He didn't look back, but he could feel every eye in the yard on him. He had no idea what they were thinking.

"You shouldn't feel too bad," Alexin assured him once they were out of earshot. "You didn't shame yourself."

"Does he do that to every new recruit?"

Alexin grinned. "Only the ones he thinks are going to be trouble."

"Did he do it to you?"

"No."

"What makes me so special?"

"Dargin just wants to make sure you know where your loyalties lie."

"By beating the shit out of me?" he asked doubtfully.

Alexin hesitated before answering. "You must know how unpopular the decision was to appoint you Regent of Dhevyn when you marry Alenor."

"I suppose."

"Then get used to it, your highness. If you plan to be regent for long, you're going to have to win these men over."

"I know," he agreed, unhappily. "It's just..."

"What?"

"I don't know. I guess I was hoping all it would take is a few rounds of drinks."

Alexin looked at him, trying to determine if he was joking, then he smiled and shook his head. "I hope you've still got your sense of humor by the end of the week, your highness."

"Could you stop calling me that?"

"What would you prefer to be called?"

"Kirsh. All my friends call me Kirsh."

"Kirsh it is, then."

Kirsh smiled, thinking that when all was said and done, he had made a good start. He had survived Dargin's beating and made the first tentative steps toward friendship with Alexin.

How bad could it get? ...

Chapter 3

Very bad, Kirsh discovered over the next two years.

The beating he had received that day was merely the first of many. Every time he stepped into the training arena, somebody managed to get the better of him. He was not badly trained, he knew that, but the men of the Queen's Guard were superbly trained, and none of them stood to lose his position if Kirsh broke a few bones. He realized now that training with his father's guard was a world away from training every day, all day, with a squad of men whose dedication to their queen was inspired by true loyalty, rather than a fat purse at the end of the week.

If he had a friend at all in the Queen's Guard, it was Alexin Seranov, the second son of the Duke of Grannon Rock. The young man was as universally liked as Kirshov was universally despised. He seemed to hold no prejudice, one way or another, about his Senetian comrade, and he was often the only one who bothered to explain rules that the rest of the guard expected him to have been born knowing. Alexin had bailed him out of trouble on more than one occasion, but Kirsh was never certain if it was because he was a friend, or that Alexin was simply a political creature, who was hedging his bets against the future.

The wake-up trumpets had long since faded when his door flew open. He must have been lying daydreaming for the better part of an hour.

"Hey! Latanya! Wake-up was sounded ages ago! Get that lazy arse of yours out of bed, or you'll be mucking out the stables with your dinner plate for the next week!"

Kirsh groaned again and rolled out of bed. He opened his swollen eyes and glared balefully at the man who had so rudely awakened him. "I heard the call, Tael."

"Then why aren't you on your feet, boy?" Tael was the second son of the Duke of Derex, a small, impoverished, insignificant

island. The Queen's Guard was the only place a second son of
Derex would be in a position to lord it over a Prince of Senet.

Kirsh gained his feet, a little unsteadily, and squared his
shoulders. He was not going to let Tael see how much pain he
was in. "I'm awake. Satisfied?"

Tael laughed sourly. "It'd take more than seeing your ugly
face first thing in the morning to satisfy me, Senet. Rove Elan
wants to see you. You're to report to him before breakfast."

"Did he say why?"

"I'm not his damn secretary, or yours either. You want to
know what the Lord Marshal wants, you're going to have ask
him yourself."

Tael left his room, slamming the door with a thump that
made Kirsh wince. He sank down on the side of his narrow
bunk and, for a moment, let the aches and pains of the past two
years wash over him, wondering if the reason Rove Elan
wanted to see him was that he had finally decided to throw him
out of the guard.

By midmorning, Kirsh had finished his interview with the
Lord Marshal and was on his way to the palace, summoned by
the crown princess. Kirsh had grimaced when Rove delivered
the order, determined to throttle Alenor when he saw her for
reminding his comrades that he was her betrothed and very
soon to be Regent of Dhevyn. He was so sick of the barbs. So
sick of hearing men laugh at him. He had privately sworn to
kill the next man who made a snide remark about "damaging
that pretty face." He was going to tear the heart out of the next
man who made a comment about not harming his reproductive
organs.

As he stewed on it all the way up to the castle, the anger
built in him like a slow boiling kettle. It was all Alenor's fault,
he concluded. If not for their betrothal, if not for that wretched
agreement between his father and Alenor's mother over the Regency of Dhevyn, they would have nothing to taunt him with.
By the time he dismounted in front of the palace, he was ready
to give Alenor a piece of his mind she would never forget.

A groom stepped forward to take his mount. Kirsh handed over the reins gratefully, careful not to turn his back on the beast. The gelding's name was Sunray, and a more unlikely name had never been bestowed on such an ornery creature. He was a slender chestnut with intelligent eyes and a mean streak as wide as the Bandera Straits. Kirsh had been issued the mount on his third day in the guard, and had been fighting with the beast ever since. Sunray snapped at him as he dismounted, but let the groom lead him away as if he was a child's pony.

"Traitor," Kirsh muttered at the beast as he trotted meekly beside the groom.

"Your highness?"

Kirsh turned to find Dimitri Bayel, the Kalarada Court Seneschal, standing in the open doorway of the palace.

"My lord."

"If you would follow me, your highness, I shall take you to the princess."

Kirsh followed Bayel, still angry with both Alenor and his treacherous horse. He knew he had been given the beast as some sort of test, and he was damned if he was going to let the ugly, four-legged fiend defeat him. Kirsh carried more than his fair share of nips from Sunray's sharp teeth, and his shins were bruised from his unpredictable hooves. But he had not been thrown yet, and Kirsh had not asked for a different horse. They were both minor victories that he clung to.

Dimitri Bayel led him through the palace and left him waiting on the terrace overlooking the Queen's Garden. The second sun was shining brightly overhead, and he was forced to squint painfully as he looked around the carefully manicured gardens. Alenor was not there, which angered him even more. It was bad enough that she had summoned him like a servant, but he did not expect to be kept waiting like one. He paced the flagstones like a caged cat, silently rehearsing the scolding he planned to deliver.

"Oh, by the Goddess! What have they done to you, Kirsh?"

He looked up to discover Alenor and her lady-in-waiting walking toward him from the gardens. She was wearing a long blue gown with a close-fitting bodice, her dark hair caught up in a jeweled clasp, the curls arranged artfully over one shoulder, leaving the other enticingly bare. Her companion stepped back discreetly as she approached him, staying in sight, but not so close that she could hear what was being said. The days when he was allowed to be alone with Alenor were long past.

It was weeks since he had seen Alenor last, and every time he did, he was struck by how much older she seemed. She was still tiny—she always would be—but she had matured in these last two years. And filled out in some rather interesting places, another, less noble part of him noticed with approval. But even that observation did not soften his mood. He was still angry with her.

"It's nothing," he scoffed impatiently, jerking his head away from her touch as she tried to reach for him. "Why did you summon me?"

Alenor seemed surprised by his abruptness. She glanced over her shoulder at her lady-in-waiting and slipped her arm through his. "Let's walk. The gardens are looking particularly lovely this morning."

Kirsh allowed her to lead him down the red brick path into the shade toward the splashing fountain in the center of the garden. Within moments, the lady-in-waiting was out of sight, although he was quite certain that if she called out, Lady Dorra would be on them in an instant.

"The Lord Marshal told Mother that you were 'surviving' your tenure in the guard," she remarked, her arm comfortably linked with his. "I wonder what you'd look like if you weren't."

"Is that why you brought me here? To gloat?"

She stopped and turned to look up at him. Alenor knew him too well to be offended by his tone. "Self-pity ill becomes you, Kirshov."

"That's because I've never had much reason to feel sorry for myself before," he admitted.

She smiled and ran her fingers gently over his puffy, swollen eye. "You look like you've been run over by a wagon."

"I feel like it, too. I'm sure they're trying to kill me. Or drive me out of the guard, at the very least."

To his surprise, she did not scoff at his suggestion. "The latter, probably. They wouldn't dare kill you, but they don't like the idea of you being in the guard. They like it even less that you're going to be regent soon."

"I figured *that* out the day I arrived."

"Yet you continue to take everything they throw at you. You'll have earned their respect, if nothing else."

He smiled crookedly, his earlier anger fading. Alenor, first and foremost, was a friend, and he could talk to her in a way he could never talk to his compatriots in the guard. "They treat me as if I'm an idiot who thinks he's better than everybody else."

"Really? I wonder how anybody could think that of you."

He glared at her, not at all pleased by her mocking smile. "What's that supposed to mean?"

"Well, you can be rather arrogant, Kirsh."

He opened his mouth to deny the accusation, and then closed it again. "Am I really that bad, Alenor?"

"No. And you're better than you used to be. But you still speak before you think, sometimes. And I suppose you can't help who your father is."

"My father!" he exclaimed sourly. "By the Goddess, I never thought I'd rue the day I was born a Prince of Senet. It's all his fault, you know. Everybody expects me to be just like him. I'm not. I'm nothing like him."

"You're the spitting image of your father, Kirsh, which doesn't help your cause, but they'll learn in time that you're a different man. Don't let them defeat you."

"That's much easier advice to give than take, Alenor."

"Do you really want me to do more than offer useless advice? I could, you know. One word from me and nobody would lay a hand on you."

"I'd rather die," he declared, alarmed that she might actually do something so humiliating. "Don't you dare even think about doing that!"

"I won't," she assured him. "I'll stand back and let them kill you, if I have to, rather than do anything that might dent that awesome Latanya pride."

"You sound like Dirk," he complained, and then regretted

it immediately, when he saw the shadow of pain that darkened her fair face. "I'm sorry, I shouldn't have mentioned..."

"I still miss him so much, Kirsh," she sighed. He was surprised to find her eyes glistening with tears. "Even after all this time."

A small spear of jealousy pricked him. Dirk had been missing for nearly two years. While he knew the cousins had been close, it annoyed him a little that Alenor still grieved him like a long-lost lover, even though Kirsh was sure their relationship had been boringly honorable.

"Oh, Kirsh, it's like the whole family is cursed," she said, wiping away her unshed tears. "First your mother, then Dirk, and now the duke and Lady Morna..."

"What are you talking about?" Kirsh asked, feeling rather stupid for his earlier suspicions. "What about them?"

"That's why I sent for you," she told him with an inelegant sniff. "Wallin Provin is dead, Kirsh. His heart just gave out at dinner one evening. And now Lady Morna has been arrested. Your father is going to burn her at the next Landfall Festival."

Kirsh stopped walking, shocked beyond words. "When did you hear of this?"

"My mother received a letter from the new Duchess of Elcast, Faralan Provin, yesterday, begging the queen's intervention."

She was fighting back tears. Kirsh gathered her into his arms and held her, wishing he could explain why, but knowing that he could not. He knew his father had threatened to drive Dirk out of hiding, but the past two years of relative quiet had lulled him into believing that the Lion of Senet was over his obsession with Dirk Provin.

"I wish there was something I could do, Allie."

She looked up at him hopefully. "This is monstrous, Kirsh! They arrested her at Wallin's funeral! Can't you speak to your father?"

Kirsh looked away, knowing how useless any plea for clemency would be. Antonov was not interested in saving Morna. He wanted to force Dirk Provin to return to Avacas.

"I doubt there's anything I could do..."

She pushed him away, annoyed, or perhaps hurt, that he would not help her. But how could he explain it to her? How could he justify what his father was doing when he didn't agree with it either? And how could he admit that he knew why this was happening and was powerless to stop it?

As if she sensed something was awry, Alenor glanced up at him. "Kirsh?"

"I love you, Alenor," he blurted out, as if he could assuage his guilt by the admission. He was not lying. He did love her. But he didn't burn for her the way he burned for Marqel...

"Oh, Kirsh, I know you love me," she said, reaching up to put her arms around his neck. He pulled her closer and kissed her. Her lips tasted faintly of berries. Another memory flashed to mind. Another time, another kiss. Marqel tasted like a heady wine.

It was a chaste kiss that he shared with his betrothed and it did not last long. But it left her gasping. When they broke apart, she looked up at him, her eyes shining. It was almost suffocating, being loved so completely.

He gently peeled her arms from around his neck. "Enough, Alenor. I don't fancy being run through by some wildly protective lady-in-waiting armed with a tapestry needle."

She sighed and stepped away from him to a more respectable distance as her lady-in-waiting rounded the corner of the path.

"Mother is sending a letter to Lady Faralan. What shall I tell her?" she asked.

"That I wish I could help," Kirsh replied. "But I fear there's nothing I can do."

"Your highness, the ambassador from Necia will be arriving shortly," Dorra informed them. "We will be late."

"I'm coming, Dorra," she promised and then turned to him. "I'm sorry, Kirsh, I really have to go. Necia and Colmath are squabbling about their fishing grounds again. Mother wants me to be there when she tries to sort it out."

He bowed again, lower this time, and took her hand in his. His kissed it gallantly. "Then you'd best go. I'll see you again soon. At the Landfall Festival, if not before then."

Her eyes narrowed at the mention of the Landfall Festival. "Perhaps. Mother is talking of visiting Grannon Rock this year."

"Not Elcast?"

She shook her head. "No. Not Elcast."

"Then I will pray to the Goddess that I'll be lucky enough to accompany you and the queen as part of your guard," he said. Then he added in a low voice that only she could hear, "Provided I live that long."

She smiled faintly and withdrew her hand. "You'll survive, Kirsh."

Alenor swept up her skirts and followed her companion back toward the palace. Then she turned suddenly and looked back at him. "Oh, by the way, I heard that Misha has taken a turn for the worse. I hope it's nothing too serious."

"Misha's survived worse than this before," he assured her. "He'll recover."

"I'll pray for him," she promised, which was an odd thing for Alenor to say. But Kirsh was not worried about his brother. Misha would pull through. Misha always pulled through.

As Kirsh watched her leave, another thought occurred to him. If the queen was going to Grannon Rock for the Landfall Festival, there was a good chance that he would be chosen for the guard that must accompany the queen. Rove would have to consider him, even if only because he was Dhevyn's future regent.

He did not let himself consciously consider the other reason that the idea appealed to him so much. A part of Kirshov knew, with a certainty that bordered on blind faith, that if he was anywhere other than Kalarada come Landfall, the Goddess would see to it that Marqel was there, too.

Chapter 4

It had become the High Priestess's habit of late to join Antonov each evening after dinner for a nightcap. While she had always been a frequent guest at the palace in Avacas—she had her own suite of rooms permanently at her disposal—she found it beneficial to catch Antonov when he was at his most relaxed. And his most vulnerable.

He had been preoccupied lately; so much so that the last young woman she had arranged to keep him entertained had lasted barely a month before Antonov wearied of her and sent her away. It was unlike him to be so fickle.

Belagren knew what was bothering him, and it was not the approaching wedding of his son to the future Queen of Dhevyn. It wasn't the continuing irritation of the Baenlander pirates who harassed their shipping lanes. It wasn't even the failing health of his eldest son.

No, what vexed the Lion of Senet was the continuing absence of Dirk Provin.

Antonov's fixation with the boy was a constant source of irritation to Belagren. She had her own reasons for wanting to get her hands on Dirk, and they had little to do with Antonov's obsession. She had tried to point out that he did not really need the boy. Kirsh would marry Alenor soon. Within a few weeks, his own son would be Regent of Dhevyn. With luck, within a year, he would have a grandchild to name as heir. He didn't need Dirk Provin to claim Dhevyn. For all intents and purposes, he already owned it.

But the Lion of Senet's plans for Dirk Provin had little to do with logic—and even less to do with reason. In Belagren's mind, it was as though Antonov was still trying to prove to Johan Thorn that he had won, despite the fact that the King of Dhevyn had been dead for two years, killed by the bastard son he never knew he had, right here on Antonov's terrace.

Pointing that out to Antonov, however, was akin to opening a vein with a rusty blade, so she was forced to take a more subtle tack.

Subtlety was wasted on the obsessed, Belagren had discovered.

"Looks like rain," Antonov remarked as he stepped onto the terrace. The sky was overcast and low, the clouds stained red by the evening sun. It was late, and the last of the dinner guests had only recently departed. A trading delegation from Talenburg, come to Avacas to promote their fine carpets, beg tax concessions from the Lion of Senet and probably cheat on their spouses while they were in the big city, away from the prying eyes of their neighbors. Belagren found the evening particularly trying.

"Well, if it does rain," she remarked sourly, "I hope it rains all over those damn Talenburg merchants' carpet samples and shrinks them down to match the size of their brains. Did you hear them going on and on about repairing the levee walls in the city? They'll be asking you to pay for that, you mark my words."

Antonov came to stand beside her, sipping a glass of wine. He smiled. "Shouldn't you be bestowing the blessing of the Goddess on our guests, not wishing them ill?"

"I am the Voice of the Goddess, Anton. I'm quite certain the last time we spoke she mentioned nothing about suffering the ill manners and banal conversation of the Talenburg Chamber of Commerce."

"You're becoming a cynic in your old age, my dear."

She smiled at him. "Isn't that a privilege we earn as we get older?"

"Perhaps," he agreed, still studying the bloodstained sky. "Some seem to think they earn the right much younger."

She looked at him quizzically. "Did you have anyone particular in mind?"

"Morna Provin."

"I hear you've had her arrested."

"I promised Wallin no harm would come to her while he lived. I kept my word."

"What are you going to do with her?"

"I thought Landfall might be appropriate. What do you think?"

Belagren glanced at him with a frown. "While I'm sure the Goddess will appreciate the irony of sacrificing Morna Provin to her, Anton, are you sure it's wise, politically? Some of the ruling houses of Dhevyn might get a little nervous if you start disposing of members of their class in such a fashion."

Antonov seemed unconcerned. "Morna is a special case. It's no secret she's only lived this long thanks to the protection of her husband. Nobody will think it odd that on his death that protection ceased. And I don't imagine Dirk will be too pleased when he hears."

Belagren sighed. *I might have known...*

"You're assuming he *will* hear about it. Suppose he's fled into Sidoria? Or he sailed south to Galina?"

Antonov shook his head confidently. "He'll hear about it. And he'll try to put a stop to it. I'd wager my kingdom on it."

Belagren was tempted to point out that that was precisely what he was doing. But she didn't. Despite the folly of such a scheme, Antonov was right about one thing: if Dirk Provin learned his mother was destined to be burned alive at the Landfall Festival, it was very likely that he would try to do something to prevent it. The trouble was, Dirk was not like Antonov. The boy had brains, and he was not the sort to go barging in thoughtlessly with nothing more than his sword and his noble heart to protect him. While she was quite certain that Antonov had thought about little else lately, she was not convinced that he fully appreciated who he was dealing with.

"The boy isn't stupid, Anton. He'll know it's a trap."

"I'd be disappointed in him if he didn't."

"Yet you expect him to walk into it?"

"He has no other choice. His mother is on Elcast, and that's where she will burn. If he wants to prevent it, then he must go to Elcast to do it. I could line the streets with soldiers and hang out 'Welcome Home, Dirk' signs, and he would still have no choice but to be where I want him, when I want him."

"It's a huge risk, Anton," she warned. "Even if you ignore

the discontented rumbling from the Dhevynian nobility, you risk making a mockery out of the Goddess's ritual. I'm not sure she would appreciate being used in such a manner. And have you thought about the reaction in Damita? Morna Provin is a Damitian princess."

"Prince Baston of Damita would slay his sister, Morna, himself if I ordered it, and the Goddess will understand."

He was right about Baston. The man had raised the art of groveling to new heights. Or was it new lows? But it was her job, not Antonov's, to decide what the Goddess wanted. "What would she understand? That you are using her celebration to further your own goals?"

"My goals are the Goddess's goals," Antonov informed her, with the absolute assurance of a true believer. She didn't like it when he talked like that. It made her feel obsolete.

"I will bring Dhevyn to the Goddess through the son of the man who denounced her," he continued. "It's the only way to completely rid Dhevyn of the heresy that poisons it."

"Even so—" she began, but Antonov cut her off.

"I'm not so blind to the feelings of Dhevyn's people as you think, Belagren. I know they accepted Rainan as their queen begrudgingly, and I know that they will accept Alenor even more reluctantly, given the circumstances of her ascension and the fact that Dhevyn will have a Senetian regent until Alenor comes of age. But think about it. If I could give them Johan's son—if I could place the true heir on the Eagle Throne—there'd be barely a voice raised in protest."

She nodded reluctantly. He had a valid point, and that made arguing against it even more difficult. "But even if you could find Dirk Provin, what makes you think he has any interest in becoming what you want him to be?"

"He killed Johan Thorn."

"Was that because he wanted to aid you or to prevent you from learning what Thorn knew?" Belagren asked.

"I've asked myself that same question a number of times," Antonov admitted.

"And what answer did you settle on?"

"You weren't there, Belagren. You didn't see him do it.

There was no fear in the boy's demeanor, not even a moment of hesitation. The boy has huge potential. Under my tutelage, Dirk Provin will become what his father could have been."

"I'm more concerned that Dirk Provin will become what his father *was*," she warned.

"You still think he fled to the Baenlands?"

"He helped Reithan Seranov and Tia Veran escape the palace after Johan's death. It seems a reasonable assumption."

"Dirk Provin *murdered* Johan Thorn," Anton reminded her with a shake of his head. "The Baenlanders would kill him, not shelter him."

"And have you considered the possibility that is precisely what *did* happen? Have you even allowed for the fact that you haven't heard from Dirk Provin these past two years because Reithan Seranov and Tia Veran used Dirk to aid their escape, and left him lying in a ditch somewhere with his throat cut?"

"I've thought about it. But I don't believe it. The Goddess wants me to bring Dhevyn to her. You've told me that any number of times. To do it properly, to do it *completely*, I need the son of Dhevyn's true king. The Goddess would not have allowed any harm to come to him until his destiny has been fulfilled."

This is what I get for being such a good liar, Belagren grumbled silently.

"Then I will pray that the Goddess looks favorably upon your endeavors," she promised. It was useful being able to fall back on the Goddess. If Antonov failed, she could always pass the blame to her deity.

Antonov nodded and took another sip of his wine, turning back to stare at the turbulent sky. "He will come, Belagren. I'm sure of it."

Chapter 5

Marqel stood at the window of the room belonging to the Crippled Prince, and looked down over the broad paved terrace where the Lion of Senet and the High Priestess stood, engrossed in a private conversation. *Are they discussing Misha?* she wondered. Or was something else consuming the attention of the two most powerful people in the world? Marqel watched them with a degree of envy. What must it be like to be so certain of your power that you never need fear that it might all be taken from you at any moment?

A muffled groan came from the bed, and Marqel turned to look at Misha Latanya. The ailing prince was still unconscious, but he had come back from the depths of the coma that had wrapped him in its smothering embrace. She looked at Ella Geon, who was bending over the bed, dribbling fluid into Misha's mouth from a small cup.

"Will he be all right, my lady?"

"He appears to be out of danger now." She put down the cup and beckoned Marqel to the bed. "Keep applying the compress. I don't want his temperature going up again."

Marqel swapped places with Ella and dabbed gently at Misha's forehead, stifling a yawn. They had been watching over him for days now as he fought the effects of the overdose he had inadvertently consumed. It had been a tense time for everyone. Marqel had barely left the Crippled Prince's side as they fought to bring the young man back from the brink of death.

"If he doesn't make it . . ." she began hesitantly. "I mean, it's not that bad, is it? Prince Antonov has a second son."

Ella turned on Marqel. "It would be a disaster, Marqel. Kirshov is engaged to Alenor *because* he is Antonov's second son, not his heir. If Rainan thought that Kirsh would inherit his father's throne, she'd call off the betrothal in a heartbeat."

The unconscious prince stirred uneasily on the bed. Marqel

wrung out the cloth and wiped his fevered brow again. She nodded in understanding as she dropped the cloth back into the bowl. "Does this mean you won't be leaving Avacas with Prince Antonov, my lady?"

"Oh, I'll be attending the Festival in Elcast," Ella replied with a smile. "Even another Age of Shadows couldn't keep me from seeing Morna Provin burn. Besides, Misha appears to be over the worst of it now. I'm sure he'll live until we get back for the wedding."

"What do you want me to do, my lady?"

"I want you to help Yuri and Olena look after Misha while I'm gone. And you can see to it that my trunks are sent down to the *Calliope* before she sails."

"Won't I be coming with you to Elcast, my lady?"

"Are you so anxious to see the Duchess of Elcast burn?"

Marqel remembered Morna Provin as a tall, aloof woman with the same unforgiving steel-gray eyes as her son Dirk. She also remembered that the only time the duchess had ever deigned to notice her, she had looked at Marqel as if she was a feral animal.

"I've never seen a noblewoman burned alive."

Ella shook her head with a frown. "You're not coming to Elcast. The execution of a member of a ruling family is a very delicate matter. We can't risk anything going wrong."

"You think I can't be trusted."

"I think it's nothing to do with you. Stop being so impatient, child. Your time will come."

"Yes, my lady."

If Ella noticed her disappointment, she chose to ignore it. "If you want to do something useful, see that Caspona and Laleno are ready to leave for Grannon Rock on time. They will be attending the Landfall Feast there this year."

Laleno and Caspona were the other two acolytes assigned to the palace. Marqel's suggestion that she stay in the Lion of Senet's palace under the tutelage of Ella Geon had had an unexpected outcome. The High Priestess had really warmed to the idea—so much so that she sent three trainees to work under Ella, not just Marqel. The other girls were a constant source of irritation to Marqel, and she spent much of her spare time trying to come up with ways to discredit them in the eyes of Ella and Belagren. So far, she had been spectacularly unsuccessful in her efforts to rid herself of either girl.

"I saw the Grannon Rock Landfall Festival when I was an acrobat." She shrugged, thinking that she would have the run of the palace for a few weeks, with Ella and the other girls away. "It was a fairly subdued affair, as I recall."

Ella nodded. "Grannon Rock considers itself a sophisticated island. They want to be considered the prime center of learning in Dhevyn and are very jealous of Avacas's older and more prestigious reputation. Of course, they wouldn't dare refuse to hold the Landfall Feast outright, but they tend to play it down. It's the reason the High Priestess makes a point of sending additional Shadowdancers out to the island every year for the Festival. It never hurts to remind people where their loyalties should lie."

"Shouldn't they just obey the law?"

Ella smiled at her ignorance. "Never, for a moment, assume that just because a thing is law, people will automatically follow it, Marqel. The price of ultimate power is eternal vigilance."

"Why Caspona, though?" Marqel did not particularly care that her rival had been chosen over her to attend Landfall on boring old Grannon Rock, but she never missed an opportunity to cast aspersions on Caspona's competence. "Is she ready for such responsibility?"

Ella glared at her. "You've a nerve, child, to question the High Priestess so."

"I'm sorry, my lady," Marqel replied hurriedly, dropping her eyes.

The Shadowdancer laughed sourly. "Oh, please, Marqel, don't even try that nonsense on me. You're not sorry. You're envious. You think all the important events are going to happen somewhere else and you want to be there. You're like a sleepy child who doesn't want to leave the party, afraid she'll miss something exciting."

Marqel looked up at her mistress defiantly. "Is that so wrong?"

"Not if you aspire to high office. But the High Priestess is still sending Caspona to Grannon Rock and not you. The queen is attending the festival there this year."

The young Shadowdancer was silent for a moment as the implications of that news sank in. "Then she'll take her guard."

"Most certainly."

"I see."

"Do you, Marqel? Do you really understand how important this is?"

"Belagren wants to be sure of Kirshov before he takes the throne of Senet."

"She wants more than that, child. We want to own him. We want to own him body and soul, the same way we once owned his father. The Shadowdancers cannot risk losing the support of the Lion of Senet. Belagren had her hand wrapped around Antonov's heart so tightly he slit his own son's throat at her behest. We must own his heir as well."

"Then why send Caspona and Laleno? If anyone has a chance of ensuring that Kirshov—"

"We would be incurring Antonov's wrath if we sent you to Grannon Rock, particularly this close to the wedding. Caspona will be charged with ensuring Kirshov's heart doesn't wander too far from the Goddess."

"Caspona hasn't got what it takes," Marqel objected. She could not believe that Belagren was sending that vacuous little bitch to seduce Kirshov. *He's mine.*

"Neither have you, it seems."

"It wasn't my fault that Kirsh was sent to Kalarada," she pointed out. When Ella seemed unmoved by her reasoning, she resorted to more direct methods. "My lady, please. Can't you speak to the High Priestess? Let me do this."

The Shadowdancer studied her for a moment then shook her head. "No, Marqel. This is too important. We cannot risk annoying Antonov at this critical stage. Caspona and Laleno will go to Grannon Rock. You will stay here in Avacas and continue your studies. I'm actually quite impressed with your progress in the area of herb lore." The Shadowdancer smiled, as if the compliment would somehow compensate for Marqel's disappointment. "Now see to it that the High Priestess's orders are carried out and I'll hear no more about it."

Marqel lowered her eyes so that Ella would not see the defiance lurking there, and curtsied in acquiescence. "As you command, my lady."

Marqel closed the door behind herself, careful not to let it slam and give Ella any reason to suspect her anger. She turned toward the stairs and the third floor, where Caspona's room was located, trying to work out where she had gone wrong. Two years as a Shadowdancer here in the Lion of Senet's palace had put Marqel in a strong position, but apparently it was not as strong as she thought. Belagren should have considered sending no one else but *her* to Grannon Rock to be with Kirsh on Landfall night. The idea that Caspona might have the power she believed would one day be hers was unconscionable.

She wished she were better at politics. She could manipulate men well, but she had never really been able to crack the secret of getting what she wanted out of Ella Geon or the High Priestess. It had something to do with being Senetian, she concluded. It was as if there were unwritten laws, and you had to be born Senetian to understand them. She wished she had someone to guide her; someone who could give her an edge over girls like Caspona and Laleno. Someone whose only interest was in helping Marqel get to the top—fast.

There was no such person, of course. Everyone was out to look after themselves.

Marqel took the stairs to the third floor, where the Shadowdancers' rooms were located, stewing about it. There had to be a way to get to Grannon Rock for Landfall, but she couldn't think of one. Her brilliant idea about staying in the palace under the tutelage of Ella Geon had proved a waste of time. For a few, short, glorious days she'd had everything she ever wanted out of life, then Kirshov had been sent to Kalarada. After that, she was just another acolyte learning the arts of herbs and poisons and the rituals of the Goddess under the distrustful eye of Ella Geon. She still had to study, still had to spend hours laboring over boring, incomprehensible texts that she struggled to understand.

Admittedly, she had learned a great deal from Ella during her time here, but once Kirsh had left, there was no point in staying to help tend the Crippled Prince. Marqel had requested she be moved back to the Hall of Shadows to continue her training under the High Priestess, but had been refused. "You wanted to be at the palace," Belagren had said, "so you are. I've no intention of moving you every time you get bored, young lady."

So she was stuck here nursing the Crippled Prince, with Ella's suspicious looks, Caspona's snide condescension and Laleno's smug disapproval. And now, after two years of living in limbo, who was going to Grannon Rock for Landfall? That sly, insipid, vacuous, insufferable cow, Caspona Takarnov.

She knocked on Caspona's door and waited, thinking that the nicest thing she could wish on her opponent was a galloping dose of the pox.

"Marqel!" the older girl exclaimed as she opened the door. "To what do I owe this remarkable honor?"

"I've an assignment for you from Ella. Can I come in?"

Caspona stepped aside to allow Marqel to enter. Caspona's room looked out over the gardens. *My room doesn't even have a view,* Marqel noted with a slight frown.

"So?"

Marqel turned to look at Caspona.

"The assignment? What is it?"

"Nothing terribly taxing." Marqel shrugged. "She's sending you to Grannon Rock with Laleno for the Landfall Feast this year."

"Why Grannon Rock, of all places?" Caspona asked. She did not look pleased that Ella had sent Marqel with her orders, rather than sending for her and delivering them personally.

"Because the Queen of Dhevyn will be attending the Festival there this year." The words almost stuck in her throat. But she was not going to let it show—certainly not to Caspona.

Caspona smiled knowingly. "Which means Kirshov Latanya will probably be there. I'll bet you're just squirming over
the thought that I'll be having your lover while you sit here in
Avacas holding the hand of the Crippled Prince while he sweats
out his last dose of poppy-dust."

Marqel clasped her hands behind her back. It gave the impression she had everything under control. In truth, she had
clasped her hands together to stop herself grabbing Caspona by
the throat. "I'm sure Prince Kirshov wouldn't even remember
me," Marqel replied with a careless shrug. "He's like that, you
know. Once he's had you, he'll cast you aside like a soiled shirt."

"He won't cast me aside," the Shadowdancer announced
confidently. "I'll give him a night he'll never forget."

"He'll forget," Marqel assured her. "Either the Milk of the
Goddess or your own...mediocrity...will see to that. All
you're going to do is be his whore for the night."

The older girl glared at her. "I am no man's whore. I'm a
Shadowdancer. Of course, you wouldn't appreciate the difference, would you? Not someone with your dubious back-
ground."

Marqel clenched her hands together even tighter. The
desire to throttle her companion was almost overwhelming.
"You should be grateful you're a Shadowdancer, Caspona.
You'd starve if you had to rely on *your* talents as a whore to earn
a living."

"Well, I guess I'll have to take your word for that, Marqel,"
Caspona replied sweetly. "I don't have the benefit of your firsthand experience selling myself to every man with a pulse and
purse between here and Damita."

"Just be ready to leave on time," Marqel snapped, furious,
but unable to think up a suitable retort.

"Shall I give Prince Kirshov your regards?"

Marqel slammed the door behind her as she left the room.

Chapter 6

Misha Latanya's latest brush with death seemed closer than the others—more real somehow, as if this time he really would simply fall into unconsciousness and never awaken. He was not sure why he felt that way. It just seemed as if this time, rather than walk past death's door, he had actually stopped and considered it for a while.

He often wondered if it would matter if he died. Misha was not suicidal but, in his more maudlin moments, he sometimes wondered if his death would simply remove the burden he was to others. Misha despised being a burden. He despised his own weakness, a fact not helped by the look in his father's eye whenever Antonov came to visit him. It was not just because he was crippled. Misha favored his mother in appearance. He had her dark coloring, her blue-gray eyes, her slender build—but not, perhaps, her nature. Kirsh had inherited that.

Misha could just remember Analee. He treasured his earliest memories of his mother, when she seemed so full of joy, so full of life. He quite deliberately blocked out the more recent memories, the ones just before she took her own life, when it seemed she was always crying, or fighting with his father over things he was far too young to understand.

He knew Antonov tried not to let his disappointment in his eldest son show. The Lion of Senet went to great pains to make Misha feel as though he were a contributing member of the family. But he sent his eldest son agricultural reports to study or asked him to consider minor, unimportant requests from outlying duchies. The important things, however, the things that really mattered to Antonov, were rarely brought to Misha's attention.

Not that he really blamed him. Antonov was a man of action. He would rather spend all day watching his men training for a horse race than an hour going over the problems with grape harvest with his advisers. He did not ignore such things—he was too astute a ruler for that—but he made sure the people who were responsible for overseeing them were competent and trustworthy so he did not have to bother with the details.

His eldest son was quite the opposite. Bedridden much of the time by his withered left side and the strange turns that caused his fits and fevers, Misha was the antithesis of everything Antonov admired in a man.

Misha knew, without doubt, that Kirshov was the son Antonov adored—Kirshov, for whom no physical challenge posed an obstacle. Misha smiled to himself, wondering how his brother was faring in the Queen's Guard. *He's probably loving every minute of it.* Misha hoped so. But he knew that Kirsh was in for a rude awakening when he became Regent of Dhevyn. Administering that cluster of rebellious, fractious islands would take more political skill than Misha thought his younger brother possessed. Two years in the guard might have matured him a bit, Misha thought hopefully, and although she was still quite young, Alenor had a good head on her shoulders.

Misha had never really gotten the full details of how his father managed to arrange for Queen Rainan to abdicate on Alenor's sixteenth birthday, but that important date was approaching soon and, before long, Kirsh would be a ruler in his own right. Misha envied his brother a little. He did not envy him his strength, his good nature or his golden good looks. He envied his *responsibility*. As Regent of Dhevyn, Kirsh would have a chance to make a real difference. If he used his head, Kirsh might even be able to heal the breach between Senet and Dhevyn, which had started during the Age of Shadows with Johan Thorn and culminated in a ruinous war that neither side could really afford.

Misha was quite a student of history. He was knowledgeable in a great many things—scholarship being the only thing he was better at than his brother. For that reason also, he quite missed Dirk Provin. His young Elcastran cousin had a fiendishly clever mind, and Misha had enjoyed playing chess with him.

There'd been a temporary laundry maid, too, that Misha had become quite fascinated by. He learned later that she was a spy. The heretic Neris Veran's daughter, no less, sent to Avacas to try to free Johan Thorn. She had not succeeded, of course, but Misha missed having someone around who would argue with him, rather than nod and smile and say, "If you say so, your highness," whenever he expressed an opinion.

The door to his room opened and he turned his head to see who had disturbed him. He was still too weak to get out of bed, but his mind was clearer than it had been for days.

"I'm sorry, Misha," Ella Geon said when she realized he was conscious. She had tended him since he was a small boy and rarely addressed him by his title unless there were others present. "Did I wake you?"

Misha shook his head weakly. "No. I've been awake for a while. What time is it?"

"Well past second sunrise," she told him. "Are you feeling up to some breakfast?"

"I think so. I was just thinking about Dirk and Tia."

Ella bustled over to the windows and threw back the drapes forcefully, flooding the room with light. "It was never proved that girl was my daughter."

"Neither was it *disproved,*" Misha pointed out, struggling to sit. Ella hurried over to the bed and helped him up, rearranging the pillows for him. "I spoke to her at some length, you know, while she was here in the palace. She was very intelligent."

"Neris didn't have a monopoly on intelligence, Misha," Ella snapped. "Just because the girl had half a brain, it did not necessarily follow that her father was Neris Veran."

"It was rather a coincidence, though, don't you think?"

Ella scowled at him. "You must be well on the way to recovering if you've got time to dwell on such things. I'll let your father know. I'm sure he can think up something more useful to occupy your mind than remembering things better left forgotten."

Misha smiled wanly. "Are you mad at me, Ella?"

"Of course not, your highness. Now, if you will excuse me,

I'll arrange some breakfast for you. Did you need anything else?"

A body that works properly wouldn't go astray, Misha thought wryly, but he shook his head. "No, thanks. Just breakfast will be fine."

Ella must have meant what she said about informing Antonov about his improvement. His father came to visit him later that day, just before dinner. Misha knew Antonov frequently chose that time to visit him, because it gave him an excuse to leave early. "My guests are waiting," the Lion of Senet would say, in a voice filled with regret. "Next time I come, we'll spend more time together. I promise." Misha wished he had a dorn for every time he had heard his father say that. He could buy one of the Dhevynian islands by now.

"Ella tells me you're feeling much better," Antonov said, as he strode into the bedroom. His father filled the room with his presence, as if the force of his personality was too large to be contained within the man. He paced it like a caged cat, the smell of sickness making him uneasy. Or was it the smell of weakness that he despised?

"Much better, thank you," Misha agreed.

"Perhaps you'll be recovered enough to attend the wedding?" Antonov suggested as he walked to the window and glanced down over the lawns. If he could possibly avoid it, Antonov rarely looked at his eldest son, and when he was forced to do so, he studiously looked Misha in the eye. Misha suspected he did it to avoid looking at his son's weak and crippled body.

"I'd like nothing more than to see Kirsh and Alenor wed, sire, but I'm not sure how I'd handle the journey to Kalarada."

Antonov looked relieved. He did not like reminding the world that his heir was a cripple, and every man and woman of note in Senet and Dhevyn would attend the wedding. Misha knew that. It was the reason he claimed he would be too ill to attend—he did his best to spare his father embarrassment whenever he could.

Not that Antonov ever noticed.

"Perhaps it's wiser that you stay here, then," Antonov agreed. "We're going to Elcast first, to attend Landfall there before we go to Kalarada. It will be a long trip."

"I heard that Duke Wallin died, just before I got sick. Is that why you're going to Elcast?"

His father nodded. "It's time to put an end to Morna Provin."

Misha frowned. "Is that wise?"

Antonov looked surprised that his son was questioning him. "Are you suggesting that Morna Provin should go unpunished for her treachery?"

"I was thinking more along the lines that it might upset the Dhevynians if you sacrifice one of their duchesses."

"I'll take that risk. Besides, it will drive Dirk out into the open. I'm sick of waiting for him. It's high time that boy came to his senses."

Misha was used to his father's obsession with finding Dirk Provin. It had governed almost every action the Lion of Senet had taken these past two years. He knew Antonov was convinced that the only way to bring Dhevyn to the Goddess was through the son of the man who denounced her. It did not disturb him, however, the way it disturbed his brother. Misha was used to being overlooked.

"I really should get going," Antonov added, before Misha could say anything further. "My guests are waiting. Next time I come by, we'll spend more time together. I promise."

"Of course," Misha said. "I'll see you later, Father. Thank you for stopping by."

Antonov nodded uncomfortably and let himself out of the bedroom with almost unseemly haste.

Once he was alone again, Misha closed his eyes and leaned back against the pillows, wondering about the wisdom of executing an essentially powerless woman simply to force her son into doing something foolish.

Privately, Misha thought his father optimistic in the extreme. Dirk Provin was far too smart to walk into such an obvious trap, and although he would enjoy having Dirk back in Avacas, he would be extremely disappointed in him if he did.

Chapter 7

From the ledge outside Neris's cave high above the Baenlands, Tia Veran watched the *Wanderer* tacking through the delta, unable to hide her relief at the thought that Reithan was home again. She worried about him constantly when he was away, always afraid the Prefect of Avacas, Barin Welacin, would finally catch up with him, or the Brotherhood would decide there was more profit in selling him out than buying poppy-dust from him. Or worse, the ever-present fear that this time, this trip, Dirk Provin would betray him.

"Is that the *Wanderer*?" Neris asked, coming to stand beside her. Her father had been quite lucid for the past few days and had even found time for a bath. Tia found it heartbreaking, sometimes, to realize this was what Neris had been like before Ella Geon came along—articulate, intelligent—not the insane wretch he was most of the time. His periods of sanity never lasted long, but they always left her with a deep sense of loss for the man he had once been.

"Yes, that's Reithan," she agreed.

"And Dirk?"

Tia turned to look at Neris, a little put out by his eager question. "Unless Reithan finally woke up to him and shoved him overboard, I suppose Dirk is with him."

"You tell him he has to come visit me. As soon as he can."

"Why? All you ever do is argue with him, Neris."

"That's because he's the only one who *will* argue with me," Neris replied. "You just boss me around."

Tia did not respond to the accusation, quite irritated by the friendship between her father and Dirk Provin, even though she was the one who had encouraged it. *Probably because so little has come of it,* she concluded. Her hope that Dirk might be able to extract from Neris the secret of when the next Age of Shadows would return had proved a futile hope. Neris had not told

Dirk anything useful at all. Or so Dirk claimed. The only things Neris Veran and Dirk Provin did were play chess and argue for hours about subjects that frequently made no sense to anybody but the two of them.

"Did you want to come down to the village with me?" she asked.

Neris shook his head. "I want Dirk to visit me. Now he's back, you tell him he has to come visit me. We can play some more chess. I'll beat him this time."

"I thought you always beat him, anyway."

"He lets me win. He thinks I'm mad and that I'll do something dreadful to him if I lose."

"Would you?"

"Would I what?"

"Do something dreadful to Dirk if you lost?"

Neris thought about it for a moment before he answered. "I don't know. I never thought about it. Do you think I should do something dreadful to him?"

"Sure. I'll even help you think of something, if you like," she offered with a smile. Tia uttered the words out of habit as much as anger these days. Two years had done much to dull her fury, although she had never been able to totally shed the core of suspicion that resided in her belly whenever she thought about Dirk Provin.

Tia still had no satisfactory reason why Dirk was here in Mil, when he could be living the high life in Avacas with the Lion of Senet. And she had never forgiven him for what he did in Avacas. She doubted she ever would. For a moment, she glanced down at her left hand. Like the little finger that had been amputated at the first knuckle, her heart had healed, but there would always be a piece missing.

"You just tell him to come visit me," Neris repeated. "Or I'll think of something dreadful to do to *you*."

"You really like him, don't you?"

Neris shrugged. "Dirk's all right. He's not as smart as me, though. He still hasn't figured out what I know, so there's no point you harassing him about it."

She frowned. "What makes you think—"

"Because you set him onto me," Neris cut in.

Tia opened her mouth to object, but Neris gave her no chance to defend herself. "I'm mad, Tia, not stupid. I know why you brought him here. He's clever, I'll grant you that. But I won't tell him. I won't tell you. I won't tell anyone what I know."

Tia shrugged helplessly. She knew better than to argue about it. Her father's intransigence on the matter was legendary.

"I'll tell him to come visit you," she promised. "Will you be all right?"

Neris nodded. "You go down and visit your boyfriend. I'll be fine."

Tia looked at him curiously. "Reithan's not my boyfriend."

Neris smiled knowingly. "I wasn't talking about Reithan."

By the time Tia had rowed back across the bay to the village, the *Wanderer* was anchored off the beach and there was no sign of Reithan or Dirk. Tia pulled the dinghy up onto the black sand and headed up toward Johan's stilted house overlooking the delta, certain that was where she would find them. Everyone in Mil still called it Johan's house, even after all this time.

Reithan and Dirk had been to Kalarada to deliver another chest full of poppy-dust to the Brotherhood. Tia was not pleased with the thought of Dirk going to Kalarada. Suppose he ran into Alenor while he was there? Of course, as Reithan had pointed out, the chance of bumping into the Crown Princess of Dhevyn while transacting an illicit poppy-dust deal with the Brotherhood in some seedy tavern by the wharves was highly unlikely. But it still made Tia nervous. Dirk was not unknown to the Queen's Guard. Some of them—the two who had watched him murder Johan Thorn in particular—would probably never forget his face.

She found them on the veranda with Lexie. Reithan was sitting next to his mother; Dirk was perched on the railing. She almost gasped when she saw him, struck, once again, by his resemblance to Johan. It was easy to forget about it when she saw him every day, but at times like these, when she had not seen him for several weeks, his dark hair and metal-gray eyes always took her by surprise.

"Tia!" Lexie exclaimed with a smile, looking up at the sound of her footsteps on the wooden decking. "I thought you were up with Neris."

"I saw the *Wanderer* heading in. Good trip?" She directed her question at Reithan, quite deliberately ignoring Dirk.

"Well, we survived it," Reithan said with a smile. "Does that qualify as good?"

"Good" would have been if only one of you had survived it, Tia was tempted to reply, but Lexie got upset when she needled Dirk, so she smiled pleasantly. "I suppose it does. Hello, Dirk."

"Tia."

He said nothing else, did nothing to provoke her, yet still she felt her ire rising. It did not seem fair that he was so much a part of the family these days. Reithan treated him like a brother; Lexie treated him like a son. Mellie adored him with almost the same ridiculous enthusiasm that Eryk did. Neris treated him like a best friend. Dal Falstov had taken him out on the *Orlando* twice now. Everyone in the whole damn village liked him. Even Porl Isingrin, the captain of the *Makuan,* and the one person Tia was certain would see through Dirk's facade, was warming to him.

Why is it only me who can see Dirk Provin for what he really is?

"Do you have any news?" she asked, taking the seat on the other side of Lexie, where she could keep her eye on Dirk.

"Quite a bit actually," Reithan said. "Alenor D'Orlon and Kirshov Latanya are getting married on her sixteenth birthday."

Tia looked directly at Dirk. "So all you did was buy us some time. Dhevyn will still have a Senetian regent. The next heir to Dhevyn will still be the Lion of Senet's grandchild."

"What do you mean, Tia?" Lexie asked curiously. "How did Dirk buy us time?"

"Dirk arranged for Alenor and Rainan to get out of Avacas

before Antonov could force the wedding to happen two years ago," Reithan explained with a warning glare at Tia.

To this day, nobody in Mil but the three of them knew that it was Dirk who had killed Johan. Tia had promised to keep it a secret for Mellie's sake, only to watch Dirk ingratiate himself into her village, her life, into the very heart of her family, where they all thought he was merely the son of a man they had worshipped as a hero. Nobody but Tia and Reithan knew that he was a cold-blooded killer.

I should tell them. I should tell everyone in the Baenlands that it was Dirk Provin who drove a knife into Johan's throat...

"Your resourcefulness never ceases to amaze me, Dirk," Lexie said with a warm smile in Dirk's direction.

Oh please... I think I'm going to be sick...

"Tia does have a point, though, my lady," Dirk replied, surprising her with his support. "All I did was buy a little time."

"What does Alexin say? Is there any way to prevent the wedding taking place?"

"His father has invited the queen to Grannon Rock for the Landfall Festival," Reithan told her. "We're hoping to make contact with Rainan while she's in Nova."

"But what can we do? I fear the wheels of fate will trundle right over us in this, with little care about what we might try to do to prevent them."

"Maybe we should kidnap Alenor," Tia suggested. "She can't marry Kirshov Latanya if she's not there."

"You'd just bring Antonov's wrath down on the whole of Dhevyn," Dirk warned. "I wouldn't lay a finger on Alenor, if I were you. Not unless you want to wake up one morning to find the *Calliope* sailing through the delta with a dozen warships in her wake."

"And how would Antonov know how to get through the delta, Dirk? Are *you* going to tell him?"

Lexie frowned at her. "Tia, he just meant that we shouldn't take any action that is likely to drive Antonov to anger."

"Perish the thought that we might do *anything* to irritate his good friend, the Lion of Senet," she snapped, annoyed that he was right, even more that it was Dirk who had pointed out the flaw in her plan.

"That was uncalled for, Tia," Lexie scolded. "I don't know why you're being so hard on Dirk. What has he ever done to you?"

Reithan glared at her, silently warning her not to answer Lexie's seemingly innocent question. She glanced up at Dirk. He was looking straight at her, too, his expression resigned, as if he expected her to expose him.

Tia forced a smile and shrugged. "I'm sorry, Lexie. I guess I'm just a bit touchy at the moment. Neris has that effect on me. And you're right. We're not in a position to challenge Senet so openly."

"And you're never going to be," Dirk counseled. "Unless you can get Neris to tell you what he knows."

Tia thought it interesting that even after all this time, Dirk still said "you," not "we." It was one of the reasons she didn't trust him.

"Have you had any luck?" Lexie asked.

Dirk shook his head. "Neris is insane, but he's as cunning as an outhouse rat. He never says anything he doesn't mean to. And he's not a fool. He knows what I'm after."

"You sit up there talking with him for hours at a time. Hasn't he told you *anything* useful?" Tia was not convinced that Dirk spoke the truth. *Maybe he already knows. Maybe that's why he wanted to go on this trip with Reithan. Maybe he found a way to get the information to the High Priestess. Maybe . . .*

"The only thing he's ever said was something along the lines of the 'secret lies within the Eye of the Labyrinth.'"

"He's talking about Omaxin," Reithan said.

"I gathered that much. But honestly, I think the idea that Neris is going to blurt out his secret is a futile hope."

"So that's it, then?" Tia asked. "We just give up and let Antonov have Dhevyn?"

"That might be your only alternative," Dirk said.

Tia glared at him. "I can't believe you have the gall to sit there and suggest that!"

"You have four choices, Tia," Dirk replied. "You can fight

Senet head on and lose. You can discover when the next Age of Shadows is due and bring Senet down through their religion, but Neris won't tell you the secret, so that's not going to work. You can decide to throw everything you have into making Dhevyn so hard to govern that it becomes easier for Antonov to let it go than to hold it. Or you can give it up and get on with your lives here in Mil, where at least you're safe and you have some chance at a normal life."

"He speaks a plain but bitter truth, Tia," Lexie agreed. "Johan thought the same."

"Well, I'm sorry I don't agree that rolling over and dying is our best option."

"The reality is that it may well be your *only* option, Tia," Dirk said.

"Giving up is the coward's way out."

Dirk didn't answer her. He just shook his head and looked out over the balcony.

"I don't think we should do anything until the *Makuan* and the *Orlando* get back," Reithan suggested. "Porl or Dal may have more information. And I'd like to see what Rainan has to say after we've been to Grannon Rock."

"She gave up her throne and agreed to hand it over to Kirshov Latanya with barely a whimper," Tia reminded them. "What makes you think she has any interest in stopping the Lion of Senet swallowing up Dhevyn?"

"She's managed to stall the abdication for nearly two years," Dirk pointed out, his eyes still fixed on the view. "Just because she managed to do it without shedding any blood doesn't lessen the achievement."

"You're a fine one to talk about bloodless coups," Tia snapped.

Lexie turned to her with a horrified expression. "Tia! Please! I'll ask you not to behave so gracelessly while under my roof. If Dirk has done something to warrant such anger, then tell me what it is and I will deal with it. But unless you can justify this continuous litany of snide remarks and savage jibes, I will ask you to behave in a more civilized manner."

The scolding wounded Tia more than she thought possible. She turned to Reithan for support, but he would not meet her eyes. Dirk also avoided her gaze, but at least he had the decency to look a little uncomfortable. Lexie stared at her expectantly, waiting for her reply.

"I'm sorry," she muttered, then rose to her feet and fled the balcony, almost overwhelmed by a feeling of helpless rage.

Chapter 8

Eryk saw the *Wanderer* sailing toward the village from high up on his perch near the goat hut. He had been working with the goats for about a year now, delighted that Lexie considered him responsible enough to be given such an important job.

Eryk liked the goats. He liked feeding the orphaned kids. He liked the sound of their clunking bells. He liked helping with the milking and watching old Dragili make her pungent cheeses. She let him watch sometimes as she gently ladled the curds into the molds. He even got to help pull up the cloth occasionally to reduce the wrinkles that would set creases into the finished cheese. In fact, Eryk was happier in Mil than he could ever remember. He did not miss Elcast the way Dirk did. The life he had left behind held little attraction for him. Here in the Baenlands he had an important job. He had real friends. He had Mellie.

For a moment, Eryk wished he could go down to the village to greet Reithan and Dirk, but decided against it. He had a much more important task to take care of, and anyway, Dirk would be up at the house with Reithan and Tia and Lady Lexie for ages yet, talking about boring things happening in the world outside Mil that Eryk had no interest in.

He was much more concerned about the present he was making for Mellie. He planned to give it to her at the Troitsa festival in two days' time. The day was widely celebrated in

Dhevyn every year, several weeks before the bigger and more elaborate Landfall Feast. On Elcast, the houses in the village were decorated with fresh green branches, and a maiden's clothes were hung on the young birch trees bordering the common at the back of Elcast Keep. The village children (and more than a few adults) floated garlands in the bay, made of birch branches and flowers, in the hope that they would forecast the future, specifically who they would marry. Once the second sun had set, the villagers would then gather on the common, singing and dancing around the decorated birch trees until the ale ran out and they staggered home, drunk and sated on the generosity of the duke.

Of course there were no birch trees here in the Baenlands, but the festival was just as much fun here as elsewhere in Dhevyn. More fun, perhaps, because here in the Baenlands, nobody celebrated the Landfall Festival.

Eryk had given a lot of time thinking about what he would make for Mellie. He wanted it to be special. He wanted his gift to say more than just "Happy Troitsa." He wanted her to understand how he felt...

"Eryk!"

He hastily threw a sack over the incomplete carving and jumped to his feet as Mellie and her best friend Eleska Arrowsmith clambered up the slope toward him. He brushed the wood shavings from his trousers and smiled as they approached, thinking that Mellie grew more beautiful every time he saw her.

"Did you see, Eryk?" Mellie called out. "The *Wanderer*'s back. Reithan and Dirk are home."

"I thaw...saw them," he stammered.

"I'm so glad they got back before Troitsa," Eleska puffed as she climbed the steep slope beside Mellie. She was as fair as Mellie was dark, and just as full of fourteen-year-old self-confidence as her best friend. "I'm going to make Dirk dance with me all night, and then when I float my garland, I'll bet it says he's going to marry me."

Mellie stopped climbing for a moment and turned to stare

at Eleska. "Don't be stupid, Eleska! Why would Dirk want to marry you? He's going to marry Tia."

"But Tia hates him!" Eleska scoffed. "She's always picking on him. Aren't I right, Eryk?"

The youth nodded, a little uncertainly. "I think she must, Mellie. She never says anything nice about him."

"I know, but she'll get over that eventually. I mean, she can't stay mad at him forever, can she? Anyway, I think they're perfect for each other. Neris thinks so, too."

"Neris is insane, Mellie," Eleska pointed out.

"That doesn't mean he's wrong."

"But why do you care?"

"Because Dirk is my brother, and if he marries Tia then she really will be my sister, so I've decided that it has to happen."

"Just because *you* decided?" Eleska asked with a frown. "But why can't she marry Reithan? He's your brother, too. Then I can have Dirk."

Mellie thought on that for a moment. "I suppose. But Reithan's a bit old for Tia, isn't he?"

"Reithan and Tia are perfect for each other," Eleska declared as she reached to top of the path. "And that way, I can marry Dirk. Who are you going to marry, Mellie?"

Mellie flopped down on the ground beside Eryk and looked out over the delta with a thoughtful expression. "I haven't decided yet."

"How about Tabor Isingrin?" Eleska suggested, taking a seat beside Mellie.

"He's an idiot," Mellie said. "And he has bad breath."

Eleska laughed. "And how did you get close enough to find that out?"

Mellie laughed, too, giving her friend a playful shove. "You're revolting, Eleska."

"Well then, what about Panka Droganov? He's kind of cute, don't you think?"

"Cute? Are you mad, Eleska? He's a moron! I'd rather marry poor Eryk here, than have Panka Droganov waking up next to me every morning for the rest of my life!"

"I'll marry you if you want, Mellie," Eryk offered, as he sat down beside her, his heart almost bursting to hear her make such a declaration.

Mellie laughed. "Why thank you, Eryk, that's very nice of you to offer. There you go, Eleska. I'm going to marry Eryk, you're going to marry Dirk, and Reithan is going to marry Tia. That rounds it out quite nicely, don't you think?"

Mellie and Eleska continued to chatter away, but Eryk was no longer listening to them. *Mellie wants to marry me,* his heart sang. He surreptitiously moved the carving around behind him, determined to stay up all night if he had to, just to have it finished in time.

And then in three days' time, he would give it to her at the Troitsa Festival. It would be her betrothal present and they could tell everyone they were going to get married...

"Are you listening to me, Eryk?" Mellie demanded.

"What? Thorry...I was thinking..."

"I asked you if you're coming up to the house for dinner tonight, now that Dirk's home."

He shook his head. "I'll see him later. I've got thome...I mean *some*thing...I have to do."

"I'll tell Mama you're coming by tomorrow then," Mellie said, climbing to her feet. She looked over the delta and smiled. "You've got the best view from up here. No wonder you like it so much."

Eryk stared up at her, his eyes shining with happiness. "The most beautiful thing in the world," he agreed.

And she wants to marry me...

Chapter 9

It was later that afternoon that Dirk rowed across the bay to the small beach beneath the goat track leading up to Neris's cave. He scrambled up the path to the ledge, and was a little surprised to find the madman sitting cross-legged in the cave's entrance, apparently engrossed in a diagram he was making. The ledge was stifling, the bare rock reflecting the heat of the second sun like a cooking stone.

"Hello, Neris."

The madman did not acknowledge his presence. As he drew closer, Dirk saw that he was sketching a series of concentric circles on a scrap of parchment that looked as if it had been torn out of a rather expensive book.

"I have a present for you."

"I'm busy," Neris replied without looking up.

"Fine. I'll just give these books to Alasun down in the schoolhouse then, shall I?" Dirk replied, turning away.

Neris scrambled to his feet and hurried after him. "Books? What books?"

"Just some books I found in the Kalarada markets, but if you're too busy—"

"Give them to me!"

Dirk was tempted to demand that Neris say "please," but decided against it. The madman snatched the books from him, hurried back into his cave and knelt on the rocky floor, shuffling through the pile.

"Have you seen Tia yet?" Neris asked as he flicked through the pages, hungry for anything new to relive the tedium.

"Oh, yes," Dirk replied with feeling, sitting himself down on the floor in front of the madman. "She said she'd be over to visit you later. After I'm gone."

The madman's eyes narrowed cannily. "Why does she hate you so much?"

"I don't know."

"You're lying."

Dirk shrugged. "All right, I'm lying. But it's still none of your damn business."

"Why won't you tell me? Don't you trust me with your little secret?"

"Why should I?" he asked with a smile. "You won't trust me with yours."

"That was very good, Dirk." Neris chuckled. "Is that your strategy now—you tell me your secret and I tell you mine? Two years and you still haven't had any luck, eh? You're persistent, I'll give you that much."

"I'm persistent? I think you hold the honor for that, Neris."

"Don't get snippy at me, boy, just because you can't outwit me."

"Actually, I was referring to your ability to keep beating yourself up over something that happened twenty years ago."

"It was nineteen years ago, actually. And I'll beat myself up over it as much as I please."

"Don't you think it's about time you accepted that it is Belagren, not you, who's responsible for fooling the world into believing a lie?"

Neris looked at him and shook his head sadly. "Even now, you mouth the words but you don't understand their significance. Don't you ever wonder how she could do that, Dirk? Don't you ever ask yourself how one moderately attractive, not-very-bright Sundancer rose from total obscurity to control of half the world in less than two decades? You've met the woman. There's nothing special about her. So why do men who in every other way are reasonable and intelligent people fall for her lies? How does she manipulate a man as powerful as Antonov Latanya?"

"You tell me. You're the one who helped her."

Neris frowned at the reminder, but Dirk had learned a lot about him these past two years. Everybody was so afraid of setting him off that nobody dared mention that it was the information he provided to the High Priestess that gave her power. But

Neris *wanted* to talk about it. He badly wanted to share his guilt, as if it somehow made it less. And he burned with the need for vengeance. The madman's true torment, Dirk often thought, was not what he had done, but that he was powerless to undo the damage.

"I helped her by telling her when the second sun would return. I never had anything to do with the Milk of the Goddess."

"What's the Milk of the Goddess got to do with it?" Dirk asked.

"It's the key to sustaining Belagren's power...that and the Shadowdancers...At least it's how she's got away with it for as long as she has." Then he smiled slyly and added, "The Goddess certainly hasn't been speaking to her much lately."

"I don't see the connection."

The madman stared at him owlishly. "And Tia said you were as smart as me?"

"Fine, then don't explain it," he shrugged. "You *are* mad if you think there is any sort of connection between the orbit of our suns and something the Shadowdancers make you drink to get aroused."

Neris grinned. "You think that's all it does? You're not just dim, you're actively stupid."

There was such a glint of mischief in the older man's eyes that Dirk could not help but smile. "What are you saying, Neris? That it's the Milk of the Goddess that gives her power?"

"Have you ever tried it?"

Dirk shifted uncomfortably as he thought of Marqel and his one encounter with the Milk of the Goddess. "Once."

"Then you've some idea of what I'm talking about."

"Actually, Neris, I have *no* idea what you're talking about."

Neris sighed heavily. "Oh, very well, I'll explain it to you, seeing as how you're too stupid to work it out for yourself. And I'll use lots of small words so I can be certain you understand it."

"I'd appreciate that," Dirk replied wryly.

Still clutching the books, Neris assumed a lecturing tone. "The second sun vanished when I was a boy. The suffering was indescribable. Our crops failed. Our cattle died. It was cold, the seas started to drop, and then the earthquakes started and volcanoes that had been dormant for centuries suddenly began to wake. There was only darkness during the day and the red light from the first sun at night. Not long after that, I was sent to the Sundancers at the temple in Bollow."

"Did your parents swear you to the Goddess?"

"Not really. Mostly I was sent there because my family was facing starvation. The Sundancers were willing to take in unwanted children, provided their parents swore an oath to follow the Goddess. I became a Sundancer because that meant there was one less mouth to feed."

"What happened after you got there?"

"I'll tell you, if you ever stop interrupting."

"Sorry."

"I was thirteen years old when I arrived. They put me to work in the kitchens. One day, I was taking a tray to some scholars working in the library. They had a mathematical problem written up on the wall that they couldn't solve."

"And you solved it?"

Neris looked incredibly smug. "After that, I didn't work in the kitchens anymore."

"Is that when they sent you to Omaxin?"

The madman shook his head. "No. But it wasn't long after that Ella Geon arrived. She is a truly evil woman, Dirk, worse than Belagren, worse than Antonov..." Neris's voice trailed off, as if it was too difficult to continue.

"What happened?" Dirk prompted gently.

"I studied. I learned. I'll spare you the boring details." Neris's eyes glazed over as he lost himself in the memory of it. Then he shrugged and looked down, as if ashamed. "Unfortunately, I also fell in love with Ella. Not that she ever noticed I was even alive in those days...Anyway, it was seven or eight years later that Paige Halyn sent us to Omaxin to see if there was anything in the ruins that might help us. That's when I discovered the hall with the Eye and told Ella and Belagren about it..." Neris laughed, but it was full of bitterness and pain. "You want to know what's really funny? I tried so damn hard! I thought that if I discovered something useful, something that Ella wanted, or needed, she'd love me. And I even deluded myself into believing that it worked. After I told Ella and Belagren what I'd discovered, Ella came to me the very next night, just like I had always dreamed..."

"It's not your fault, Neris. You couldn't have known what they'd do with the information."

"I should have known. Perhaps I did know and just pretended not to see. Anyway, Ella and Belagren had one more weapon in their arsenal that I didn't know about until it was too late. That made all the difference."

"The Milk of the Goddess?"

He shook his head. "Poppy-dust."

Neris closed his eyes for a moment. "Goddess, I can still remember the first time I tried it. It was like I'd discovered a new plane of existence. You've no idea what it felt like. Suddenly, I saw things differently. When I took the dust, I was a different man. It made me smarter. I would have giant leaps of intuition and reasoning. It made me more articulate, more confident, more...more everything! I thought I was invincible!" He opened his eyes and stared at Dirk balefully. "Do you see the irony, Dirk? I was only capable of working out *exactly* when the second sun would return while I was lost in the drug."

"Why didn't you stop taking it?"

"I didn't *want* to stop! I still don't! How can I make you understand? Poppy-dust is a demanding mistress, Dirk. At first, you want her. Then you need her. Then you crave her. Before long, you can't function without her. I reached that pathetic milestone in record time. Then Ella told me if I ever shared what I learned with anyone else, she'd take it away from me. That's *why* it's my fault. Because I'm weak. Antonov's baby son, his wife who killed herself, all the people who died in the war, all the people who die each year at the Landfall Feast—their blood is on my hands! I made it happen. I gave Belagren and Ella the knowledge they wanted in order to ease my own suffering."

"And what about the Milk of the Goddess? Where does that fit in?"

"You've seen the mushroom, Jaquison's Blight?"

Dirk shook his head. "I've heard about it. I can remember

somebody finding a patch in Elcast when I was small. Mother had them burn half the damn forest down to be certain they were destroyed."

"Your mother is a wise woman, Dirk, if a little excessive. The Blight only thrives during the Age of Shadows. It can't survive the light and heat of two suns. Distilled, the mushroom is a powerful aphrodisiac. But more important, it destroys reason. You wanted to know how Belagren gained so much power? She introduced the Milk of the Goddess to the Landfall Festival."

He stared at Neris, not sure if he believed the madman. "But how? ..."

"How does she do it? It's painfully simple, Dirk. If Belagren has a gift at all, it's that she understands man's baser instincts. She understands what it means to strip away our veneer of civilization, our thin human skin, even if only for one night of the year. You've no idea the power that gives her. You've no concept of how seductive that can be."

"If that's the case, why is it only the unmarried men and women who take part in the ceremony?"

"Bah! Unmarried! Why do you think the participants are masked, Dirk?"

He thought about that for a moment, not completely convinced. "When I drank the Milk of the Goddess all it did was convince me I never want to touch the stuff again."

"Did you sample the delights of a Shadowdancer while you were under its influence?"

Dirk hesitated before he answered. "Yes."

"And what was that like?"

"It was the stupidest thing I've ever done."

"You say that now. But what was it like at the time, Dirk? What was it like when you *didn't* care? What was it like to let out that animal that resides within us all? Don't you remember what it felt like? Don't you recall how intoxicating it was? Don't you sometimes wake up at night, dreaming of her ... dreaming of recapturing that feeling?"

"No," he declared emphatically.

"That's a lie. Of course you do. It's why the Milk of the

Goddess works so well—because every man and woman who takes it hungers for that release. They hunger for that one night of the year when they can delude themselves into thinking that they are masters of their own destiny. Only a few of the very strong can resist it."

Dirk thought about it, consciously trying to remember a night that, for two years, he had quite deliberately blocked out. "It was like a nightmare," he admitted finally. "Like I was someone else. It was like...I don't know...I mean...I knew who I was, but it wasn't really me...It's hard to explain."

"You don't need to explain. I've been there."

"Is that what drove you mad?"

Neris stared at him for a moment and then shrugged. "I'm not mad, Dirk. I'm far saner than I want to be. Actually, I would love to be truly insane. I wouldn't have to care, then."

Dirk nodded in understanding. How much easier life would be, how uncomplicated, if he could simply do what Neris had done and give himself over to the dark side of his nature, rather than face the consequences of what he had done.

"That night...I recall every detail. But after the Landfall Festival, nobody remembers anything. Why?"

"They remember, Dirk. But how many of them are willing to admit it?" Neris studied him closely. "You hide dark secrets, Dirk Provin, and my daughter despises you for them. Is it that you've tasted the Milk of the Goddess? Is it that you've been in the arms of a Shadowdancer? Is that why she doesn't trust you?" When Dirk did not answer, he chuckled. "I'd not boast about having slept with a Shadowdancer to anyone else in Mil, if I were you. Tia wouldn't be the only one to look at you askance if they realized how close to the heart of the beast you've lain."

"And how close is that, exactly?" Tia asked from the cave's entrance.

Dirk jumped to his feet and turned to stare at her, appalled to think she may have overheard their discussion. She met his eye for a moment, then turned and stalked off.

"Tia!" he called after her.

Neris chuckled softly and began to sing softly, "You're in trouble now... you're in trouble now..."

Cursing the madman, Dirk ran after Tia, scrambling down the perilous goat track to the beach. "Tia!"

She stopped when she reached the beach and turned to face him. Her small dinghy was pulled up beside his on the sand. He slithered to a halt on the beach in front of her, but before he could say anything, she tried to hit him with her clenched fist. Dirk saw it coming and dodged. Tia drew back her arm for another attempt, but he caught her wrist before she could do any damage.

"Let me go!" she snarled.

"Tia, you didn't hear all of it. It's not what you think..."

"It's *exactly* what I think, Dirk Provin!"

"It didn't happen the way—"

"Don't bother explaining it, Dirk. I know what happened. I saw you."

Dirk let go of her wrist with a shove.

"I saw you! That night in Avacas. The night before you killed Johan. I saw you with a Shadowdancer. Goddess! How could I forget about that! I was so right about you! You're so deep in the Lion of Senet's pocket they even let you have a Shadowdancer of your own!"

"She claimed I raped her!" he shouted at her, stunning her into silence. Then, in a much more reasonable tone, he added: "It's why Kirsh put a reward out on me. It had nothing to do with Antonov. The Shadowdancer in question isn't even Senetian. She's a Dhevynian thief Belagren recruited in Elcast. She spiked my drink with the Milk of the Goddess out of nothing more than spite because Alenor and I found her in the woods fooling around with Kirsh. The next day she turned up covered in bruises claiming that I raped her. Kirsh nearly killed me over it."

"Why would she claim you raped her?"

"I don't know."

"You didn't think to *ask*?"

"Well, I didn't really have the time to launch a full investigation," he snapped. "You see, the very next day I killed my own father and things got a little hectic after that."

Tia didn't say anything for a while; she just stared at him, her suspicion and distrust so tangible Dirk could almost touch them. He sighed helplessly. "Look, I'll go. Why don't you go up and visit with Neris?"

"Has he told you anything useful?"

Dirk shook his head. "More of the same. He keeps talking about the Eye, but other than that..."

Tia nodded. "I'll see you later then." She pushed past him and began climbing the goat track up to Neris's cave.

"Tia!" he called after her.

She stopped and turned back to look at him. "What?"

I'm not what you think, he wanted to explain. *I'm not a monster. I'm not a murderer. I'm not a rapist. If I'm guilty of any crime, it's the crime of being a fool.* But he could not find a way to say it without sounding like he was just trying to compensate for his own guilt. "It doesn't matter," he said.

Tia studied him thoughtfully for a moment then turned back to climbing the track up to her father's cave.

Chapter 10

Dirk returned to Neris's cave the following morning only to find it empty. There was no sign of the madman, the fire was cold and his bed was neatly made. Neris was not the type to make his bed when he got up in the morning, so it was a fair bet that Tia had made it for him the day before and he had not slept in it that night. Dirk walked back outside and looked up at the overhanging ledge. As he suspected, Neris was sitting there, still as a lizard, staring up at the second sun. He had probably been up there all night.

"Neris!"

The madman looked down at him, not surprised to find he had a visitor. "Hello, Dirk."

"What are you doing up there?"

"I was considering doing my Deathbringer routine," Neris

told him, sounding quite reasonable. "Haven't done it for a while. People might start to think I'm not crazy if I don't give them a show every now and then." He looked thoughtful, rather than maniacal, which was a good thing. "I don't think I'll bother now. It doesn't seem to have the same effect on you as it does on Tia. Is that because she's a girl? Or because you couldn't really care less if I jumped off this ledge or not?"

Dirk smiled. He had learned very quickly that the more you tried to coax him down, the more Neris liked to pretend he was going to jump. The first time he had come to visit Neris without Tia, the madman had threatened to throw himself off the ledge. Dirk had shrugged disinterestedly and headed back down to the beach. A few moments later Neris had scrambled down the path after him, begging him not to leave. There had not been any trouble with Neris threatening suicide since, although he'd had no luck trying to convince Tia she should stop reacting to her father's threats by panicking. They'd had a rather heated argument about it, actually. Tia was not impressed that after a few days, Dirk thought he knew more about handling her father than she did.

"Well, if you are going to jump, can you wait until I've gone? I don't need Tia blaming me for your death as well as..." he stopped himself before he could say anything to incriminate himself.

Neris stared at him cannily. "As well as *who*?"

"Nobody," Dirk shrugged.

"You're never going to win this fight if you can't learn to lie better than that, Dirk Provin."

"Who says I'm trying to win *any* fight?"

Neris did not answer him. He climbed to his feet and stood on the edge of the precipice for a moment, as if considering whether to throw himself off, and then, with a shrug, he turned and disappeared from view as he headed for the small path that led down to the cave and the lower ledge where Dirk waited.

"If you don't want to fight, then why are you here?" Neris asked a few moments later, as he squeezed himself through the tight gap in the rocks that gave access to the upper ledge.

"I thought you wanted to play chess."

"I don't mean here and now, you idiot boy. I mean, what are you doing here in Mil?"

"I don't really have much choice, Neris," he pointed out, following the madman into the cool dimness of his cave.

"Not at first, perhaps," Neris agreed, as he picked up the kettle, peered inside to see if there was enough water and carried it over to the fireplace. "But it's not as if you're a prisoner here. You've been in Mil long enough to call yourself a Baenlander. Why do you stay?"

"Why do *you* stay?" Dirk asked in reply.

Neris poked around the dead coals with a frown. "That's easy. They feed me and they keep me supplied with poppy-dust. What's your excuse?"

"Well...they feed me..." Dirk said with a smile.

Neris scowled at him. "So for the sake of a few regular meals, you plan to waste the rest of your life playing chess with a madman? And they say *I'm* the crazy one."

Dirk was not sure he liked what Neris was implying. "What should I be doing then?"

"Righting the wrongs of the world."

"That's a bit rich, coming from the man who caused most of them."

"But I didn't cause them, remember?" Neris retorted, straightening up from the fireplace. "You told me that yesterday. You said I should stop blaming myself."

"So now you're blaming me?"

"I'm not blaming you. Not yet, anyway."

"Not yet?"

He smiled. "You've a little while to go before I decide it's all your fault."

"I don't follow your reasoning, Neris."

"That's because I'm mad," the older man replied cheerfully, squatting down by the kettle and tossing a few sticks on top of the charred remains of the previous day's fire. He began to strike the flint, but seemed more interested in the sparks and the noise than actually lighting the kindling.

Dirk shook his head in confusion, wishing Neris would find

something else to talk about. The madman's logic frequently left him with a headache. "Did you want me to light that?"

"Just because I'm insane doesn't mean I can't use a flint," he snapped defensively.

"I was only trying to be helpful ..."

"If you want to help, why not do something really useful?" Neris suggested, still striking the flint as if he was tapping out the rhythm for a dance. "Save the world. Go back to Avacas and bring that bitch Belagren to her knees."

"Then tell me when the next Age of Shadows is due."

"You don't need to know that to bring Belagren down."

"It would help."

"Yes, but that would be taking the easy way out. I'd rather see you use that mind of yours for something really challenging." He suddenly tossed the flint to Dirk and stood up. "Here, why don't you light it?"

Dirk caught the flint and squatted down beside the fire, arranging the kindling so that it might actually burn.

"Do you know what would happen if Belagren dropped dead tomorrow?" Neris asked as he watched Dirk light the fire.

Dirk didn't answer. He had gotten the kindling smoking and was blowing on it gently, coaxing the tiny flame to life.

"I'll tell you what would happen," Neris continued in a lecturing tone. "Not a damn thing. The world would continue on, just as it is today. Both suns would still rise, the rain would still fall, the volcanoes would still erupt and I'd still want my blincakes made just the way I like them. Nothing would change but the name of the person perpetrating the lies. The lies themselves would continue. They have a life of their own now."

"Then what's the point of killing Belagren?" Dirk asked.

"There isn't one. And you don't need to kill a person; you need to kill an idea. That's a much harder thing to do."

Dirk sat back on his heels and looked up at the madman thoughtfully. "How do you kill an idea?"

"That's the challenge," Neris replied with a smile. "Haven't you got that fire going yet?"

"It's coming. Don't be so impatient."

"I could make it not burn."

"What?" Neris's inability to stay focused on the one subject for long drove Dirk to distraction.

"I can make the wood impervious to flame," the madman announced.

"How?" Dirk asked skeptically.

"Ever seen the stuff they use to clean mold off old stone?"

"I never really paid much attention to what the servants were cleaning."

"That's because you're highborn. You think these things happen by magic."

Dirk sighed. "I still don't see what cleaning mold has to do with making wood impervious to fire."

"That's because you keep interrupting me before I can explain."

"I'm sorry. Please explain it to me."

"There's nothing to explain. If you soak a piece of wood in sinkbore, it won't burn. That's all."

"Sinkbore?"

"That's the stuff they use to clean mold off the stone. They make it in Sidoria, up near the salt lakes...foul-smelling place that it is. But sinkbore works a treat. A little bit of zinc...a little bit of boric acid...a few other goodies thrown in for luck...remarkable stuff."

"When did you become an alchemist?"

"I dabbled in it for a time. When you're addicted to something like poppy-dust, it pays to have a bit of knowledge about chemistry. You never know when you're going to need it. Anyway, I grew up near a zinc mine. There's nothing quite like the smell of burning calamine and wool."

"And exactly what does this have to do with Belagren and the Shadowdancers?"

"Absolutely nothing. Although haven't you ever wondered how they get the wicker suns at the Landfall Feast to burn in different colors?"

"They treat the wood," Dirk answered. "The red flame comes from pinewood pitch, doesn't it?"

"How should I know?"

Dirk smiled and moved the kettle over the flames. "You never answered my question."

"What question?"

"We were talking about killing an idea. At least we were... until you decided to give me a chemistry lesson."

Neris stared at Dirk for a moment and then shrugged. "I don't think you can kill an idea, Dirk. You can change it, maybe, but I don't think you can actually kill it."

"And while ever we believe that, Belagren will keep on getting away with what she does," Dirk pointed out.

"And that's why Johan failed. He was fighting an idea as much as he was a battle. Even if he'd had the strength to defeat Antonov, he still had Belagren and her religion to contend with. I tried to point that out to him, of course, but people tend not to take you very seriously when you're foaming at the mouth."

Dirk smiled thinly. "By the time he'd had his arse kicked by Antonov until it bled, I imagine he'd figured it out. And he never tried again because he couldn't find a way to kill the idea."

"There may be hope for you yet, boy," Neris remarked.

"Why didn't *you* figure out how to do it?" Dirk asked him, a little peeved by Neris's patronizing tone.

The madman shrugged. "Not my area of expertise, I'm afraid. Ask me how much the world weighs and I'll figure it out for you, Dirk, but to destroy a whole religion... that takes a special sort of skill that I don't have. It takes political cunning, not mathematical ability. And nerves of solid steel," he added with a grin. "I'd rather face an army of trained killers any day than a handful of religious fanatics. Anyway, it wasn't my job. The one who should have killed the idea, the only person with the power to nip it in the bud, did absolutely nothing about it."

"Who was that?"

"The Lord of the Suns, Dirk. Paige Halyn."

"His brother, Brahm, was our Sundancer on Elcast when I was a child. I met Paige Halyn in Avacas once. He seemed a harmless old coot."

"He is," Neris agreed, "which is largely the problem. Remember, the Shadowdancers are a part of his Church, and subject to his authority—in theory, if not in practice. If he'd denied Belagren's visions when she first claimed to have them—if Paige Halyn had denounced her prophesies as heresy from the outset—Belagren would never have become as powerful as she is."

"Why didn't he?"

Neris shrugged. "I don't know. But I tried to tell him what she was doing. I even explained about the ruins in Omaxin...I told him all of it. But he didn't do a damn thing."

"Maybe he was afraid of casting doubt on the validity of his own beliefs," Dirk suggested. "If Belagren claimed to speak for the Goddess and he publicly denounced her visions, where does that leave him? How could he prove the unprovable, when Belagren had the second sun poised to reappear to back up her claims and he had nothing but his faith?"

Neris thought about that for a while, and then nodded. "You may not be as smart as me, Dirk, but you've a better head for politics than I ever had. Belagren did, too, which is why I could never get the better of her. She was livid when she learned I'd been to see the Lord of the Suns, though. It was after that that she sent me back to Omaxin to seal the cavern and build the Labyrinth. Is that kettle boiled yet?"

"Give it time," Dirk told him.

Neris smiled suddenly. "That's the answer, you know."

"The answer to what?"

"To all your questions. When is the next Age of Shadows due...how do you kill an idea? Just give it time, Dirk. Just give it time."

Chapter 11

For days, Tia fretted about what she had overheard Dirk telling Neris in his cave. For days she could barely think of anything else.

Tia had promised two years ago to not to reveal that it was Dirk who had killed Johan Thorn. But she had agreed reluctantly, mostly because she was desperate to protect Johan's daughter from the pain such a revelation would bring. She was not sure she could hide the truth for much longer.

How much pain would Mellie suffer if the Lion of Senet ever found his way through the delta? The short-term hurt of Mellie learning her newly acquired brother was the man who killed her father might well be the lesser of two evils.

By the time Troitsa came around, Tia had made up her mind. She could not keep her awful secret any longer.

She waited in her room until the house was almost empty, her heart constricting as she heard Mellie chattering away to Reithan and Dirk about what she was going to wish for when she floated her garland. Tia waited until the voices had faded to nothing before making her way through the house to Johan's study, where Lexie was putting the final touches on her own garland. To her surprise, Porl Isingrin was with her. She had not realized the pirate captain had returned from his last voyage.

"Tia!" Lexie exclaimed as she looked up. "You're not ready yet."

Tia glanced at Lexie and the captain with the feeling she had interrupted something important. "I'm not going."

Lexie put down the ball of string she was using to tie off the garland. "What's wrong, dear?"

"I have to talk to you, Lexie. Alone."

"That sounds rather ominous. What did you want to talk about?"

"Dirk."

"What a coincidence," Porl said. He was standing near the open doors that led onto the balcony. "We were just talking about him,"

"What's he done now?" she asked.

"Wallin Provin is dead."

"Oh," Tia said, feeling a little guilty. She had not expected that.

"We were just debating the advisability of telling Dirk," Lexie explained.

"I'm sure he'll get over the grief in record time."

"That's not the problem, lass," Porl said. "Morna Provin has been arrested. She's to be executed at the next Landfall Feast."

Tia was not sure what to say. She had a rather low opinion of Morna Provin, but despite what she thought of the woman who abandoned Johan for a life of comfort as the Duchess of El- cast, nobody deserved to die like that.

"Are you afraid of upsetting him, or that he'll do some- thing stupid?"

"The latter mostly," Porl agreed.

Tia shrugged. "Tell him. If he wants to go charging off to Elcast to rescue his mother, then good riddance to him, I say. Maybe we'll get lucky and he'll get himself killed in the process. Anyway, you can't hide that sort of news for long. Dirk is going to find out eventually, and I imagine he'll be rather peeved at you for keeping it from him. And perish the thought we might do anything to upset our precious Dirk."

"Tia, what is the matter with you?" Lexie sighed. "Have you nothing kind to say about that poor boy?"

"*Poor boy?*" she repeated incredulously. "*Poor boy!* God- dess, Lexie, do you know what he is! Have you any inkling of what he's done?"

"What did he do, Tia?" Lexie asked, sitting down in the big leather chair that had once been Johan's.

"Dirk is the one..." She found couldn't do it, could not bring herself to say it.

"Who killed Johan?" Lexie finished for her.

Tia burst into tears as two years of pent-up secrets suddenly found release. Porl looked away uncomfortably as Lexie rose from the chair and walked around the desk. She took Tia in her arms and held her while she sobbed, muttering soothing non-sense words, as she had when Tia was a small child. "There, there, darling, you don't have to hold it in any longer."

"I'm so sorry, Lexie," she sobbed. "I know he reminds you of Johan. But he's a killer. He murdered his own father..."

"I know, Tia, I know..."

Tia lost herself in the comfort of Lexie's arms for a time, and then she pulled away, staring at her foster mother. "What do you mean, you *know*?"

Lexie pulled a kerchief out of the sleeve of her gown and handed it to Tia before she answered.

"About three days after you brought him to Mil the first time, Dirk came to see me, Tia," Porl said. "I brought him to Lexie. He told us what happened. He told us about Johan, about the Shadowdancer they claim he raped, even about how he ac-quired the dubious title the Butcher of Elcast."

"So you got his nicely sanitized version of events," Tia con-cluded, after blowing her nose loudly on the kerchief. "And now you're on his side. Damn, he really is clever, isn't he?"

"I doubt anything Dirk told us was sanitized for our bene-fit, Tia," Lexie said. "In fact, he was quite distraught. I suspect he confessed to us in the hope that we might punish him in some way. I think he was trying to relieve the pain he was in."

"He never suffered a moment's remorse over what hap-pened," she objected. "I was there, Lexie. I saw it happen."

"You're wrong, darling. I don't think a day goes by that Dirk isn't tormented by what he did. I suspect it will haunt him for the rest of his life."

"Good!" she declared with an inelegant sniff.

Lexie sighed. "Sit down, Tia."

"Why, so you can convince me how wrong I am about Dirk Provin? Don't waste your breath."

"No, I think I need to convince you how wrong you are about Johan."

Tia stared at her in confusion, taking the seat facing the

desk. Lexie dragged another chair over to face her and sat down. "Describe Johan for me, Tia."

"He was tall...sort of, with dark hair and brown eyes..."

"Not his physical description. Tell me what sort of person he was."

"Brave. Noble. Compassionate...I don't see the point of this, Lexie."

"You remember Johan as a hero," Porl remarked.

Lexie nodded in agreement. "You never saw the man, Tia, only the tragic figure of a deposed king who was robbed of his kingdom by an evil warlord."

"But that's exactly what happened..."

"In your mind, certainly," Lexie agreed. "But you weren't there. The fact is Johan lost Dhevyn because he invited Antonov in. Worse than that, he begged the Lion of Senet for help, and he allowed the true love of his life—"

"He loved you, Lexie!"

"Johan loved Morna, Tia, more than you will ever understand, unless you've loved someone the same way. Johan and I came together for comfort as much as love, and we were happy enough together, but his last thoughts were of Morna, not me."

Tia did not want to admit such an unpleasant truth. *Give my love to your mother.* It was the last thing Johan said. And he said it to Dirk.

"But he—"

"No, let me finish. Johan allowed the love of his life to marry the man Antonov chose because he was too afraid to deny him."

"Johan wasn't afraid of anything!" she declared hotly.

"Don't be ridiculous, Tia. Johan was as full of fear as any other man. Why do you think he never tried to take Dhevyn back? The Johan you have built up in your mind is ten feet tall and made of solid gold. The real Johan was a thoughtful man, a cautious man, and one who spent his entire life paying for his mistakes. Think about it, Tia. Why do you think Johan left orders to kill him if he was ever captured? He wasn't a martyr by nature. He was a realist."

"I still don't see how any of this excuses what Dirk did."

"Do you know why Morna left Johan, Tia?"

"Because she was a coward."

Lexie shook her head. "She left him because she thought Johan was the coward. Morna was a passionate young woman in those days. A bit like you, now that I think about it. She wanted to set the world on fire. When we suffered such an appalling defeat at the end of the war, Johan decided not to try again. We were weak, hungry, demoralized and decimated. Morna disagreed. She wanted to keep on fighting."

"So she left him and went back to her husband? Where's the logic in that?"

"I don't think her plan was to sit quietly as the Duchess of Elcast for long," Porl suggested. "She went back to Elcast to claim her eldest son, but when she got there, Antonov and Belagren were waiting for her. She was tried and sentenced to death. Wallin begged Antonov for her life and he relented, but only as long as Morna agreed never to leave Elcast again."

"So she pretended that Dirk was Wallin's son, and quietly raised her boys on Elcast for the next sixteen years? Some revolutionary she turned out to be."

"That's a reality of life you've yet to learn, Tia," Lexie warned. "You can start out with the best of intentions in the world; but somehow one day turns into another and before you know it your children have grown and you haven't done half the things you set out to do when you were younger."

"I still don't see the point..."

"The point is, Tia, you're judging Dirk when you could not possibly know how he feels. He did a very courageous thing, and—"

"*Courageous?*" she cried in disbelief, jumping to her feet. "Lexie! He killed your husband!"

"And I'll mourn Johan until the day I die. But what I *won't* do is condemn a decent young man who saved my husband from months—possibly years—of torture at the hands of Antonov Latanya by doing what Johan asked of him."

Tia sank down on the chair again. "Lexie, why is it only me that thinks he's dangerous?"

"Because nobody else has quite the same black-and-white

view of the world that you have, Tia. In real life, good people sometimes do bad things and bad people are not all totally evil. Dirk lives with what he's done every day of his life. Just because he doesn't wear his heart on his sleeve, doesn't mean he isn't punishing himself over it. He certainly doesn't need you twisting the knife at every opportunity."

"It's so unfair! He kills Johan and somehow I'm the one in trouble!"

"Perhaps you should think about apologizing."

"To Dirk Provin? The second sun will freeze over before that happens."

"Well, if you can't bring yourself to apologize, at least give him the benefit of the doubt."

"You really don't resent him, do you. He's Morna's son, for Goddess's sake! How can you even bear to have him in your house?"

"I have a penchant for taking in lost children, Tia."

She looked away guiltily. "You both think I'm being unreasonable, don't you? I know Reithan does."

"I think you're still grieving for a man you loved like a father. But he's been dead for two years, Tia. It's time to let it go."

Tia wiped her eyes with the kerchief. "I can't just forgive and forget, Lexie. I was there. I saw it happen."

"Nobody expects you to forget. But I think it's time you forgave Dirk." She held up her hand when Tia tried to object. "When you harbor bitterness, my dear, happiness will find another port to dock in. I'm not saying this for Dirk's benefit. While I'm sure he'd appreciate hearing a civil word from you on occasion, I think that young man is more than strong enough to weather your rage. But I worry about you. You cannot go on living in a state of constant fury. Your anger will destroy you long before it destroys Dirk." She took Tia's hands in hers and forced a cheery smile. "Now, why don't you go wash your face and put a dress on and we'll go down to the beach with the others. It's not often we get to have a party here, and we shouldn't miss this one."

"I suppose," she agreed glumly. "But I'm not wearing a dress."

"It was worth a try, Lexie," Porl said with a smile.

Tia wiped her eyes, sniffing back the last of her tears. "I'm sorry, Lexie."

"You don't owe me an apology. Now, off you go, or we'll miss the garland floating."

Tia walked toward the door, turning back to look at Porl when she reached it. "Who else knows, Captain?"

"A few of the council we thought could be trusted."

"You never told Mellie?"

"No. You were right to keep it from her, Tia. Mellie doesn't need to know."

"I miss him so much, Lexie."

"We all do, Tia. But life goes on. Johan wouldn't want you to waste your life fretting over something you can never change."

Tia nodded silently and walked back to her room.

Chapter 12

By the time they arrived on the beach, most of the children were caught up in a boisterous game of stingball. The game involved a circle of players, armed with a hard leather ball, aiming it at the mass of children gathered in the center, with the intention of striking them, thus eliminating them from the game. It was called stingball, because as the younger, less agile children were eliminated from the circle, the game frequently became quite savage, as the sole aim of the outer circle was to hit the remaining participants hard enough to bruise.

When Tia and Lexie arrived, there were only seven players left in the center, among them Mellie and Eleska, who squealed with triumph every time they managed to successfully dodge the ball. Reithan and Dirk both stood in the outer ring, laughing almost as hard as the girls as they hurled the ball across the circle, trying to get the few remaining players out.

Tia watched the game for a while, laughing as Reithan caught Eleska a stinging blow on the shins. She limped out of the circle and the game carried on, the children who had already been eliminated cheering on their faster, stronger teammates.

"That really hurt!" Eleska exclaimed as she hobbled over to where Lexie and Tia were standing.

"Well, Eleska," Lexie said with an unsympathetic smile, "if you want to play with the big boys, you have to be able to take it."

"Still, they shouldn't throw so hard."

"It wouldn't be any fun if they did that, Eleska," Tia pointed out. "Mellie seems to be keeping up, though."

"I bet they don't throw it so hard at her."

"On the contrary," Lexie corrected. "It is the sacred duty of all brothers the world over to brand their little sisters as hard as possible when playing stingball. It's in the rules."

"What rules?"

Before Lexie could answer, Mellie let out a howl of pain and the game halted while she limped from the circle, rubbing her behind with a sour look.

Tia smiled as Mellie approached, looking mightily put out. "Never turn your back on the ball, Mel, you should know that by now."

"It wasn't fair! I wasn't ready for it!"

"Who got you?"

"Dirk, the rotten bastard."

"Mellie!" Lexie cried, shocked by her vulgarity. "Mind your tongue!"

"I didn't mean *that* sort of bastard, Mama," Mellie explained. "I mean the hits-you-on-the-bum-when-you're-not-ready-for-it sort of bastard."

"Oh," Tia said, biting back a smile, "that sort."

Lexie rolled her eyes. "Dear Goddess, to think that in other circumstances she'd have been raised at court!"

"That's right!" Eleska exclaimed. "I keep forgetting you're a princess, Mel."

"So does Mellie, I fear," Lexie muttered, smiling fondly at her daughter.

A cheer went up from the circle as Tabor Isingrin was struck. There were only four boys left in the circle now, and the game was getting quite rough and very fast. Tia watched Dirk, Reithan and the other half dozen young men in the outer circle hurling the ball to and fro, thinking Mellie and Eleska had no idea how much they'd held back to prevent doing the girls any serious harm. There was an unwritten rule among those who were old enough to man the outer circle. You never aimed above the waist, and you always let the little kids think they were winning for a while. But once they were gone, once the only players left were the young, fit and rather cocky youths of the village, then nobody held back.

"Holen Baker will win," Mellie predicted as yet another player was struck down. "He always does." She looked around, trying to find someone in the crowd. "Has anyone seen Eryk?"

"He got hit just after the little Jarik twins," Eleska told her. "He was a bit upset he got out so soon."

Mellie sighed. "I'd better go find him. I promised he could float his garland next to mine."

"That was very thoughtful of you, Mellie," Lexie told her. "You go find him then and we'll meet you down by the water."

"I'll fetch the garlands," Eleska offered, hurrying off in the opposite direction, her limp forgotten. Another cheer went up as two more boys fell victim to the ball in quick succession.

As Mellie forecast, Holen Baker was the only one left standing and the other children swarmed him as he whooped with delight over his victory. The outer circle broke up as Reithan caught sight of them. He signaled to Dirk and they both headed over to where Lexie and Tia were standing.

"I'm getting old," Reithan complained when they reached them. "I swear stingball never used to be that much hard work."

"Don't expect any sympathy from me," Lexie laughed. "If you insist on volunteering for these things, you can't complain about them afterwards."

"Can't I? What's the point then?"

"You complain all you want, Reithan," Tia consoled him. "Nobody's going to listen to you anyway, so what difference does it make?"

"You're a heartless fiend, Tia," Reithan accused. "Now I know where Mellie gets it from."

"What about you, Dirk?" Lexie asked. "You appear none the worse for the wear."

"Well, I'm younger than Reithan," Dirk replied with a grin. "I suppose when I get to his advanced age, I'll be feeling it, too."

"Hey! You're supposed to be on my side!"

"I *am* on your side," Dirk assured him. "I'll fetch your cane and your shawl any time you're ready for them."

Tia watched them joking and laughing, feeling like an outsider. She wondered for a moment if that was what she really distrusted about Dirk. No matter what she did, Tia would never be truly a part of Johan's family. She was not blood—not like Dirk and Mellie and Reithan. She was the lost child taken in because her mother was a coldhearted bitch and her father was a wasted drug addict.

"Very droll," Reithan said with a scowl. "I'll remember who thinks he's younger and fitter the next time we have to reef the mainsail in a storm."

"If you had any brains, Reithan, you wouldn't have the damn mainsail set in a storm in the first place," Porl Isingrin remarked as he came up behind Tia.

"I can't win. They're either younger and fitter or older and wiser..."

"Life's like that," Porl agreed. "Nice game, by the way. Although I think someone should check on Holen Baker."

"Why? The little weasel didn't even look like getting hit."

"That's my point," the pirate laughed. "There's something wrong with that boy. Nobody should be able to move that fast."

Their conversation was suddenly halted by a high-pitched scream echoing across the beach. Everybody froze at the unexpected sound.

"That's Mellie," Tia said.

She had barely uttered the words before Reithan and Dirk

were running in the direction of the screams. Without even thinking, she raced after them, a sick feeling in the pit of her stomach. Mellie screamed again. They followed the sound, crashing through the scrubby undergrowth that fought to survive near the beach. Dirk streaked ahead of Reithan and she could hear Porl Isingrin's labored breathing behind her.

They found Mellie in a small clearing. She was lying on the ground, with Eryk sitting astride her, his hand over her mouth as he tried to stop her screaming. Tia arrived in time to see Dirk haul the boy off her. Then he hit him so hard that Eryk's feet left the ground and the boy flew backward, landing on his back several feet from Mellie. Tia raced to her and gathered the child into her arms. Mellie was sobbing uncontrollably.

"What in the name of the Goddess is happening?" Porl bellowed as he reached them. He took in the scene with a glance and paled. "Did he? . . ."

"I don't think so," Dirk said, panting heavily.

Eryk tried to sit up, but Reithan turned on him savagely. "You stay right where you are, boy!"

"Reithan, get Mellie up to the house," Lexie ordered calmly as she stepped into the clearing.

Tia marveled at her composure. She wanted to kill someone, starting with Eryk. And then she would probably strangle Dirk Provin next, for bringing him to Mil in the first place.

"Porl, would you see to Eryk, please?"

The pirate nodded and looked at Dirk. "We'll take him up to the longhouse."

Dirk bent down to haul Eryk up by his shirt. The boy's face was streaked with tears, his expression stunned, his nose dripping blood unheeded down the front of his shirt.

Lexie turned to address the rest of the crowd that had followed the screams. "The rest of you, get back to the party. The excitement is over."

Through force of habit as much as anything else, the villagers complied with her orders. Dirk shoved Eryk in front of him, wearing that same icy expression Tia remembered from the night he killed Johan. She shuddered at the recollection as she helped Reithan scoop Mellie up into his arms.

Eof the labyrinth

"It's all right, Mel," she whispered soothingly. "It's all over."

Reithan glared at her for a moment then turned to watch Dirk and Porl escorting Eryk away. "It's not over, Tia. Not by a long shot."

Lexie and Finidice put Mellie to bed, leaving Reithan and Tia with nothing to do but anxiously pace the balcony. When Lexie finally emerged from Mellie's room, her expression was grim.

"She blames herself," Lexie told them, as she sank wearily down onto a chair.

"That's ridiculous!" Tia cried. "She's fourteen!"

"Keep your voice down," Reithan warned.

"It's ridiculous however loud you say it, Reithan," she snapped.

They heard footsteps on the veranda and turned to find Porl Isingrin and Dirk had arrived.

"How's Eryk?" Lexie asked.

"Confused," Dirk said. "He's not sure what he did wrong."

"Well, you would defend him, wouldn't you?"

Dirk seemed quite offended. "If I thought for a moment that Eryk seriously wanted to hurt Mellie, Tia, I'd kill him myself."

"Settle down, both of you," Lexie ordered impatiently. "Mellie says Eryk tried to kiss her. She got a fright so she screamed, he tried to shush her, they fell over and that's when we found them."

Porl nodded in agreement. "That's much the same story we got from the boy. He's quite distressed that he might have hurt her."

"He can afford to be," Tia remarked sourly. "He was the one on top."

"Tia, please!"

She turned away from Lexie's accusing stare only to find Mellie standing on the veranda in her nightgown.

"You're talking about what to do with Eryk, aren't you?"

"Mellie, you should go back to bed..." Lexie began.

"You shouldn't be mad at Eryk, Mama. It wasn't his fault."

"Don't worry about him, Mel," Reithan told her. "We'll take care of it. Go back to bed."

"No! Not until you listen to me. It wasn't his fault. It was my fault. Eleska and I went up to visit Eryk the other day and we were fooling around, talking about who was going to marry who and...I said I wanted to marry Eryk."

"And he believed you?" Lexie asked.

Mellie nodded. "He doesn't understand, Mama. He didn't realize we were joking. He'd carved a doll for me and when he gave it to me, he said it was my betrothal present. He said all this other stuff too, about loving me, and being so happy that I wanted to marry him, too...Then he tried to kiss me. He didn't even try that hard, and I didn't mean to scream like that...I just got such a surprise, we fell over, and you found us. It looked a lot worse than it really was. Please don't hurt him."

"Nobody's going to hurt him, lass," Porl assured her.

"Dirk hit him pretty hard."

"He'll get over a few loose teeth," Dirk said.

"You have to promise me. It truly wasn't his fault. He's not mean or vicious and he wasn't trying to hurt me. He's just... different."

"You have my word that no harm will come to him, Mellie," Lexie promised.

Mellie studied their faces in the red sunlight and then nodded and left the balcony without another word.

Porl Isingrin broke the uncomfortable silence. "Despite what it looked like, I believe Mellie may have the right of it."

"How can you say that?" Tia demanded. "She's a child!"

"In his head, at least, Eryk is probably younger than Mellie," Reithan pointed out.

"Aye, but that child's mind is in the body of a young man," Porl reminded them. "How old is he now? Fifteen?"

"Sixteen," Dirk corrected.

"Even worse. We look at him and see the child in his mind. We forget about the fact that he's almost a man, with a man's wants and needs..."

"Oh, please! *Spare* me!" Tia cried. "If he's old enough to

have *urges,* then he should be damn well old enough to control them."

"You can start lecturing us on control when you learn to control *your* temper, young lady," Porl retorted impatiently. He turned to the others before she could add anything further. "I agree Eryk probably meant Mellie no harm this time, but if he thinks he's in love with her, that could cause problems in the future."

"What do you suggest we do, Porl?" Lexie asked. "I can hardly post a guard on Mellie on the off chance that Eryk might one day decide to pursue her."

"No, of course not. What do you think, Dirk?"

They all turned to look at him. "Send him out to sea."

"You callous bastard," Tia accused. "You'd set that boy afloat on the open sea?"

"Tia, what goes on inside that head of yours?" Reithan asked, shaking his head. "He meant putting him to work on one of the ships." He turned to Dirk and added cautiously, "That is what you meant, isn't it?"

"I meant find him a berth on a ship. That way he'll be away from Mil a good part of the time. It will give him time to get over his obsession with Mellie."

"Oh," Tia said, feeling like an idiot. "That's not a bad idea, actually."

"It's an excellent idea," Lexie agreed. "Can you arrange it, Porl?"

The pirate nodded. "He can come with us to Nova. I'll find him something more permanent when we get back. Perhaps the *Orlando* could find room for him."

"You'll take him to Grannon Rock for Landfall?" Lexie asked thoughtfully. "Then perhaps you should go, too, Dirk."

Dirk shrugged. "If you think it will help."

Tia looked at Lexie. *Why did it make any difference . . .* and then she realized why Lexie had suggested it. If Dirk went with Porl and Reithan to Nova for Landfall to meet with the queen, then he would be isolated on the *Makuan* and unlikely to hear about his mother until it was too late. A part of Tia was uneasy with the decision to conceal the truth from him. If it was her mother about to be burned, she would want to know.

"I'll go, too," she offered, thinking that if Dirk was going to cause trouble, she would see it coming before anybody else did. The rest of them trusted him far too much for her liking. "Is that all right, Captain?" She deliberately did not ask Reithan's permission, certain he would have denied it.

"This voyage is starting to take on the air of a damn pleasure cruise," Porl complained.

"I won't be in the way," she promised.

Porl shrugged. "Aye, I suppose you can come."

"Just don't let her near the galley," Reithan suggested with a sour look.

"Then we'll leave it at that. For now," Lexie announced. "And hopefully that will be the end of it."

Tia nodded her agreement with the others; unable to shake the feeling that Lexie's statement fell into the category of famous last words.

Chapter 13

The High Priestess left for Elcast on the *Calliope* with Prince Antonov the day after Troitsa. A Shadowdancer named Marika Torna had been left in charge in the Hall of Shadows and the High Priestess had left quite specific instructions about what was expected in her absence.

The Landfall Festival was the busiest time of year for the Shadowdancers, and everyone had work to do. The Avacas Landfall Festival was a huge event, involving every Shadowdancer still in the city. Marqel's role was minor, a fact that was even harder to stomach knowing that while she suffered through the raging lust of some minor noble out of his mind with the Milk of the Goddess, that conceited, loathsome...*she-goat*, Caspona Takarnov, would be wrapped in the arms of

Kirshov Latanya on Grannon Rock. Although the knowledge gnawed at Marqel, she could do nothing about it while Ella or Prince Antonov was in the palace nor while the High Priestess was still in Avacas, for that matter.

She had a plan, but for it to work she needed to set the wheels in motion at the very last minute.

Prince Misha was out of danger, although the overdose had left him even weaker than normal, and there were real fears that he would never completely recover. Marqel checked on him the night before Caspona and the others were due to leave, although her attention was not really required. Olena Borne was still in the palace, and Yuri Daranski, Antonov's personal physician from the Hall of Shadows, always tended Misha during Ella's absence. Marqel was still an apprentice, and the care of someone as important as Misha Latanya would never be left solely in the hands of an inexperienced acolyte.

It was late when Marqel visited the Crippled Prince. The red sun flooded the room, making his complexion appear much healthier than it did in the harsh light of the second sun. Misha smiled wanly at her as she placed a cool hand on his forehead. He was much more lucid these past few days, and obviously in pain now that the worst of the drug had worn off.

"You've been watching over me, haven't you?" he asked weakly.

Marqel got along well with Misha. He was easy company and appreciated the attention of a beautiful young woman. In different circumstances, were he not a cripple—were he not destined to die in the High Priestess's grand scheme—she might be quite interested in fostering his obvious attraction.

"I've just been doing my job, your highness."

"I remember you being here...at odd times. I think you've done more than duty calls for, Marqel."

"If I have, it's because you're worth it, your highness," she replied with a coy smile.

Misha was not fooled. "Now you're trying to flatter me."

"Is it working?"

He forced a smile. "Yes."

"Good," she declared, taking a seat beside him on the bed.

"My evil plan to win you over with my beguiling charms is working."

"And once you have me, what are you going to do with me?"

For a fleeting moment, the thought crossed her mind that maybe Misha would not die. Suppose Belagren changed her mind? Suppose something happened to Kirsh and Misha lived to inherit the throne of Senet? She could have Misha with a snap of her fingers if she wanted him. His left side was weak, certainly, but she had nursed him for long enough now to know that the rest of his anatomy functioned quite normally. *What would he give,* she wondered, *for the chance to feel like a real man?* What would he be willing to pay?

She placed her hand on his thigh, making it appear accidental as she turned to smile at him.

"What would you like me to do, your highness?" she asked softly.

Misha stared at her. He was in too much pain to act on her invitation, but he knew it was there. She recognized the look, the need, the desire...

Then sanity returned and she jumped to her feet, assuming an air of professional concern. *Dear Goddess! What am I thinking?*

"I'm sorry...I really have to go now. Yuri is here in the palace if you're in need of anything."

Misha looked rather disappointed, but he nodded in understanding. "I'm still tired. I'll probably just sleep."

"Then sleep well, your highness," she said and hurried from the room before the Crippled Prince could think up a reason to ask her to stay.

After she left Misha's rooms, Marqel headed for the kitchens, then a little while later, bearing a tray and three cups of steaming tea, headed back upstairs to Caspona's room. She knocked and waited until the other girl opened the door.

"I've come to apologize," Marqel said, with a tentative smile. "I shouldn't have said what I did the other day. Will you accept a peace offering?" She held up the tray. Steam rose off the cups, scented faintly with peppermint.

Caspona stared at her warily. "Why?"

"Because you were right. We're not whores. I'm just disappointed, that's all. I so wanted to see Grannon Rock."

Although she was clearly suspicious of Marqel's motives, Caspona stood back to let her in. Marqel smiled wider and entered the room placing the tray on the table near the window. She schooled her features into a pleasant expression and turned back to the other Shadowdancer.

"Did you want some help packing?"

"I'm almost done."

"You should be getting to bed soon. You have an early start in the morning."

"Your concern is touching," Caspona remarked with a frown.

"To be honest, Caspona, it's not you I'm thinking of. Ella ordered me to make sure you and Laleno got away on time." *That explanation should satisfy her.* Caspona knew her well enough to doubt that anything Marqel did came from any innate generosity of spirit.

Picking up one of the cups, Marqel pretended to sip the tea, and then placed it back on the tray. "Come on. Drink it before it cools."

Caspona stared at her for a moment, and then reached for her tea, quite deliberately taking up the cup that Marqel had just put down. Marqel smiled at the gesture.

"Do you distrust me that much?"

"I wouldn't trust you to throw me a line if I was drowning in a puddle," the other girl told her pleasantly. "Now, why don't *you* drink it before it cools?"

Unconcerned, Marqel picked up the untouched cup and took a small swallow of the peppermint tea. The two girls stared at each other over the rims of their cups, the silence thick between them. Caspona drained hers and placed the cup on the tray with a thump.

"Thank you, that was very thoughtful of you, Marqel. Now if you don't mind, I need to finish packing."

Putting her half-finished cup down, Marqel picked up the tray. "Don't stay up too late."

Caspona opened the door for her. "I won't."

Marqel did not look back as she left the room and headed down the broad tiled hall toward Laleno's room. The older girl was already in bed when she knocked, and did not appreciate being woken.

"What do you want, Marqel?" she snapped as she opened the door.

"I just came to check that you're all ready to leave tomorrow."

"I am," Laleno replied. "Was that all you wanted?"

"Yes, but..."

"Then good night!" The acolyte slammed the door in Marqel's face.

With a smile, Marqel turned for the staircase and the kitchens. She would wash the cups herself, to make certain no trace remained of the poison. The tiny sip she had imbibed shouldn't do her any lasting harm, but she knew Caspona distrusted her. It had been the only way to get her to take the tea.

Marqel had learned a great deal since she had joined the Shadowdancers and she was a gifted student when it came to poisons. The concoction she had brewed was a particularly virulent blend of poppy-dust and nightshade.

They would find Caspona in the morning. The poor girl would appear to have died in her sleep, choking on her own tongue during a fit. Everyone would think it was the result of an overdose. It was not common for a Shadowdancer to be addicted to poppy-dust, but neither was it so rare that anybody would think to look for another cause. And it did not matter that Laleno would not let her in; made no difference to her plans that Laleno had not drunk the tea. In fact, it was better this way.

Marqel hummed a cheery tune to herself as she made her way downstairs.

Chapter 14

Marqel took breakfast the following morning in the vast dining room that served highborn residents of the palace. There were few people in attendance this morning. With Antonov on his way to Elcast, many of his staff had taken the opportunity to visit their own estates, or simply take advantage of his absence by sleeping in. Even when he was in residence, the Lion of Senet rarely joined his guests for meals unless it was a formal dinner. He was an early riser and had usually spent time praying in his small private temple and broken his fast long before the rest of the palace was awake.

The room was long and narrow and faced the east, so it was one of the first rooms in the palace to catch the rising of the second sun. The long table was a forest of crystal and silverware. On the western wall, under huge silver domes, platters of several different types of cooked meat, perfectly poached eggs, freshly baked bread and delicate little pastries were constantly replenished by a small army of servants whose job it was to keep the highborn residents of the palace fed. Breakfast went on for quite a while in the Avacas palace. It was not uncommon for the servants to be tactfully shooing out the last of the diners so they could set the table for lunch.

She picked at her food, trying to look as bored and unimpressed by the wealth surrounding her as the highborn who took this place for granted. Even after two years living amid such fabulous wealth and plenty, Marqel still had to stop and pinch herself occasionally, to remind herself that she was not dreaming. On more than one occasion, she'd had to stop herself from pocketing the odd piece of silverware as a hedge against the future. Every now and then, she would look back over the series of events that led her to this place and shake her head in wonder. Her life as a nameless Landfall bastard, scratching for a living as an acrobat with Mistress Kalleen's troupe, seemed as if it had been lived by someone else. She was *somebody* now. She was a Shadowdancer. And soon, if everything went according to plan, she would become even more important.

Across the table from Marqel, the Shadowdancer Olena Borne, Ella's assistant, was tucking into a hearty breakfast. Beside her sat some visiting lord from western Senet, stuffing his face as if it was his last meal. Marqel could not remember his name, but knew that he had been staying at the palace for the past week or so and was due to leave later today. Farther down the table sat two other men, palace functionaries whose names Marqel could not remember. She thought the taller one was a distant cousin of Antonov's, which was how he had secured a position in the palace. The shorter one she did not know much about at all. They seemed to be lingering over their meal, deep in conversation about something to do with last year's maize harvest.

"My lady?"

Marqel glanced up at the servant who had entered the dining room and stopped behind Olena's chair.

"Master Daranski sent me to fetch you, my lady," the girl explained, rather nervously.

"Now?" Olena asked, glancing at her meal.

"One of the Shadowdancers is ill, my lady. He said it was urgent."

Olena muttered a curse under her breath as she pushed her chair back. "You'd better come, too, Marqel," the Shadowdancer ordered as she rose to her feet.

Marqel followed Olena and the servant from the dining room, quite pleased that she had been invited along. She was a little concerned, however. The servant had said one of the Shadowdancers was *ill*.

If everything had gone according to plan, the servant should have announced that one of the Shadowdancers was dead.

"What's wrong with her?" Olena demanded of Yuri as she followed the servant into Caspona's room. The physician was bent over the bed, examining Caspona's limp form. Marqel tried to look past Olena and Yuri to see if she was breathing, but it was too difficult to get a good look at her without being obvious about it.

Yuri straightened up, dismissed the serving girl and waited until she had closed the door behind her before he answered.

"She appears to have taken an overdose of poppy-dust," he announced with a frown.

Olena stared at the young woman in shock. "*Caspona?* Do you know anything about this, Marqel?"

The question caught her off guard. "Er…no, my lady. I didn't know she was an addict."

"She shows no sign of a regular habit," Yuri remarked, glancing down at the young woman. Marqel could not tell if she was still alive, but she supposed a coma would do just as well. The important thing was that Caspona was not able to travel to Grannon Rock.

"Is she dead?" Olena asked. She sounded irritated, rather than upset.

Yuri nodded. "Since some time last evening, I'm guessing."

Marqel was very careful not to let her relief show. She also thought it high time she established her alibi.

"But…I spoke to her just before she went to bed! She seemed…well, the same as usual…"

"What were you doing here in Caspona's room last night?" Olena asked suspiciously. "I was under the impression that you two barely spoke to each other."

Marqel did not hesitate with her reply. "Ella told me to make sure Caspona and Laleno were ready to leave for Grannon Rock today, my lady. I was just checking that she was packed and ready to go. I checked on Laleno, too." And when she was questioned, Laleno would remember Marqel waking her for that very reason…

It was all too easy, really.

Olena cursed in a very unladylike fashion. "I forgot they were due to leave for Grannon Rock this morning. Damn!"

"Did you want me to send to the Hall of Shadows, my lady?" Marqel offered helpfully. "The ship doesn't sail for at least another hour. I'm sure Lady Marika could find a replacement for her."

"In an hour?" Olena scoffed. "Marika's probably not even out of bed yet, if I know her." She looked at Marqel thoughtfully. "Pity I can't send you in her place."

Marqel nodded in understanding. "I know. Ella explained how annoyed Prince Antonov would be if I went to Grannon Rock. Can't Laleno simply go on her own?"

Olena shook her head. "Daena Lorinov is due to give birth any day. That's why we were sending two Shadowdancers to Grannon Rock in the first place. She's in no condition to take part in the Landfall Festival."

"I'd not wish to cause trouble for Prince Kirshov, my lady."

Olena thought on it for a moment. "Of course, Laleno will be there, too," the Shadowdancer mused, "so it's not as if you'd have to even see Kirshov..."

Marqel tried very hard to appear nonchalant while Olena sweated over the decision.

"Well, whatever you decide," Yuri warned, "do it quickly, Olena. I need to get Caspona out of the palace and back to the Hall of Shadows before the manner of her demise becomes public knowledge."

"Can I trust you to do as you're ordered?" Olena asked Marqel with a frown.

"Yes, my lady," Marqel promised meekly.

The Shadowdancer had little choice in the matter, Marqel knew, but she was still torn with indecision. "I don't know..."

"Oh for pity's sake! Send the girl in Caspona's place," Yuri advised impatiently. "There's little for her to do here in the palace at present. Now, do you think we could get on to more important matters?"

Olena nodded doubtfully. "Can you be ready in time?"

"I'll try, my lady."

"Then go," she ordered with a wave of her hand. "And stay out of trouble."

"Yes, my lady." Marqel dropped into a quick curtsy and hurried from the room. As she turned to close the door behind her, Yuri turned his attention to Olena.

"Thank the Goddess this didn't happen while Antonov was in residence," he said. "How are you going to explain it?"

"You're the physician," Olena pointed out testily. "Surely you can think of an acceptable reason why she died."

"I can say it was a weak heart, I suppose," Yuri agreed. "You'll have to let Belagren know."

"It can wait until she returns from Elcast," Olena replied. "Right now it's more important we make certain that nobody in the palace gets wind of the fact that one of our Shadowdancers living under the Lion of Senet's roof was a poppy-dust addict."

Marqel closed the door with a smile and headed back to her room where her bags were packed and ready to be taken down to the ship that would deliver her to Grannon Rock.

PART TWO

OF

DECEIT

AND

VENGEANCE

Chapter 15

Grannon Rock came into view through a haze of low-slung cloud. The morning air misted across the deck of the ship with a rain so fine it was little more than a heavy fog.

Nova was a relatively new city and much of it reeked of damp and recent construction. The city had an aroma of freshly sawn timber, stonecutters' dust and wet mortar. Although it was almost two decades since the return of the second sun, many of the buildings were still encased in scaffolding, and there were piles of dressed stone, particularly marble, stacked untidily along the shoreline, where the salvage crews had dumped them after they were recovered from the drowned city beneath the sea.

The harbor was new, too; so new that the seabed still had to be regularly dredged to rid it of the sunken debris that fouled the water and made it perilous for shipping. During the Age of Shadows, and the Age of Light before it, Nova had been situated much lower down the mountain. The earthquakes and tidal waves that accompanied the departure of the second sun had shattered the city, and the return of the sun had brought with it floods that covered what was left.

Dirk was quite impressed by Nova's grandiose, albeit recycled, architecture. The city sprawled over the peak of the submerged mountain. The more impressive buildings were high on the slopes overlooking the harbor. The meaner dwellings closer to the docks had an air of impermanence about them. Everyone assumed that the oceans had risen as much as they were going to, now that the second sun was firmly established in the sky, but there was no guarantee. The people who lived closest to the shore might wake one morning to find their homes under water.

"They're building a new library," Reithan remarked, pointing to an enormous half-completed building near the peak. They were standing on the foredeck of the *Makuan* as she sailed through the heads. Porl Isingrin could be heard yelling orders to his crew over the creaking of the rigging and the snap of canvas. Although they had offered to help, Tia, Reithan and Dirk were passengers on this trip, and Porl had advised them to make the most of their brief holiday and enjoy the view.

"It's supposed to be twice the size of the one at the university in Avacas," Tia remarked.

Dirk had seen the university's library. It was huge. "Why build so large a library?"

"Jealousy, mostly," Reithan surmised with a shrug. "Dhevynian academics still resent their exclusion from Avacas."

"Well, why shouldn't they resent it?" Tia asked. "It's ridiculous banning people from the Senet University just because of their nationality."

Reithan nodded thoughtfully. "I never understood the logic behind that, myself. You'd think the High Priestess would want to keep the Dhevynian scholars in a place where she could keep an eye on them. Allowing them their own center of learning away from the supervision of the Church just allows heresy to ferment."

Dirk shrugged as he looked out over the harbor. "She probably thinks it's better to let a little rebellion ferment and keep it manageable, than to try to smother it completely and have it blow up in her face someday."

"I never realized you knew the High Priestess so well, Dirk. Is this something you should have shared with us before now?"

Dirk turned to look at Tia, shaking his head. "You know, one day, Tia, I'm going to say something that you actually *can't* find a way to twist around into proof that I'm a Senetian informer."

She smiled. "Really? I can't wait."

"Tia…" Reithan warned.

"Oh, settle down, Reithan. I'm only teasing. Dirk's a big boy. He can handle it."

Dirk grinned suddenly. "How do you know I'm a big boy, Tia? Have you been peeking?"

It took Tia a moment to realize what he was suggesting. She blushed crimson and punched him painfully on the shoulder. "You're disgusting!"

Without waiting for his response, she stalked off toward the stern. Reithan looked at Dirk and sighed heavily. "You really can't help flirting with danger, can you?"

"I'm sorry. I just get a little fed up with her relentless hatred sometimes."

"You do bear her torments with a remarkable degree of stoicism," Reithan agreed. "If it was me, I'd have throttled her long ago."

"Don't think I haven't been tempted on more than one occasion."

"You know, I don't think she *really* hates you...maybe she really likes you and just doesn't want you to know it," he suggested with a grin.

"Well, if that's her plan, Reithan, it's working. Really, *really* well."

Reithan laughed as Porl came forward to join them. He pointed to a compact, three-masted, square-rigged ship anchored at the docks that bore the royal insignia of Dhevyn. "The queen's arrived already." Then he turned to Dirk curiously. "What did you do to upset Tia?"

"I woke up this morning."

"Ah," Porl said, nodding in understanding. "That would do it."

Reithan smiled and turned his back on the view to face Porl. "We'll need to contact Rainan as soon as possible."

"Alexin promised to broach the subject with the queen as soon as he could. Landfall night will probably be the best time to meet with her. There'll be plenty of strangers around and most of the Senetians on the island will be at the ritual once the second sun sets."

"Aren't you risking an awful lot, being seen openly?" Dirk asked.

"In Nova I'm just another trader captain." Porl shrugged. "I've been coming here for years and never had much trouble. Besides, we have a few friends in high places. We'll be safe enough. I don't like *your* chances, though, should anybody recognize you."

"Don't worry, I'll keep my head down," Dirk promised. "I'm getting very good at it, actually."

"You do that, lad." The captain hesitated for a moment, as if debating something with himself. "There's something else I to want you to promise me."

Dirk looked at Porl curiously. "Name it."

"I want your word that you'll not do anything reckless while we're here."

"Are you worried that I might?"

Porl shrugged uneasily. "Nova's a busy port. There's lots of rumors flying around, gossip, that sort of thing. Don't listen to it, Dirk."

"If it makes you happy," Dirk agreed, thinking it the strangest thing anyone had asked of him since he had arrived in Mil. He glanced at Reithan, wondering if his stepbrother had any idea of why Porl Isingrin would deliver such a warning. For some reason Reithan looked away uncomfortably and refused to meet his eye.

A little puzzled by the behavior of both Reithan and Porl, Dirk turned to the captain. "Do you really think Rainan will agree to meet with us?"

"There's no way of knowing," Porl admitted. "But with the wedding so close, she might be willing to clutch at anything to delay it."

"She's just as likely not to want anything to do with you for the same reason," Dirk pointed out. "It's odd, though, don't you think, that Antonov is staying in Avacas for Landfall? You'd think this close to the wedding he would want to keep an eye on the queen himself."

"I'm sure the Lion of Senet has plenty of other more diverting pastimes than looming over the Queen of Dhevyn every chance he gets," Reithan remarked with a forced laugh.

"Actually, I disagree," Dirk said, shaking his head. "Ruling Dhevyn, even by proxy through Kirsh, means everything to Antonov. I can't imagine what he would find more important than that."

Reithan and Porl exchanged a nervous look, making Dirk highly suspicious.

"Well, whatever it is, it's hardly going to affect us while we're here on Grannon Rock," Reithan declared, deliberately putting an end to any further discussion. "By the way, Porl, I've been meaning to ask you...how's young Eryk doing?"

"Not too bad," Porl answered, apparently just as relieved to be discussing something else. "The lads have been giving him a bit of a hard time, but he can follow instructions if they're clear enough. He'll make a fine sailor in time."

"What do you mean they've been giving him a hard time?" Dirk asked. He had hardly seen Eryk on the voyage, and when he had, the boy had been morose and untalkative. Dirk glanced back over the deck, but could see no sign of his young friend.

Porl slapped his shoulder reassuringly. "Don't panic, lad. It's just the normal sort of roughhousing you'd expect with a young 'un. It's like an initiation. He's fine."

"Don't interfere, Dirk," Reithan warned. "If the boy is going to make his own way in life, you can't keep protecting him."

"I know, it's just..."

"Reithan's right, lad," Porl agreed. "Leave well enough alone. My lads won't do him any lasting harm."

Dirk nodded uncertainly. After years of watching over Eryk, he was uncomfortable with the idea of leaving him to fend for himself among the pirates who crewed the *Makuan*. But they were right. At some point, Eryk was going to have to make his own way in life, and the best thing Dirk could do for him now was allow him to stand on his own two feet.

But it did not feel right. Dirk turned back to watching the *Makuan* slice through the waves toward the city of Nova, unable to shake the feeling that both Reithan and Porl were keeping something from him, but whether it was to do with Eryk, or it was something more sinister, he could not tell.

Chapter 16

The queen and her party were met by the Duke of Grannon Rock when they docked in Nova and taken by carriage to the duke's residence on the peak of the mountain. The rain dissipated quickly once the second sun was fully risen, leaving the air humid and uncomfortable.

Alenor had only met the duke once before, when he had visited Avacas several years earlier, and she could barely remember him. Saban Seranov proved a surprisingly cheerful man with brown eyes and gray-streaked hair that fell across his face constantly. He always seemed to be brushing it aside. He greeted the queen formally, sparing a brief smile for his son, Alexin, when he noticed him among the guard.

"Your eldest son is not in residence at the moment?" Rainan inquired, once the introductions had been made.

"Raban will be home tomorrow, your majesty. He's out checking on the reconstruction in one of the villages on the other side of the island. I apologize if you're offended that he's not here to welcome you."

"No offense taken, my lord. I was merely curious. I imagine Alexin is looking forward to catching up with his brother."

The duke smiled briefly. "I believe, your majesty, that separating my sons was one of the more intelligent decisions I've made in my life. I'd not be too eager to see them reunited."

"Don't they get along?" Alenor asked curiously.

"On the contrary, your highness, they get along famously, which is mostly the problem. It's paying for the damage they cause in their enthusiasm that concerns me."

Alenor glanced at Alexin. The captain of the guard was looking rather embarrassed. "I can't wait to hear all about their escapades, my lord," she said, turning back to the duke. "Alexin is always so...proper...at court."

The duke smiled. "I'm beginning to wonder if we're talk-

ing about the same man. But come, your highness, let me see
you and the queen settled and provided with refreshments. Perhaps later I'll tell you about some of the pranks my sons are famous for."

"I look forward to that," Alenor replied, smiling at Alexin.
The captain rolled his eyes but said nothing. Kirsh stood a few
paces from Alexin, his blue-and-silver uniform making him
unremarkable amid his fellow guardsmen. Rainan made no attempt to introduce him to the duke, but if he was offended, he
gave no sign of it.

The Duke of Grannon Rock's residence was too big to be
called a house, but not really large enough to be called a palace.
Constructed of wood and stone, it was a rambling structure that
sprawled over the peak of a hill, and seemed more a cluster of
connected buildings than one large house. They were met by an
honor guard made up of the household staff. Alenor stepped
down from the coach and glanced back over the island. The
rain had lifted, and in the distance, she could just make out a
ship sailing through the heads toward the harbor.

Duke Saban led them through the honor guard into the
house. He showed them their rooms, and then had Alexin show
them to the communal bathhouse that served the whole complex. It was fed by a hot spring, and the room stank of sulfur,
but Alenor was delighted at the prospect of soaking away the
grime of her journey in the luxurious pool.

"Just let me know when you wish to use the baths, your
highness," Alexin told her. "I'll have a guard posted to ensure
you're not disturbed."

"Thank you, Captain," she said, glancing across the steamy
room at Kirsh. Her betrothed was on his best behavior, she
noted, doing nothing to draw attention to himself. He had not
even blinked when Rainan failed to introduce him to the duke.
Kirsh was here as a member of their guard, not the future Regent of Dhevyn, and seemed quite content in that role. He
smiled at her, but did nothing more.

Rainan saw his smile and turned to Alexin. "Just be certain
you handpick the guard, Alexin. Her highness has a reputation
to uphold."

"Never fear, your majesty. The Princess Alenor's virtue is safe in the hands of the Queen's Guard."

Alenor glared at the queen, quite annoyed to be discussed in such a manner. "I rather think my virtue would be better served if the Queen's Guard kept their hands to themselves, don't you, Mother?"

Alexin bit back a smile and looked away. Alenor liked Alexin. She knew he was the closest thing to a friend that Kirsh had in the guard. That reason alone was enough to make her look favorably upon the young man.

Rainan stared at her daughter for a moment and then shook her head. "You deliberately misunderstand me, Alenor."

Alenor did not answer her mother. She turned to Alexin instead and smiled brightly. "So, Captain, is there anything else we need to know about?"

"Not that I can think of at present, your highness."

"In that case we shall return to the house and get ready for lunch," Rainan decreed. "If that's all right with you, Alenor."

"It is."

Alexin snapped his fingers and their escort filed out of the steaming bathhouse, but before Alenor and her mother could follow, the captain stepped in front of them, blocking their way.

"Captain," Rainan said. "Is there a problem?"

Alexin glanced around the room to be certain they were alone before answering. His demeanor was almost...furtive, Alenor thought curiously.

"I have...a message, your majesty," Alexin began, a little uncertainly. "One that I must ask you to keep in the strictest confidence."

"You have me intrigued, Alexin. What is this mysterious message?"

Alexin coughed to clear his throat before continuing. "Ah...there are some...people...coming to Nova who would like to arrange a meeting with you. To discuss matters of great importance regarding Dhevyn's future."

Her mother did not display any obvious sign of surprise. "I see. And why do your friends wish to discuss Dhevyn's future with *me*?"

"I never said they were my friends, your majesty."

Rainan smiled. "Very well then, your associates."

"Neither are they my associates. I am merely passing on a message."

"You haven't answered my question."

"I believe they feel that an alliance may be worth discussing."

"Mother—"

"Later, Alenor," the queen said sharply, before returning her attention to Alexin.

"Why are they doing this now?"

"I couldn't say, your majesty. But they are most anxious to meet with you."

"My answer is no, Alexin."

The Guardsman nodded. If he was disappointed, Alenor couldn't tell. "I understand, your majesty." He bowed and took a step backward before turning for the door.

"Alexin," the queen called after him.

"Ma'am?"

"This is a dangerous game you have involved yourself in."

"I happen to think it worth the risk."

When he was gone, Alenor sank down on the edge of the baths, feeling light-headed and more than a little shocked. Although she had heard Antonov complain about them when she lived in Avacas, this was the first overt sign she had ever seen that the Queen's Guard were actively working against Senet.

"Alenor?" her mother asked. "Are you unwell?"

"You think this offer comes from the Baenlanders, don't you."

She shrugged, and seemed unsurprised. "It's not an unreasonable assumption. Alexin's cousin, Reithan, is very highly placed with the pirates. He may even be their leader now that Johan is gone. On the other hand, Alexin is Saban Seranov's son. This might be some twisted game of Antonov's designed to test my loyalty."

"It seems a little subtle for the Lion of Senet. It sounds more like a plot Belagren would hatch. Besides, I thought you trusted Alexin."

"I do trust him," Rainan said. "I just don't trust his father."

"Why won't you meet with them?"

"I don't think I can risk it, Alenor."

"But if they could help us—"

"If they could help us, Alenor, they would have done it long before now, when Johan ruled them. The truth is, the Baenlanders are probably falling apart without his leadership and need our help. I can't afford to become involved. Not now. Not with the wedding so close."

"But couldn't you just meet with them? Find out what they want?"

"No, Alenor," the queen replied emphatically. "And I'll thank you not to raise the subject again."

"But, Mother—"

"I said no, Alenor."

With that, the queen swept up her skirts and followed Alexin outside, leaving Alenor staring after her.

Chapter 17

The queen arrived in Nova two days after the Shadow-dancers, but Marqel saw little of either Rainan or the Princess Alenor, and nothing at all of Kirshov. Somewhat to her annoyance, the Shadowdancers were not guests in the duke's residence, but were accommodated in rooms attached to the Temple of the Suns.

The Sundancers had been resident in Nova for centuries and they still nominally had control over the temple there. The Sundancer in charge was a tall, heavily built woman named Jalena Arkin. She welcomed Laleno and Marqel with barely disguised hostility. The animosity between the Sundancers and the Shadowdancers was never more apparent to Marqel than in the barely civil greeting they received when they arrived.

There were two other Shadowdancers based permanently

in Nova, but one was away in Cashton, the other major city on the island, and the other, Daena Lorinov, was heavily pregnant with a child that was rumored to be the bastard of Raban Seranov, the duke's eldest son. Daena greeted them briefly, looking bloated and unattractive, then retired to her rooms. Marqel watched her leave, thinking that she would never let that happen to her body. No child would ever ruin her figure like that.

Jalena arranged for them to go hawking a couple of days later—mostly, Marqel suspected, to get them out of her way. The Duke of Grannon Rock loaned them horses and his hawkmaster, and provided an elaborate picnic. Marqel spent the morning bored witless. She considered hawking to be the most useless pastime she had ever encountered, and could not understand how anybody could think it even remotely entertaining. Laleno, on the other hand, was having the time of her life.

The other Shadowdancer was several years older than Marqel, a tall slender brunette with the polished manners of a noblewoman. Although a Landfall bastard like Marqel, she had been raised in the home of the Duke of Versage. Her mother had given birth to her and then married the duke's Seneschal not long after her second birthday. Consequently, Laleno was educated and refined in a manner that Marqel could never hope to emulate.

They rode out from the temple before the second sun rose and the heat became unbearable. For much of the morning they followed the duke's handsome young hawkmaster and his well-trained birds as they swooped on the rabbits that crowded the hills of Grannon Rock. With the sea level rising, much of the game had sought higher ground, and the rabbits in particular were on the point of becoming vermin.

At midday they stopped for lunch in the shade of a grove of trees, near the sheared-off edge of Mount Grannon. One of the earthquakes had sliced half the mountain away, leaving a raw scar on the hill, exposing layers of sedimentary rock that striped the cliff-face in a dazzling array of vibrant colors. The hawkmaster told them about it as they ate a cold lunch of game meat, flavored breads and sweet red wine.

Laleno hung off his every word, as if he was her intended target, not Kirshov. That annoyed Marqel intensely, even though she suspected Laleno was just flirting for practice. Marqel still had not worked out exactly how she was going to stop Laleno from having Kirsh on Landfall night, but at least she was here on Grannon Rock, where she might be able to do something to prevent it. Perhaps an opportunity would present itself, but Marqel was becoming a little concerned. Landfall was only a few days away. She was running out of time.

"The view sounds most impressive," Laleno was saying to the hawkmaster, fluttering her eyelids with a coy smile. "I would love to see it."

"I'd be delighted to show you, my lady," the hawkmaster offered. "It's not a place you should venture near without an experienced guide. The ground is still very unstable in places, but it's worth the effort."

Laleno glanced at Marqel, who was sitting with her back to a tree, giving the appearance that she was dozing in the warm afternoon sun, as she tried to puzzle out the problem of Laleno and Kirshov.

"Marqel? Would you mind waiting?"

"I suppose not," she replied, scowling as the hawkmaster held out his hand to help Laleno up and then led her toward the cliffs. The servants began clearing away their picnic as Marqel settled herself back against the tree, pulling her broad-brimmed straw hat over her face.

"Don't let me sleep too long," she ordered one of the nearby grooms. "We need to be back in plenty of time for dinner tonight."

Marqel dropped the hat over her eyes and settled herself more comfortably against the tree, but resting was a singular waste of time. Her mind would not let go of the idea that Kirsh was here in Nova and Laleno was going to have him. She opened her eyes in annoyance, and then glanced at the grooms, who were standing near the horses. They were chatting among themselves, not even looking in her direction.

She climbed to her feet and looked around, then, on impulse, set off in the direction that Laleno and the hawkmaster had disappeared.

Marqel followed their tracks in the soft earth through the trees for quite some time before she heard them. Concealed behind the undergrowth, she stopped to watch. They were right on the edge of the cliff. As Marqel had suspected, Laleno was more interested in the handsome young hawkmaster than the view. The Shadowdancer had cast aside her shirt and was naked to the waist. The hawkmaster was sucking on her nipple as she threw her head back, moaning with pleasure. Even from where she was hidden, Marqel could see the bulge in his tight leather trousers. As she watched, he lifted his mouth from her breast and kissed the Shadowdancer on the mouth. His hands were pulling up her riding skirt as she fumbled at the buckle of his belt.

Marqel studied them curiously. The hawkmaster was so anxious to possess the Shadowdancer that she could be standing over them and he wouldn't notice a thing. They were so close to the edge, too. That was probably Laleno's idea. She liked the idea of danger. It heightened her pleasure.

They were so lost in their lust neither of them noticed her approach. The hawkmaster was smothering Laleno's throat, her breasts, her navel with kisses. Laleno had wrapped her fingers through his dark hair and was pulling him to her, forcing his head downward. This was about Laleno's pleasure, Marqel noted with detached interest, not the hawkmaster's. He would do what she wanted.

Laleno opened her eyes and caught sight of Marqel as the hawkmaster dropped to his knees before her on the very edge of the cliff. He did not see her approach; his face was covered by Laleno's skirts. The Shadowdancer stared at her uncomprehendingly for a moment.

Marqel smiled. Laleno probably had no idea what Marqel intended until she shoved them backward with all the strength she could muster. The Shadowdancer did not utter a sound as she and the hawkmaster plummeted over the edge of the cliff.

The hawkmaster cried out, but he was still tangled in Laleno's skirts, which muffled his screams of terror as the ground below rushed to meet them.

It took a long time for them to fall. Marqel had time to note that the hawkmaster had spoken truly—the cliff really was an impressive sight with its colorfully striped layers of rock. She waited patiently, as first Laleno and then the hawkmaster landed on the jagged rocks at the foot of the mountain.

Marqel watched the broken bodies at the base of the cliff for a while longer, making certain that neither of them was moving, before she turned and called for help.

Had Marqel realized the fuss it would cause, she might have thought twice about disposing of Laleno in such a dramatic fashion. Jalena was distraught when she learned of the accident, and spent the rest of the day trying to organize a rescue party to recover the bodies from the foot of the cliffs. Looking convincingly pale and distraught, Marqel retired to her rooms to savor her accomplishment, while pandemonium erupted around her. Daena came to visit her, to offer her sympathy, which Marqel suffered through nobly, choking back false tears and letting Daena stroke her hair comfortingly with her pudgy, swollen fingers.

She begged off dinner, eating in her rooms, but the pregnant Shadowdancer seemed determined not to let her out of her sight. In an effort to be rid of the clinging woman, Marqel announced that she would light a candle for Laleno, and requested some time alone to beseech the Goddess to watch over Laleno in the afterlife.

Both Jalena and Daena nodded sympathetically and left her alone. She took the thick red mourning candle and hurried toward the temple, glad finally to be rid of the other women.

Her moment of solitude was not to be, however. There was a girl in the temple kneeling near the altar, her head bowed in prayer, and off to the side, a sailor stood with his head down, his lips moving silently as he begged the Goddess for something . . . *probably that he gets laid tonight,* she thought uncharitably.

Marqel placed the candle on the altar and turned back, thinking she caught a movement near the door. She looked up but there was no one there. She smiled down at the kneeling girl.

"The Goddess is with you, my child," she said.

She was no older than Marqel, and seemed overwhelmed to have been singled out by a Shadowdancer. She had short, red-blond hair and was dressed like a boy. *She's probably praying for some dress sense. Or maybe a boyfriend.* She certainly wasn't going to find one without divine intervention dressed like that.

"Thank you, my lady," the girl muttered.

Marqel placed her hand on the girl's head for a moment, bestowing the Goddess's blessing on her, and then moved away. The girl looked positively terrified.

Marqel smiled. She liked having that effect on people.

She left the temple and headed back to the residence, hoping that Jalena and Daena had not decided to wait up for her. She was sick to death of their sympathy, and if they didn't leave her alone, she might have to do something about them, too.

Then she thought about the girl in the temple with a smile. She had been so pathetically grateful to receive a blessing from a Shadowdancer.

Defiantly, Marqel took the path toward the road. There were plenty of taverns in town where a Shadowdancer would be welcomed, she knew, and she would prefer to spend the evening in the company of people who wanted to enjoy themselves, rather than the wailing and moaning going on up at the residence. If she was caught, she could always claim she had been ministering to the general population, making sure they were committed to attending the Landfall Festival. If anything, her dedication in the face of today's tragedy might be applauded.

Besides, Marqel had killed two people today. She could really do with a drink.

Chapter 18

It was long after first sunrise before Reithan, Dirk and Tia ventured off the *Makuan* and into Nova for a look around the city. Neither Tia nor Dirk had been to Nova before, and after days aboard the cramped and crowded pirate ship they were anxious to stretch their legs on dry land. Tia seemed to be in a good mood, which was a nice change, but Dirk was certain he would only have to look at her the wrong way to set her off again.

Reithan led them to a tavern near the docks named the Drowned Sailor, which was crowded with sailors and the whores who made a tidy living keeping them entertained. A few of the men glanced at Tia speculatively as she entered, but lost interest quickly when she glared at them. They found a table near the door and waited in silence as Reithan fetched ale for them. Dirk looked around with interest.

"Stop it," Tia ordered impatiently.

"Stop what?"

"You're gawping like a country boy on his first trip out of his village."

"Is 'gawping' actually a word?"

"You're the clever one, you tell me."

"I can't leave you two alone for a minute, can I?" Reithan complained good-naturedly as he dumped three foaming tankards on the table between them.

"He started it," Tia snapped out of habit, and then she rolled her eyes. "Goddess! I sound like Mellie. Will Alexin get here soon, do you think?"

Reithan shrugged. "It'll depend on when he can get away. There's no guarantee he'll even show up tonight."

"I'm still surprised that *any* of the Seranovs are sympathetic to your cause," Dirk remarked, taking a sip from his ale. The hum of conversation was like a blanket over the whole room, broken occasionally by the raucous laughter of the sailors near the bar.

"You always say that," Tia pointed out with a frown.

"Say what?"

"Yours, not ours."

"It's just a figure of speech, Tia," he shrugged. "It doesn't mean anything."

"Actually, they're more sympathetic than you think," Reithan told them in a low voice, glancing around the over-crowded tavern to ensure that they were not attracting any un-wanted attention.

"I'm with Dirk on this," Tia said. "I don't trust any Sera-nov."

"Well, that's got to be a first. And what do you mean, you don't trust any Seranov? I'm a Seranov."

"You know what I mean."

"Lucky for you I do."

"Will he meet us here?" Dirk asked.

Reithan shook his head. "We'll meet at the temple."

Dirk smiled. "There's a certain irony in that."

"I think it's a stupid idea," Tia objected. "What if someone sees us?"

"So what if they do? We're merely poor sailors come to beg the Goddess's blessing."

"Suppose someone recognizes you. Or Dirk."

"If anyone was going to recognize me in Nova, they'd have done it years before now, Tia. And nobody knows Dirk here in Nova. Or anywhere in Dhevyn, for that matter. Provided he stays away from Elcast and Avacas, he's as anonymous as the next man."

"I still think it's crazy," Tia muttered unhappily into her ale.

"Your objection is noted," Reithan said, taking a good swallow. "Now drink up, or we'll be late."

The Temple of the Suns in Nova had been spared the upheavals of the rest of the city, a fact that the Shadowdancers made a great deal of fuss about. It was, they claimed, proof that Nova had been destroyed because of the Goddess's wrath. The temple sat amid an acre or so of carefully manicured gardens, and was home to half a dozen members of the Church, Sundancer and Shadowdancer alike. The temple itself was a large circular building with a domed roof, which sat a little apart from the larger residence behind it. The red sun reflected off the copper dome, making it look like a giant red onion.

Inside, the floor was tiled in an intricate geometric pattern that drew one's eye to the altar at the far end, where two golden suns rested, one slightly larger than the other. There were a number of people in the temple kneeling in prayer, their lips moving silently as they begged the Goddess for whatever it was they thought she could provide.

Tia glanced around, but there was no sign of Alexin.

"He's not here," she whispered. "What now?"

"We pray," Reithan said. He turned to Dirk. "Stay near the door. When Alexin arrives, I want to be sure he's alone."

Dirk nodded and moved back toward the entrance. Reithan whispered something to Tia and she moved away from him and then knelt closer to the altar, where she could watch the rear entrance that the Shadowdancers used to enter the temple. Dirk bowed his head as if in prayer, unable to bring himself to kneel. One of the old women struggled stiffly to her feet and shuffled out of the temple, followed a few minutes later by a young pregnant woman with a tear-stained face. Dirk wondered what she was crying about. Was she afraid for her child? Had the child's father abandoned her? Did she really think an imaginary Goddess would listen to her?

As the evening progressed, the temple slowly emptied of worshippers until the only three left were Reithan, Tia and Dirk. As the last man departed, Tia climbed to her feet, rubbing her knees with a frown. She looked toward the door and then glanced at Reithan, who shrugged silently. She opened her mouth to say something, and then shut it hurriedly at the sound of a door opening behind the altar. Tia quickly resumed her kneeling position, bowing her head as a Shadowdancer stepped out from behind the altar.

Dirk's stomach lurched. He took a step backward into the shadow of the entrance. Marqel stepped up to the altar, dressed in the red robes of her order, her long flaxen hair hanging loose, her slender wrists clanking softly with the weight of golden bracelets. She was carrying a thick red candle, which she carefully placed between the two golden suns. It was a mourning candle, Dirk noted, wondering who had died. Then she turned and glanced around the temple. Dirk's heart pounded loudly in his ears, his breathing stilled, willing her not to notice him. Her eyes passed over the shadowed entrance without pausing.

Marqel noticed Tia then, and smiled. "The Goddess is with you, my child," she said.

"Thank you, my lady," Tia muttered, determinedly staring at the floor.

Marqel placed her hand on Tia's head for a moment in a blessing, and then moved away, back behind the altar. A few moments later, they heard the door close and the sound of footsteps fading on the gravel path behind the temple.

Dirk sagged against the wall and closed his eyes. *Marqel the Magnificent.* What was *she* doing here in Nova? He discovered he was trembling, but he was not sure if it was his close brush with discovery, or the memories she evoked in him that caused it. Before he could decide the reason, he felt the cold touch of steel against his throat.

"One usually keeps his eyes *open* when he's a lookout, Dirk Provin," Alexin advised softly.

Dirk's eyes flew open to find the Guardsman standing before him, his unsheathed blade pressed across his throat.

"I'll remember that next time," Dirk promised warily.

Alexin grinned and lowered the blade. "Where's Reithan?"

"Inside."

Alexin replaced his dagger in its sheath and walked into the temple. Dirk glanced outside but the path was deserted so he followed Alexin inside.

"That was close," Tia said, glancing in the direction Marqel had disappeared, as she climbed to her feet.

"Closer than you know," Dirk said. "That Shadowdancer knows me."

"I told you it was a bad idea meeting here," she grumbled. "Hello, Alexin."

"Tia."

"What news?" Reithan asked as he joined them. This was neither the time nor the place for pleasantries.

"She doesn't want to meet you," Alexin informed them without preamble. He did not have to explain. There would be no mention of names, just in case they were overheard.

"Did you explain? ..." Tia began, obviously thinking that Alexin had somehow botched things up. Dirk thought Tia probably could not imagine the Queen of Dhevyn not wanting to plot the overthrow of Senet.

"She understood well enough. She's just not interested."

"What about Al— her daughter?" Dirk asked.

Alexin shrugged. "She seemed a bit more amenable to the idea, but her mother overruled her."

"I don't think we should have anything to do with the daughter," Tia said. "She's far too attached to her fiancé for my liking."

Dirk nodded reluctantly in agreement. The Alenor he remembered was besotted with Kirshov. Had two years back home on Kalarada done anything to dim her affection? There was no way of telling.

"I can ask again, if you want me to," Alexin offered, "but she's suspicious. She probably thinks it's a trap."

"Isn't there anything you can say that will convince her it isn't?" Reithan asked. "I hate to think we've come all this way for nothing."

Alexin shrugged. "I can try. But I can't afford to press the issue. If my father got wind of it..." He let the sentence trail off, and turned to Dirk. "You'd be well advised to keep your head down, too. Your old friend is here as part of the guard, and with Antonov and Belagren on Elcast at Landfall..."

"Why have they gone to Elcast for Landfall?" Dirk asked suspiciously.

Reithan refused to meet his eye. "We'd best be going before that Shadowdancer comes back."

Alexin nodded. "I'll go first. I'll send a message down to the ship if anything changes. Tia. Dirk."

The Guardsman left without waiting for a response, leaving Dirk no chance to question him. He turned on Reithan, grabbing his shoulder, forcing his stepbrother to look at him.

"What's going on?"

"Not here," Reithan warned, shaking off Dirk's arm. He strode toward the entrance and Tia hurried in his wake, also refusing to meet his eye.

Dirk caught up with them as they turned out of the gardens and onto the road that led back into the town.

"What's going on?" he demanded again. "You told me Antonov was staying in Avacas. Why is he going to Elcast?"

"Who knows why the Lion of Senet does anything?" Reithan shrugged.

"You obviously do."

Reithan stopped walking and turned to look at him. Tia stopped beside Reithan and shrugged. "He knows something is up now, Reithan. You might as well tell him the whole story before he hears from someone else."

Reithan nodded reluctantly and took a deep breath. "Wallin Provin died a few weeks ago, Dirk. I'm sorry. They say his heart gave out."

Dirk stared at Reithan in shock. "And you're only telling me this *now*?"

"We were concerned that you might..."

"What? Do something stupid?" he snapped. "Goddess! I am so *sick* of you people not trusting me. What do I have to do, Reithan? Tattoo 'I love Dhevyn' across my forehead? What did you think I would do? Go charging off to Elcast to mourn him? Why? Wallin is dead. There's nothing I can do to bring him back."

"I'm sorry, Dirk," said Tia. "You're right. We should have told you sooner."

She reached out her hand to him, but he turned away. "Don't waste your false sympathy on me, Tia. Just leave me alone."

Dirk left them there, standing in the middle of the road, bathed in red sunlight, as he strode down the road toward the town, his vision misted by grieving, angry tears.

Chapter 19

With the Lion of Senet absent from Avacas, Crown Prince Misha was—supposedly—left in charge. It was Antonov's way of making everybody think he trusted his heir, but it didn't really fool anyone. Misha's power was severely limited. His father's people showed Misha only what they thought he needed to know about, not wishing to bother the ailing prince (so they claimed) with anything that might disturb him.

Misha was well aware that what he was given to sign and approve had been heavily censored, and it annoyed him. Just because he couldn't walk properly didn't mean he was incapable of making a decision. He could read a balance sheet better than his father. He knew more about the history of every province and duchy in Senet than anybody else in the palace. But it just took one twitch, one tremble, and they looked at him like he was a brainless fool, gathered up their reports and hurriedly excused themselves before they had to suffer the embarrassment of watching the Crown Prince of Senet foaming at the mouth and twitching on the floor like a decapitated chicken.

Misha had learned the hard way that the best time to meet with the Chancellor of the Exchequer or the Palace Seneschal, or Barin Welacin, the Prefect of Avacas, was in the morning right after he had taken his tonic, when he was at his most alert. Then he could question them with a steady voice, ask for details that were, quite often (he suspected deliberately), excluded from their reports, and make decisions that had half a chance of being implemented. The Lion of Senet had never questioned a decision he had made in this manner, nor seen fit to overrule him, which gave Misha some hope. But neither did he trust his son with anything terribly important, so it probably mattered little to Antonov, one way or the other.

Misha was feeling particularly peeved about the whole arrangement this morning. His father had been gone for more than a week, but he had still not seen anything more interesting than the estimates for next year's maize harvest. And now, Lord Palinov, the Chancellor of the Exchequer, had brought him a request from the city elders in Talenburg, asking for a grant of ten thousand gold dorns to strengthen the levee walls around their city to prevent Lake Ruska's yearly flooding of the lower parts of the city after the spring rains. Lord Palinov had handed him the letter with a heavy sigh and a recommendation that they grant Talenburg two thousand dorns and let them find the rest of the money somewhere else.

The letter advising the elders of Talenburg about the Lion of Senet's decision was already drafted, and required nothing more than Misha's signature and that he apply his father's seal to the finished document.

"A number of people were drowned in last year's floods, as I recall," Misha remarked as he read through the letter.

"But only in the poorer quarters of the city, your highness," Palinov assured him. "Nobody important was killed."

"I imagine the people who died were important to somebody," Misha replied. "A child who lost his mother in the floods would disagree with you, I think, as would any struggling family who lost their breadwinner."

"You know what I mean, your highness," Palinov shrugged with an oily smile. "Like you, I grieve for the loss of any person, no matter what their station in life. But in granting this request we would be setting an extremely bad precedent. If we say yes to Talenburg, the next thing you know Bollow will be asking for the same consideration, then Tolace will want something, then Paislee, then Versage...By the end of the week, every city in Senet will find they suddenly have a need for large amounts of our cash for urgent capital works."

"And if we only grant them a fifth of what they ask for? How will they raise the rest?"

"Talenburg could easily levy a tax on its own citizens to raise the necessary funds, your highness."

"So the poor get to drown in the floods or pay taxes they can ill afford to repair the levee walls," Misha concluded.

"Your highness," Palinov sighed condescendingly. "You must realize that these requests are always outrageously inflated. Talenburg probably doesn't need to spend anywhere near ten thousand dorns to repair the levee walls. They simply ask for that amount, knowing that we will only grant part of it. It's a game they all play. You mustn't let yourself be swayed by emotional pleas to save the lives of a few starving peasants, when the vast majority of the money is liable to wind up lining the pockets of the Talenburg city elders."

"Is this all they sent?" he asked, holding up the letter. He was pleased to see the parchment was steady in his hand.

"There was some supporting documentation," Palinov admitted. "Estimates, a few engineering diagrams and the like, but..."

"I want to see them."

"Your highness?"

"I will see what else they sent, my lord," Misha insisted. "Or I will cross out the figure of two thousand dorns and replace it with the ten thousand dorns they originally asked for and grant their request for the full amount right now."

"As you wish," Palinov said, backing down with a shrug. *He's humoring me. He probably thinks I won't understand a word of it.* "Was there anything else, my lord?"

"I merely require your signature on a few other things, your highness," the chancellor said, holding up a sheaf of official-looking documents. "I can show you where to sign."

"Leave them on the desk. I'll read through them later."

"Your highness really doesn't need to bother himself," Palinov advised, as if Misha was just a little bit odd for suggesting such an unheard-of thing. "They are simply administrative matters that your father did not have time to deal with before he left for Elcast. Even he would not waste time going over every little detail."

"I'm not my father," Misha pointed out coldly.

The chancellor looked at him strangely for a moment, and then rose to his feet. "No, Prince Misha, you certainly are not."

Misha wasn't sure how to take the comment, but he was fairly confident Palinov didn't mean it as a compliment.

Later that afternoon, one of Palinov's scribes arrived with a bundle of documents that turned out to be the "supporting documentation" the chancellor had so blithely dismissed as irrelevant to Talenburg's request for assistance. Misha frowned when he saw the pile, and dismissed the scribe with a wave of his hand. He was not feeling nearly so enthusiastic about looking through the pile of documents as he had been this morning.

"Perhaps you should review them tomorrow," Olena suggested, when she noticed the look on his face. "Palinov can wait another day for your decision."

That will just give him another day to find a way to thwart me, Misha thought, but he did not share his sentiments with Olena. If the Shadowdancers had their way, he would not be bothered by Lord Palinov at all. He had argued with both Ella and Olena in the past about his responsibilities as the crown prince. They were firmly convinced that Misha was overextending himself by attempting to take an active part in the governance of Senet, and that he would be much better off if he left it to those paid to deal with such things.

"I'll look through them later," he told her. "After dinner, perhaps."

"Well, don't stay up too late," the Shadowdancer warned. "You're still very weak. You need your rest."

"You fuss over me like I'm made of glass, Olena. You're worse than Ella, I swear."

"You may not be made of glass, your highness, but you're certainly not made of diamond, either. You'll suffer for it if you do too much."

Although she sounded concerned, Misha could not avoid the feeling her words contained a veiled threat. Like Ella, Olena always called him "your highness" when she was peeved with him.

"I know my limits," he assured her. "Better than anyone."

"Then let me help you back to bed..."

"No," he said, reaching for the pile from Talenburg. "I've changed my mind. I will look at these now."

With shaking hands he unrolled the largest document and spread it out on the desk. Olena glanced at the diagram curiously. "Can you make any sense of that?"

"More than Lord Palinov, I'll wager. Could you fetch me some tea?"

"I'll have some sent up," Olena promised. "Did you want me to send someone to sit with you?"

She meant: *Do you want me to send someone to watch over you in case you have another fit?* But Misha was feeling reasonably sound, although his trembling was slowly getting worse.

"No. I'll be fine. Just have the tea sent up."

"As you wish, your highness."

They were always saying that to him, he mused as Olena left the room and he turned his attention to schematics of the Talenburg levee wall.

As you wish.

As if his will carried weight, and the title of Crown Prince of Senet actually meant something.

Chapter 20

Alenor was furious when she learned that Marqel was part of the Shadowdancers' delegation to Grannon Rock for the Landfall Festival. So furious, in fact, that she did something she had promised Kirsh she would never do. She sent for Alexin, and specifically forbade Kirshov from taking part in the Festival.

"Your highness, it might be a bit difficult..." Alexin began, when she told him what she wanted.

"How is it difficult? You're the Captain of the Guard. He is one of your officers. I should think it would be a simple matter."

"Simple, perhaps, but not wise. Kirshov is Senetian. For him, the ritual of the Landfall Feast is very important."

"And since when do the desires of a foreign prince outweigh those of your crown princess?"

Alexin bowed apologetically. "They don't, your highness, of course. I'm sorry if I gave you that impression. I will assign Kirshov to the guard escorting you and the queen on Landfall night. That should keep him occupied and out of trouble."

"Thank you, Captain," she said with relief. "I don't suppose I need to point out that I would rather Kirsh didn't know of my interest in his duties during the Landfall Festival?"

Alexin smiled thinly. "No, your highness, I don't suppose you do."

Once the captain had left, Alenor turned to stare out over the lawns. They were deserted, this late in the afternoon, except for the lone figure of a small boy chasing a puppy toward the bathhouse.

The door opened and her mother entered the room, dressed in a dark mourning gown. She had been paying her respects to the Shadowdancers in the temple in town—out of politeness, if not genuine regret that one of them had died so tragically.

"Well, that's that rather onerous duty taken care of," Rainan sighed, pulling her gloves off.

"Did you find out what happened?" Alenor asked, turning from the window.

The queen unpinned her veil and tossed it on the side table. "Apparently Laleno was wandering too close to the edge of the cliffs when the ground gave way. The hawkmaster died trying to save her."

Alenor's first hopeful thought—that it was Marqel who had plunged to her death—proved to be an idle one.

"I wonder if that will dent their enthusiasm for the Landfall Feast."

The queen shrugged. "Somehow I doubt it. The Sundancer in charge of the temple spent much of the day making arrangements to ship poor Laleno's body back to her family in Versage, but I'm quite certain the Shadowdancers won't let the inconvenient death of one of their sisters get in the way of the Landfall Feast."

"At least this unfortunate incident has spared us the need to socialize with them."

Rainan smiled sadly. "You're becoming a cynic, my dear. Was that Alexin I saw leaving?"

Alenor nodded. "I was just checking on the arrangements for Landfall."

"You mean you were checking on Kirshov."

"Is that so wrong?" she asked, a little defensively.

"Not wrong, Alenor, but foolish. He doesn't want your interference, and Antonov won't appreciate you trying to manipulate circumstances to suit yourself."

"Antonov does nothing *but* manipulate circumstances to suit himself," she pointed out sourly.

"All the more reason not to let him catch you at it."

Alenor glared at her mother. "Why do you put up with him? Why do you let him dictate to Dhevyn? He should have no say over what we do!"

"Don't you think I would defy him if I could?"

"I don't know. Sometimes I think you give in far too easily."

The queen sighed again and walked to the window to stand beside her daughter. "Johan tried defying him, Alenor, and more than half the dukes of Dhevyn sided with Senet. I won't start another civil war."

"I still don't understand how that happened, either. You should have hanged them all for treason. They should have backed Johan."

"By the time Johan tried to rebel against the yoke of Senet, the damage was already done. The reality is that by the time they met on the battlefield, Johan was already fighting a lost cause. Only people like Johan and Morna Provin refused to admit it. And then Antonov sacrificed his son, and that very morning the second sun appeared in the heavens for the first time in a decade. We had no chance after that."

"You threw away our independence," Alenor accused. "We're nothing more than a subject province of Senet now."

"Perhaps," the queen conceded. "Temporarily. But once you and Kirshov are married and Misha rules Senet..."

"Antonov is expecting the opposite. He thinks my marriage to Kirshov will seal Dhevyn to Senet forever."

"Then it will be up to you to prove him wrong."

Alenor looked at her mother, suddenly understanding what she was getting at. "Which is why you don't want me doing anything to interfere with Kirsh and the Landfall Festival, isn't it? You don't want me to tip my hand. Should I countermand the order I just gave Alexin?"

"No. The damage is done. In truth, I would rather Kirshov didn't take part in the Festival, either. Just be more cautious in the future, my dear. Until you're married, we are treading a very thin line."

Alenor sighed. "Will I ever stop making such blunders?"

"It's not a blunder," she assured her. "Well, not a serious one. You're young and in love. The chances are Antonov would see it as nothing more than the childish interference of a young woman jealously protecting what she considers her property."

"Kirsh would be furious if he found out."

"Then hope he doesn't, Alenor."

"Is it always like this, Mother?" she asked, turning back to stare out of the window. "Will I never be able to take a breath without considering the implications?"

"Not if you plan to remain Queen of Dhevyn for long."

"How do you bear it?"

"I try not to think about it," Rainan shrugged. "But it's not so bad. And it does have its compensations."

"I hadn't noticed any."

Rainan smiled. "Well, at the very least, it means you always get served first at dinner."

Alenor smiled at her mother's wan attempt at humor. *If only it were that simple,* she thought wistfully. But it was nice to share a private moment with her mother. They had so few of them.

"Mother, about Alexin's offer to meet with—"

"I told you, Alenor, I won't discuss it."

"Why not? Shouldn't we at least consider the idea?"

"No. And that is my final word on the subject. I will not risk everything just to meet in a seedy back room somewhere and have a bunch of fanatical exiles tell me how I should be running my kingdom."

"You let Antonov tell you how to run it."

Her mother glared at her. "You don't know what you're talking about, Alenor."

"Then explain it to me, Mother. In a few weeks I'm going to be sixteen. I will be married and a queen, with a regent whose every move will be dictated by Avacas. On that day you'll lose your damn kingdom anyway, because the day I marry Kirsh, we effectively hand ourselves over to the Lion of Senet. Haven't you seen the people he's placed in our court already? Why are you so determined to do this?"

"I am determined not to cause our people any more suffering, Alenor. I am also determined not to hear any more about alliances with the exiles in Mil. Now please, do not mention it again."

Alenor knew it was futile to discuss the matter any further, but she could not help wondering if, just for once, someone in the Dhevynian royal family should take a risk.

Then she sighed. If someone was planning to take a risk, it certainly wasn't going to be her.

Chapter 21

Morna Provin found herself spending much of her days lost in thought. There was precious little else to do as she counted down the sunrises until the Landfall Festival. She thought a great deal about the past, and tried very hard not to think about the future.

Tovin Rill was holding her in the cells of the Senetian Garrison on the outskirts of Elcast Town. Built hastily after the return of the Age of Light, it was not a particularly aesthetically pleasing fortress, its functionality taking precedence over its appearance. Her small cell was in one of the outbuildings, constructed of roughly dressed stone, the only light provided by a tiny barred window, too high in the wall to offer a view of anything but a small patch of sky. Her bed was a straw pallet, her toilet a wooden bucket in the corner.

For the most part, her guards were considerate, and for all that she was trapped in a cell normally reserved for thieves and murderers, she had not been unbearably uncomfortable. Captain Ateway had brought in some debtor slaves to clean the cell before incarcerating the dowager duchess, and he made sure the bucket was regularly emptied. Faralan had also sent down quite a few of her personal possessions, and she had been allowed writing materials to enable her to put her affairs in order. All in all, the whole thing was being handled in a very civilized manner, except for the fact that at the end of it lay a burning pyre and inevitably, her death.

Morna had always thought that she would have to be dragged kicking and screaming to her execution, but now that she was actually faced with it, she found herself quite philosophical about the whole idea. The reason, she concluded, was that she had little to live for any longer. There were no sons left to raise, not even a decent fight left to fight. Johan was dead, and so was Wallin. Dirk had vanished. Rees no longer needed her, or wanted her, it seemed. Her purpose in life was gone. In a few weeks, Alenor D'Orlon would marry Kirshov Latanya, and Dhevyn would have a Senetian regent.

Antonov and Belagren had won.

If Morna regretted anything about her life, it was that she did not perish in the last great battle at the end of the Age of Shadows. Those who died in that fight at least went to their graves believing that they were dying for something worthwhile. She understood now the futility of what she and Johan had attempted. She thought a lot about Johan these days. It was almost as if she could feel him waiting for her on the other side.

How much harder it had been to live on, to learn the bitter truth that good did not always triumph over evil. She had discovered the hard way that right was not enough when people were frightened and hungry. And who got to judge what was "right," anyway? In the eyes of Antonov Latanya, she was evil personified. Her story, told from his perspective, cast her as the villain. They had lost that last dreadful battle, in part, because at least half the dukes of Dhevyn had preferred the Lion of Senet's version of right over Johan's.

Morna smiled faintly, thinking it would have been so much easier if Antonov had been short and fat, or ugly, or horribly scarred, or drooled when he ate. But there was nothing about the man that hinted at the darkness in his soul. No outward manifestation of evil that made it simple to look at him and say "Beware!"

Then she wondered about her own reasoning. *If there is no Goddess, does that mean humans have no soul?*

"My lady?"

Morna looked up from the small desk they had provided for her in the cell. She had been composing letters to be read after she was gone; hence her rather maudlin train of thought. She welcomed the interruption.

"Yes, Captain?"

"Lady Faralan is here to see you."

"Thank you, Captain. Please show her in."

We're all being so polite, so terribly courteous about this. Perhaps that was the true measure of nobility, this remarkable gift for accepting everything with grace and elegance, when any normal, rational person should be howling in protest.

"How are you today, my lady?" Faralan inquired as Ateway opened the cell door for her. He locked it again once she was inside, but moved to the other side of the guardroom to give them at least the semblance of privacy.

"I'm well, Faralan. And you?"

Faralan lifted the basket she was carrying onto the bunk. Morna glanced at it, wondering if Ateway or one of his men had searched it before allowing her daughter-in-law to bring it to her.

"I brought you some food. Welma baked herb bread for you."

Welma had been the baker in Elcast Keep since before

Morna arrived on Elcast as a seventeen-year-old bride during the Age of Shadows. The brusque, unforgiving baker had been very understanding of a young princess raised for a life of luxury and leisure who suddenly found herself married to a complete stranger, and mistress of an enormous keep that required an army of servants just to ensure it ran smoothly from one day to the next.

"Does she worry that I'm not thriving on a steady diet of gruel?" Morna asked with a small smile.

Faralan returned her smile cautiously. "I'd quite a job assuring her that you weren't down here being stretched over a rack. She's very loyal to you, my lady."

"Then do something for me, Faralan. Tell Welma to forget me. It will do none of us any good if she voices her displeasure in the hearing of the Lion of Senet."

"I will," Faralan promised. "He'll be here tomorrow."

"Antonov? He's cutting it a bit fine, isn't he? It's only a few days until Landfall." She said it without even thinking about what Landfall meant to her. Faralan looked away, unable to speak so calmly or openly about the perilous future that awaited her mother-in-law. Perhaps she should have said, "It's only a few days until I die." What would poor Faralan do then?

"I suppose there's little chance that Rees is planning to petition Antonov for my life?"

"I'm sure he will," the girl hurried to assure her. "I've spoken to him about it on a number of occasions."

"Faralan, don't you think it odd that Rees needs to be coerced into asking for his mother's life?"

The poor child looked away in shame. "It's not that he doesn't want to..."

"No. It's that he's studied his options and decided prosperity lies with following Antonov. I've no one to blame for that but myself, I suppose. He never said anything to me directly, but I know he thought Dirk was my favorite."

"Is it true?..." Faralan began, and then she appeared to change her mind, obviously embarrassed.

"Is what true, dear?" When the girl didn't answer, Morna

smiled. "If you have any questions, you'd best ask them now. I'll not be in a position to answer them after Landfall."

Faralan took a deep breath. "Rees says...he got a letter from Prince Antonov. He says Antonov claims Dirk...that he was..."

"Johan Thorn's bastard?" Morna finished for her. So Antonov had told Rees the truth. Well, that explained why Rees was being so cooperative. The Lion of Senet would have worded the letter in such a way that Rees would have felt totally betrayed by the revelation. The secret that Morna had kept for so long to protect one son was now the ammunition the other son would use to destroy her.

How naive I was to ever imagine I could fight you and have a chance of winning, Antonov Latanya.

"It's true then?" Faralan looked genuinely shocked.

"Yes, it's true."

"But you let Dirk leave! You sent him to Avacas!"

"I've done many things in my life, Faralan. Not all of them have been wise."

"Do you think he's dead?"

"Who? Dirk? Of course not," she scoffed. "If my son was dead, Antonov would have hung his head from the gates of his palace in triumph the day it happened."

"Where do you suppose he is, then?"

Morna wondered at the question. Was Faralan genuinely concerned for Dirk, or was she fishing for information at Rees's behest? *Was there ever a time I trusted anyone?*

"I've no idea."

"Do you think he'll come to? ..."

"Why don't you say the rest of it, Faralan? Do you think he'll come to watch me die? I certainly hope not."

"My lady, that's not what I meant."

Morna sighed. Perhaps she was being too hard on the child. Faralan had been married to Rees for a bare four months. Her annual visits to Elcast had trained her to run a household, not deal with the politics of deceit or vengeance.

"I'm sorry, Faralan. I don't mean to snap at you. None of

this is your fault. I just find myself leaning toward the maudlin the closer I come to dying."

Faralan nodded warily, trying to give the impression that she had some notion of what Morna was going through, then glanced over her shoulder to ensure that Captain Ateway was still out of earshot.

"Master Helgin asked me to give you something," she said, lowering her voice. She reached into the basket and picked up a small loaf resting on the top of the herb bread and fruit that Welma had sent.

"I didn't realize Helgin had taken up baking as a hobby," Morna remarked, accepting the loaf from Faralan's out-stretched hand.

"He said it might make things easier...when the time comes," Faralan whispered cautiously.

Morna glanced down at the loaf. What had he done? Laced the dough with nightshade? Or had he and Welma actually baked the bread with something hidden inside? She bit back a smile. Surely nobody actually did that? Not in real life.

"Does Rees know about this?" she asked curiously. It was odd that the thought of suicide no longer disturbed her. For the first time in her life she understood how Analee had been able to take her own life. Strange that, of all the outcomes of her impending death, the most unexpected was that it had allowed Morna to finally forgive her sister.

"No."

Morna frowned. "I appreciate your help, Faralan, but if I can give you one piece of advice before I die, let it be this: don't set yourself up in opposition to your husband. Not if you wish to be happy."

"But what if I think what he's doing is wrong?"

"Then run, child," she suggested, sadly. "Run away now. Run as far and as fast as you can, because I can guarantee that you will spend the rest of your life regretting it if you stay."

Chapter 22

Kirshov Latanya was rather annoyed when he discovered he had been assigned to the Queen's Guard detail, instead of being allowed to take part in the Landfall Festival. He had been planning to complain to Alexin about it, too, until it occurred to him that this was the first time in almost two years that he had been assigned to anything remotely useful, and it might be smarter to follow orders. He had never imagined that it would be so hard to win the trust and confidence of his comrades-in-arms. Perhaps finally, the Lord Marshal was convinced that he was worthy of his commission in the Queen's Guard, and Alexin had assigned him to guard the queen on Landfall night for that reason.

Objecting to his assignment might set his cause back by years.

The Grannon Rock Landfall Festival was probably going to be disappointing, in any case. It was held in the confines of the town square, and was smaller almost than the Elcast Festival. Rainan and Alenor would leave the square as soon as the drums began to pound, so he would have no chance to see Marqel, and certainly no chance to do anything else with her.

He had heard she was among the Shadowdancers brought to the island to conduct the ritual, but the closest he came to her was when he caught a glimpse as she rode out to go hawking with the other Shadowdancer the day before. One of them had been killed in an accident, he had heard, but nobody could tell him who. He didn't think it was Marqel. For some reason he felt he would know if something happened to her.

Alenor knew the identity of the late Shadowdancer, but Kirshov was not so foolish as to broach the subject of Marqel with his betrothed. They had an unspoken agreement: Marqel did not exist, and if they both pretended that was the case, they could maintain a harmonious peace.

Kirsh was relieved at midnight, when the next detail arrived in the wing of the duke's house where she was quartered to assume the protection of the queen. There was not much point that Kirsh could see. Grannon Rock was a safe island and the duke's house was well guarded. The chance that some fanatical Dhevynian was plotting dastardly deeds against the queen was remote. However, he did not relax his guard either, and the men who took over from him were nervously alert, as if they were expecting an assassin to jump out from behind the tapestries at any minute.

Once he was off duty, Kirsh debated heading into the city to see what was happening. It was well into the night, and he knew there would be nothing much going on now, but he decided to seek out Alexin, who had mentioned plans to meet some friends in a tavern somewhere. He could not remember if Alexin had given the name of the tavern, but Nova was not so large that Kirsh could not check them all if he had to.

With no other purpose in mind than a drink with a friend, Kirsh woke the grooms in the duke's stables, arranged to borrow a horse and headed into town.

He found Alexin in the third tavern he tried. It was near the docks, and was remarkably subdued, given the lateness of the hour. With all the other entertainment available in Nova so close to Landfall, the tavern was feeling the pinch. The innkeeper stood behind a long, polished bar that was dented and battered from the frequent fights that broke out in the taproom. He looked up with pathetic eagerness when Kirsh stepped into the room. Any customer on a night like this was welcome.

Kirsh glanced around, ordered ale and headed to the corner where he had spied Alexin's familiar profile through the dusty window. The Guardsman was deep in conversation with another man, a sailor. Neither man noticed Kirsh approach.

"...*if* she says yes," Alexin was saying in a low voice, as Kirsh neared the table. "As I told the others, she wasn't very enthusiastic about the idea."

"We don't have time to sit here and wait for her to think it

over. We have to get this done quickly," his companion remarked. Kirsh noticed that his face was scarred on the right
side, as if he had been badly burned.

"I agree," Alexin shrugged. "But I'm not certain—" Alexin
shut his mouth abruptly as he glanced up and caught sight of
Kirsh. The Guardsman looked as guilty as if Kirsh had just
caught him stealing the crown jewels. His companion was staring at him with open hostility. "Kirshov!"

"Alexin," Kirsh greeted him warily. "I'm not interrupting
anything, am I?"

"Of course not!" Alexin declared with false cheer. "I was
just catching up with Captain...Borus, here. He's an old friend
of the family. Borus, this is Kirshov Latanya."

Captain Borus looked like anything but the type who
might call himself an old friend of the Seranov family. He
glared at Kirsh with a calculating stare. "So, you're Antonov's
cub."

Kirsh bristled at the contempt in the man's voice. "You
seem to have a problem with that."

The captain smiled coldly. "You look like him."

"You know my father?"

"By reputation only, I'm afraid," he replied, although for
some reason, Kirsh was sure he was lying. "How are you finding life in Dhevyn, your highness? Must be a bit of a comedown
for someone like you, mucking it out in the barracks with the
commoners."

Kirsh didn't know who this Captain Borus was, but he
took an instant dislike to the man. "It's none of your damn business what I think about Dhevyn."

"Ah, but that's where you're wrong, your highness. When
the prince of a foreign nation is about to become Regent of
Dhevyn, I think it's the business of every citizen in Dhevyn to
know what he thinks of us. More to the point, I think we have a
right to know where his loyalties lie. Don't you agree?"

"What are you implying?" Kirsh demanded, his ire rising.
Alexin was shaking his head at the sailor, warning him to cool
down.

"I'm not implying anything," the sailor shrugged. "I'm saying it straight out. Whose side are you on, Kirshov Latanya? If we went to war with Senet tomorrow, who would you fight for?"

"Dhevyn is not at war with Senet," Kirsh pointed out, a little disturbed by the question. Who *would* he fight for, if Dhevyn and Senet went to war? He was appalled to discover he could not answer the question, even to himself.

"We're not at war *today*," the sailor agreed. "But unless you're a prophet, son, you might want to give the matter some thought. I'd hate to be one of the men under your command, my life hanging in the balance, while you make up your mind."

Somehow, being called "son" by this boorish sea captain seemed even worse than the man's accusations.

"I am not your *son*, sailor," he said icily. "You will address me in a manner befitting my rank, or better yet, don't address me at all." Without waiting for Borus to reply, he turned to Alexin. "I'm sorry to have disturbed you, Alexin. Perhaps we can have a drink together some other time. In more congenial company."

"Tomorrow, maybe?" Alexin suggested, deliberately avoiding the eye of his companion. He neither apologized for the sailor nor seemed unduly concerned that Kirsh was leaving.

"Tomorrow," Kirsh agreed.

He turned on his heel and strode toward the entrance, tossing a coin to the tavern-keeper for the untouched ale that stood waiting for him on the counter.

Kirsh rode through the deserted streets for a while, still angry at the sailor's words. What did it matter whose side he was on? Dhevyn and Senet were allies. He was going to marry their future queen. The two nations were tied together by proximity and economic necessity. Even in times past, when they had been less than friendly, they had never actually fought each other. In fact, the only war that had happened in recent times was the one led by Johan Thorn against the Lion of Senet and the forces loyal to the Goddess. Borders and nationalities had meant nothing during that conflict. You were either on the side of the Goddess or you were not.

He was wandering the streets aimlessly as another thought occurred to him. What was Alexin doing in that tavern with such a man? He tried to recall what little he had overheard before the men had halted their discussion. They were obviously discussing something of import, but he had no inkling as to what that might be. It disturbed him. Alexin was a loyal Guardsman, but that did not mean he wasn't a loyalist. Antonov had warned him before he left Senet that the guard was full of seditious fools. Was Alexin plotting something with the scarred sailor?

Impulsively, Kirsh turned his borrowed horse around and headed back toward the docks. If Alexin was plotting against the queen, it was his duty to learn what was afoot. If he was plotting something against his father, Kirsh felt just as duty-bound to discover it. Of course, he would then be confronted by the very dilemma the sailor had posed. If he uncovered a plot against Senet involving the queen or her guard, who would he report it to?

He was still no closer to an answer when he was hit from behind by what felt like a tree trunk. He had only just turned onto the street facing the docks when his attackers struck. Black lights swam before his eyes as he fell from the saddle, landing heavily on the ground, then all light vanished as a dark hood was pulled over his head. He struggled wildly to regain his feet, but received a sledgehammer-like fist in the gut for his trouble. Gasping for air in the smothering hood, he lashed out blindly with his feet. They kicked him again, this time in the lower back. He grunted with pain as he was pushed down, face first onto the cobbled street. His hands were pulled back behind him and expertly tied, then lashed to his ankles. Finally, the rope was looped around his throat. He quickly discovered he couldn't move his feet without choking.

His assailants had not uttered a word from the moment they had surprised him, and it was that which alarmed Kirsh the most. These men were not simple cutpurses looking for an easy mark. They were efficient and thorough and knew exactly what they were doing. He stopped trying to struggle against the ropes that bound him; it was fruitless, and every movement threatened to strangle him.

"What do you want?" he gasped, his voice muffled by the rough cloth of the hood. Silence followed his question. Although he couldn't see what was happening, he got the feeling his attackers were waiting for something. "What do you want, damn it!"

"What do we want?" a voice finally answered. Although he couldn't be certain, he thought it might be the sailor from the tavern. "We want nothing, your highness, except to be left alone."

The statement puzzled Kirsh, but he was too busy gasping for air to pay much attention to it. The hood reeked of old fish and the smell alone was enough to make him gag.

Then the man spoke again, but it was to someone else. "Work him over good, Kurt, but don't kill him." He laughed harshly, confirming Kirsh's suspicions about the identity of the man. "Just make sure you hit him in a manner befitting his rank."

After that, Kirsh had no time to spare wondering about his attackers.

There were three of them at least, he thought, and they proceeded to beat him with frightening precision. One pain blurred into another as they pounded into every vulnerable point in his body. They broke no bones, nor hit him anywhere likely to prove fatal, but that still left an awful lot of places he could be hurt. Helpless to defend himself, he teetered on the edge of unconsciousness as they punched him relentlessly, no thought left in his mind except the hope that eventually the torment might stop. He was trussed up like a turkey and could do nothing to shield himself from the blows. All he could do was remain silent, as if by not crying out, he was somehow fighting back. It was the only weapon left to him, so he bit back his howls of agony and let them think he wasn't hurting.

"Goddess! What are you doing?"

A voice from the past. He wasn't sure if he heard it or simply imagined it. *How could Dirk be here?* Kirsh wondered if they had slipped up and killed him after all, despite their orders to the contrary. *Am I dead? Is this the afterlife?* Right at that moment, the mere idea that the pain might stop at any moment was close enough to paradise to satisfy Kirsh.

"This is none of your concern." It was the voice of the sailor from the tavern, he was certain. Kirsh was a little surprised to discover he was still there. He thought he had left. There was a moment's tense silence before the older man spoke up again. "All right, you can cut him loose, Kurt."

The voice belonging to the one called Kurt muttered something that sounded like an order, and a few moments later the pressure eased around his throat as the ropes were cut. Kirsh groaned weakly and rolled onto his side, hoping to find a place that didn't hurt, but there was none.

"You shouldn't even be out here," the sailor warned. "Suppose someone sees you?"

"Suppose someone sees your thugs beating a man to death not fifty paces from the ship?" the one who sounded like Dirk retorted. "At least they could have had the brains to take him somewhere else."

"Who is he, anyway?" a female voice asked curiously.

"The Lion of Senet's cub."

From the scuffling sounds near his head, Kirsh wondered if the one who sounded like Dirk was trying to come to his aid and the others were holding him back.

"Why are you *doing* this?"

"Why do you care?" the girl asked.

They must think I'm unconscious, Kirsh realized, endeavoring to remain still. If he could learn the identity of his attackers, or even the reason for it, he could do something about settling the score later. Right now, surviving this seemed more important than revenge.

"Kirsh was my friend, Captain."

"You know," the female voice remarked, "I really wish you'd stop reminding us about your rather dubious coterie of friends."

Kirsh muffled a groan.

"Beating Antonov's son half to death isn't going to achieve

anything," the one who sounded like—but could not possibly be—Dirk pointed out angrily.

"Oh? I don't know. At the very least it'll knock some of the arrogance out of him."

"He's not moving," the girl said. "Suppose you've killed him?"

"Then I'll be heartbroken," the sailor replied with obvious insincerity. "I think we can safely assume our work here is done," he added, perhaps to the men who had beaten him. "You'd best get him out of here, Kurt, before his friends come looking for him. Assuming he has any friends. And don't leave him lying about near the ship. Throw him over his horse and dump him in the town somewhere before you take that hood off."

His mind reeling from the pain and the implications of a conversation Kirsh was sure he must have imagined, he lost consciousness as they dragged him upright. The men who had beaten him slung his limp and battered body between them, then hauled him to his borrowed mount and draped him inelegantly over his saddle before leading him away from the docks.

Chapter 23

It was the early hours of the morning before Marqel left the tavern and headed uphill toward the road that led to the temple. Red-stained clouds had built up, threatening rain. The sky was low and heavy and the air felt moist. It began to rain, not heavily but enough to make her shiver as her red tunic gradually became soaked. She walked on, heedless of the weather. Perhaps, when she arrived back at the temple looking forlorn and drenched, the others would assume she was stricken with grief, rather than the truth, which was that she had spent a very agreeable evening in a tavern getting pleasantly drunk.

Most of the shops in the center of town were still closed. On the other side of the square an early rising merchant was lifting the awning on her fruit stall to catch the first customers of the day. The rain was falling harder now, tiny rivulets forming between the cobbles as the water drained toward the sewers beneath the town. Marqel heard a horse nicker softly from the shadows of a lane between the tannery and a shop displaying a sign that announced "Distinguished Pottery." She squinted curiously through the rain at the riderless horse. He was saddled, his reins dragging on the ground, and he was nudging at the rubbish thrown out from the back of the shop.

Instinctively, Marqel eyed the horse with a view to its value. Someone would surely pay to have it returned. The saddle alone was worth a fortune; the fittings appeared to be solid silver and worked with exquisite attention to detail. She smiled to herself, thinking how some habits were so ingrained in her, that even after more than two years in the Goddess's service, she still could not help but wonder about the reward she might claim for retrieving something so valuable.

She called softly to the horse as she entered the lane, speaking nonsense words in a soothing tone so as not to startle the beast. There was no sign of his owner. When she was close enough, she reached up slowly for his bridle and was rewarded with a friendly push. Marqel smiled as the gelding rubbed his wet, velvety muzzle against her cheek.

"Aren't you beautiful?" she murmured as she patted him.

The horse tossed his head with a shower of raindrops, nodding as if he agreed with her. Carefully, she gathered up his reins and threw them over his neck to prevent him stepping on them. She made no attempt to mount him. Marqel still had little experience with riding and was not so foolish that she would attempt to mount an unknown horse, regardless of how friendly he might appear.

"Come on, gorgeous," she coaxed, tugging on his bridle to move him forward. "Let's go find out who owns you."

Even with the promise of shelter in the offing, the horse refused to budge. She tugged a little harder, but the gelding was adamant. Marqel sighed impatiently as she looked around for

something that might entice him, some scrap of food or an errant weed poking through the cobbles that might tempt the
beast to move. As she did, the rubbish heap beside her moved.

With a squeal of fright, Marqel jumped backward. The
horse seemed unconcerned. Instead, he lowered his head and
pushed at the rubbish. A glimpse of royal blue poked out from
under the discarded packing left over from the pottery shop.
When the pile moved again and groaned, Marqel realized that
it was a man. Quickly, she tore away at the piled-up rubbish until she was able to drag the limp body clear of the pile.

He was dressed in the blue-and-silver uniform of a Queen's
Guardsman. She rolled him onto his back and gasped aloud.
He was so battered and bruised, she almost didn't recognize
him.

"Oh, Goddess! Kirsh? Kirshov? Answer me!"

He groaned, but that was all the sense she could get out of
him. Oblivious to the rain, Marqel checked him over carefully,
but it appeared that nothing was broken. She frowned suspiciously, recognizing the work of professional thugs. Kalleen
had occasionally hired out Sooter and Murry to the moneylender on Bryton because they could deliver the same sort of
precise beating: the kind that would leave a man pissing blood
for a week, but wouldn't kill him. The moneylender was quite
firm on that point. He wanted his errant debtors alive to pay
their debts. Kirsh, too, had been worked over by experts.

"Oh, Kirshov," she cried, cradling his head in her lap.
"Who did this to you?"

The horse pushed against her back to remind her he was
still there. Marqel glanced around the lane, but there was nothing there she could use to bathe his wounds, and she would not
leave him. Not like this. Tears streamed unheeded down her
face, mingling with the rain. It all made sense now. Why she
had come here, why circumstances had conspired to bring her
down this particular lane at this precise moment.

Kirshov needed her and destiny had guided her to him.

Marqel's cries for help eventually roused the pottery store
owner. She ordered him to send his son to the duke's house for
help. Marqel did not want to involve the Queen's Guard, but

she knew she couldn't care for him alone. He needed to be moved, for one thing, and she had no hope of performing that feat on her own.

It was well into the morning before help arrived. The second sun had risen behind the clouds and the rain had settled in to a steady downpour that had hardly faltered as she sat in the lane, holding Kirsh to her, urging him to wake. She was soaked to the skin, her long fair hair plastered to her head, but she didn't notice her own discomfort.

Several Guardsmen accompanied the storekeeper's son on his return. They lifted Kirsh into an open wagon—none too gently, she noticed with a scowl—then, with Kirsh's horse tied to the back, headed up the hill toward the duke's house. They did not ask for an explanation, nor seem to expect one. She got the impression they rather expected Kirsh to get himself into trouble and, if anything, his injuries were his own fault. Marqel rode with Kirsh in the wagon, refusing to let the Guardsmen near him.

When the wagon arrived at the duke's house, the captain of the guard hurried out to greet them with Alenor close on his heels. The dark-haired princess was distraught when she caught sight of Kirshov, even more so when she realized that it was Marqel who held his head in her lap. The rain quickly drenched the princess, ruining her pale silk gown and destroying hours of work by her hairdresser. Within minutes, her Royal-Bloody-Highness was looking as disheveled and unkempt as a gutter rat.

"Who did this to him?" Alenor demanded of Marqel angrily.

"You would know better than I, your highness," Marqel replied as she relinquished Kirshov to the Guardsmen. "Perhaps this was meant as a warning to you."

"What do you mean by that?"

"Later, your highness," the captain advised. "We need to get him inside."

"Of course," the princess agreed, stepping back to let the Guardsmen lift him clear. Marqel noticed that with Alenor present, they were much gentler in their handling of the Senetian prince than they had been in the town. Alexin led the way as they carried him into the house.

Marqel jumped down from the wagon and made to follow him inside. She was determined not to let Kirsh out of her sight, but the little princess blocked her path. Marqel was a head taller than Alenor, but that didn't seem to cow the younger girl. The rain had soaked her though. Her carefully arranged curls lay flat against her head and her skin had taken on a faintly blue tinge as the cold rain began to take its toll.

"Where do you think you're going?"

"To tend the prince," Marqel replied.

"The duke's physician can take care of him now. I thank you for your assistance, my lady Shadowdancer, but it is no longer required."

"But I'm trained—"

"I know what you're trained in, Marqel," the princess informed her icily. "And Kirsh doesn't need your help. Not now. Not ever."

For a long moment, the young women stared at each other.

"My lady?"

They both turned toward the Guardsman who stood on the step near the open door to the duke's hall. If he noticed anything amiss, he was wise enough not to let it show.

"What?" Alenor snapped, automatically assuming that the man was addressing her.

"The prince is conscious, your highness. He's asking for the Shadowdancer."

Marqel felt a surge of triumph as she stared at the princess. Alenor looked so deflated, so hurt, that Marqel almost felt sorry for her. Almost. The sorry little bitch deserved everything she got. She was a princess; she was rich. One day she would be a queen. That should be more than enough for anybody. What made her think she could have Kirshov as well?

"I'll be right there," Marqel informed the Guardsman, although her victorious gaze never left Alenor's face. The little princess seemed to be fighting back tears. Drenched and devastated as she was, Marqel thought she had never seen such a pathetic sight.

"It seems Kirshov does need me," she said softly.

Alenor didn't reply. With a triumphant smile, Marqel pushed past the princess and hurried inside to tend Kirsh.

Chapter 24

Alenor slammed the door of her room and began tearing off her sodden clothes, blinded by tears of anger and humiliation. The rain rattled against the window, making the room almost as gloomy as her mood. When the door opened without warning, she turned to yell at whomever it was that dared disturb her. She didn't want to see anyone. She simply wanted to die.

"Alexin told me what happened," Rainan explained, closing the door behind her, before Alenor could say a word.

"Oh, Mother!" she cried, hurling her sodden gown to the floor. "How could he betray me like that?"

"Betray you?" the queen asked curiously. "I'm not sure I follow you, Alenor."

"How could Kirsh ask for that damn Shadowdancer instead of me? And in front of the Guardsmen? What must they think? What was *he* thinking?"

"From what Alexin tells me, he's barely conscious." The queen walked into the dressing room and reappeared a moment later with a towel. She handed it to Alenor and then picked up the ruined gown from the rug where Alenor had thrown it. Rainan walked across the room and draped it over the back of a chair, where at least it wasn't dripping on the Duke of Grannon Rock's carpet. "I'm not sure Kirshov knew what he was saying, darling."

"But that just makes it worse!" Alenor declared from under the towel as she tried to dry her hair. She rubbed at it vigorously for a moment then looked up at her mother. "Don't you see? He called out to *her*. Not me!"

"I assume we're talking about the Shadowdancer who found him?" Rainan asked. "I know her from somewhere, don't I?"

"She was in Avacas. She was the one who claimed Dirk raped her."

"And Kirsh attacked him for it, as I recall. Quite a catalyst for disaster, your little Shadowdancer."

"She's a thief and a liar and she's been after Kirshov since we first met her on Elcast."

Rainan seemed unconvinced. "Alenor, by all accounts she saved his life. Aren't you overreacting just a little bit? She had been with him for quite some time before help arrived. He's delirious. Kirshov was probably just calling for the most recent familiar face, darling. It's you he loves. You've told me that a thousand times."

"No, he was calling for Marqel because she's the one he truly wants."

Rainan's reaction to her angry announcement was guarded. The queen took over from the mother. It hurt Alenor a little to think that her mother's response was politically motivated, rather than guided by maternal feeling.

"Are you certain of that?"

Alenor shrugged and sank down on the edge of the bed. "Yes."

"I see."

"You don't sound surprised."

"To be frank, Alenor, I was more surprised to learn that you loved Kirsh, or that he seemed to love you. Falling in love is a luxury for someone in your position."

"Did you love my father?"

"I liked him well enough, certainly, and I grieved for him when he died, but I never loved him. Like your future consort, your father was chosen because of who he was, not for what I felt for him."

"How can I marry Kirsh now, Mother? Knowing that he doesn't love me?"

"For one thing, you don't know he doesn't love you. Your entire hypothesis is based on the delirious babbling of a barely conscious young man. And second, even if you loathed him, Alenor, the wedding would still go ahead. The only chance we have of protecting Dhevyn's sovereignty is to ensure that the next king or queen of Dhevyn after you is of Senetian *and* Dhevynian blood."

"Won't that achieve the exact opposite? If Kirsh and I have a child, then we're all but handing Dhevyn to the Senetians."

"On the contrary, my dear, we are securing its future. Antonov wishes to own Dhevyn, make no mistake about that. He will do it peacefully by marriage, or he'll do it the hard way and take us by force, but one way or another, he intends to claim us."

Alenor nodded thoughtfully. "So you think that if the next heir to Dhevyn is Antonov's grandchild, he'll think that he's achieved his goal?"

"Exactly," the queen agreed. "By the time your child inherits the throne, we'll have been able to negotiate a much more reasonable and secure agreement regarding Dhevyn's future with Misha."

"With our luck," she sighed miserably, "Antonov will live to be a hundred and fifty and poor Misha will die before he can inherit anything."

"If Misha dies, Alenor, you won't be marrying Kirshov. I'll not have Dhevyn absorbed by Senet because we suddenly share an heir."

"I heard Misha was really sick."

"But well on the way to recovery," Rainan assured her. When Alenor looked at her questioningly, she smiled. "I'm not entirely reliant on the information fed to me by Antonov and Belagren."

"You have spies in Senet?" Alenor asked in surprise.

"Sympathizers." Rainan smiled. "Now, why don't you finish getting changed? I'm going to be busy for a while drafting a letter to Antonov, trying to explain this rather unfortunate accident."

"It wasn't an accident, Mother, someone beat him up."

"Alexin seems to think it was cutpurses. Apparently he was drinking with Kirshov in a tavern by the docks in the early hours of the morning. He claims Kirsh was quite drunk when he left him. I guess we won't know the whole story until he recovers."

"Do you think it was cutpurses? Or because of who he is?"

The queen shrugged. "I'm very fond of the cutpurse theory myself. When Antonov hears about this, I'll have enough to account for, without trying to explain away an attempt on his son's life."

"Does Antonov need to know?"

"I don't think there's any way to stop him finding out." The queen smiled comfortingly. "Why don't you go up to the bathhouse and have a good long soak? Things will look a lot less drastic when you're clean and dry."

Her mother's reassurances did little to placate Alenor, but she could see there was no point arguing about it.

"Yes, Mother."

Rainan stepped forward and kissed her cheek. "It will all work out, Alenor, I promise. We've survived so far."

Rainan let herself out of the room, leaving Alenor staring thoughtfully after her.

We've survived so far. It was true, she knew, but it wasn't enough. In a few weeks, Alenor would be Queen of Dhevyn, but she was not so foolish to believe that she would have any control at all over her kingdom or her own fate. Kirsh didn't really care about being regent, and she knew he would allow the underlings his father had placed in Dhevyn's court to run things as they saw fit. She would be lucky if she questioned anything. All he wanted was that damn thief.

It's up to me, she realized with an overwhelming sense of despair. *Mother can't do anything, Kirsh won't do anything. If anyone is going to put things to rights, then it has to be me.* The unfairness of it all seemed to swamp her for a moment. *What can I do? I'm fifteen years old, and I'm surrounded by people who are too afraid to sneeze in the direction of Avacas for fear of upsetting Antonov and Belagren...*

Then she thought of Alexin and his cryptic offer.

Maybe she was not as alone as she thought.

Her hair still damp, but dressed in dry clothes, Alenor hurried through the duke's sprawling house to the wing where the Queen's Guard were quartered. She badly wanted to check on Kirshov, but didn't want to risk running into Marqel, so she gave his room a wide berth. Perhaps later she would visit him, when he was fully awake and aware of his surroundings.

Mother's probably right. He didn't know what he was saying. If she told herself that often enough, she might even come to believe it.

"Your highness!" a startled voice declared as she burst into the dormitory, where the off-duty Guardsmen were lying about on their bunks in various states of undress. She had no time to be embarrassed.

"I'm looking for Captain Seranov."

"I ... er ... I believe he's in the bathhouse, your highness," one of the guards told her, as his companions hurriedly began to cover themselves. "I can have someone fetch him for you, if you wish."

"Thank you, but I can take care of this myself."

She smiled suddenly, realizing that the guards were more embarrassed than she was.

"As you were, gentlemen."

Alenor hurried across the lawns toward the bathhouse. The rain had stopped and the heat of the second sun was making the ground steam as it burned off the excess moisture. The bathhouse was steamy and stank of sulfur.

"Alexin?" she called through the mist. Fed by a hot spring, the baths had been bricked in to form two large pools, separated by a low stone wall.

"Your *highness*?" a disjointed voice answered.

"Are you decent?"

"No!" He sounded quite alarmed. "What are you doing here?"

Alenor emerged out of the steam to find him treading water in the center of the pool. "I wanted to talk to you."

She suddenly realized the danger she was putting them both in. Nothing would get Alexin hanged faster than being caught alone, naked and swimming with the Crown Princess of Dhevyn in the Duke of Grannon Rock's baths.

"Couldn't we wait—" he began. She was sure he was going to ask, "Couldn't we wait until I've got some clothes on?"

"This is the only chance we'll have to talk," she informed him as she sat on the edge of the pool.

With some reluctance, Alexin nodded and swam closer to the edge, so they could speak without being overheard, even though it was the middle of the day and, except for Alexin, the bathhouse was deserted.

"Is something wrong?"

"Why do you assume there's something wrong?"

"You're willing to risk your reputation and my neck to come here, your highness. That would seem to imply that something out of the ordinary is going on."

Alenor trailed her fingers in the warm water. "You saw what happened when they brought Kirsh back to the house this morning?"

"Yes," he agreed cautiously.

"He didn't want me. He wanted someone else."

"Kirsh was semiconscious, your highness. He probably had no idea what he was saying."

"That's what Mother said." She sighed heavily. "I'm sorry. I didn't come here to whine about Kirsh. I wanted to ask you something else."

"I'm at your disposal, your highness."

"I want to meet your friends."

Alexin stared at her. "I *beg* your pardon?"

"The Baenlanders. I want to meet with them."

"Does the queen know about this?"

Alenor rolled her eyes impatiently. "Don't be stupid, Alexin, of course she doesn't know! She's made her position on this matter quite clear."

"And you still want to defy her?"

"I want to do the best thing for my kingdom. Anyway, in a

few weeks it won't matter what my mother thinks. *I* will be Queen of Dhevyn."

"With Kirshov Latanya as regent," Alexin pointed out warily.

"All the more reason to meet with them now."

The captain was silent for a moment. "You do realize the danger involved, your highness?"

She nodded. "I wouldn't have risked meeting you like this otherwise, Alexin. Will you arrange it? Do you think they'd want to meet with me?"

"I'll see what I can do," he agreed, although he sounded rather doubtful.

"Thank you." She stood up, and glanced at her skirts with a frown. There was a large damp patch where she had been sitting on the pool's edge. She would have to get changed again. At this rate, she would have worn everything she brought with her by the end of the day.

"Alenor."

She glanced down at Alexin. He had never called her by name before. "Yes?"

"Are you doing this for Dhevyn, or just to get back at Kirshov?"

She hesitated before answering, not certain she knew herself. "For Dhevyn," she said eventually, almost believing it.

"Are you sure? If I do this, it's not just you that will be in danger. We can't afford to have you change your mind in a few days just because you've forgiven Kirsh—"

Cutting off his warning, Alenor impulsively leaned down, took his head in her hands and kissed him. There was nothing chaste or pure about it. She opened her mouth willingly, almost wantonly; leaning so far over she was in danger of falling into the pool. Alexin suffered a moment of stunned immobility then he kissed her back. It was then that Alenor came to her senses. She broke off the kiss and stared at him in surprise.

She had not expected to feel so...*wanted*.

"If I was planning to get back at Kirsh I'd be doing something like that," she said, in a voice barely more than a whisper, then she turned and fled the bathhouse before he could respond, or she could do anything more to embarrass herself.

Chapter 25

I've reviewed Talenburg's request for assistance," Misha advised Lord Palinov, several days after the matter had been brought to his attention, "and I have decided that you were right. We shall only grant them two thousand dorns."

Misha was feeling much better today—so much better that he had insisted he be carried down to his father's office to meet with the chancellor. The sun streamed in through the eastern windows, bathing him in light. Misha suspected he didn't present nearly as daunting a figure as his father did in the same position, but it was a timely reminder to the Chancellor of the Exchequer that one day, Misha Latanya would be the Lion of Senet. Misha had no interest in making Palinov believe that the chancellor would be answerable to him when that far-off day arrived. When Misha ruled Senet, he had already decided that the first person to go would be Lord Palinov.

"A wise decision, your highness," Palinov replied, carefully, but not completely, hiding his sneer.

"As for the rest of the funds, we will offer Talenburg a loan of eight thousand dorns to be repaid over the next ten years at a reduced interest rate."

"A *loan,* your highness?"

"They need the money, my lord. I've taken a good look at their estimates and I find them thorough, well thought out, and not in the least bit inflated. If anything, I feel they might be a little optimistic in their projections, particularly in their assumptions regarding the cost of the granite required. It will have to be shipped across the lake from the quarries in Laska, and I fear they've not allowed enough for such an expensive undertaking."

"We are not moneylenders, your highness," the chancellor reminded him, obviously horrified by the suggestion. "This is unprecedented. What will your father say?"

"He says it's a wonderful idea," Misha informed the chancellor, playing his trump card with glee. "I knew you'd be reluctant to do anything so radical without his approval, so I sent a message to him on Elcast asking for his advice. He seems to think my plan is a very satisfactory solution to the problem."

Palinov looked quite stunned. The last thing he expected was for Misha to go over his head to Antonov. The Crippled Prince was suddenly filled with a warm feeling of affection for all well-trained carrier pigeons. And mightily relieved that his father had replied to his request so promptly.

"You seem to have thought of everything, your highness."

"Well, you were right about setting an awkward precedent, my lord," Misha told him graciously. "At least this way, if any other city wishes to prevail upon the generosity of the Lion of Senet, we'll actually make a profit from it."

"I . . . I don't know what to say, your highness," Palinov admitted, which was probably the most honest statement Misha had ever heard him utter.

"You've no need to say anything, my lord. Just see to it that the appropriate agreements are drawn up and I'll sign them as soon as they're ready."

"His highness has demonstrated an unexpected talent for statesmanship."

"Why is it so unexpected, my lord?" Misha asked bluntly. "Do you think my brain is as withered as my leg?"

"Of course not, your highness!" he gushed hurriedly. "I never meant to imply anything of the kind!"

"I would hope not."

Palinov rose to his feet and bowed. For the first time in his life, Misha saw a hint of genuine respect in the old man's eyes.

"I will see to it that your orders are carried out at once, your highness."

"You do that," Misha said.

By lunchtime, Misha's euphoria over beating Palinov at his own game had faded somewhat, and he began to feel quite ill. He asked to be taken back to his rooms, canceling his scheduled meeting with the Prefect of Avacas. It was easy to find an excuse not to meet with Barin Welacin. Misha despised the man.

Barin would be the second person forcibly retired when Misha became the Lion of Senet.

Not that he was likely to inherit his father's crown anytime soon, Misha realized, as he collapsed with relief against his pillows and ordered the servants from the room. Antonov was not yet fifty, in the prime of life, and showed no hint of slowing down. Misha was doomed to suffer the fate of all heirs: he had to bide his time, learn what he could, and hope that when the time came, he could do as good a job as his father had done.

That Antonov was an astute and competent ruler was never in doubt. But he had made a few decisions that Misha would not have, had it been up to him.

While he had no personal gripe against the High Priestess, Misha was a little concerned at how much influence she had over his father, and was determined that when he ascended to the throne, the separation between Church and crown would be much more clearly defined. Misha believed in the Goddess, and he had no reason to question the High Priestess's claims that she was the Goddess's voice on Ranadon. But in his mind, there were a few too many decisions taken that placed the wishes of the Church over the welfare of Senet.

He turned his face from the window, the light bothering his eyes, as he thought that the execution of Morna Provin was one such decision that was extremely ill advised. It would do nothing but stir up old memories that had almost faded into history. So what if Morna Provin lived? She had not raised a finger in rebellion in nearly two decades. She had been so quiet that many people thought her already dead. It was foolish to so forcibly remind everyone that she was not.

Of course, her execution had much more to do with her son than actually disposing of a traitor. If it were not for Dirk,

Antonov might have left Morna to die of old age on Elcast, forgotten if not forgiven. His father had a lot invested in Dirk. He had known, since Morna gave birth to him, that the child could not possibly be Wallin's son, and he had bided his time, waiting for Dirk to grow up; waiting for the right opportunity to use the knowledge of his true parentage to the best advantage.

Why did women think that men couldn't count off the months of their confinement as well as any woman could? Misha wondered idly.

But whatever the circumstances of his birth, Misha did not think Dirk was stupid enough to walk into such an obvious trap. Nor did he think Dirk would ever willingly return to Avacas. The boy he remembered was not interested in seeking power or glory. And he was Dhevynian enough that he would probably consider joining the Lion of Senet in any venture tantamount to betraying his own people.

Misha sighed heavily, as even thinking about the situation on Elcast became too much of an effort. Maybe Olena was right, after all. He had overextended himself and now he was suffering for it. He lay back against the pillows and debated calling for her. There was a bell by his bed that he often used to summon a servant. Sometimes it was all he could do to ring it.

Misha closed his eyes, cursing his own weakness. His victory over the chancellor had been so sweet, but he was paying for it now. By sheer force of will he had kept the tremors at bay long enough to wipe that smug, patronizing smile off Palinov's face.

What would it be like when he really *was* in charge? When there were no others around to cover for his weakness? Could he actually rule Senet if he had to hide away every time he began to feel a little shaky? Would he be taken seriously by anybody if they saw him, rigid and unconscious, too weak to control his own limbs?

Misha knew that people called him the Crippled Prince. Nobody ever said it to his face, of course, but that's what they called him. Would his father's title be amended when his son inherited the crown? Would he be known as the Lion of Senet or the Cripple of Senet?

Misha was finding it increasingly difficult to concentrate. He was shivering violently, and white spots danced before his eyes, as if he was looking at the world through a gauze scarf filled with holes.

The Cripple of Senet.

The title seemed to taunt him as his vision became increasingly blurred. Misha reached for the bell and shook it weakly, suddenly crying out as his stomach cramped savagely.

The bell tumbled to the floor with a clatter. Misha was already unconscious by the time Olena answered his summons.

Chapter 26

Alexin arranged the meeting with Alenor to take place the day before the Landfall Festival. The meeting place was a deserted building several miles from Nova that Reithan's father had used as a hunting lodge back before the Age of Shadows. The building was a ruin now, but its advantage was that it was built in the lee of a small hill that gave a wide view of the surrounding countryside. Porl posted several lookouts on the hill to watch out for the princess, and to ensure she was not being followed.

"She's taking her time," Tia remarked impatiently.

She was sitting with her bow resting on her lap next to Dirk on the steps leading to the entrance of the lodge, which was nothing more than a gaping hole where the doors had once hung. The only thing left of the lodge now was the masonry and the beams that supported the upper floor, and even they were slowly being carted away by local farmers looking for stone and wood to repair their fences. The paneling, the door frames and the windows were long gone, probably taken by those same farmers for firewood.

"I imagine they're taking a rather roundabout route," Porl replied, apparently unconcerned. The pirate captain was behind them, poking about in the ruins to relieve the tedium of waiting.

"Why do you suppose she wants to meet us?"

"Maybe because *we* asked for the meeting?" Dirk suggested.

She glared at him. "That's not what I meant."

"Alexin seems to think she's genuine," Reithan remarked. He was sitting on the ground with his back against a large oak that shaded the ruin; his feet stretched out in front of him, making the most of the shade.

"How do we know she's not doing this at Kirshov Latanya's behest?" Tia persisted. "For all we know she went straight to her boyfriend after Alexin spoke to the queen the first time and blabbed the whole thing to him."

"I doubt Kirshov Latanya's in much of a state to do anything at the moment," Porl reminded her with a grin, as he stepped back out onto the remains of the veranda. Dirk glanced up at him. Porl grinning was never a pretty sight.

Dirk made no comment about the beating Kirsh had received. He was alone in his condemnation of that dreadful deed, and it did nothing but aggravate his companions to remind them of it.

"Tia's got a point, though," Dirk said thoughtfully.

"I do?" Tia asked in surprise. She always seemed surprised when he agreed with her.

"Alenor only changed her mind about meeting with us after Kirsh was hurt."

"Do you think she's connected the two?"

"We'll find out soon enough," Reithan said, climbing to his feet. "There's the signal."

Dirk glanced up and caught sight of a bright flash coming from about halfway up the hill behind the house where the lookouts were posted.

Tia glanced at Dirk. "Nervous?"

"Why would I be nervous?"

"Well, you haven't seen your little cousin for a while, and the last time you saw her she couldn't decide whether to hug you or hang you."

"Leave him alone, Tia," Porl said as he walked down the steps to stand beside Reithan, who was watching a small group of riders approaching from the west.

"I wasn't picking on him," she called after him, and then she turned to Dirk. "Do you pay them to do that?"

"Do what?"

"Stick up for you all the time."

"Tia!" Reithan called sharply.

"What?"

"Get up to the first floor. And keep an arrow nocked."

"What's wrong?" Dirk asked, wondering at the sudden change in Reithan's demeanor.

"That's Raban Seranov," he said, pointing at the horseman in the lead of a group of four riders heading in the direction of the lodge. "Not Alexin."

"The first sign of trouble, you put an arrow through that smug little bastard's left eye, Tia," Porl ordered.

Tia nodded wordlessly, picked up her short bow and the quiver of arrows and disappeared into the ruined lodge. Dirk walked forward to stand between Reithan and Porl.

"You sound worried," he said to Reithan.

"Alexin I trust. His brother I'm not so sure about."

"Why not?"

"Raban makes all the right noises about being on our side," Porl explained. "But we always seem to run into trouble when he's around. Trouble he manages to weasel out of—like he's been greased."

"Raban is supposed to see to it that we don't get unduly bothered by the customs men in Nova," Reithan added. "The last time the *Makuan* was in port she was boarded and searched."

"Did they find anything?" Dirk asked curiously.

"We wouldn't be here telling you about it if they had." Porl laughed grimly.

"Dirk, why don't you stay out of sight until we know what's going on?" Reithan suggested.

It seemed like good advice, so Dirk turned toward the ruin. On impulse, he clambered up the remains of the stone staircase after Tia. She was standing in the shadow of a tall window opening, an arrow nocked and waiting, although she had not drawn it yet.

"What are *you* doing here?" she asked without looking back.

He took up a position in the shadows on the other side of the window. "I thought the view might be better."

Tia didn't answer him. The riders cantered closer to the lodge and, for the first time, Dirk could clearly see Alenor riding at the right hand of a heavyset man with dark hair and a hooded falcon resting in his gauntleted left arm. She was wearing a dark blue, elegantly cut riding habit, with a matching wide-brimmed hat to shade her creamy skin from the harsh light of the second sun.

Reithan and Porl waited near the big oak as the riders halted before them. There were two other men with Alenor, besides Raban Seranov, wearing the black-and-green livery of Grannon Rock. Dirk guessed they were members of the duke's personal guard.

"I might have known you'd be the reason for this clandestine meeting, cousin," Raban called cheerfully to Reithan as he dismounted.

Tia raised the bow and began to draw back slowly.

"I'm surprised to see you, Raban," Reithan replied, walking forward to meet him. "I thought you'd be too busy inventing new and ever more imaginative ways to kiss Antonov's arse."

The heir to Grannon Rock walked back to one of the riders and handed him the falcon, before turning to help Alenor out of her saddle.

"I would not be here but for Alexin *and* Raban's assistance, my lord," Alenor said as she dismounted. "I rather think the question is not so much if I can trust *him,* but if I can trust *you.*"

Reithan bowed to Alenor. "I didn't mean to offend you, your highness. It's just the last time we were forced to rely on Raban's assistance, we barely escaped with our lives."

"That wasn't my fault, Reithan," Raban said.

"So you keep saying," Porl remarked skeptically.

Alenor glared at Reithan and Porl as she removed her hat. "Is this your idea of a meaningful dialogue? You endanger us all by asking for a meeting just so you can argue with my escort?"

"Of course not, your highness," Reithan said.

"I only agreed to this meeting because Alexin thinks you can help us," Alenor explained, fidgeting with her riding crop, the only sign of her nervousness.

"We'd very much like to help, your highness," Reithan agreed. "If you'll let us."

"How?"

"Stopping the Lion of Senet gaining control of Dhevyn would be a good start," Porl suggested.

"And how do you plan to do that?" Alenor asked, a little impatiently. "Do you have plans to assassinate him? Or Kirshov, perhaps? I won't be party to anything that involves needless bloodshed."

"One could argue that killing a Latanya doesn't really qualify as *needless*," Porl remarked with a faint grin.

Alenor glared at him. "If that's all the help you can offer me, then I should never have come! Perhaps my mother was right. You Baenlanders *are* nothing but trouble."

"Your highness, we want the same thing you want," Reithan assured her, with a rather irritated glance at the scarred pirate.

"But how do I know I can trust you, Reithan Seranov? The last time we met you were a prisoner of the Lion of Senet and slated for torture and execution. Now here you are, alive and well, trying to draw me into a plot to overthrow him. What proof do I have that he didn't break you? How can I be sure you're not simply an agent sent by Barin Welacin to test my loyalty?"

Dirk listened to the conversation, thinking Alenor had grown up a great deal in the two years since he had seen her last. She seemed much more confident, much more sure of herself. Or it might just be the riding habit she wore. It made her look much older than her fifteen years.

"I should put this arrow through *her*," Tia muttered beside him, her arm trembling from the effort of keeping the string taut for too long. "That would solve most of our problems right there."

"Don't even joke about it, Tia," he said softly, not sure if she was serious.

Below them, Reithan studied the princess for a moment, and then he glanced up at the window where Dirk and Tia were concealed, before turning back to Alenor.

"Perhaps if I can't convince you of our sincerity, your highness, someone else can?"

Tia slowly let the string go slack and turned to Dirk. "That sounds like your cue, long-lost cousin."

"Just watch who you're pointing that bow at," he warned as he turned for the stairs. "I don't want you shooting me by accident."

She smiled. "If I ever shoot an arrow into you, Dirk Provin, it won't be by accident."

"...and I can't imagine what either of you can say that will convince me you can be trusted," Alenor was saying as Dirk emerged into the sunlight from the ruins.

"Then why did you come?" Dirk asked, walking toward the small group gathered in the shade of the massive oak tree.

The dappled light danced over Alenor's face as she looked up at the sound of his voice. *"Dirk?"*

"Hello, Alenor."

She hesitated for a fraction of a second, and then rushed across the small distance that separated them and threw her arms around him, sobbing with relief at the sight of him.

"Well, I guess this means you're glad to see me," he remarked, hugging her tightly.

Alenor sniffed and looked up at him, wiping away her tears. She held him at arm's length for a moment, drinking in the sight of him. "Oh, Dirk, what happened to you? Where have you been all this time? Why didn't you let us know you were alive? You're so tall now, and so... We must get a message to Elcast. And Kirsh! Oh... poor Kirsh... did you hear what happened to him?"

"It seems Kirsh got drunk and copped a beating down near

the docks a couple of days ago," Raban explained before Dirk could betray them by not looking surprised.

"Is he all right?" Dirk asked, genuinely concerned.

"He'll live," Raban assured him.

"I'm so glad you're here, Dirk," Alenor sighed, and then turned to the others with a commanding air. "I wish to speak to my cousin, gentlemen. Alone."

"Your highness—" Raban objected, but Reithan cut him off.

"Leave them be, Raban. Let her talk to Dirk."

"And while they're talking, you can explain how it wasn't your fault you set the excise men onto us," Porl added.

Alenor slipped her arm through Dirk's and led him away from the house, still clutching her wide-brimmed hat. They walked toward another large shady oak some fifty feet from the ruin. Alenor stopped when they reached the tree and sat down on the grass. Dirk glanced back at the house warily.

"They can't hear us from over there," Alenor said.

Dirk was actually more worried that they were still in range of Tia's bow, but he could hardly tell Alenor that. He sat down beside her, placing himself between Alenor and the lodge.

"I can't believe you're really here," she said, putting aside the hat and taking his hands in hers. He was surprised at how small her hands were. Far too small to carry the burden she must soon assume. "I've missed you so much, Dirk. You must promise me you will never, ever leave me again."

"You know I can't promise that, Alenor."

"I know," she sighed. "But it's nice to pretend for a moment. Are you really a pirate now?"

"Not really. More an occasional drug runner, sometime goatherd and full-time chess player."

"You disappear off the face of Ranadon for two years to play *chess*?"

"I have a worthy opponent," he explained with a smile.

"Who? Misha used to claim that the only person who'd have a chance at beating you in chess would be..." she faltered for a moment, then nodded in understanding. *"Neris Veran."*

"If Reithan realized I'd let it slip that Neris still lives, we'd be lucky to leave here alive."

"Well, *I'm* not going to tell him. Are you?"

"No."

"Then we have nothing to worry about, do we?"

"*Nothing* to worry about?"

She smiled wistfully. "Like I said. Sometimes it's nice to pretend."

"Why did you come, Alenor?" he asked curiously.

She let go of his hands and looked out over the rolling fields that stretched away toward the hills in the distance, a sea of golden grass that rustled and whispered in the slight breeze as if each seed-head had a secret to share with its neighbor.

"Do you remember when we first met on Elcast? I told you I was going to put an end to the Landfall Festival."

"I remember."

Alenor smiled thinly at her own foolishness. "I had this idea that it would be easy. Well, not easy, perhaps, but at least possible."

"And now you think it's impossible?"

"Now I've learned the meaning of the word *compromise,*" she corrected. "It's all I hear. We have to give in a little bit here, Alenor, a little bit there, Alenor, just to hold on to the little bit we have left, Alenor. But it's eating us alive. Every little piece of Dhevyn that we surrender to Senet is gone forever, and when I marry Kirsh…"

"You risk losing it all," Dirk finished for her. "I thought you loved him."

"Unfortunately, Kirsh doesn't seem to reciprocate my feelings with quite the same enthusiasm," she said with undisguised bitterness. "He's found someone else he finds more… appealing."

"Marqel the Magnificent?" Dirk asked intuitively.

She looked at him in surprise.

"I saw her the other day in the temple," he explained. "I wondered what she was doing here on Grannon Rock."

"I'm not even going to ask what you were doing in a temple, Dirk," she said with a faint smile, and then sighed. "But you're right. She's with him now, I suppose, nursing him back to health."

"Is that why you're here?"

"Alexin asked me the same thing."

"What did you tell him?"

Unaccountably, Alenor blushed and looked down at her hands. "You don't want to know."

He waited for her to say something further, but she seemed reluctant.

"You can't stop the wedding, Alenor," he said gently, guessing that was at the core of her torment. She had loved Kirsh all her life, and now, when he was within her grasp, she realized that she loved a dream, an illusion. The Kirsh that Alenor had loved as a child probably never even existed.

"Why can't I stop it?" she demanded petulantly. "If I don't marry Kirsh, then he can't become regent and—"

"And Antonov will have your mother executed and the whole of Dhevyn under martial law while you're still trying to return the wedding gifts."

"So that's it? You think I should just marry Kirsh and let him ruin what's left of Dhevyn in his father's name?"

"I don't think Kirsh would deliberately ruin Dhevyn, Alenor."

"That doesn't mean he won't. It's killing me to think that I'm a party to this. I want to end it. I want it over and done with!"

"Then marry him. Let him have Marqel as his mistress."

"Are you mad? You think I should allow Kirsh to take my kingdom while he entertains himself with that...that... whore?"

"I think, Alenor, that if Kirsh is busy entertaining himself with that whore, then he's going to be far too busy to do anything but sign whatever you put in front of him. You can't fight them from the outside, Alenor. The only way to win this is to keep what little power you have. I'm sure Johan Thorn would have been the first to tell you how little real impact you can make from exile."

Alenor was silent for a long moment, then, slowly, tentatively, she smiled. "You really are quite devious, aren't you, Dirk?"

"Don't take such a step lightly, Alenor," he warned. "People can be very cruel. You may find the humiliation of having your husband openly flaunting a mistress more than you can bear."

"I could bear it. If I knew there was an end in sight."

"What do you want of us?"

"The Baenlanders? It's odd thinking of you as one of them. I don't know what I want, Dirk. A magic wand would be nice. Something I could wave over Dhevyn and make everything right again."

"Damn," he said with a smile. "I left my magic wand back in Mil."

"What am I going to do?" she asked, as if he knew the answer. "I can't do this on my own."

"Reithan was hoping to find a way to delay the wedding, too."

"Then he's more guilty of wishful thinking than I am. Antonov will make certain that it goes ahead. Anyway, I'm beginning to think that maybe it's not such a bad idea that my mother abdicates. She is far too willing to give in to Senet. But then I look at *why* she gives in so easily and I realize I probably won't do any better. I can't fight Antonov any more effectively than my mother can."

"You're never going to win Dhevyn back by fighting for it, Alenor. Even Johan understood that."

"Then how do I do it?"

"You have to expose Belagren. That, in turn, will destroy Antonov."

"Far easier said than done," she pointed out with a frown. "Unless your new chess partner happened to mention when the next Age of Shadows is due."

"If only," Dirk said with a short, skeptical laugh.

"Why can't *you* do it, Dirk?"

"Me?"

"You're as smart as Neris, aren't you?"

"No!"

"Don't be so modest. Why don't you go to Omaxin and work it out? If we knew that *one* thing, we could crush Belagren in a matter of days."

"I really don't think it's that simple, Alenor."

She smiled at him and squeezed his hand comfortingly. "I'm sorry. I shouldn't even ask it of you. You must be out of your mind over your mother."

"What's my mother got to do with it?"

She stared at him with a puzzled frown. "Surely you know what's going to happen on Landfall?"

When Dirk responded with nothing more than a baffled shrug, her eyes filled with tears.

"Your mother was arrested at Wallin's funeral, Dirk," she said. "I thought someone would have told you. Antonov and Belagren are going to burn her at the Landfall Festival tomorrow."

Chapter 27

Tia watched Dirk and Alenor for a long time as they sat under the tree not far from the house, lost in a conversation that excluded all others. The cousins' obvious closeness irritated her. The princess had greeted Dirk like a long-lost lover; all his past deeds apparently both forgiven and forgotten. She could not understand what it was about Dirk Provin that made people react to him like that. She couldn't understand why he engendered such a feeling of trust in others, when his actions should attract quite the contrary.

Alenor was holding both his hands in hers as they spoke. *What's he telling her?* she wondered. *What is she saying to him? Are they just catching up on old times, or are they plotting something?* She was suspicious of Alenor, even more so of Dirk. How did one trust a girl in love with the Lion of Senet's son, and friends with the man who had killed Johan Thorn?

There was simply no way to tell what they were discussing, so she moved back to the window near the front of the lodge and looked down on the others. The two guards Raban had brought with them were still mounted, one of them holding the falcon on his left arm. Raban, Reithan and Porl were standing under the tree talking.

"...it'll take place in Kalarada," Raban was telling Porl and Reithan. "The invitations have already gone out."

"Was there any mention of the abdication?" Porl asked. Tia guessed they were talking of Alenor's upcoming wedding to Kirshov Latanya.

"No. But don't get your hopes up," Raban warned. "It could just mean that Antonov wants to spring it on the guests at the wedding, before anyone has time to object."

"It's an open secret though, surely?" Reithan suggested.

"Yes and no. I mean, the rumors are fairly accurate, but for the most part, Rainan hasn't been acting like she's about to abdicate, so people prefer to believe that she won't."

"Is there any chance that she won't?"

Raban shook his head. "Alexin thinks not, and from what I've seen since she's been here in Nova under my father's roof, I'm inclined to agree with him. Rainan is cautious—cautious to the point of being ineffectual, actually. Our young princess over there has more spunk in her little finger than her mother ever had."

Reithan glanced over at the couple under the tree and suddenly straightened as he saw Dirk and Alenor heading back toward them. Alenor was holding Dirk's hand and had obviously been crying. Tia looked at Dirk and experienced a moment of dread. He had an oddly familiar expression on his face. It was that same flat, dangerous look in those steel-gray eyes that she had seen the night he killed Johan Thorn.

Cautiously, Tia nocked her arrow again.

"Your highness," Raban said with a bow as they approached. "Is everything all right?"

"Yes, my lord," the princess replied. "Dirk and I just had some catching up to do." She turned to Reithan and Porl. "Dirk tells me you were hoping to find a way to delay the wedding."

"That's right, your highness," Reithan agreed. "We thought that—"

"It can't be done," Alenor announced. "Nor do I think it should be done."

"But your highness—"

"None of us is in a position to challenge Senet, Reithan, and one furtive meeting does not constitute an alliance. You have no plan. We have nothing but a common purpose. Noble as that might be, it's not going to free Dhevyn."

"But once Kirshov is regent," Porl pointed out, "it will be too late to do anything."

Alenor glanced at Dirk before she answered. Tia saw the look and wondered about it. What had they cooked up between them?

"You let me take care of Kirshov. I believe I know him better than you."

"Well enough to control him?" Porl asked.

"And even if you can control Kirshov Latanya, your highness," Raban added, "you'll still have all his lackeys to deal with."

"Then find a way to free Dhevyn, gentlemen. Come to me with a plan that has a hope of succeeding and we have ourselves an alliance. Until that day, don't make my life any more difficult than it already is. We should get going, Raban. We can't afford to be away from the rest of the hunting party for too long." The princess turned to Dirk and smiled at him warmly. "Good luck, Dirk."

Good luck? Why was she wishing him luck?

"Remember what I said," he answered cryptically.

"I will," she promised. Alenor stood on her toes and kissed Dirk's cheek, then put on her wide-brimmed hat and tied it under her chin before allowing Raban to assist her into the saddle. Once she was mounted, she gathered up her reins and looked down at Reithan and Porl. "I appreciate that your people want to help Dhevyn, but good intentions alone are not enough. Get a message to Alexin or Raban if you have something constructive to offer, and I promise I will get a message to you if a solution somehow magically presents itself to me. In the meantime, let's not endanger everyone by meeting like this again, unless the risk is truly worth it."

With that announcement, Alenor kicked her horse into a canter, heading back in the direction they had come. The two guards rode behind her, followed a few moments later by Raban.

They watched her leave in silence, then Porl turned to Reithan and Dirk.

"Well, she's not exactly what I imagined," Porl remarked.

"Raban was right about one thing," Reithan agreed. "She certainly has spunk. What were you two talking about for so long, Dirk?"

Tia waited for his answer. When he didn't respond immediately, she lifted the bow and began to draw back on the string, the arrow aimed squarely at Dirk's back.

"Which one of you," Dirk asked in a flat, toneless voice, "decided that I didn't need to know that Antonov and Belagren are going to execute my mother at the Landfall Festival on Elcast?"

Reithan and Porl exchanged a concerned glance before Porl answered him. Tia drew back the arrow until the fletching brushed her cheek.

"Now, lad, I can understand that you're a bit upset—"

"A *bit* upset?"

"We thought it better that you didn't know, Dirk," Reithan told him.

"*We?*" Dirk demanded angrily. "Who is *we*? Who the hell do you think you are that you can decide such a thing on my behalf?"

Reithan reached his hand out to his stepbrother. Dirk reacted as if he had thrown a punch. He took a swing at Reithan, but the older man ducked and grabbed Dirk, swung him around and slammed him against the trunk of the tree.

"Settle down, Dirk!" Reithan yelled at him.

Dirk tried to hit him again, but Reithan had Dirk's right wrist pinned in a tight grip above his head and his other arm across his throat. Dirk was finding it difficult to breathe. Tia trembled as she watched them struggle, the muscles in her arm crying out in protest. Dirk thrashed against Reithan's hold but could not break it. In desperation, his left hand reached down to the dagger at his belt.

Tia let the arrow go. It thunked solidly into the tree a whisker from Dirk's left ear. Reithan jumped back in alarm. Dirk turned to look at the arrow in shock then stared up at Tia, who had already nocked and drawn another arrow.

"Get your hand off that dagger, Dirk Provin, or I swear I'll put the next one between your eyes," she called down to him.

Without hesitating, Dirk brought up his hand to show that he believed her. Reithan turned to stare up at her, looking almost as pale as Dirk. "Get down here!"

Tia slowly let the string go slack and turned for the ruined stairs. It only took a minute to reach the ground floor. When she emerged into the sunlight, Reithan turned on her angrily. "Do you know how close that was?"

"Do you know how close he was to gutting you?"

Tia walked over to the tree where Dirk was still leaning against the trunk. "Believe it or not, I happen to think they *should* have told you," she said as she began to work the arrow loose. "But that doesn't give you an excuse to pull a knife on anyone."

He stared at her, wide-eyed and pale, as she jerked the arrow free and replaced it in the quiver on her belt.

"You knew about this, too?" he asked.

"We all did. Lexie thought it best that you weren't told. Porl and Reithan agreed with her."

Dirk looked past her at Reithan. "I have to go to Elcast."

"There'd be no point, lad," Porl told him sympathetically. "We'd barely make it in time and even if we did, there's nothing you can do to save her."

"You don't know that for certain."

"No, he doesn't," Reithan agreed. "But what we *do* know for certain is that Antonov is on Elcast with the High Priestess, and your brother Rees is actively aiding him. Just what do you suppose you can do against those sorts of odds?"

"You can't expect me to stay here and do nothing!"

"Dirk, think about it..." Porl began, but Dirk was in no mood to be reasonable.

"I am thinking about it, Captain, and all I can see is that you and Reithan and Lexie conspired to prevent me from saving my mother from being burned alive."

"Even if we got there before Landfall, Dirk," Reithan pointed out, "there's nothing we can do to save her. Morna Provin was condemned to death before you were born."

"I don't care. I'm going to Elcast," Dirk announced. "If you won't help me, I'll find my own way there."

"Be sensible about this, lad!" Porl said. "You've spent the past two years trying to stay out of Antonov's way and now you want to reappear right under his nose for the sake of a useless gesture. Damn it, boy, he's probably expecting you to turn up!"

"You think trying to save my mother from being burned alive is a useless gesture?" Dirk asked incredulously.

"That's precisely what it is," Tia agreed. "And Porl's right. This is as much about driving you out into the open as it is about your mother." Dirk glared at her, but before he could respond she added, "But in your place I'd want to do exactly the same thing."

"Don't encourage him!" Porl snapped.

"Johan would have tried to do something," she reminded them, turning to look at the captain. Her words silenced the argument like a wet blanket thrown over a fire. Porl Isingrin shook his head and then looked down at his boots.

"If we leave Morna Provin to die without trying to do *something,* then we're no better than Antonov," she added.

Reithan turned to Porl. "Maybe Tia's right. Maybe we should try."

"It's a waste of time," Porl insisted.

"We *could* get there by Landfall, though, couldn't we?" Dirk asked.

"If we leave on tonight's tide," Porl agreed reluctantly. "If we don't have any trouble clearing the harbor. If we get favorable winds the whole way. If nothing breaks. But once we get there, what are you going to do? Drop anchor in Elcast harbor and lower the longboat? Even if I could get you there in time, even if you could get past the Lion of Senet's guards and some-how find a way to free Morna, even if by some miracle you got her back to the *Makuan,* how would we escape? The *Calliope* would run us down in a matter of hours."

"We could get to Yerl in a night," Dirk said. "And then I could go overland to Elcast Town on horseback."

"Alone?" Porl scoffed.

"If need be," Dirk retorted.

"I'll go with him," Tia volunteered.

"You?" Reithan asked in surprise.

"Well, someone has to make sure he doesn't do anything stupid."

Reithan stared at her for a moment and then shrugged. "In that case, I suppose you'd better count me in," he told them. "Someone has to make sure *you* don't do anything stupid, Tia."

The captain debated the issue for a moment in silence then he threw his hands up in defeat.

"This is foolish in the extreme," he warned. "But if you re-ally must do this, I'll do my best to get you to Yerl by morning. But after that, you're on your own. I'll weigh anchor outside El-cast harbor until second sunrise the day after Landfall. If you haven't found your way back to the ship by then, I'll assume you're not coming back."

"Thank you, Captain," Dirk said.

"If we're shipping out tonight, we'd better get moving," Reithan suggested, turning toward the ruins where their bor-rowed horses were tethered.

"Tia," Dirk called as she turned to follow Reithan.

"What?"

"Thank you."

"Don't thank me. I was aiming for your forehead. I missed."

"I meant for sticking up for me. You didn't have to. I ap-preciate it."

Tia was not even sure why she had spoken up on Dirk's be-half. It was not as if she actually wanted to help him. And she was certainly not happy with the idea that she had just con-vinced Reithan and Porl to put Dirk within the grasp of the

Lion of Senet. Perhaps it was because she still didn't trust him, and it was easier to go along with him than risk letting him out of her sight. But somehow the decision felt right, even if she couldn't explain it.

"Nobody deserves to be burned alive, Dirk," she said with a shrug. "Not even your mother."

Chapter 28

Marqel was forced to leave Kirshov for a few hours to go into the town to find some bromelain extract, imported from the distant Galina islands, to help relieve his pain and bruising. She had tried explaining what she wanted to one of the duke's servants, but the half-witted fool had returned with nothing more useful than a packet of turmeric, so she decided to undertake the task herself.

The marketplace was crowded. This close to the Landfall Festival the city was packed with visitors and traveling performers. She watched a troupe of acrobats performing for a while, thinking they weren't nearly as good as she had once been, although there were more of them in the troupe and, by the quality of their costumes, they appeared to be making a tidy living.

It was a long time since Marqel had spared her former life a thought. She wondered for a moment what had become of Kalleen and Lanatyne, Murry and Sooter and the insufferable Vonril. She decided she didn't care. Marqel had moved up in the world, a fact that was driven home to her time and again as she browsed the markets, looking for a decent herbalist. People hurried out of her way. They made a path for her through the crowd as if her red robe was surrounded by an invisible shell that others could not penetrate.

Almost...

She was nearly bowled over by a rough-looking boy

EYE OF THE LABYRINTH

dressed like a sailor who barreled straight into her. He smelled like he hadn't bathed in a month, walked with his head down and his unruly dark hair was probably riddled with lice.

"Idiot!" she snapped. "Why don't you watch where you're going?"

"Thorry..." the young man muttered without looking up.

Marqel pushed past him and then stopped suddenly and turned to look at the boy. He had grown somewhat in the two years since she had seen him last, but there was no mistaking that lisp. "Eryk?"

The boy stopped and turned to look at her blankly. "My lady?"

"Goddess! It is you! Don't you remember me, Eryk? Marqel? The acrobat? From Elcast?"

Slowly she saw the light of comprehension glimmering in his dull eyes. "But you're a Shadowdancer."

"That's right. Don't you remember? That's why I was on the ship with you on the way to Avacas. So I could join the Shadowdancers."

The boy nodded, suddenly cheered to see a familiar face. "What are you doing here, then?"

"I was about to ask you the same thing."

The stroke of good fortune that had made Eryk cross Marqel's path left her almost dizzy. In truth, she couldn't have cared less about seeing Eryk again, but one thing was certain— where Eryk went, Dirk Provin was sure to be close by. *Is he here now? If I look up will I be looking into those cold, unforgiving eyes?* Almost fearfully, Marqel glanced around, studying the faces in the crowd, wondering if she could spot him, but there were too many people.

Marqel looked back at Eryk with a smile. In the hands of this half-witted man-child lay a future she had not dared dream about. That she might be the one to discover where Dirk Provin was hiding when all of Prince Antonov's efforts to flush him out over the past two years had failed was more than she could have hoped for; more than she could have imagined in her wildest fantasies.

"Why don't we go somewhere quieter, Eryk?" she suggested. "Somewhere we can talk."

"If you want," Eryk agreed readily.

Marqel took his grubby, calloused hand in hers and led him to an inn on the other side of the square. Her status as a Shadowdancer secured them a private room without so much as mention of a payment. She ordered wine from the innkeeper, then changed her mind and ordered ale instead. Eryk would prefer ale, she guessed.

"You've been away a long time," she said, taking a seat beside him on the small settee by the window. "I was worried about you."

"You were?" he asked in surprise.

"Of course I was! You and Dirk disappeared so suddenly, we were all afraid that something terrible had happened to you."

"We was fine, Mar— my la— What do I call you now?"

"Marqel is fine, Eryk. We're old friends, remember?"

He nodded eagerly. "We've been in the Baenlands," he volunteered. "But it's a secret. Nobody's supposed to know we're there."

"Never fear. I'll not tell," she lied with a comforting smile. "It must be terribly harsh, living with all those pirates."

"I really liked it," he told her, and then he frowned. "Well, I did until I tried to kiss Mellie. I hurt her, I think. I didn't mean to, truly, but she said she wanted to marry me and then she screamed and Dirk hit me and Reithan got really mad at me, too, and they wouldn't let me see Mellie and then they put me on the ship with Cap'n Isingrin and they all pick on me 'cause I'm slow and ..." His incomprehensible babbling trailed off unhappily.

"Who is Mellie?" she asked curiously.

"She said she was going to marry me."

Marqel smiled. "You said that. Why did she scream when you kissed her?"

"I don't know ..."

"Had you ever kissed a girl before Mellie?"

The boy shook his head, his eyes downcast.

"Then maybe you just weren't doing it right," she suggested.

He looked up hopefully. "What do you mean?"

"I mean, maybe this Mellie of yours just got a fright because you didn't know what you were doing."

"I suppose," he conceded. "But it doesn't matter now. They're never going to let me see her again."

"Oh, I don't know. Perhaps that's why they sent you out on a ship—so you could get out into the big wide world and gain some experience."

"How?" he asked.

"You could always pay someone to show you what to do, Eryk."

The boy shook his head. "Even if I could afford a whore, Lord Dirk says I shouldn't go near them 'cause they've got diseases."

Marqel bit back a smile. *How typical of Dirk Provin.* Then another thought occurred to her. Eryk was more than just a lucky break. He could do more than tell her where Dirk was. If she handled him correctly, he could be an unending source of information that she could use to advance herself into the High Priestess's favor.

"There are other ways to learn, Eryk."

"I don't understand."

Careful not to startle him, Marqel gently placed her hand on Eryk's thigh. "I could show you."

He stared down at her hand with wide eyes. "You? But you're a Thadow...I mean a *Shadow*dancer!"

"It is my job as a servant of the Goddess to help people, Eryk." She smiled warmly at him. "You could do me a favor in return."

"What sort of favor?"

"I'm not sure..." she said, making a great show of giving the matter serious thought. "I know...how about telling me all about what Dirk's been up to?"

"Why do you want to know that?"

She shrugged. "I don't really. Personally, I don't care what he's been doing these past two years. But Prince Kirshov and

Princess Alenor miss him terribly. You know what good friends they all were. If you can tell me all about him I'd be able to pass it on to them, to stop them worrying about him."

"I don't know ..." he said uncertainly.

"I understand it's a secret, Eryk, and I promise I wouldn't tell anyone else but Alenor and Kirsh. It would mean so much to them, especially Kirsh. He's very sick at the moment."

Eryk nodded. "Will he be all right? Lord Dirk was really angry about that. He said they shouldn't have done it."

It was her turn to look surprised. "*You* know who beat up Kirsh?"

He looked away guiltily. "I'm not supposed to say."

"Then I won't ask you to betray your friends," she promised. She didn't need to ask, anyway. If Eryk knew who Kirsh's assailants were, then it was a fairly safe bet they were part of the same crew he belonged to. And better yet, Dirk Provin was on the same ship ...

But Eryk was not quite as stupid as she remembered. He was reluctant to divulge anything regarding Dirk. For that matter, Marqel did not even know the name of his ship. All she really knew was that Eryk was lusting after some girl called Mellie.

"Let's not worry about Dirk, for the time being," she declared. "Let's deal with your problem first. Show me how you kissed Mellie."

Eryk stared at her. "Here?"

"There's nobody watching."

"Are you sure?"

"Of course, I'm sure. Come now, don't be shy. How can I help you if you won't show me where you went wrong?"

Eryk thought it over for a moment, and then he nodded. "I kissed her on the mouth."

"Like this?" Marqel leaned forward and kissed him, teasing his mouth open with the tip of her tongue.

Eryk cried out in alarm.

"What's the matter?"

"It weren't nothing like that!"

"Did you like it?" she asked, trying to hide her smile.

"Well…" he mumbled uncertainly. The boy had blushed a bright shade of crimson. *Pathetic little creep.*

"Don't you think your Mellie would like to be kissed like that?"

"I suppose…"

"Then we have our work cut out for us, Eryk," she announced in a businesslike tone. "And when we're done, you can tell me all about Dirk."

Chapter 29

Her mind still reeling from the information she now had in her grasp, Marqel hurried back through the duke's house toward the room where Kirsh lay. The halls in this part of the house were gloomy, even in the middle of the day, the only light coming from a narrow window at the far end of the long corridor. As she turned the corner she spied a familiar figure heading in the same direction and cursed under her breath. The last person she had wanted or expected to see on her return was the princess.

"Did you enjoy your ride, your highness?" she called.

Alenor stopped and turned to face Marqel. "What are you doing here?"

"I was about to ask you the same question, your highness. I left orders that the prince wasn't to be disturbed."

Strangely, her declaration seemed to have little impact on the little princess. "*You* left orders, Marqel?"

"I am responsible for his care, your highness."

"A task you appear to be undertaking with great enthusiasm."

Marqel frowned. Why was Alenor so smug, so unperturbed?

"I don't answer to you, Princess Alenor."

"Not yet," she agreed. "But you will. One day."

Marqel bit back the retort that leapt to mind. She did not have the time or the inclination to get into an argument with the princess. What she wanted was to return to Kirsh, to tell him what she had learned about Dirk Provin.

"Do you know if there's been any news on who attacked him?" she asked, deliberately ignoring Alenor's thinly veiled threat.

"Not yet. Although it was fortunate that you chanced to be walking past the lane where he was attacked, just so you could come to his aid."

"The Goddess led me to him," Marqel replied.

"Do you truly believe that, Marqel?" she asked.

"Of course I do."

Alenor was silent for a moment, and then she nodded. "Then I trust you'll pray for Kirsh's speedy recovery."

Marqel stared at her suspiciously, but she could detect no hint of cynicism in Alenor's tone. "I will."

Alenor turned toward Kirsh's room.

"Your highness!"

"Yes?"

"The prince is sleeping at the moment and I'd prefer it if he wasn't disturbed. I can send someone to fetch you when he's awake."

Alenor hesitated, and then she nodded. "As *soon* as he wakes, Marqel. I'll be in the library."

"Yes, your highness," she promised.

Marqel reached Kirsh's door and knocked before entering. The prince was lying on the bed, covered by a thin sheet that was already bloodstained in several places. His face was bruised and bloodied, as was the rest of his body. There was barely a part of him that had not been hit.

"Kirsh?" She asked the question softly, in case he really was asleep.

Kirsh moved his head gingerly and squinted at Marqel. "Am I still dreaming?"

"You're not dreaming, Kirsh. It's me."

Kirsh pushed himself up onto his elbow. The effort it took was a testament to the pain he was in. They had done a real job on the Senetian prince. Marqel marveled that he was still alive—let alone conscious and coherent.

"I dreamed about you. You came to my rescue." He shook his head slowly. "I thought I was dead. I thought you'd come to escort me through the afterlife."

"What makes you think you're special enough to warrant an escort through the afterlife?" Marqel asked with a smile. "And even if you did, what makes you think *I'd* come looking for you?"

Kirsh tried to smile, but his split lip opened again and began to bleed afresh. He groaned and flopped back onto the pillows. "I'm so glad you're here, Marqel."

"Who did this to you, Kirsh?"

Kirsh's puffy eyes narrowed. "Shut the door."

Curious, she obeyed, and then came back to sit on the side of the bed. Kirsh pushed himself up again with a groan. "I don't know who to trust anymore. They told me that Alexin claims I was drunk and set upon by thieves down near the wharves. But I wasn't drunk. He's lying. Whoever attacked me knew who I was."

"Are you saying you think this was deliberate? That the Queen's Guard is somehow involved?" In light of what she had learned about Dirk, that put a rather interesting slant on things.

"I spoke to Alexin not long before I was attacked. He was drinking in a tavern near the docks with a man whom I believe to be a pirate, or at the very least, an associate of theirs."

"You do know what you're accusing them of, don't you?" Marqel asked.

"I know, which is why I'm so glad you're here. I don't know who to trust. At least I can be sure of you."

Marqel smiled. This put a whole new complexion on things. She suddenly decided not to mention anything to Kirshov about what she had learned from Eryk. The boy had not even hinted about a Guardsman being involved and, until she had proof, it might be wise to keep what she had learned to herself.

"I don't know how high this goes," Kirsh continued. "Is Alexin working on his own? Is he in league with the Baenlanders? Or is this something that infects the entire Queen's Guard? It would explain why they've been so determined to drive me out."

"Aren't you making a great deal out of nothing, Kirsh?" she asked cautiously, trying to divert him. Her secret would be worthless if Kirsh worked it out on his own. "Alexin might simply be trying to cover his rear. It really doesn't look good that you were attacked on his father's island. He'll have to explain what happened to both your father and the queen, and it makes Grannon Rock look a lot less culpable if you actually contributed to your own downfall."

Kirsh hesitated for a moment. "I never thought of that."

Marqel took his hand in hers and squeezed it gently. "Then it's a good thing you told me your dire conspiracy theory before you opened that big mouth of yours and started accusing the Duke of Grannon Rock and the entire Queen's Guard of treason."

"But I could be right," Kirsh insisted, not quite ready to abandon his theory.

"Yes, you could be right. But you might also be very, very wrong. I wouldn't go making accusations like that unless you have proof, Kirsh."

"Then I'll find the proof!" he declared. "Will you help me, Marqel? You're the only person in Dhevyn I trust."

"Yes, Kirsh, I'll help. Now why don't you rest? You look like shit."

"I feel like shit. I'm so tired."

"Then why don't you try to get some more sleep? Did you want me to fetch anything for you?" she asked, rising to her feet.

Kirsh closed his eyes and nodded slowly. "Can you find Alenor and send her to me?"

You'll see Alenor when I'm good and ready to let her in, Marqel replied silently, but she smiled at Kirsh. "She's gone hawking for the day with Raban Seranov and a company of his friends, I believe."

"Really? I always thought she didn't like him much."

"Well, with you incapacitated, she had to find something to do to entertain herself, I suppose."

"Will you ask her to visit me when she gets back?"

"Of course," she promised. "Now rest. I need to prepare a lotion to help ease your bruises. I'll be back in a while."

"I missed you, Marqel," he murmured drowsily.

"I missed you, too," she replied, but it was doubtful he heard her. By the time she reached the door, he was already snoring softly through his bruised and swollen nose.

Chapter 30

The Duke of Grannon Rock's library was quite paltry considering the man ruled over the island that fancied itself the greatest center of learning in Dhevyn. The small collection of books barely covered two walls of the room. The others were hung with numerous oil paintings of the Seranov family dating back several generations, including, Alenor noted with interest, Drogan Seranov, Reithan's father and the man the current duke had denounced in order to claim his brother's title. Raban stood beside her, identifying the men and women in the portraits and providing mildly amusing anecdotes about each one as they worked their way around the room.

The queen sat at the long polished table reading through yet another draft of the letter she must send to Antonov, explaining what had happened to his son. She had been working on it for hours, and was still no closer to completing it than she had been this morning before Alenor left to meet Dirk and the Baenlanders.

"I'm sure this sounds like I'm trying to cover something up," Rainan complained, tossing the quill on the table.

Alenor glanced over at the queen. "You can only tell him the truth, Mother."

"And the truth is I don't know what to say," she sighed. "Why couldn't Kirsh have just fallen from his damn horse and broken his leg? That would be so much easier to explain away."

A knock at the door interrupted them and Raban called permission to enter. When the door opened, Alenor was surprised to see Marqel entering the room, escorted by Alexin. The Shadowdancer curtsied gracefully to the queen before she spoke.

"You have news of Prince Kirshov, I take it?" Rainan asked.

"He's awake and asking for Princess Alenor, ma'am."

Rainan smiled at Alenor. "There you are, dear. I told you there was nothing to worry about."

"How is he?" Raban asked.

"Recovering, my lord, although it will be some time before he's able to resume his duties as a Guardsman, I suspect."

"I believe that's not really any of your concern, Marqel," the queen pointed out.

"I think Marqel was merely offering her expert medical opinion, Mother," Alenor suggested sweetly. Marqel stared at her in shock. The sight left Alenor feeling strangely euphoric.

Thank you, Dirk. For the first time in my life, I feel like I'm in control of it.

"In fact," she continued pleasantly, "I've been quite impressed by this Shadowdancer's dedication to her work. My betrothed would be in serious trouble without her."

They all stared at her in total bewilderment.

"If Marqel is agreeable, I was going to suggest that after the Landfall Festival we ask the High Priestess if Marqel could be posted to our court in Kalarada. Kirsh will need continuing care in the short term, and I'm sure he would benefit from the spiritual guidance of having his own personal Shadowdancer at court. What do you think, Mother?"

Rainan was speechless. Marqel looked dumbstruck. Raban seemed confused. Only Alexin looked at her suspiciously.

"Well!" she declared, when nobody answered her. "As there seem to be no objections, I guess that settles it."

"Alenor..." the queen began.

"Yes, Mother?" she replied innocently.

"Are you sure about this?"

"I've never been more certain of anything in my life," she assured her mother confidently, although her eyes were fixed on Marqel. *What are you thinking, you sly little bitch?*

Marqel stared her down. Alenor knew in her heart that she had lost Kirsh. If she had ever really owned him. Her worship of Kirsh was something rooted in childhood. Seeing Dirk today had reminded her of that. But she was about to become queen. It was about time she started acting like one.

"Is there something wrong, Marqel?" Alenor asked. "You look quite pale."

"Er...no, your highness, I'm quite well," the Shadowdancer replied, covering her shock and suspicion well. "Your generous offer has taken me by surprise, that's all."

Alenor smiled with venomous sweetness. "Don't you like surprises?"

Marqel didn't answer her for a moment, then she smiled at Alenor with the same poisonous charm. "Actually, I have a surprise for you, your highness. When I was in town today, I learned who was responsible for the attack on Prince Kirshov."

The momentary feeling that she was in control vanished with Marqel's statement.

"Who was it?" Alenor demanded.

"It was the crew from a Baenlander ship called the *Makuan*," she informed them. "And I believe the one who instigated the attack was Dirk Provin."

"Dirk Provin is here? In Nova?" the queen gasped, which was fortunate. Alenor was certain her own alarm and guilt was written clearly on her face for all to see.

"That's not possible, your majesty," Raban assured the queen with a careless wave of his hand. He was much better at dissembling than Alenor was. "He'd be arrested the moment he set foot on Grannon Rock."

"He's here," Marqel insisted.

Raban turned to Marqel, full of blustery indignation. "What proof do you have of this? I'll have you know that I mightily resent the implication that we allow pirate ships to dock in our harbor, or that we are sheltering a wanted man. You need to be a tad more sure of your facts before making such spurious accusations, young lady. That red robe doesn't give you the right to accuse innocent people!"

"Nevertheless," Alexin said, sounding eminently reasonable, "we should investigate this."

How do they do it? Alenor wondered. *We're all pretending that we don't know anything about this. Why am I the only one who's shaking?*

"If there really is a Baenlander pirate ship in port," Alexin continued, "then we most definitely should do something about it. But I have to agree with my brother, my lady Shadowdancer. Dirk Provin disappeared two years ago. We don't even know that he still lives. I'd be very surprised to find him here in Nova."

"I agree," Alenor said, trying to find even a trace of her earlier confidence. "If Dirk is anywhere at the moment, he's headed for Elcast, surely?"

"He's here. *In Nova,*" Marqel repeated with conviction.

"Then perhaps you should look into this, Captain?" Alenor suggested, hoping she sounded regal, rather than terrified. *If Marqel knows that Dirk is here in Nova, what else does she know?*

Alexin bowed smartly. "At once, your highness. Raban? I may need your help with the harbormaster."

"Of course," his older brother agreed. "If you will excuse us, your majesty?"

Rainan nodded wordlessly, the whole situation taken out of her hands by the three conspirators before her. Alenor dared not look either Alexin or Raban in the eye for fear of giving away their secret. Raban followed Alexin from the library, leaving Marqel alone with Alenor and the queen.

"That will be all," Alenor told the Shadowdancer.

"Shall I tell the prince to expect you, your highness?"

"No. I'd like to surprise him."

"As you wish." Marqel curtsied again to Rainan. "Your majesty."

"You may go."

Marqel closed the library door behind her, leaving Alenor to face her mother.

"Alenor, what in the name of the Goddess are you up to?"

"I'm acting like a queen."

"By inviting the woman you suspect your consort loves to court?" she scoffed. "That's not the act of a queen, Alenor, it's the act of a willful child."

Alenor met her mother's eye defiantly. "You did your best for Dhevyn, Mother, and now it's my turn. My methods just happen to be different from yours."

Rainan shook her head uncomprehendingly. "You will be the ruin of us all, Alenor."

"Then I should carry on the family tradition quite nicely, don't you think?"

Chapter 31

Captain Ateway warned Morna that Antonov was coming. It was not much of a warning, but it was enough for her to take her seat in front of the small desk and appear totally engrossed in her correspondence when the Lion of Senet marched into the guardhouse. She heard that he had arrived on Elcast the day before, amid his usual pomp and ceremony, and was a little surprised that Antonov had chosen to visit her, rather than demand she be brought before him.

"Everybody out!" Antonov ordered.

Morna glanced up with a serene smile as the guards hurried to obey. She was not surprised to find the High Priestess at his side. Antonov was wearing white, as he usually did. His shirt was exquisitely embroidered with golden lions, his knee-high boots tooled in a similar fashion. *He's such a vain man,* she realized. *He must be sweltering in all that finery.* Belagren was dressed in the red robes of her office, dripping with diamonds at her throat, wrists and fingers, her long hair unbound and brushed to a shine. But the color was unnaturally even. She had aged, Morna noticed with a degree of spiteful satisfaction. How old was she now? Almost fifty? How much longer did she think she could keep Antonov interested in her by dying her hair and draping herself in jewels?

"Anton! How nice of you to drop by," Morna said pleasantly as soon as they were alone. "And look who you've brought to keep me company! Hello, Belagren. You're looking well. Have you put on weight? It suits you, I think."

"You appear to have *lost* weight," Belagren retorted. "But then, I understand prison cuisine isn't very appetizing."

Morna rose gracefully from her stool and faced them, separated by the bars of her cell and a lifetime of animosity. "Perhaps, if the Goddess answers my prayers, you might find out for yourself someday, my lady."

"You actually *pray,* Morna?" Antonov asked in surprise. "Does this mean that are you are finally willing to accept that there is a Goddess?"

Poor Anton. He'll never give up. He had never abandoned the hope that Morna would see the error of her ways, even after all this time. *Was that the true definition of faith, this blind, obsessive need to believe that everything would go your way in the end? To believe—even in the face of incontrovertible proof to the contrary—that you were right?* It was something of a shock to Morna to realize that she no longer feared Antonov Latanya. She pitied him.

"Would it make the slightest difference to my fate if I did?"

"It might."

She shook her head. "Even if it meant a life of comfort and luxury until I die of old age tucked in my own bed, I still couldn't bring myself to pretend I believe in your false Goddess, Anton."

"You're as foolish and obstinate as your sister was," he sighed, obviously disappointed.

"But not as courageous, I fear. My sister had the strength to take her own life rather than live with your lies. I think I actually envy her that."

"Analee wasn't brave," Belagren sneered. "She was weak. And easily led. You and Johan corrupted her."

Morna stared at the High Priestess, as if seeing her for the first time. "There are times when I could almost forgive Anton, Belagren. He's misguided, but at least he honestly believes in what he's done. But you? You know the truth and still you allow the lies to be treated with the respect that only the truth deserves. No, it's worse than that; you actively encourage them for your own ends. This world is ill, Belagren, and you are the most visible symptom. You are the open, festering sore on Ranadon's face, and you infect everything you touch with your poison."

"You will not gain my favor by insulting the High Priestess, my lady."

"I don't want your favor, Anton." She smiled faintly, experiencing a moment of startling clarity. Everything seemed so clear now that she had nothing to lose. "Don't you understand? I don't *care* any longer. You've won. You've taken everything you can from me—the man I loved, both my sons, even my country—all of it. I have nothing left for you to take now except my life, so you might as well have that, too. I have no further need of it."

"You'd die for your sons?" Antonov asked, curiously. "I wonder, would you live for them?"

His question took her completely by surprise. "What do you mean?"

"Give me your youngest son, my lady, and I'll let you live."

Morna stared at him in shock. "Dirk? You're doing this for *Dirk's* benefit?"

"I warned him before he left Avacas that his only future was with me. Apparently, he didn't get the message the last time. I intend to make myself much clearer in the future."

Morna could not believe what she was hearing. "Even if I wanted to be party to such a monstrous bargain, I couldn't tell you what you want to know. I have no idea where Dirk is. I've not seen my son since you took him from me."

Antonov smiled. "I'm aware that you don't know where he is. Trust me, if you'd been in contact with Dirk at any time these past two years, I would know of it."

"Then what's your point, Anton?"

"This time it is *your* life on the line, Morna. I'm willing to bet that he'll not stand by and let you die if he thinks he can prevent it."

"Then I trust he has the wisdom to realize that he can't prevent it, and stays well away from Elcast on Landfall." She laughed humorlessly. "Do you forget who you're dealing with, Anton? Even if he was foolish enough to come home, Dirk will take one look at the men you have gathered against him and run like hell."

"Then I'll just have to make sure he doesn't see what I have gathered against him. In fact, I'm quite willing to give him a free run all the way up to Elcast Keep. It will only be after he springs my trap that he will realize he can't defy me and win."

"You're a fool if you think Dirk will fall for anything so transparent."

"We'll see who the fool is tomorrow night at the Landfall Festival, Morna," Belagren said. "By the way, did you have a preference for which sun you wish to represent? I thought the second sun would be appropriate, don't you?"

She stared at the High Priestess for a moment, wondering at the woman's callousness, and then turned her attention back to Antonov, deciding that Belagren's question did not deserve to be dignified with an answer.

Besides, nothing irritated Belagren more than to be ignored.

"Even if you succeed, Anton, what then? Even if you manage to capture Dirk, what will you do with him? You can't seriously believe that he'll ever follow you willingly."

"Why not? Isn't that the motto of the Royal House of Damita: 'Whose side am I on this week?' Your family isn't exactly renowned for having the courage of their convictions, my lady. Your father took Johan's side against the Goddess during the Age of Shadows, yet your brother Baston grovels so hard for my favor he'd lick my boots clean if I asked. Your sister Analee took a solemn oath to obey the will of the Goddess when we married, and abandoned it as soon as she was asked to do something that didn't suit her. Then she killed herself rather than face the consequences. And look at you! You declared war on me for what you purportedly believed in, and then, at the first sign of trouble, you fled your lover and cowered here in Elcast for twenty-odd years just to save your bastard son's neck and your husband from disgrace. Why shouldn't I believe that your son will do as I want if I offer him sufficient incentive?"

"My son is better than that!" she declared.

"Your son is a bastard who raped a Shadowdancer, killed his own father and then ran away like a mongrel dog, Morna," Belagren reminded her cruelly. "I would think the least of our concerns is what it might take to turn him to our cause."

"Don't you dare stand there accusing my son of rape and murder!" Morna snapped. "You're responsible for more deaths than I can count. Both of you! And you hide behind your false Goddess, as if that justifies everything you do."

• Antonov studied her for a moment then shook his head sadly. "I had such high hopes for you once, Morna. In a way, I hope you do die before Dirk gets here tomorrow. I'm very fond of the boy and it would break his heart to see how far you've fallen." He turned abruptly, startling Morna with his sudden yell. "Captain!"

Ateway must have been waiting just outside. He hurried back into the guardhouse and saluted smartly. "Sire?"

"You are to strip Lady Morna's cell. Remove everything, including the bed. If she needs to relieve herself, she can ask for a bucket. She will only eat what you yourself have sampled. You will also remove her outer garments and post a guard in this room at all times. She is not to be left alone. If she tries to harm herself, you will restrain her. Is that clear?"

Ateway spared Morna a rueful glance but did not question his orders. "Of course, your highness."

"Are you afraid I'll kill myself before you can, Anton?" she asked with a weary smile. *If only I was so brave as to eat that loaf Helgin sent me . . .*

"It's not an unreasonable fear. Your family is rather fond of suicide, my lady."

"Only when they're forced to deal with you, Anton," she replied.

Chapter 32

Dirk watched the eastern horizon nervously as the *Makuan* sailed toward Elcast, watching for any hint of yellow or blue staining the sky. He was not sure how long it was until the first sun would set. While the sky was red, while there was still no sign of the second sun rising, he could still pretend he had another day. He could still imagine it was not too late; still convince himself that they might make it to Yerl in time to save his mother.

"You're going to wear a hole in the deck if you keep pacing like that," Tia remarked, turning from watching the smudge in the distance that was the southern tip of Elcast.

"What time is it?"

"About five minutes since you asked me the last time." She glanced at the eastern horizon. "We've got an hour, maybe less, until second sunrise."

"We're not going to make it," he concluded grimly.

"We might," she shrugged. "Don't be such a doomsayer."

Dirk didn't answer her. Tia's sudden decision to take his side in this dangerous enterprise was vaguely unsettling, but he was too familiar with her mercurial mood swings to question it closely. He didn't know what drove Tia to do anything, and had long ago given up imagining that he ever would.

"Have you seen Eryk?" he asked instead. He hadn't seen the boy since the night Kirsh was beaten, and was a little concerned. They had departed Nova in such haste that at least two crewman he knew of had been left behind.

She shook her head. "Kurt probably knows where he is. Why?"

Dirk glanced back over his shoulder toward the stern where the first mate was standing behind the helmsman, yelling orders to the men clambering over the rigging. Since he saw him work Kirsh over so efficiently, Dirk had little inclination to even acknowledge the mate's existence, let alone get into a conversation with him.

"I want to explain to Eryk what's happening. I don't want him hearing it from anyone else."

"The chances are he knows by now, Dirk," Tia reasoned. "It's the worst kept secret on the ship. Everyone knows why we're so unexpectedly rushing off to Elcast."

She was right, Dirk knew. There was not a man aboard who had not somehow discerned the reason for Porl Isingrin's sudden decision to depart Nova and sail for Yerl, an insignificant port they rarely visited in the normal course of events. He wondered how many of the crew thought as Tia did. None of them, he guessed, had any particular affection for Morna Provin, but they were all quite happy to be doing something that might result in someone being saved from the sacrificial fires of Landfall.

The wind was brisk and the ship cut through the choppy straits between Grannon Rock and Elcast bathed in the red sunlight of the first sun. Gripping the railing as he walked, Dirk headed toward the stern, sidestepping the sailors who scrambled to obey Kurt's bellowed instructions. The *Makuan* was a tightly run ship, and there was little effort wasted as the sailors went about their duties.

Kurt glanced up and saw Dirk. He was not a particularly tall man. His eyes were brown, like most Dhevynians, but his hair was so blond it was almost white, which made him appear much older than his thirty-five years.

"We're already doing eight knots," Kurt informed Dirk as he approached. "Which is faster than I thought this bucket could move. Don't waste my time asking if we can go any faster."

"I was looking for Eryk, actually."

"He's working. You can socialize with him when he's finished his watch."

Dirk was a little taken aback by Kurt's brusque retort. "I just wanted to check that he got back to the ship..."

"He's fine, Dirk. He looked so happy when he came on board I thought he must have got laid. Now, unless you have something useful to tell me, I'm busy trying to get this lumbering bitch to pretend she's the *Calliope*."

Feeling rather chastened, Dirk returned to the bow.

Tia grinned when she saw his frown. "Did I forget to mention that Kurt's in a foul mood?"

"Why?"

"He has a sister on Nova who's about to have a baby. This desperate dash to Morna Provin's rescue has seriously interfered with his plans to be there for the child's birth."

He glanced back at the first mate, suddenly feeling a little guilty. "I didn't realize..."

"You never do, Dirk," she shrugged. "Like most of your kind, you think the world begins and ends with *your* problems."

"My *kind*?" Dirk stared at her, wondering what he had done in the few minutes it had taken him to walk to the stern and back that would make her turn on him again.

"The highborn. You're all the same. You think an accident of birth makes you better than the rest of us."

"That's ridiculous. Anyway, what's this 'better than the rest of us' nonsense? Your mother was highborn. Even worse, you were born of Senetian nobility, right in the Hall of Shadows itself! If you want to start keeping score on who's got the most dubious ancestry, Tia Veran, you might want to take that into account."

Tia didn't look pleased at the reminder. "It's not the same thing. I was raised in Mil."

He nodded in understanding. "Ah...I see. And in your eyes, that makes you better than me, doesn't it?"

"No, Dirk," she said, meeting his eye defiantly. "I didn't kill my own father. *That's* what makes me better than you."

She pushed past him and headed aft, leaving him staring after her, wondering what it would take for Tia to ever forgive him. Then another thought occurred to him. Why did he care anyway? It was not as if he needed her forgiveness. The truth was, even if she got down on her knees and *thanked* him for killing Johan Thorn, it made no difference.

Dirk would never forgive himself.

It made the urgency of his present mission even more pressing. He had been able to do nothing to save his father. Dirk was fairly certain he would not be able to live with himself if he did not at least try to save his mother.

The second sun was rapidly overtaking its companion before they were close enough to Yerl to lower the longboat. Dirk was chafing at the delay, but did his best not to let it show. He knew Porl Isingrin and his crew had worked miracles to get them to Elcast as fast as they had, and he would achieve absolutely nothing by complaining that it still had not been fast enough.

Kurt relented and sent Eryk to say good-bye to Dirk as he was waiting for the sailors to winch the longboat down to the water. The boy looked tanned and fit, and much happier than when Dirk had seen him last. Perhaps Reithan had been right. Left alone to find his place in the crew, he was starting to settle into his new life.

"Kurt said you wanted to th— see me, Lord Dirk," Eryk said, consciously correcting himself as he came up behind him.

Dirk sighed as he turned around. He had given up trying to break Eryk of the annoying habit of referring to him as "Lord Dirk" a long time ago. He studied the boy closely for a moment, but he seemed none the worse for his time as a sailor. "I just wanted to see how you were doing, Eryk."

The boy shrugged. "I'm all right."

"They're not picking on you too much, are they?"

Eryk shook his head. "Not really. Derwn was worse."

Dirk had not spared the son of Elcast Town's butcher a thought since he had left home. It reminded him sharply that he was about to face more than the threat of Antonov's wrath. His whole life had been spent on Elcast, and he was not sure what it would be like to suddenly find himself home again, a stranger and an outcast.

"Well, you keep working hard, and if it gets too much for you, make sure you tell Captain Isingrin."

"Don't tell him that, Dirk," Tia scolded, coming up behind

Eryk carrying her knapsack and her bow. "Snitching is the worst crime a sailor can commit."

"I thought that was mutiny?"

"Only if you get caught. Hello, Eryk."

"Are you going with Lord Dirk, too, Tia?" he asked, taking in her traveling garb.

"Yes," she replied with a smile. "*Lord* Dirk needs someone to keep an eye on him."

The boy nodded thoughtfully. "That's good, Tia. Lady Morna was really nice to me. I'm glad it's going to be you that saves her."

"We'll try, Eryk," she promised, a little uncomfortably, and then she looked at Dirk. "You ready?"

He nodded. "We're just waiting for Reithan."

Tia said good-bye to Eryk and squeezed past them to the longboat where the sailors had almost finished launching it. Dirk turned back to Eryk. "The captain said he's going to try to meet up with the *Orlando* in Kalarada. He seems to think he can get you a permanent berth with Captain Falstov's crew."

"They visit Mil pretty often, don't they?" Eryk asked hopefully. "I'll be able to see Mellie again, won't I?"

"Eryk..." Dirk began uncertainly. How could he explain it? How could he tell Eryk to leave Mellie alone without breaking the boy's heart? "About Mellie."

"It's all right, Lord Dirk. You don't have to tell me. I understand what I did wrong."

"You do?" he asked in surprise.

Eryk nodded. "I won't do it again. I know that now. Next time, I'll know what to do."

"Dirk!" Tia called. "Are you coming or not?"

"I have to go," he explained. "But I'm glad you understand about Mellie."

"Dirk!" Reithan bellowed, adding his impatience to Tia's cry.

"Good luck, Lord Dirk."

"Thanks, Eryk." He ruffled the boy's head fondly and hurried over to where Reithan was waiting for him with Porl Isingrin. Tia was already in the longboat with the crewmen who were manning the oars.

"We should be in sight of Elcast harbor a few hours after first sunrise," Porl was telling Reithan as his stepbrother tossed their packs down to Tia. "I'll have the longboat waiting where we arranged to meet. We'll hang around as long as we can, but if you're not at the rendezvous by the time the second sun rises tomorrow morning, we can't risk waiting for you."

"If that happens, we'll make our own way back to Mil," Reithan agreed. "For that matter, you should run at the first hint of trouble. I don't want you risking your whole ship for this."

"Don't worry about me, Reithan," the pirate assured him, grinning crookedly. "I was dodging the Lion of Senet's excise men while you were still sucking on your mama's tits. I know how to keep my head down." The captain turned to Dirk. "Good luck, lad. Don't be too hard on yourself if this all comes to naught."

"I appreciate your help, Captain."

"I've not done much but get you here," the pirate shrugged. "It's up to you now."

"Are you two coming, or are you planning to stand up there gossiping all day?" Tia called impatiently from the longboat.

Porl smiled. "You take care now. Both of you. And don't let Tia needle you too much, Dirk."

Dirk climbed over the railing and slid down the rope ladder, jumping the last few feet into the boat. Tia caught his arm as he almost overbalanced.

"Careful!" she snapped. "You nearly capsized us!"

Up on the deck of the *Makuan,* Porl watched Dirk take his place in the bow and turned to Reithan. "I'm letting him go against my better judgment."

"He'll be all right, Porl."

"Don't get me wrong. I think he's a good lad, but that's not my point. We can't afford to send him back to aid our enemies. Do whatever it takes, Reithan, but don't under *any* circumstances let that boy fall into the hands of the Lion of Senet or the High Priestess."

"You worry like an old woman, Porl. I'd kill Dirk before I let that happen."

Porl Isingrin frowned and replied in all seriousness, "You may have to, Reithan. You may just have to."

Chapter 33

Dirk was not so well known in Yerl that his presence would raise suspicion, but just to be on the safe side, Tia insisted that he keep out of sight while Reithan arranged to purchase horses for their journey. He was not happy leaving the task in Reithan's hands. Unquestionably, of the three of them, Dirk was the most knowledgeable when it came to horseflesh. Tia had rarely ridden. Reithan was a little more experienced, but he was still a sailor first and foremost. Despite Dirk's objections, they overruled him, and it was left to Reithan to find them mounts. There was not much available. Yerl was a fishing port, and a small one at that, but he was able to find three average-looking beasts that seemed to have the legs required to get them across the island.

Tia glanced at the horses warily when Reithan rode up towing the two other horses behind him. They were waiting a little out of town in a small clearing near the north road. Reithan dismounted when he reached them, handing the reins of all three horses to Dirk.

"The dun looks like he's going to drop dead halfway there," Tia complained, as Dirk began to inspect Reithan's purchases.

"Which is why you're going to have to ride him," Dirk said, as he checked the shoes of the sturdy looking chestnut. "You're the lightest."

Tia glared at him suspiciously. "Are you sure it's not because you're hoping he *will* drop dead and I'll break my neck when I get pitched to the ground?"

Dirk looked up and smiled faintly. "Well, there is that..."

"Cut it out, you two," Reithan ordered impatiently. "What do you think, Dirk? Are they worth what I paid for them?"

"How much did you pay?"

"Thirty-four silver dorns, but that included the saddles and the tack."

"I think that horse thief saw you coming," Dirk told him with a frown, and then he shrugged. "But they should survive the trip."

"How far is it, anyway?" Tia asked.

"Eighty miles, give or take," Dirk said, moving on to the dappled gray.

"Eighty *miles*?" she gasped in horror. "You want us to ride eighty miles in a *day*?"

"You could do it on foot in less than two days," he informed her. "In theory."

"How do you *know* that? Did you get bored one day and decide to work out how fast a man can walk?"

He looked at her as if she was just a little bit crazy. "I was born here, Tia. Don't you think I'd know something like how long it takes to get from one end of my own island to the other?"

She hadn't thought about that. She was so used to Neris working out strange things like how far a man could walk in a day, or how long it would take to bore a hole through a piece of granite using water drips, that she just assumed Dirk was fond of the same useless pastimes.

"We'll have to pace the horses," Dirk warned Reithan. "But we should be able to make it to Elcast Town before the second sun sets if nothing goes wrong."

"Then let's get moving," Reithan suggested. "We've a long way to go, and we're not gaining any time standing around here talking about it."

"Good idea," Tia agreed, taking the reins of the dun from Dirk. "And while we're riding, Mister I'm-the-smartest-person-in-the-world here can do something really useful."

"Like what?" Dirk asked, looking rather offended.

"Like coming up with a plan, Dirk," she said, as she swung

into the saddle. "Call me picky, but I just can't help feeling I'll
be a lot happier about this heroic little adventure we're about to
embark upon if we're actually still alive at the end of it."

Tia's prediction that the dun would drop dead halfway to Elcast
Town proved prophetic. It did not actually drop dead, but it
went lame about twenty miles from the town. They had ridden
through the day, alternately walking and cantering the horses.
As the second sun traveled slowly across the sky, they had
walked the horses for longer and longer periods, their bursts of
speed becoming shorter and shorter as the animals wearied. Tia
was exhausted, sore, dirty and hot—almost as bad as the poor
horse. She leaned against a nearby tree wearily, resting her foot
on a small post sunk into the ground on the side of the road.

Dirk examined the horse with concern and turned to look
at her. "He's done for. You can't ride him any farther."

"What are we going do?" she asked.

"We'll have to double up. And change horses as often as we
can to ease the load."

"How far is it to Elcast Town?" Reithan asked.

"Seventeen miles."

"And I suppose you *know* we're exactly seventeen miles
from Elcast Town because you were born here?"

"No. I know we're exactly seventeen miles from Elcast
Town because you've got your foot on the mile marker," he told
her.

She snatched her boot from the post and looked down.
Sure enough, carved into the weathered wood was the letter *E*,
under which was carved the number seventeen. She looked up
and glared at Dirk in annoyance. It wouldn't be so bad if he
didn't always look so smug when he managed to get one up on
her.

Even Reithan managed a weary smile. "You walked into
that one, Tia. Come on. You can ride with me for the first few
miles." He reached down and offered her his arm. They both
grunted with the effort it took to swing her up behind him on
the gray.

Dirk pulled the saddle from the lame dun's back then slipped the bridle from his head and let the animal hobble away toward a patch of succulent grass on the verge. He piled the tack by the saddle, handed Tia her pack and glanced up at the sky with concern. "It's going to slow us down, riding double. Perhaps I should ride ahead..."

"No," Reithan declared flatly, surprising Tia with his determination. "We do this together or not at all, Dirk."

Dirk looked as if he might object, then he nodded in agreement. "Let's ride then," he said, swinging into his saddle. "It's almost second sunset. We're running out of time."

They reached the outskirts of the town about an hour and a half later. Dirk halted near a small crossroad. The intersecting track led down to the harbor, while the road they were on changed from a rough dirt surface to cobblestones. Dirk was riding a little ahead of Reithan and Tia. He hauled his mount to a stop, then turned and waited for them to catch up.

"This is where we part company."

Reithan swung his leg over the gray's neck and jumped to the ground as Tia slid forward in the saddle and picked up the reins. She had strung her bow a little way back and had it slung across her shoulder.

"Do you remember what I told you about finding the Outlet?" Dirk asked Reithan.

"I turn left about half a mile from the town off the road to the Keep."

Dirk nodded. "Good luck."

"You, too, Dirk. Don't do anything stupid."

"He won't," Tia promised on his behalf.

They both turned to look at her, and then Reithan shook his head. "Be nice, Tia."

"Be careful, Reithan."

He smiled. "I will. I'll meet you back at the Outlet. Don't be late."

Reithan shouldered his pack and headed down the track toward the harbor without looking back. Dirk glanced at Tia.

"This close to the Festival the town will be all but deserted, so we shouldn't have any problems getting up to the Keep. Think you've got enough left in you for a gallop?"

"More to the point, have the horses got enough left in them?"

"Barely."

She took a closer grip on her reins. "Let's do it then."

They cantered through the town and, as Dirk had predicted, there was barely another soul to be seen. Tia glanced around with interest as they rode, finding it hard to think of this place as Dirk's home. It was so...ordinary. The houses were neat, the town square bordered by a variety of shops—just like a score of other towns she had seen on islands all over Dhevyn. Then she glanced up and got her first sight of Elcast Keep.

Tia gasped at the sight of it. The massive, ancient Keep loomed over the harbor, its tall central tower reaching up eight stories and topped by a massive dome painted gold by the setting second sun. Dirk urged his horse into a gallop as they reached the other side of town where the road curved sharply and steeply around the bay. Tia glanced at the sky in the east. Was that a tinge of red on the horizon?

The Keep gates stood open and unguarded. *Like an open mouth waiting to snap shut on us the moment we're inside,* she thought nervously. She knew this was a trap. Reithan knew it was a trap. Even Dirk knew it. The question now was whether they had anticipated the trap well enough not to be caught in it. They galloped through the gates and came to a halt before a set of broad granite steps that led to two massive bronze doors in the central tower. The courtyard was deserted.

Dirk dismounted and turned to wait for Tia, looking around at the Keep with an odd expression on his face. It was more than two years since he had been home, she recalled. She wondered what he was thinking. Was he glad to be back? Maybe not, given the circumstances, but with Dirk it was hard to tell. He had one of those faces that betrayed nothing unless he wanted it to.

She dragged on the bit and brought her exhausted mount to a halt before jumping to the ground and unslinging her bow.

"Put that away," Dirk ordered.

"You don't know what's waiting for us in there, Dirk."

"Women and children, mostly," he shrugged. "Everyone else will be down on the common."

Dirk turned and took the granite steps two at a time. Tia was far too stiff and sore to do anything so agile. She followed him up the steps at a much more sedate pace and waited as he pulled the massive door open.

Tia stepped inside and looked up in amazement. One really didn't get a sense of the size of the place until inside, dwarfed by the huge circular tower and the staircase that ringed it. It was as if the whole building had been bored out of living rock.

Dirk nudged her when he caught her gaping, and began to walk through the hall toward the high table on the other side. There were several women sitting at the tables talking among themselves. At one, a woman softly strummed a balalaika, at another, several small children appeared to be having a party. These were the children of the Keep, Tia guessed, deemed too small to attend the Festival. Their footsteps caught the attention of a plump blonde dressed in a plain but well-cut green dress. She looked up curiously, and then stiffened in shock as she caught sight of Dirk.

Now is when this all goes to hell, Tia thought. *If she raises the alarm, we're done for.*

The girl hurried toward them.

"Hello, Faralan."

She stopped a few paces from Dirk and studied him for a moment before she returned his greeting warily. "Dirk."

"You're married to Rees now, I hear."

She nodded. "You shouldn't have come. Antonov is waiting for you."

"I know," Dirk agreed calmly. "How many men has he got?"

"Several hundred at least. The woods and the Festival are riddled with them, and there's more waiting here in the Keep."

"Where are they?" Tia asked, looking around. There was nobody she could see but the women and children.

"They've orders to stay hidden until I raise the alarm."

"Are you going to raise the alarm?" Tia asked.

"I have no choice," the girl shrugged. She appeared to be genuinely sorry about it, but that was not going to help them much if she started screaming.

Dirk nodded in understanding. "How long can you give us?"

Tia's attention was diverted by a sound she almost thought she imagined. She stilled, trying to filter out the sound of Dirk and Faralan talking, the balalaika and the chatter of the children at the table. She felt it as much as heard the sound in the distance, deep and rhythmic.

"Drums."

Dirk and Faralan both stopped to listen.

"You must hurry, Dirk," Faralan warned. "There's not much time."

He nodded. "Can you do anything about the guards here in the Keep?"

"She can't," a male voice behind them said, "but I can."

Tia and Dirk spun around to find a portly old man with a gray beard and a fond smile on his face standing behind them. She had been so absorbed in listening for the drums, she had not heard him approach.

"Helgin!" Dirk cried, embracing the old man warmly.

"Now, now, enough of that," the old man muttered, pushing him away. "The drums have started and you don't have much time. But don't worry about the Lion of Senet's men here in the Keep. Most of them will be asleep until tomorrow morning. With luck a few of them won't wake up at all."

"You drugged Antonov's guards?" Faralan gasped. "Master Helgin! How *could* you?"

Tia glanced up and noticed that the beams of sunlight crisscrossing the hall through the arrow-slit windows were reddening rapidly. "Dirk, we're running out of time..."

"Go," the old man urged.

"Antonov will kill you for this, Helgin."

"My problem, Dirk, not yours. Now *go*!"

"Here," Faralan added, picking up two masks from a discarded pile on the table near them. "You'll need these."

Dirk accepted them from her, and then clasped her hand for a moment. "Thanks, Faralan."

She smiled. "Good luck, Dirk."

They ran from the Hall without looking back. Outside, the drums were much louder, much more insistent, and the first sun was well and truly on the rise. Dirk ran toward the postern gate with Tia close on his heels.

The drums began to pound faster.

Chapter 34

They came for her just before first sunrise. Morna was composed and ready to die, and determined not to humiliate herself.

Ateway opened her cell door and stood back. He had a full escort waiting to take her to the common. Every man was Senetian, and not one familiar face among them.

"I have letters that I'd like distributed after I'm gone," she informed the captain.

"I'll see to it, my lady."

She smiled at him. "You've been very considerate, Captain Ateway. I do appreciate it."

"Thank you, my lady."

Lifting her chin proudly, she stepped out of the cell and was immediately surrounded by the waiting guards. She felt so small, yet oddly, so important.

Ironically, the next hour might prove to be the most memorable of her life. Until she passed from this world, every eye on Elcast, and many other places in Dhevyn and Senet, would be fixed on her. Antonov was taking a huge risk in executing her. There had not been a member of a Dhevynian ruling family executed for treason since the end of the War of Shadows. To do it at the Landfall Festival, to associate her death so closely with the High Priestess, was doubly dangerous. Hopefully, her death would stir up resentments long thought buried; fears that had been dormant for years. The thought gave a small measure of comfort.

I achieved so little in my life—it would be nice to think that at least my death might prove useful.

The guard escorted her on foot to the common, the wall of leather and steel keeping her hidden from the view of her people. *My people? They were Wallin's people, not mine. They tolerated me for his sake.* Her death might stir up political turmoil, but except for a few, like Welma and Helgin, she realized she had no friends who would genuinely grieve her passing.

Is this what they mean when they say your life flashes before your eyes when you're about to die? She didn't like the feeling at all. Morna did not wish to be reminded of the mistakes she had made.

It took the best part of an hour before they reached the common. The second sun was almost completely set by then and the drums had started pounding. Morna had always hated that sound but now, when the drums did nothing but herald her impending death, she found she welcomed them. It meant that it would be over soon.

Morna had a plan. She knew that if she could inhale sufficient smoke, she would pass out quickly and avoid the worst of the pain. All she had to do was breathe, as deeply and as fully as possible. She steadfastly refused to think of the flames.

And she would not scream. She was determined about that. Antonov and Belagren might enjoy watching her burn, but they were not going to have the satisfaction of seeing her reduced to a screaming, sobbing wretch, begging for mercy.

She would breathe deeply, look them in the eye, and let the smoke take her.

The people were masked by the time she was led to the post on top of the pyre representing the second sun. The decorative masks of the celebrants were not a very effective disguise, and she could make out Rees's curly dark hair as he stood there un-complainingly as they tied his mother to the stake. The mask he wore covered only his eyes, and formed the head of a bird. The beak protruded out over his nose and the feathers over the eye-holes glinted red in the ruby light of the evening sun. The mask had been a gift from Antonov the first year he came to Elcast.

Rees shouldn't even be here, Morna thought. *He's married now. Does he hate me so much that he wants to watch me burn?*

The young Duke of Elcast stood a few paces from Tovin and Lanon Rill. The governor's son looked away uneasily when she caught his eye. *How strange that my own son is so keen to see me die, but the son of a Senetian nobleman has the decency to feel guilty about it.*

She looked around for Antonov. His mask was made of gold-tipped white feathers. With his customary vanity, it per-fectly matched the gold embroidery on his white jacket. He met her gaze without flinching, and then looked away, scanning the crowds, looking for someone.

He's looking for Dirk, she realized. *Oh, please, if there really is a Goddess, keep my son away from here tonight.*

The drums grew more insistent and the crowd separated into two circles, men in the inner circle, women forming the outer, encircling the wicker suns. By the altar, where a large bowl filled with dark liquid sat ready and waiting, Belagren stood, her expression smug, as she gave the signal for Ella, Madalan and a male Shadowdancer Morna did not recognize to pass out the small silver cups. Morna noticed there were many more men in the crowd than normal. They were masked as if they were part of the Festival, but they were armed, and few of them let the silver cups do more than touch their lips before passing it on.

Please, Dirk, be far from here tonight. Don't try to save me.

On her left, another man with a pockmarked face and the dull eyes of heavy sedation was being tied to the post on the pyre of the first sun. He was Stanislav Denov, a fisherman from Yerl who had murdered his pregnant young wife in a fit of jealous rage not long before Wallin died. She glanced at Rees in the crowd again. Had he condemned the man to death? She watched as her son took a sip from the little silver cup then handed it on to the next man. He was swaying on his feet.

In fact, everyone was swaying now in time to the primal beat of the drums. She saw Ella walk to the center of the inner circle. She could see her lips move as she chanted a prayer to the Goddess, calling down her blessing on those present.

Everyone but me, that is.

Morna caught sight of Belagren as she moved away from the altar, clutching a flaming torch in her hand. The spectators cried out their encouragement.

"Please, let it be over quickly," she whispered to nobody in particular.

Belagren danced toward the wicker sun, where the drugged Yerl fisherman slumped against the post. The crowd fell to their knees as the High Priestess cried out something Morna could not quite make out, then she touched the flaming torch to the dry kindling piled at the base of the sun. The wicker caught with a whoosh, the flames leaping upward. The smoke was heavy in Morna's nostrils. She drank it in greedily. Perhaps the fumes from the first pyre would make her unconscious even before the flames of her own pyre reached her.

Once Belagren was satisfied that the first sun was well and truly alight, she danced back to the second sun and hesitated for a moment, staring up at Morna.

"There'll be a reckoning for this," Morna warned, meeting Belagren's eye defiantly.

"Not in your lifetime," the High Priestess responded in a voice meant only for her.

Then she smiled triumphantly and touched the torch to the pyre.

Morna managed to keep her composure. She stared silently down at Belagren as the flames caught, breathing through her mouth, hoping the smoke would take her soon. She could hear the flames crackling beneath her; feel the heat on her bare feet as it built up momentum.

Then the flavor of the smoke changed, and she realized her shift was smoldering. She fought down her panic, forcing herself to take great heaving gasps of the choking smoke. She coughed as her lungs rejected the poison she was trying to inhale; her eyes watered as the smoke billowed around her. Belagren stood watching her, waiting for her to crack.

I won't give you the satisfaction, you black-hearted bitch.

The flames licked higher and Morna felt the first real pain as they reached the soles of her feet. She bit down on her bottom lip to stifle her screams as the smell of her own burning flesh mingled with the wood smoke. Then her dress stopped smoldering and burst into flame. The fire raced toward her face, her loose hair crackling around her with a sickening stench as it burned.

She took another gasping breath of smoke but unconsciousness refused to save her. Her eyes were blurred with tears and pain. She glanced at Rees one last time. He had not moved, transfixed by the sight of his mother consumed by flames.

Then for some reason, a movement on the slope toward the Keep caught her eye. There were two figures running toward the common. A couple of latecomers no doubt, hurrying to watch the Duchess of Elcast burn...

Her feet were on fire, the flesh blackened, the smoke billowing as the moist flesh simmered and burned. She could taste blood in her mouth. She had bitten right through her bottom lip to stop herself from screaming.

Morna closed her eyes, willing herself to bear the agony, willing herself to ignore it. But the flames had hold of her now and would not let her go. The heat seared her flesh even in places it had yet to touch.

"I'm sorry, Johan!" she cried out silently, no longer able to contain her suffering, no longer caring that she wasn't going to die well. "I tried to be strong..."

And then she began to scream.

Chapter 35

Dirk and Tia were halfway down the slope when they heard the screams. Dirk began to run faster, streaking ahead of Tia.

"Dirk! No!"

She slipped her bow over her shoulder and put on an extra burst of speed, forcing her stiff, aching muscles to move. When she was within a few steps of him she threw herself at Dirk and tackled him to the ground. They rolled the rest of the way down the slope and came to a stop with Tia sitting astride him. Dirk struggled to get free of her, but she held him down, through sheer force of will as much as physical strength.

"It's too late!" she cried, as she tossed the bow aside, relieved to see that she hadn't broken it in her desperate lunge to stop Dirk from throwing his own life away.

But the screams and the drums were all he could hear. There was a wild, feral look in his eyes. She doubted he heard a word she had said.

"It's too late," she yelled at him again, slapping his face to reinforce her point. "You can't save her!"

The slap brought some semblance of sanity back into his eyes. "Let me up, Tia."

He sounded calm, but she wasn't fooled.

"You can't do anything, Dirk."

The screams kept on relentlessly. *Dear Goddess, why doesn't she stop?* Dirk tried to push Tia off him, but she had his arms pinned with her knees. She snatched up the bow and pushed it down across his throat until he was gasping for air.

"It's too late. There is nothing you can do," she repeated slowly. "When I let you up we're going to turn around and run like hell. Is that clear?"

"Yes," he agreed, far too meekly.

"Let me put it another way, Dirk. You take one step in the direction of that pyre and I'll put an arrow in your back."

He looked as if he believed her, but she wasn't sure. The drums and his mother's tormented screams as she was roasted alive were likely to have much more impact on him than Tia's rational argument about the futility of a rescue attempt. But she had no choice. As they rode double toward Elcast Town, in a low voice that Dirk would not hear, Reithan had given her very specific instructions about what she must do if Dirk looked like he was going to be captured. If she was certain of anything at all, it was that the Lion of Senet and his henchmen were waiting for him down there on the common.

She eased the bow a little and when he made no attempt to struggle, she warily climbed off him. He sat up, his face streaked with tears as Morna Provin's screams tore through his soul. Tia stood up, nocked an arrow, drew the string back against her cheek and pointed it straight at him.

"Get up."

Dirk did as she ordered, but moved no further. He could clearly see the pyre from where they were standing. There was perhaps a hundred yards of open space between where they had fallen and the edge of the crowd. The wicker suns were well alight, both figures tied to them swathed in flames.

"End it, Tia," he said in a dull voice.

"*What?*"

The screams intensified, as if the flames had tightened their grip on the duchess.

"End it. Don't let her suffer. If we can't save her, let's do that much at least."

Dirk was looking not at her, but at her bow and the arrow she had drawn. Tia realized what he was asking of her as the unremitting screams tore through the red night.

Horrified by what he wanted, she relaxed the string and offered him the bow. "You do it."

He shook his head. "You're the better shot. And the moment that arrow hits they'll know we're here. We've one chance at this, that's all."

She hesitated, appalled by what he had suggested. Morna's screams were drowning out all reason.

Why hadn't they drugged her, like they did the other victims of Landfall?

"For pity's sake, Tia!" he cried urgently. "That's my mother down there! You said it yourself! Nobody deserves to die like that! End it! *Please*."

The screams were unbearable. Dirk's eyes were haunted. Tia took a deep breath and drew the arrow back again, pointing it at Dirk. Then without allowing herself time to question what she was about to do, she swung the bow around and took aim on the burning pyre. She let out the breath slowly, unconsciously judging the distance, then, between one breath and the next, she released the string. The arrow arched over the common and hit the pyre.

It struck Morna Provin in the eye, instantly cutting off the dreadful sound.

The silence was a relief, but the other things Tia felt were too confused, too difficult to confront. To kill in cold blood . . . to quite deliberately take a life, even for a humane purpose . . .

Tia shook herself and glanced down at the crowd. All hell was breaking loose as the soldiers hidden in the crowd realized what the arrow meant. They had already been spotted, and several guards were running across the open ground toward them.

"That's torn it," she remarked. It was odd, but she felt nothing. The doubt, the recrimination, the guilt—they would come later, she guessed, when she let herself think about it.

Dirk muttered something that sounded like a curse and grabbed her hand. He dragged her up the slope back toward the Keep. The postern gate seemed to be a lifetime away. They would never make it. As they neared the looming bulk of the Keep, Tia could hear the labored breathing of the soldiers who pursued them. They scrambled up the steps cut into the last part of the slope, when suddenly the gate opened for them and slammed shut as soon as they were through, the locking bar dropping into place behind them.

Panting heavily, her heart pounding, Tia turned to discover their benefactor was the old man they had met earlier in the Keep.

"Quickly," he urged as the guards started pounding on the postern gate. It was only a matter of minutes before they would be at the front gate as well.

Dirk and Tia followed him across the courtyard, where there were two fresh horses saddled and waiting for them, held by two young grooms. Tia ran to the nearest mount and jumped into the saddle. She turned, expecting Dirk to follow, but he had stopped to talk to the old man.

"Come with us, Helgin."

"My days of running and hiding are over, Dirk," the man replied with a rueful shrug. "Save yourselves. Don't worry about me."

Dirk muttered a curse and turned to Tia. "Get down."

She dismounted, wondering what he was up to now. Dirk turned to the grooms. "Mount up. Ride toward the Yerl turnoff and then cut across country. Let them get a good look at you. As soon they look like catching you, surrender to them. Tell them I threatened to kill you if you didn't do as I bid."

The boys followed Dirk's orders without question. Tia watched their fresh horses galloping out of the Keep with despair. "Send our only means of escape off with the grooms! Why didn't I think of that?"

"Shut up, Tia," he ordered, before turning back to the old man. "You're coming with us, Helgin."

"No, Dirk, I must—"

"What? Stay here and give Antonov someone to vent his wrath on? Don't be an idiot."

"I'd slow you down..." the old man objected.

"No, you won't. We haven't got that far to go."

In the distance, Tia heard a shout, as the guards closing in on the main gates caught sight of the two figures on horseback galloping away from the Keep.

"Which way?" Tia asked, deciding that maybe sending the grooms off as a decoy wasn't such a bad idea after all.

Dirk pushed the old man ahead of him toward the gate. "Follow me."

A few paces from the main gates to the Keep, Dirk led them onto a faint track that wound down through the brush toward the beach. He led the way in silence, stopping occasionally as the sound of shouted commands and galloping horses on the cobbled road above them drifted down. Helgin kept up pretty well, and Tia started to wonder who he was. She did not object to his presence, though. The old man had aided them enough that she was satisfied he was on their side, but if they collected any more exiles from this damn island, they would have rename Mil New Elcast.

They hurried through the red night, past a small waterfall and a clear pool that steamed faintly with a whiff of sulfur, until they broke out of the woods and reached the beach. Not far from where they emerged, the longboat was waiting. Tia recognized Kurt and, with some relief, Reithan, standing on the beach, their swords drawn. Two archers stood either side of him. An arrow thunked into a tree near Tia's head as the pirates caught sight of them.

"Hey! It's us!" Dirk cried in a loud whisper.

The archers lowered their weapons. Kurt and Reithan hurried forward to meet them.

"Who's that?" Kurt demanded suspiciously when he spied Helgin.

"A friend," Dirk replied shortly, before turning to Reithan. "How did it go?"

"Fine. Let's get the hell out of here." He glanced at Tia then looked over her shoulder, as if he expected someone else. "You weren't able to..."

"No," Tia told him flatly.

Reithan looked at her for a moment, and then decided not to pursue the matter. "Come on. I don't know how long we've got before my diversion isn't a diversion any longer."

Tia helped Helgin into the boat and took a seat in the bow as the sailors stowed their weapons and picked up the oars. Dirk helped Reithan and Kurt run the boat into the water before jumping aboard. Reithan and Kurt took up the other pair of oars, and the longboat cut swiftly through the water toward the heads, leaving the small beach behind them. Dirk clambered forward and came to sit beside her.

"Are you all right?" he asked cautiously.

"Leave me alone."

He put his hand on her shoulder. "You're trembling."

She shook him off impatiently. "I'm fine. Just leave me alone."

"Tia..."

"What?" she snapped.

Dirk stared at her for a moment. "Thank you."

Tears welled up in her eyes. The fear of capture, the adrenaline rush of their escape, had kept the full impact of what she had done at bay. Dirk was right. She was trembling. And she wanted to cry.

"Look," he said gently.

"At what?" she muttered, hanging her head so that he wouldn't see her tears.

"Reithan's diversion."

Tia looked up, wiping her eyes. He was pointing around the bay at the wharf where the *Calliope* was tied.

The Lion of Senet's magnificent ship; his pride and joy, with its golden gunwale, proud masts and sleek lines, was furiously ablaze.

"Was that your idea?"

He nodded. "Seems like justice, don't you think? Now Antonov and I have both lost something we loved tonight."

A sob she could not stifle rocked her suddenly. Dirk put his arm around her and held her while she cried, as the longboat slipped silently though the heads toward the waiting *Makuan,* the night lit brightly by the red sun and the roaring flames of the *Calliope* as she burned.

PART THREE

NEW FRIENDS, OLD ENEMIES

Chapter 36

The days following Landfall were strange for Dirk. The grief he felt for his mother was tempered by the knowledge that Antonov had not gone unpunished. The sight of the *Calliope* going up in flames had a cathartic effect on him. He could remember Wallin Provin telling him when he was a small child that vengeance served no purpose, but Dirk was inclined to disagree. Now that he had tried it, he decided vengeance tasted just fine.

Stooping to avoid hitting his head on the low beams of the *Makuan*'s companionway, Dirk made his way aft through the gloom to the mate's cabin, where Tia was quartered. He had hardly seen her since they had left Elcast, and was fairly certain she was avoiding him.

Dirk felt more than a little guilty about what he had asked of her, although he was not sorry he'd been able to end his mother's torment. He regretted that he'd had to ask Tia to do it. It was his decision, his responsibility, and he should have been the one who'd carried it out, but he was no marksman. A shot like the one Tia had made was far beyond his skill. But now he had burdened Tia with the guilt of taking another human life, and for that he was genuinely sorry.

Dirk knocked on the cabin door and waited for a moment, then knocked again when he received no answer.

"Who is it?" came the muffled reply.

Dirk said nothing, certain that if he identified himself, she would refuse to open the door. He knocked again and heard her moving about inside the cabin, followed by the lock turning. Tia jerked the door open and made to slam it in his face as soon as she realized who it was.

Dirk pushed his hand against the door to stop her closing it.

"Go away."

"I need to talk to you."

"Well, I don't need to talk to you. Leave me alone."

He pushed the door open a little farther, and she threw her hands up in defeat, taking a step backward.

"Say what you have to say and go."

He closed the door behind him and leaned on it, looking at her with concern. "You look terrible."

"Thanks. Did you come here to tell me that? Fine. Now you can leave." She turned her back on him and pretended to straighten the bedding on the narrow bunk.

"I am leaving, Tia. That's what I came to tell you."

She turned to stare at him suspiciously. "What do you mean, you're leaving?"

"I'm going to Omaxin."

"Why?"

"Because I've had enough. I've spent the last two years pretending that if I kept my head down, Antonov would forget about me. Maybe I hoped it would all just go away. But it won't. Not now. I risked everyone trying to save my mother, and all I've achieved is hurting you and provoking Antonov."

"Nice of you to figure that out *after* the fact."

"He was looking for me before, Tia. Now he's going to be actively hunting me. I don't want to spend the rest of my life hiding from him."

"So you're going to run away to Senet? That makes sense. Go and hide right under his nose. You really are the clever one, aren't you?"

"Actually, Senet is probably the last place he'll look for me, but that's not why I'm going. I want to end this, Tia. I want to bring him and Belagren and their whole twisted, sick religion down so badly that I can taste it like ashes on my tongue."

She said nothing for a time, perhaps trying to decide if he meant what he said. "Do you really think you'll find the answers in Omaxin?" she asked eventually.

"I don't know. But if Neris won't tell me what I need to know, the only other option I have is to go to the source."

"Why are you telling me this?"

"I want you to come with me."

She was clearly shocked by the suggestion. "Me! Why?"

"There's only one other person on Ranadon who's spent as much time as I have trying to extract the truth from Neris, Tia, and that's you. Between us, we know everything Neris has ever said about the place. I'm going to need that information if I have any chance of working out how to get through the Labyrinth or when the next Age of Shadows is due."

She shook her head in disbelief. "You're out of your tiny little mind if you thought I'd agree to this!"

"What's the alternative, Tia?" he asked. "Are you going back to Mil to wait for Antonov? You know he'll come. It may not be next week, or next month even, but we lit a fuse on Elcast and it's going to explode in our faces if we don't do something to stop it."

"And whose fault is that, Dirk Provin? We tried to tell you it was foolish to attempt a rescue. But you had to try, didn't you? And now you're going to destroy us all."

"You agreed with me," he reminded her.

"If I'd known you were going to ask me to kill your mother for you," she retorted bitterly, "I might have had second thoughts."

Tia was not nearly as tough as she pretended, Dirk thought. He was also sure that she was a lot tougher than she knew. He did not flinch from her accusing eyes. He empathized with her anger. He just couldn't think of a way to make her understand that.

"You're blaming me, aren't you?" he asked, hoping to somehow impart his sympathy for her plight. Not that she was all that interested in sympathy from him.

"You're damn right I'm blaming you!" she cried. "As if it wasn't bad enough watching you kill your own father, I let you talk me into killing your mother for you, too. Got any plans for your brother you'd care to let me in on?"

"Until you appeared on that terrace in Antonov's palace in Avacas, Tia, I'd never killed anyone, either," he said.

"You acquired a taste for it quick enough, didn't you?"

"I killed Johan to save your life," he reminded her.

"Nobody asked you to save my life, Dirk. Don't try justifying what you did by making it my fault."

"I asked you to kill Morna to save her from unbearable suffering. You didn't have to do it, but you couldn't bear her pain any more than I could."

His words silenced her. She said nothing for a time, then, as if she had come to a decision, she squared her shoulders and glared at him, a little of the Tia he knew before Landfall showing through.

"Suppose you do this; suppose you somehow manage to cross Senet without getting caught. Suppose you get to Omaxin and find a way through the Labyrinth without getting killed. Can you actually work out when the next Age of Shadows is due?"

"I don't know," he told her honestly. "For that matter, I don't even know if having that information will help. All I'm certain of is that I have to try. I can't promise any more than that."

She nodded slowly. "We'd better speak to Reithan, then."

"Does that mean you'll help me?"

"If you're determined to do this, Dirk Provin, there is *no* chance I'm letting you loose in Senet on your own."

Dirk nodded with relief, glad that she had agreed with his plan, while a small voice in the back of his head warned him that she had only agreed to it because he hadn't told her everything.

They met in the captain's small stateroom a few hours later, where Dirk outlined what he had in mind. Porl Isingrin objected immediately to what Dirk proposed. Reithan, however, was a little more thoughtful.

"It's a huge risk, Dirk," he warned, "with no guarantee of success at the end of it."

"That doesn't mean we shouldn't try."

"Can you do it, though?" Porl asked. "Are you really smart enough to work out what Neris learned in those damn ruins?"

"Everyone keeps telling me I am." Dirk shrugged. "I won't

know until I get there and see this Eye of the Labyrinth for myself."

"So, in other words, you might risk your life and Tia's for a solution that doesn't even exist?"

"Yes."

"It's worth a try, Captain," Tia insisted. "All we've done for twenty years is hide in the Baenlands waiting for Neris to give up his secret. And Dirk's right when he says the Lion of Senet is going to want revenge. Even if we go back to Mil, the chances are we're all going to be dead by next Landfall. Antonov will offer a reward for the secret to sailing through the delta so large that even you'll be tempted. We might as well give ourselves some small chance."

"I think I preferred it when you two didn't get along," Porl complained. He looked across the chart table at Reithan. "What do you think?"

"I think it's dangerous, risky and doomed to fail," he said. Then he smiled. "But I also think it might be worth a try."

"You can drop us off in Tolace," Tia suggested. "They won't be looking for us in Senet. Anyway, I'm Senetian, and Dirk was in Avacas long enough to act like one. Come to think of it, he acts like a Senetian most of the damn time, anyway. But we can blend in. We'll just be two travelers heading north."

"And what happens when you get to Omaxin?" Reithan asked. "Belagren has had her Shadowdancers working those ruins for years. How are you going to get past them?"

"We need to get them out of there," Dirk told them.

"How?" Reithan asked.

"By giving them what they're looking for."

They all stared at him suspiciously.

"They're after the same thing we are," he explained. "If they think they're going to find it someplace else, they're not going to waste time and energy scratching through the ruins of Omaxin to find it."

"I'm not as smart as you, lad," Porl said. "Would you like to go back and explain that again?"

"There are only two ways anybody will ever learn when the next Age of Shadows is due," Dirk said patiently. "One is the ruins in Omaxin, but by far the easier way is to get the information from the one who already has it."

"You'd better not be suggesting what I think you are," Tia warned.

"You want to give them Neris?" Reithan asked in a carefully guarded tone.

He looked at them in despair, wondering what it would take to make them understand what he could see so clearly. "It's not the truth that matters; it's what people *believe* to be the truth. If Belagren thinks she knows where Neris is, then trust me, she'll abandon Omaxin so fast they probably won't have time to quench their cooking fires."

"So you want to feed Belagren false information about where Neris is?" Tia concluded. "Great idea in theory, but how are you going to manage that? Do you suggest we let one of our people be caught by the Lion of Senet, just so Belagren can have the fun of torturing the information from him?"

"No," he replied. "We use Alenor."

"What reason would Belagren have to believe anything that Alenor told her?" Porl asked. "And more important, how would Alenor explain where the information came from without endangering herself? What's she going to say to Belagren? 'Hey, I have a message from my friends in the Baenlands that you might be interested in'?"

"She doesn't have to tell Belagren anything. She tells Antonov."

"This is getting way too complicated," Porl complained.

"It's simple. Alenor tells Antonov she has information about Neris's whereabouts, and we provide her with a source of information that can't be connected to us. Even if he doesn't believe her, Antonov will mention it to Belagren, and trust me, she has no choice but to act on the information. Antonov just wants to get his hands on Neris because he's a heretic. Belagren *has* to find him, because her entire future rests on the information Neris has about the Age of Shadows."

"There's an awful lot that could go wrong…" Porl said uncertainly.

Reithan nodded slowly. "But it might work."

"Will Alenor do it, though?" Tia questioned. "She wasn't exactly brimming with enthusiasm over the idea of an alliance."

"She said to come to her with a workable plan," Reithan reminded them. "Given a healthy dose of luck, this just *might* work."

Tia smiled briefly at Dirk before turning to Reithan. "You'll let us do it then?"

He nodded slowly. "Actually, Tia, I have a bad feeling there's no way of stopping either of you." Then he turned to Dirk. "How do we provide Alenor with the information about Neris without risking her neck?"

Chapter 37

Kirsh's injuries had kept Rainan and Alenor in Nova longer than anticipated, which gave Antonov and Belagren plenty of time to receive Rainan's letter regarding Kirsh's unfortunate accident. That was how everyone was referring to the beating—an unfortunate accident—as if that somehow lessened the crime.

They had received the news that the Lion of Senet and the High Priestess were waiting for them as soon as their ship docked in Kalarada. There was no sign of the *Calliope* in the harbor. Alenor wondered if that meant the rumors she had heard on Grannon Rock were true. Had Dirk really burned Antonov's precious ship to the waterline in revenge for his mother's death?

There was no time to prepare for the confrontation. Although Rainan still nominally ruled Dhevyn, she was not foolish enough to try to stall the inevitable audience with Antonov. Alenor, Kirsh and the queen were taken from the ship straight up to the Audience Chamber in the Kalarada Palace. The city looked unchanged as they passed through it, although there were a lot of Senetians on the streets; particularly noticeable were Antonov's Palace Guard. Kalarada's red-shingled roofs clustered together almost as if the city was cowering under the gaze of what was, to all intents and purposes, an occupation force.

Why do we let the soldiers of another nation walk our streets with impunity? Alenor asked herself as the carriage clattered over the cobblestones toward the palace. Then she answered her own question, acknowledging the bitter truth with reluctance. *Because we have no choice . . .*

Antonov was waiting for them, sitting on the Eagle Throne as if he owned it. Sunlight streamed down on him from the glass panels in the roof, bathing him in light. There were also a score or more people that Alenor did not know waiting for them, all of them Senetian, she guessed by their dress.

Who are these people? Alenor wondered nervously.

There was no sign of the High Priestess, which was something to be grateful for. Lord Dimitri Bayel, Kalarada's Seneschal, also stood near the throne, wearing a look of cautious fear.

The Lion of Senet slowly rose to his feet and stepped aside as the Queen of Dhevyn approached. She seemed unconcerned that she had found him comfortably ensconced on her throne. Alenor suspected it was deliberate, as if Antonov was reminding Rainan who really held the reins of power in Dhevyn.

Her mother waited until Antonov had stepped aside before she took her seat and made a great show of straightening her skirts. When she was done, she looked down at the strangers filling her court with a frown, and then finally deigned to turn her attention to the Lion of Senet.

"I trust you didn't find my throne too comfortable, Anton?"

Antonov smiled, but said nothing.

Alenor stopped in front of the throne with Kirsh by her side. The Senetian prince was limping slightly, but other than some rather impressive bruises and his sorely wounded pride, he seemed none the worse for his ordeal.

Antonov's disconcerting gaze flickered over his son with a scowl. "Who did this to you?"

"I don't know, sir," Kirsh answered after only a moment's hesitation. Alenor breathed a sigh of relief. At least Kirsh had not blurted out his dangerous theory about Alexin and the Queen's Guard being in league with the Baenlanders. Marqel had planted that idea in his head, she was certain, and Alenor had spent much of the journey from Nova trying to laugh off his suspicions.

"Do *you* have an explanation, your majesty?" Antonov asked Rainan.

"We can only assume that Kirshov's obvious wealth attracted a rather unsavory element," she shrugged.

"Obvious wealth? He was in uniform, wasn't he?"

"Yes, Anton, but his wealth *was* rather prominently displayed. His saddle is trimmed with silver, as is his bridle. His boots are obviously well made and not standard issue. Even the sword he carries is worth more than most Guardsmen earn in a year. All these things would set him apart from other Guardsmen."

Alenor wondered if her mother was commenting on Kirsh's mode of dress or chastising him for it. There was a note of reproach in her voice.

"Yet they stole nothing," the Lion of Senet pointed out.

Rainan seemed unable to explain why, if thieves had taken such trouble to beat up Kirsh for his wealth, they would leave it behind when they abandoned him.

If you're going to lie to him, Mother, at least make it believable. "Perhaps they were disturbed before they could complete the task, your highness," Alenor suggested.

"And what was the task, Alenor? To rob my son? Or kill him?"

"Anton, I'm quite sure nobody set out to murder Kirshov," the queen scoffed. "There are much more efficient methods of killing a man, if that was their intention."

Antonov did not reply. Instead he turned to his son. "Did you get a look at your attackers, Kirsh?"

"No, sir, they took me from behind and covered my head with something...a fish sack, or the like. I couldn't see a damn thing."

"Sergey!" the Lion of Senet barked suddenly. Even Kirsh jumped at his shout.

"Your highness?" The captain of Antonov's guard stepped forward with a salute.

"You will return to Grannon Rock on the next tide. When you get back to that Goddess-forsaken island, you will turn it upside down and inside out until you have found the men who did this. Is that clear?"

"Your highness, if the men who attacked Prince Kirshov were sailors, they could be long gone before—"

"I don't care, Sergey. Find them and bring them to me, or I will pay Grannon Rock a visit personally and deal with the matter myself."

"As you wish, sire." Sergey turned on his heel and marched from the throne room to carry out his orders.

"I trust no harm came to *you* on this ill-fated journey, Alenor," Antonov asked with fatherly concern.

"No, your highness, although..." she hesitated and lowered her eyes.

"Although what, my dear?" he asked curiously. "Come now, child, we know each other too well for you to be shy with me."

"It's just...well, we heard there'd been some trouble on El-cast..."

Antonov's expression darkened. "I see. And did you happen to hear the name of the author of this trouble?"

Alenor knew she was treading on very dangerous ground, but she needed to know how far she could push Antonov, as much as she wanted to learn what had really happened on El-cast.

"Rumor has it that it was Dirk," Kirsh said, before Alenor could answer him.

"Then for once, rumor has the right of it."

"And the *Calliope*?"

"The *Calliope* is now a burned-out husk," Antonov announced flatly.

"I'm sorry, sir..."

"There's no need to apologize, Kirsh. I will see to it that Dirk is found."

"Do you know where he is, then?" Alenor asked, trying to sound as if she was only mildly interested in his fate. "It's been so long since anyone heard from him ..."

"Oh? I heard a rumor that he was in Nova while you were there, my dear. There's even a suggestion that it was he who led the attack on Kirsh."

Alenor frowned. Had Marqel already communicated her suspicions about Dirk to the High Priestess?

"Well, if he was in Nova, Anton," Rainan said skeptically, "the boy must have sprouted wings since I saw him last. He can't have been in Nova assaulting your son and in Elcast burning your ship at the same time." Alenor breathed a sigh of relief. She didn't know how Dirk had gotten to Elcast as fast as he had, but her mother's words had done much to remove the suspicion that he had been in Nova when Kirsh was beaten. In fact, the notion seemed quite absurd in light of the events on Elcast.

Unaccountably, Antonov suddenly smiled.

What's he up to now? Alenor wondered.

"Perhaps you're right, Rainan. Let's not dwell on it any longer. The important thing is that Kirsh is still in one piece, and we have the happy union of my son and your daughter to look forward to. I've brought some people with me to assist you in seeing to the wedding and the coronation arrangements. I'm sure you'll find their help invaluable. And I've decided to stay on Kalarada until the wedding, too. Just to make certain everything goes according to plan."

Although it was pleasantly spoken, there was nothing subtle about Antonov's threat. *Just what we need,* Alenor thought in despair. *Antonov's spies looking over our shoulder every waking moment. And probably while we're sleeping, too.*

"There's really no need ..." the queen began.

Antonov turned to Rainan with a menacing smile. "On the contrary, your majesty, I think there *is* a need, a very great need, for me to stay and supervise the wedding. And your abdication. Or have you forgotten about that?"

"No, I've not forgotten," Rainan replied meekly.

"I should hope not, Rainan," the Lion of Senet warned. "We wouldn't want your daughter to inherit your crown the old-fashioned way."

Chapter 38

Marqel was summoned to appear before the High Priestess almost as soon as her feet touched solid ground. The message was delivered to the ship by one of the Queen of Dhevyn's palace lackeys, so Marqel could tell nothing about the tone of the message. She had no idea if it was a warm invitation or an angry summons. Kirsh had left with Alenor and the queen as soon as their ship docked so, with some trepidation, she climbed into the open carriage sent down to the wharf to collect her and headed for the palace.

The city of Kalarada, like the island it was named after, was a steep, narrow place where the buildings loomed over each other as they peered down over the harbor. Marqel had been here several times as an acrobat, and she remembered the city more for its clientele than for its architecture. She had never been to the palace, though; never even got a glimpse of it before today. She watched it slowly emerge out of the woodlands on the outskirts of the city as the carriage moved up the steep hill. The palace was tall and narrow and picturesque, built of the same white stone as the Hall of Shadows in Avacas. It was set amid acres of woods that were carefully tended to give the impression of wilderness. Another, smaller keep, the barracks of the Queen's Guard, sat lower down the mountain in the shadow of the larger palace. She thought about Kirsh as they passed, wondering what he was doing now. Was he thinking of her? Or was he with that snotty little princess?

What a fool Alenor is, Marqel thought with a smile. *Fancy inviting me here to Kalarada to be with Kirsh. How naive could one person be?*

When she reached the palace, a servant led her through a maze of halls, up several short staircases and down several others toward the High Priestess's suite. The palace had been built around the contours of the mountain on which it sat, she suspected, which made for some interesting detours.

Belagren was in her rooms with Madalan when she arrived. The servant left her outside with a bow, and then hurried off, probably not wanting to face the High Priestess. Marqel knocked on the door and waited, trying to control her racing heart by taking deep, measured breaths. All her plans, everything she had done to get herself here, might soon prove to have been for naught if the High Priestess did not believe her story.

Madalan opened the door for her. She curtsied politely. "The High Priestess sent for me."

"Is that Marqel?" Belagren's voice called from behind the partially closed door.

"You'd better come in," Madalan suggested, standing back to let her enter.

Marqel stepped into the room and glanced around. The suite was smaller than she expected, but tastefully furnished. Kalarada did not enjoy the conspicuous wealth of Avacas, but what the palace lacked in ostentation, it made up in understated elegance.

Belagren was sitting at the small carved writing desk by the window. The room looked out over the sea. All Marqel could see beyond the High Priestess was an ocean of blue, but it was impossible to tell where the sky finished and the sea began.

When Belagren looked up her expression was cold and hostile. "I left you at the palace in Avacas. I expected to find you there when I got back."

"There was some trouble..." Marqel tried to explain as she stopped a few feet from the High Priestess.

"Ah yes, I heard about that," the High Priestess cut in. "Caspona suddenly died of an overdose. Odd that nobody suspected she was a poppy-dust addict."

"I had no idea, either, my lady," Marqel hurried to assure her. "I would have said something if I'd known."

Belagren turned in her chair to face her. "Oh, I'm quite

sure you would have, Marqel. I know how much you two loathed each other. I'm quite certain that even if you *suspected* Caspona was fooling around with poppy-dust you'd have come running to me."

Marqel breathed a mental sigh of relief. Maybe this was going to work.

"Of course," the High Priestess continued, "I find it extremely convenient that she chose to die the night before she was due to depart for Grannon Rock, and that you so graciously offered to take her place."

Marqel met the High Priestess's gaze with guileless innocence. "Do you really think she meant to kill herself, my lady?"

Belagren looked at her in surprise. "What?"

"You just said you thought it odd that she chose to die on that day. Do you really think she deliberately took her own life? I mean, it's no secret that I never liked her much, but she didn't strike me as the suicidal type. I spoke to her just before she went to bed the evening before. She didn't appear to be unhappy."

Stick as close to the truth as you can, Marqel knew. It was the only way to lie effectively.

Belagren was silent for a moment, her expression thoughtful. "You admit that you were the last person to see her alive?"

"Was I? I didn't know."

"And if you had known that Caspona was planning to take her own life," Madalan asked from behind her, "would you have done anything to prevent it?"

Marqel glanced over her shoulder at the High Priestess's right hand. "I hated her, my lady, and she hated me. Had I any inkling of what she was planning, I probably wouldn't have done a thing. But if I'd known she was an addict, I would have reported that. Cheerfully."

"I'm inclined to believe you would, Marqel," the High Priestess agreed. "You're a vindictive little bitch."

Marqel let the insult pass. *I might be a vindictive little bitch, but I'm smarter than you are, you aging old whore.*

"Of course, Caspona's tragic and untimely demise would seem a lot less suspicious had not Laleno met a similar fate in your company not more than two weeks later," Belagren remarked, watching her closely.

Marqel met the High Priestess's gaze evenly. "Laleno was with the Duke of Grannon Rock's hawkmaster when she died, my lady. I wasn't even there."

"You found the bodies, though," Madalan pointed out. "What made you go looking for them?"

"Laleno asked me to make sure we weren't late getting back to the city. I was following her instructions, my lady."

"You have a well-rehearsed answer for everything, Marqel," Belagren noted with a frown.

"I've had a lot of practice, my lady. I've been questioned a score of times since the accident."

Belagren did not look entirely convinced, but Marqel's story had stood up to close scrutiny so far, and she was growing more and more confident that it would survive the High Priestess's inquiry. "Did you have anything to do with what happened to Prince Kirshov?"

"*My lady?*" Marqel gasped in genuine shock.

Belagren smiled. "That got a reaction from you."

"My lady!" she protested. "I had nothing to do with that! I found him... I *saved* him!"

"Oh, settle down, girl," Belagren ordered. "Of all the strange things that happen around you, that's the one thing I am certain that you had no part in. What I *would* like to know is how you came to the conclusion that Dirk Provin was involved."

Marqel allowed herself a small, triumphant smile. This was the opening she needed. This was her payoff for allowing that half-witted moron to touch her.

"Because I found his servant in Nova, my lady."

"His servant?" Madalan asked.

"The half-wit. Eryk. I bumped into him... quite literally... in the marketplace in Nova. The poor boy was desperately lonely and unhappy. He was thrilled to see a familiar face. We had a very long and interesting conversation, Eryk and I."

Belagren stared at her. "You *know* where Dirk Provin is?"

Marqel shook her head. "Not exactly. But I know where he's been. And who's he's been with."

"And you're only telling me this now?" Belagren demanded angrily.

"I couldn't think of a way to get the information to you safely, my lady. I mean, it is rather...sensitive..."

"So you found a way to get Alenor to invite you to Kalarada," Belagren concluded, with a touch of begrudging admiration.

Actually, Marqel still had no idea why Alenor had invited her to Kalarada, but she was quite content to let the High Priestess think it was the result of something she had done.

"I couldn't think of any other way, my lady."

Belagren nodded. "I believe, Marqel, that even if you'd marched in here and confessed to killing both Caspona and Laleno, I'd be inclined to forgive you in light of this."

Fat chance, Marqel thought. She smiled tentatively. "I'll be allowed to stay then?"

"For reasons known only to the Goddess herself, Alenor seems to want you here," Belagren told her. "I've no wish to upset our future queen at this point. You'll certainly stay here until I leave. After that, we'll see."

"Thank you, my lady," she said with a curtsy.

"Is that wise?" Madalan asked the High Priestess. "Given the previous relationship between Kirshov and Marqel, Alenor's good will may soon evaporate if she thinks there's a chance that her beloved has a wandering eye."

The High Priestess was silent for a moment, and then she looked at Marqel. "Have you and Kirshov resumed your... friendship?"

Marqel thought about lying for a moment, and then decided against it. "I haven't slept with him again, if that's what you're asking. He's not been in a fit state to do much of anything."

"And now that he's recovered?"

"All I need do is snap my fingers in his direction, my lady."

Belagren smiled. "Vindictive *and* cocky."

"I don't believe in false modesty, my lady."

"I suspect you don't believe in modesty at all, Marqel," the High Priestess snorted. "However, it suits me to allow you some leeway in this matter. Kirshov is prone to attacks of honorable behavior. I don't want him deciding to 'do the right thing' by Alenor at an inconvenient time. You may do what you must to keep Kirshov's mind focused on the benefits of following the Goddess. Just be discreet about it. If the Lion of Senet gets wind of it, I will deny all knowledge of the affair and ship you off to the farthest outpost I can find at the slightest hint of trouble."

"I understand, my lady."

"Good," she declared. "In that case, you may pour me some wine and pull up a chair. I want to know everything you learned about Dirk Provin."

Feeling relieved and rather proud of herself, Marqel left the High Priestess's room three hours later, having delivered her carefully edited version of Eryk's tale. She was starting to realize that true power lay in knowledge; not the sort of book learning that Dirk Provin favored, but in knowing what others wanted to know.

Marqel confirmed the High Priestess's suspicion that Dirk had been living with the Baenlanders. She had related Eryk's tales about Dirk's exploits with the notorious and elusive Reithan Seranov. What she had not confirmed for the High Priestess was that Neris Veran lived and was hiding in Mil. Nor had she mentioned the existence of a young girl named Mellie Thorn. Marqel knew how touchy the nobility were on the matter of heirs, and she had no intention of muddying the waters with another potential claimant to the throne of Dhevyn.

Alenor would be queen soon, and Kirsh the Regent of Dhevyn. Any issue of theirs would be the heir to the Dhevynian throne, and when Misha died, the heir to Senet as well. Of course, that was assuming an heir came from this union, a circumstance that Marqel was quietly determined to prevent.

Marqel had changed her mind about pregnancy since meeting up with young Eryk in Nova. There was a good reason to risk ruining her figure, she had decided. If Kirsh was going to father any children, then the first should be *her* child. It would be illegitimate, certainly, but the nobility were quite happy to overlook that if it meant preserving an important bloodline. If she wanted proof of that, she need look no further than the Lion of Senet's obsession with finding Dirk Provin.

When Alenor proved barren, or unable to carry a child to term (it did not matter which; Marqel knew the right herbs to make either happen), then the only living heir would be the healthy child born of Kirshov's mistress.

Marqel smiled as she walked. *I will be the mother of a king or a queen. That bratty little princess will live to see my child elevated to heir.*

That would feel almost as good as seeing Dirk Provin brought down.

Chapter 39

The Senetian port of Tolace was home to a number of small estates belonging to noble families with sufficient wealth and leisure time to afford a holiday home on the coast. Its main claim to fame, however, was the Hospice run by the Sundancers for centuries, and now occupied by Belagren's Shadowdancers.

It was to Tolace that young women of noble birth came to deal with any unfortunate accidents resulting from Landfall. It was here, in Tolace, that the sons and daughters of Senet's more prominent families were sent when their poppy-dust addiction became serious enough to attract attention. It was to Tolace that the old and the senile were sent to die.

And it was here that Neris Veran had faked his own death.

The Hospice was a sprawling complex of small, discreet cottages set among carefully manicured gardens, connected by graveled paths to the larger, less aesthetically pleasing buildings housing the general wards where the less fortunate were cared for. The whole place was surrounded by a long whitewashed wall. The rest of Tolace was built around the wall, as if the town had no other purpose but to serve the Hospice and its needs.

"I was conceived in there," Tia remarked as she and Dirk walked alongside the wall toward the center of town. Dirk glanced at her curiously. They had said little since Kurt had delivered them by longboat to a small deserted beach some eight miles from the town.

It was midmorning, and the town around them was well and truly awake. The seemingly endless Hospice wall provided a perfect backdrop for the market set up in its shadow, and the air was filled with the shouts of merchants hawking their wares and the smell of roasting meat from the numerous stalls selling food. There were several other stalls offering a dubious, virulently alcoholic drink known as *vod'kun,* which Tia had tried once when she was in Avacas with Reithan. The drink had a faintly aniseed aftertaste and a tendency to strip the lining from one's stomach. She could not imagine anyone wanting to drink it this early in the morning.

"That's where Neris is supposed to have killed himself, isn't it?"

She nodded and pointed west where the land rose sharply, exposing a long line of jagged cliffs. "Over there, I think it was."

He nodded thoughtfully, but said nothing further, making Tia wonder what he was thinking. Dirk Provin could be the walking definition of inscrutable when he chose. She was not sure how she was going to deal with weeks, possibly months, with only him for company while they crossed Senet trying to discover the most valuable secret on Ranadon.

"You don't say much, do you?" she remarked, his silence suddenly grating.

"What did you want me to say?"

"You could tell me what the plan is," she suggested tartly. "That would be a good start. Are we going to walk all the way to Omaxin?"

"People won't notice a couple of travelers on foot," he shrugged. "If we buy horses, someone might remember us. Besides, the only coins we have are Dhevynian dorns. That will stick in people's minds."

"How are we going to change them?"

"Very carefully," he said. "And here, while we're still on the coast. Once we get inland, Dhevynian dorns will cause comment wherever we try to spend them."

"It's six hundred miles to Omaxin," she pointed out. "It's going to take us a long time on foot."

Dirk didn't seem concerned. "With luck, that will leave time for Reithan to get a message to Alexin, so that he can get a message to Alenor, so that she can let it slip that she knows where Neris is..."

"So the High Priestess can send the order to Omaxin ordering the Shadowdancers to leave," she finished for him with a frown. "There are far too many things that could go wrong with this insane plan of yours."

"You're free to turn around and go home anytime you want, Tia."

"And leave you alone in Senet? Not likely!"

"And to think I was planning to ditch you somewhere along the way so I could get back to Avacas and my old friend Antonov," he told her. "Damn, you've foiled my plans."

He had not so much as cracked a smile, but she just knew that he was laughing at her. "You know, at some stage before this journey is over, Dirk Provin, I'm probably going to end up killing you."

"Are you planning to do this before or after we've saved the world?"

She looked at him in astonishment. "Saved the *world*? That's a bit dramatic, even for you."

"Is it? Think about it for a moment. I mean, other than the obvious fact that being able to predict such an important event will shatter Belagren's whole damn religion and destroy Antonov when he realizes he's been duped, what's the most useful thing about knowing when the next Age of Shadows is due?"

"Being able to prepare for it, I suppose."

"Exactly! The last Age of Shadows lasted nearly ten years. If Johan had had any idea it was coming, he could have stockpiled food, made arrangements to deal with the refugees, made any number of contingency plans...and not have to rely on Senet, which means Dhevyn would never have been invaded in the first place."

He was right, she realized. She had just never given the long-term consequences of what they were doing much thought. Her only real interest was vengeance—for her father, for Johan Thorn, and lately, for Morna Provin.

"You do know what's going to happen, don't you? Your insane plan will actually work. We'll get to Omaxin and you'll immediately find a way through the Labyrinth, where the solution will be waiting for us, plain as day, and it'll take you no more than ten minutes to figure out that the next Age of Shadows isn't due for another thousand years, and this whole damn exercise will have been a complete waste of time!"

"It's possible," he conceded.

"And what are we going to do then? What if the next Age of Shadows isn't due in our lifetime?"

"I suppose at that point we're going to have to decide if we really care what happens a thousand years from now." Then he added mischievously, "Of course, the smart thing to do would be to decide there is a Goddess after all, beg Antonov's forgiveness, and spend the rest of my life in comfort and luxury in Avacas as the guest of the Lion of Senet."

"You know what scares me about you?" she remarked. "That you can even *think* that."

"I was kidding..."

"I know you were, but that's not the point, Dirk. Most people I trust couldn't even *imagine* doing anything so craven."

"Well, that answers your question then."

"What question?"

"Why I don't say much," he explained. "Every time I open my mouth around you, Tia, I get into trouble for it."

He strode on ahead leaving her staring after him feeling as if somehow, she was the one who had said something wrong.

"We need to think up different names. Senetian names," Dirk said later as they sat at a table outside one of Tolace's numerous taverns while they sorted through their supplies. They had spent the morning shopping in the markets, buying food and cooking utensils for their journey, spending their larger denomination Dhevynian coins on small purchases in order to get Senetian dorns as change.

Tia nodded her agreement as she rearranged her pack to fit in the wheel of cheese. "Fine. You can call me Natasha. I'll call you Little Antonov."

He frowned. "Are you going to be like this all the way to Omaxin?"

She stopped and thought about it for a moment then nodded. "Probably."

When he didn't answer her, she glanced at him and smiled. "Don't look at me like that. This trip is going to be hard enough without us arguing all the way there and back. I intend to be the soul of charm and wit every step of the way."

"I'm relieved to hear you say that, Tia," he said as he stood up, shouldering his well-laden pack with an effort. "Because I think I'd *prefer* Antonov owning Dhevyn completely to listening to you snipe at me, day in, day out for the next few months."

Tia lifted her own heavy pack onto her shoulder. "The old Tia would probably make some snide remark about you probably preferring Antonov owning Dhevyn anyway, but I'm going to be a good girl now and not say a word."

He stared at her for a moment, as if he was completely baffled by her. "You really are quite insane, aren't you?"

"It runs in the family," she agreed. She adjusted the pack on her shoulder to a more comfortable position and then looked at Dirk with a smile. "Come on, Little Antonov. Let's go save the world."

Chapter 40

As Alenor's birthday drew near, the preparations for her wedding and coronation began to take on the atmosphere of a major military campaign. The young princess was pulled in a thousand different directions at once as everyone in the palace—from the cellarmaster to the Queen's Guard—wanted her opinion on every tiny little detail, every minor point of protocol; none of which was helped by the fact that Antonov and Belagren were still in the palace, overseeing the whole circus.

Rainan did the best she could, but the closer she came to actually fulfilling the promise she had made to abdicate on Alenor's sixteenth birthday, the less enthusiastic she was about the idea. There was no way to escape it, Alenor knew, and a part of her wished the day would arrive quickly so that finally, she would be able to do something about the mess her mother and her uncle had made of Dhevyn.

She had no idea *what* she was going to do to fix things. All she was that certain of was that she probably couldn't do any worse than her predecessors.

It seemed that more and more Senetians arrived at the palace every day. The list of aides that Antonov had deemed necessary for Kirsh's regency was insanely long. He had been sending staff to Kalarada on and off for over two years now, with obscure titles like chief assistant to the undersecretary's chamberlain, but the trickle had turned into a flood since he arrived from Elcast. She didn't know what half of them were supposed to be doing, and was afraid to imagine what the other half were up to.

Alenor was helpless to do anything about it. Her mother was right about one thing: to tip her hand before the wedding—to give Antonov the slightest hint that she was not going to cower under his gaze and do exactly as he wanted—might prove fatal.

So she let it happen and waited, hoping that things would get better once she was queen.

Kirsh had proved absolutely useless in helping with the wedding arrangements. He was counting down the days before he left the Queen's Guard, and was determined to make the most of his last few days in the company. Alenor considered his attitude quite astonishing, considering his comrades in the Queen's Guard had done nothing but give him hell for the past two years. She was quite sure Kirsh had another reason to prefer his barracks accommodation to the palace, and fairly certain she knew what that reason was. She did not dwell on it, though. There were more than enough people feeling sorry for her now. She had no need to feel sorry for herself.

"Please, your highness, hold still!"

Alenor let out a long-suffering sigh as Barenka Salanvor, supposedly the most sought-after seamstress in all of Senet and Dhevyn, continued to pin the hem of her wedding gown. She was hot, her back ached and she was thirsty. And she hated the dress. It was huge and cumbersome and so heavily encrusted with crystal beading that she was sure she would keel over from the weight of it, long before she managed to complete her vows or take her crown.

"Your highness?"

Alenor glanced over her shoulder at Dorra, her lady-in-waiting. The young woman was Senetian, sent at Antonov's behest after they had left Avacas. She was pleasant enough, with dark eyes and thick blond hair, but she was Antonov's creature, and Alenor had never trusted her.

"Yes, Dorra?"

"Captain Seranov is here to see you, your highness. Shall I send him away?"

"No!" she cried, desperate for an excuse to end this nightmare dress fitting. "I want...I mean...I *should* speak with him. He'll be responsible for security during the wedding. I must be certain everything is arranged. We have a great many important people attending and I will not allow anything to happen to them. Send him in, Dorra."

"Your highness is hardly in a fit state to receive visitors."

"I'm perfectly decent, Dorra. Now send him in. Mistress Salanvor, you may take this opportunity to have some refreshment while I speak with the captain of my guard."

"As your highness wishes," the seamstress agreed reluctantly through a mouthful of pins. She climbed to her feet, dropped the pins in a small bowl on the table and then curtsied before leaving the room.

"*Now*, Dorra," Alenor commanded, when the older women didn't move.

Looking decidedly unhappy, Dorra opened the door and stood back to let Alexin in. He saluted sharply and waited expectantly for the lady-in-waiting to depart.

"You can go now, Dorra."

"Your highness, I really don't think it's appropriate that I leave you unchaperoned with—"

"Oh, for pity's sake, Dorra! What do you think can happen to me standing here like a coat rack covered in pins? Anyway, if my honor isn't safe in the hands of a captain of the Queen's Guard, where is it safe?"

Dorra curtsied, obviously unhappy. "I'll be right outside if you need me, your highness."

"Thank you, Dorra. And I promise that if the captain tries to have his wicked way with me, I'll scream for you."

Dorra closed the door behind her, scowling at Alexin, who was doing his best to hide his smile. She grinned and held out her hand to him. "Help me down, Alexin. I feel like I ought to be standing out in the garden covered in pigeon poo."

He crossed the room and held her hand for her as she stepped down from the stool, kicking the yards of material out of the way so she wouldn't trip on it.

"It's quite…an amazing…gown, your highness," he remarked carefully.

"It's all right, Alexin, you can tell me what you really think. It's hideous, isn't it?"

"It's not your usual style," he agreed with a faint smile.

"It's all the rage in Senet, so I'm told." She picked up her billowing skirts and stepped inelegantly over to the tall windows that looked out over the Queen's Garden and sat down on the sofa. "I'm going to look like a fool, standing in the temple swathed in yards and yards of virginal white while my husband forgets to recite his vows because he's too busy making eyes at his mistress." She reached down and pulled out a pin that was stabbing her in the side and tossed it on the floor. "Assuming, of course, that I haven't already collapsed from the weight of this blasted thing."

"Your highness, you can't assume—"

"I'm not assuming anything, Alexin," she said bluntly. "I know for a fact that Kirsh is with her almost every night."

"It was your invitation that brought the Shadowdancer here, your highness," he pointed out—a little unsympathetically, Alenor thought.

"I know," she sighed. Then she smiled wanly. "Don't pay any attention to me. I'm just being waspish. I have far more important things to worry about than Kirsh. Although I find it rather irritating that my fiancé can fool around with his Shadowdancer quite openly, yet I can't be alone with the captain of my guard without fearing for my reputation. What did you want to see me about?"

"I have a message for you."

She waited for him to add something further, but when he did not elaborate, she guessed instantly who the message must be from.

"Is it good news?"

"It might be."

"You're being very cryptic, Alexin."

"Cautious," he corrected in a low voice, looking pointedly over his shoulder at the door where Dorra was undoubtedly trying to listen in.

Alenor nodded in understanding. "The message is not a brief one, I assume?"

"It will take some explaining, your highness. Certainly more time than we have now."

"I shall probably want to go riding later today, Captain," she announced loudly for Dorra's benefit. "Would you be so kind as to arrange an escort for me?"

"It would be my honor to escort you myself, your highness," he replied with a bow.

"Then leave us now. And be so kind as to ask Lady Dorra and Mistress Salanvor to come back in. I wish to get this damn dress finished before the next Age of Shadows."

Alexin saluted and walked toward the door. Dorra opened it before he could reach for the knob, confirming Alenor's suspicion that she had been trying to listen to their conversation. Mistress Salanvor hurried in a few moments later. She frowned when she saw Alenor sitting on the sofa and sighed dramatically.

"Oh, your highness…look at you! Now we're going to have to start all over again."

Alenor was glad Alexin had given her an excuse to go riding. The chance to escape the palace, and that hideous dress, even for a short time, was just what she needed, although she had had to think up a long list of chores for Dorra to stop her lady-in-waiting accompanying her. That was going to be a problem in the future, she knew, which was the other reason she had insisted that she needed no other companions on her ride other than the Queen's Guard. If Alenor did not establish the habit now of riding alone with her escort, she would have no chance of doing it once she was queen. That would make it extremely awkward to speak with Alexin regarding matters that were likely to see her meet the same fate as poor Morna Provin if she were caught.

It was overcast and humid as she gave the mare her head and let her gallop along the bridle path through the woodland bordering the city with a feeling of guilty pleasure. Poor Snowdrop would have keeled over from the effort, but Circael, the spirited black mare Antonov had bought for her in Arkona when she was fourteen, relished the chance to run free. Behind her, she could hear her escort trying hard to keep up, although she wondered a little about that. It was highly unlikely, she thought, that Circael could outrun a Guardsman's mount if he seriously wanted to catch her.

She glanced over her shoulder as one of the riders drew level with her, not surprised to discover it was Alexin. Slowing Circael to a trot, she looked back at the rest of the escort who also slowed to match her pace. They hung back out of earshot, but remained in sight.

"Do you trust them?" she asked.

"Every one of them," Alexin assured her. "With your life."

She nodded, satisfied that Alexin had hand picked the men and that they were loyal to her. She wondered what it was that made the second sons of Dhevyn better men than their fathers and their older siblings.

"If we have to keep meeting like this, Alexin, I'm going to spend more time in the saddle than I will on my throne."

"I'm sure you'll sit both with equal grace and skill, your highness."

The compliment made her blush. She still had difficulty meeting Alexin's eye at times, especially when she remembered that embarrassing scene in the baths at his father's house in Nova. She had been hurting badly over Kirsh, but what on Ranadon had possessed her to kiss him like that? Fortunately for both of them, Alexin was gentleman enough to pretend it had never happened.

"So what's this message, Captain?" she asked, forcing herself to focus on the business at hand.

"The Baenlanders have a plan."

Alenor frowned. "What sort of plan?"

"Dirk Provin has gone to Omaxin."

"Omaxin!" she exclaimed, then glanced around nervously. Fortunately, the only people who might have heard her cry were Alexin's men. "He's in *Senet*?" she added in a whisper. "Oh dear! I never thought he'd actually take my suggestion seriously. What is that fool boy thinking of? Those ruins are crawling with Belagren's Shadowdancers."

"They're aware of that, your highness. That's why they need your help. We need to get them out of Omaxin."

"How can *I* get the Shadowdancers out of Omaxin?" she asked doubtfully.

"You need to speak to Antonov."

"What do they want me to do, Alexin? Walk up to the Lion of Senet and ask very nicely if he could please arrange to remove the High Priestess's Shadowdancers from Omaxin because they're in the way of my plans to destroy him?"

Alexin smiled.

I should never have agreed to meet with those damn pirates, Alenor thought. *I should never have offered them hope of an alliance. Goddess! I sound like my mother.* "What do they want me to tell him?" she sighed, thinking that she wasn't even queen yet, and she was already making stupid mistakes.

They continued at a walk along the bridle path as Alexin answered her question. The future Queen of Dhevyn listened with growing dread as the captain of her guard explained to her exactly how she was supposed to get the Shadowdancers out of Omaxin.

Chapter 41

The city of Bollow's elegant spires and green-tinted copper domes came into view some three weeks after Tia and Dirk left Tolace. Their journey had been hard work at first, neither Tia nor Dirk having spent a great deal of time walking recently, and certainly not the four hundred miles they had covered since leaving the coast. But as their packs lightened and their bodies grew accustomed to the exercise, they had settled into an easy pace that took them steadily toward their destination. They were both tanned and fit and lean, although Dirk suspected they didn't smell terribly good after three weeks wearing the same clothes and without the chance for a proper bath.

Dirk was quite enjoying the journey, although the lack of any news about what was going on in the rest of the world made him a little nervous. For all they knew, Antonov had invaded Mil, or burned every city in Dhevyn to the ground, or denounced his throne and turned into a hermit while they were cut off from civilization. He was looking forward to reaching Bollow, where they would have a chance to find out what had happened in their absence.

They had camped out most of the way, swinging well clear of Avacas and taking the back roads through the smaller farms and villages, slowly wending their way north through Senet. For most of the journey since Talenburg, the Ruska Lake had been their constant companion in the distance as they followed the shoreline toward Bollow. They kept away from the main road close to the lake, though. Their forays into the few towns they had been unable to avoid had been uneventful, although Tia gleefully insisted on calling him Little Antonov whenever they were not alone.

Without even discussing it, they had fallen into a routine of walking, resting, walking and stopping each night when the first sun rose. The weather was warm and they often didn't bother with a fire, unless Tia had managed to bring down a rabbit or a bird during the day with her bow.

Dirk was privately in awe of Tia's casual proficiency with a bow and arrow. She seemed to put so little effort into hitting whatever she aimed at. He'd never had much to do with archery. The small amount of weapons training he had received as a boy in Elcast from Master Kedron had been with a sword, which was the weapon of choice for most highborn sons.

Tia had been on her best behavior at the outset, but after a while, with nobody but each other for company for days at a time, they had unconsciously put aside their bickering. Dirk couldn't be bothered arguing with her, and Tia seemed unable to maintain her belligerent posture if he gave her nothing to gripe about. For much of the way they traveled in companionable silence, and when they did talk, by unspoken agreement, they kept to subjects that were unlikely to cause an argument.

There was also the question of their mutual survival. Tia was prone to quick anger and even quicker judgments, but she wasn't stupid. She knew that their best protection lay in watching one another's back, and she seemed determined to keep up her end of the bargain. She still couldn't resist the odd jibe about

Dirk's friendship with Kirshov Latanya, and she positively relished the pained look on his face when she called him Little Antonov. But she had not said a word about Johan's death since that night on Elcast, when she had discovered for herself what it felt like to kill someone for the sole purpose of saving him from intolerable pain.

"How much money do we have left?" Tia asked as they stopped on the rise of the last of the foothills to look down on Bollow. The many-spired city sat on the shores of Lake Ruska, the long, narrow body of water that stretched from Talenburg in the south, all the way to Omaxin in the north, some two hundred miles away yet. Dirk thought the inland sea must have been a river once, which was trapped during some cataclysmic geological event in the distant past. Perhaps the same volcano that destroyed Omaxin had been responsible for turning the Ruska River into the Ruska Lake.

"What?" Dirk asked absently, when he realized Tia had spoken.

"I want a bath. Badly."

"There's a whole lake down there," he pointed out. "Why not just go for a swim?"

"Because I want to be *clean,* Dirk, not just wet. I want to wash my hair with real soap. I want to put on clean clothes." She looked him up and down. "You'd seriously benefit from a bath, too, my lad. And a shave. Don't ever grow a beard, by the way. You'd look ridiculous."

"I suppose we can spare the coin, if it means that much to you," he said, self-consciously scratching at the stubble on his chin.

"We're going to eat at a decent inn, too," she declared. "I'm sick of rabbit. I'm sick of pigeon. And if I never see another piece of black bread or goat's cheese as long as I live it will be far too soon."

"That, I have to agree with," he said with a smile. "Although once we get past Bollow, we may look fondly on our days of rabbit and black bread. It's supposed to be pretty barren up north."

"We'll worry about it later," Tia shrugged. "After we're clean."

By late afternoon they were in Bollow. They looked around with interest as they headed toward the center of town, searching for somewhere to stay. The city was one of the oldest on Ranadon and it wore its great age like an elegant but declining old maid desperately clinging to her last vestige of beauty. The streets were paved with granite and bordered by sheltered walkways, their vine-covered trellises held up by slender, fluted pillars linked together by archways carved with a strange script that Dirk couldn't read.

"You're gawping again," Tia warned, as his head swiveled in amazement. The city was in decline, but it must have been glorious once. He couldn't help staring.

"This place must have been stunning when it was first constructed."

"I suppose," she agreed disinterestedly.

The day was bright, the weather much less humid this far north. The people of Bollow had a purposeful air about them, as if everyone had something to do or somewhere to be. Although it was almost first sunrise, the street markets were still in full swing, and showed no sign of ending any time soon. They crossed the busy streets, two anonymous travelers in a city that was full of them, heading toward the majestic domed temple that was the centerpiece of the whole city. The dome reached up twelve or thirteen stories and was visible from almost everywhere in the city. It reminded Dirk of Elcast Keep.

"Who do you suppose built Bollow?" he asked.

"I don't know. I don't really care, either."

"But don't you ever wonder?"

"About who built Bollow? It's never even crossed my mind."

"Not just Bollow. Elcast Keep. Parts of Avacas. The Elcast levee wall. The old library in Nova before it was destroyed. Omaxin. All of those places have been around for thousands of years. Don't you ever wonder how they came to be there?"

She looked at him for a moment, then rolled her eyes. "You are *so* like Neris sometimes."

By the tone of her voice, Dirk realized she didn't mean it as a compliment. "It's not an unreasonable question," he said, a little defensively.

"Dirk, this may come as something of a shock to you, but most people don't spend their every waking moment trying to solve all the riddles of the universe. In fact, some people even go as far as not caring about things like that at all."

"How can you *not* wonder about it, though? I mean it's—" Dirk stopped midsentence as he stared up the street and caught sight of several yellow-robed Sundancers walking toward them. The figure in the lead was slightly stooped, his long beard brushing the jeweled belt at his waist. Dirk didn't know the two aides that walked behind him, but he certainly knew who the old man was.

"Dirk? What's wrong?"

"We'd better get out of sight."

Tia spotted the approaching Sundancers and understood immediately. She glanced around, then grabbed Dirk's wrist, and pulled him into a shadowed alcove between two shops on the other side of the street. Dirk pressed himself against the wall, turning his face to the shadows. Tia's short curls tickled his nose as he tried to dissolve into the masonry. He was all but breathing in her ear.

"Don't you even *think* of kissing me," she warned in a whisper as the Sundancers passed by. Dirk hid his smile. Apparently, she had not forgotten the last time they had hidden in an alley together. They waited for a moment or two, then Tia turned to look at him.

"So why are we dodging Sundancers now?" she asked.

"The old man in the lead? The one with the beard? That was Paige Halyn."

"The Lord of the Suns himself?"

He nodded, glancing down the street to make certain the Sundancers had not turned back. "I've met him before. In Avacas."

"Your list of friends grows ever more frightening, Little Antonov. Do you think he saw you?"

"No. But we shouldn't hang around Bollow too long. I forgot that he lives here."

She adjusted the pack she was carrying and frowned. "I don't care if the High Priestess has decided to build a summer house here. I'm not leaving this place until I'm clean and fed. The Lord of the Suns doesn't know me from a bottle of *vod'kun*. I don't have to hide from anyone."

"We just need to be alert."

"You be alert," she muttered impatiently as she pushed past him, back into the street. "I'm going to be clean."

They found an inn not long afterward that met Tia's exacting standards, in that it had good food, clean beds and baths so deep you could swim in them. Dirk left her happily soaking away the grime of their last few weeks on the road and slipped out to take care of an errand of his own.

By the time Dirk left the inn the second sun had begun to set. He headed toward the center of the city slowly, hoping to appear nothing more than another visitor, overwhelmed by Bollow's beauty and diversity (or gawping, as Tia would have said). It was not difficult to find what he was looking for. The dome of the massive temple was like a beacon. Every road in the city eventually led to it.

He had quite deliberately not bathed yet, guessing that if he accidentally bumped into anybody who remembered Dirk Provin from Avacas, they would not associate this grubby, unshaven peasant with the well-dressed young man who had lived under Antonov's patronage in the palace. It was a reasonable assumption. He had caught a glimpse of himself in the window of a shop a couple of streets past the inn and barely even recognized himself.

As he neared the plaza that surrounded the temple, the stalls grew more numerous, the merchants more boisterous. Bollow, it seemed, did much of its commerce after first sunrise, which meant Dirk would have to wend his way through countless stalls and a dense crowd to reach his destination. After the solitude and open spaces of the last few weeks, he found the task quite daunting. It was nerve-wracking, being in such close confines, surrounded by strangers, never knowing if someone had recognized him. There was the added worry that Tia might have decided to follow him, too, although when he left her, he doubted she would emerge from her bath anytime soon. But he would not put it past her. Perhaps not unwisely, Tia did not trust him much, and he was quite certain he would not be able to offer a satisfactory explanation if she discovered where he was heading now.

Dirk crossed the broad paved plaza in front of the temple with his head down, deliberately slowing his pace as he reached the steps leading up to the gilded doors that stood open and welcoming to all who wished to offer the Goddess their prayers. He stepped into the temple and halted just inside the entrance. At the other end of the massive hall, Paige Halyn stood with his arms outstretched, offering a prayer of thanks to the Goddess for another day that the second sun had risen, beseeching her to ensure that it rose again tomorrow. Dirk had seen Brahm Halyn perform the same ritual in Elcast every sunrise since he was a small child. It was the Shadowdancers who had perverted what was an essentially harmless creed that promoted respect for all living things into something that required human sacrifices.

He worked his way around the edge of the circular hall until he was close to the door of the antechamber where Paige would retire when he finished his prayers. The old man's voice was rasping and unenthusiastic as he went about his ritual. Dirk suspected that the Lord of the Suns had long ago given up hoping that he would ever have control over his religion again, and if he could not control that, what hope did he have of making a Goddess heed his words?

Paige finished his prayers and leaned forward to kiss the two beaten gold suns on the altar, then turned and smiled at the smattering of worshippers who still kept their faith in the Sundancers. He had long ago lost most of his followers to the Shadowdancers. Why follow an old man who offered nothing but vague promises, when they could follow a priestess who brought back the second sun? Why subscribe to a religion that required you to stop and pray at sunrise, twice a day, when you could follow one that required nothing more of you than to rut like a stallion once a year at an orgy?

There was no contest, really.

Paige Halyn made his way slowly toward the antechamber. Dirk waited until the door had almost swung shut before he slipped in behind him.

The Lord of the Suns turned at the sound of the door closing. He squinted a little at Dirk, as if he was shortsighted, and then gasped in surprise. *"You!"*

"My lord," Dirk greeted him, taking a step farther into the room.

Paige Halyn backed away from him in fear. "One shout from me and my people will come running," he warned.

"I'm not here to harm you, my lord."

"Then why are you here? I want nothing to do with you, boy. Leave!"

Dirk stepped a little closer. Maybe it was a good thing Paige Halyn was frightened of him. "I need your help, my lord."

"My help?" he scoffed. "What could the Lord of the Suns do to aid the Butcher of Elcast?"

"I need you to get a message to the High Priestess for me," Dirk said.

Chapter 42

Dirk emerged from the temple a little over an hour later, feeling relieved that he had finally done what he probably should have done two years ago. He felt more than a little guilty, too. It was going to be hard on Tia when she realized what he had set in motion. Perhaps he should warn her ... then again, she would probably slit his throat before he got halfway through his explanation, so maybe it wasn't such a good idea to mention it.

The second sun was gone, and the evening market in the square was well under way in the red light of the first sun as he pushed his way back through the stalls toward the inn. He was about halfway across the plaza when he spied a troop of Senetian soldiers heading in his direction.

The stalls around him were mostly silversmiths and gem merchants, but over to the left was a multicolored pavilion filled with people. They all appeared to be watching some sort of contest in the tent, and occasionaly would break out into an enthusiastic cheer. As it was the most crowded place nearby, Dirk slipped between the two nearest stalls and ducked into the tent. He pushed through the crowd until he was certain he was hidden from view, and then turned his attention to the contest he had inadvertently come to witness.

There was a small podium in the center of the tent where two men sat. One of them was a heavyset man with an impressive beard, dressed in a flamboyant robe of purple embroidered with golden sigils. The man sitting opposite him at the table was much younger, dressed in a simple shirt and trousers. His fingers were stained with black ink, as if he was a scribe or some sort of clerk. He was staring intently at a large checkered board that sat on a table between the two men, which looked like two chessboards placed edge to edge. Behind the scribe stood another young man similarly dressed, and the two consulted each other frequently before making a move.

The pieces on the board were made of carved wood, painted black on one side, white on the other, and marked with numbers. Some of the pieces were squares, some were circles and others were triangles. There was also a stack of pieces on the board in front of each player. As Dirk watched, the young scribe finished his discussion with his friend and then moved a white circle to capture a black one next to it. He then turned the piece over so that it was now white and another cheer rose from the crowd.

"Fools!" the man next to him remarked scornfully. "They'll never win by assaulting."

"What are they playing?" Dirk asked.

"Rithma," the man told him, glancing at Dirk curiously. Then he pointed to the large bearded man in the theatrical purple robe. "That's Ingo the Invincible. Nobody's ever beaten him."

"So why do they keep trying?" Dirk asked.

The man pointed to the opposite corner of the pavilion where another large bearded man stood guarding a small chest sitting on an upturned barrel. "'Cause there's a pot of over three hundred dorns to the first person who can beat Ingo with a greatest triumph."

"What's a greatest triumph?"

The man shook his head. "You're not from around here, are you lad?"

"I'm from Avacas," Dirk explained.

The man nodded in understanding, as if anyone from Avacas would automatically be stupid. "A greatest triumph is the hardest win," his companion explained. "You need to wipe out your opponent's pyramid with your four pieces lined up on his side of the board to form all three progressions at the same time."

Dirk looked at the game thoughtfully then glanced over at the chest. Three hundred dorns was an awful lot of money. He and Tia barely had ten dorns left and they still had to buy supplies for the rest of the journey north. Returning to the inn with more money than they could possibly spend might also assuage his guilt a little...

"Explain the rules to me," he said.

"Well, white always goes first," the man told him. "The circle pieces can move one square in any direction, horizontally, vertically or diagonally. The triangle pieces can move two places and the squares move three. Now, those stacks that each player has are called pyramids and they're made up of other pieces, but they can only move the same way as their base piece can go."

"Can you jump your opponent's piece?"

The Bollow man shook his head. "No. You need a clear path. And you're not allowed to shorten it, either, or make turns."

"But you can capture them, right?" Dirk guessed, watching the young scribe turn over yet another piece belonging to Ingo so that the white side was uppermost.

"Aye. A captured piece can be turned over and used by you."

"So the object of the game is to capture as many of your opponent's pieces as possible?" Dirk asked.

"Sort of," the man agreed. "You see, there are four ways to capture your opponent's pieces: assault and ambush or sally and siege. In assault, you can capture and replace any piece of equal value. Now an ambush is when you have any higher-numbered piece next to his lower-numbered pieces whose sum or product are equal to it."

Dirk nodded and listened as the man explained the rest of the rules, and began to understand why Ingo the Invincible had never been beaten. The man spoke of sallying and sieges, of captured pieces and attacking pyramids, and of pyramids that could be captured by their total, the value of their bases, one layer at a time, or the sum of several layers at a time.

"So how do you win?"

"Well, there are eight possible ways to win, five lesser victories and three greater victories. The first lesser victory is called—"

"But you don't win the pot for the lesser victories, do you?"

"No, of course not, I just thought..."

"Tell me about the greatest triumph then."

The man shrugged. "All the greater triumphs require lining up at least three pieces in an arithmetical progression or a geometrical progression or a harmonic progression, and it can't be done until Ingo's entire pyramid has been captured. A great triumph is when you have three pieces lined up to form one of the progressions. The greater triumph is if you manage to get four pieces lined up to form two of the progressions simultaneously. The greatest triumph—and the pot—is four pieces lined up on Ingo's side of the board to form all three progressions."

"Does it matter if he manages to recapture any of the pyramid pieces?"

"No. Pyramids can't be reassembled."

Dirk thought about if for a moment. It seemed fairly straightforward. He just needed to remember the rules. The mathematics involved in the game did not faze him in the slightest, but the rules were rather convoluted. The problem was he didn't want to draw any undue attention to himself by climbing up onto a podium in a crowded tent and taking on the unbeatable Ingo the Invincible.

"Have you ever played?" he asked the man beside him.

"Aye," the man nodded with a smile. "Quite a bit. But Rithma's a game for mathematicians and philosophers. Ask anyone in Bollow and they'll tell you I'm a bit of a philosopher, but I've not got a head for the numbers."

"But you're allowed an adviser, aren't you?" he asked, pointing to the young man giving the scribe directions about where to place the pieces.

The man looked at him quizzically. "You're not suggesting I play with you advising me, are you, lad? You don't even understand the rules."

"No, I don't," Dirk agreed. "But I understand the mathematics. Care to give it a try? We can split the pot if we win."

The man thought about it for a moment and then broke into a broad grin and offered Dirk his hand. "My name's Davros. What's yours?"

"Little Antonov," Dirk replied with a grin, accepting the handshake. "What's the stake to play?"

"Ten dorns."

"I've only got five," Dirk lied. He wasn't going to gamble every last dorn he owned. It seemed only fair that Davros share some of the risk.

Davros patted his pockets with a frown. "I've not got a purse on me at present. Here! This should make up the stake." He pulled a slender silver chain from the pocket of his vest and held it up for Dirk to examine. At the end of chain was a tiny bow and arrow, wrought of fine silver.

"It's very pretty," Dirk remarked, not sure of its value.

"It's just a trinket, really," the older man shrugged. "I made it for my niece, but she's got so much jewelery now she'll not appreciate it. Tell you what—if we win, you can keep it and I'll

buy her something really impressive with my share of the winnings."

"That seems fair."

"Are you sure you want to try this?"

Dirk nodded.

"Let's do it then," Davros agreed with a laugh.

It took Ingo another three or four moves to beat the young
scribe and his friend. The two young men walked from the
table, looking forlorn and rather surprised that they had been
beaten. Ingo rose to his feet and accepted the applause of the
crowd in a manner that reminded Dirk sharply of Marqel, back
when she was just a simple acrobat on Elcast. It was something
to do with performers, he thought. They all had that same manner, that same hunger for acknowledgment, for public acclama-
tion.

"So who's next?" Ingo called to the crowd.

"That'd be me!" Davros called back, stepping up to the
podium.

Ingo turned and smiled benevolently at him. "Ah, my old
friend Davros the Silversmith! Haven't you suffered enough
public humiliation?"

"Apparently not," Davros replied. The crowd laughed and
applauded him as he took the seat opposite Ingo and began to
reset the board. Dirk moved around behind his chair and studied the placement of the pieces carefully.

"I see you've brought reinforcements this time," Ingo said,
glancing at Dirk as he resumed his seat.

"This is Little Antonov," Davros said, by way of introduc-
tion. "He's from Avacas."

"Then this shouldn't take very long at all," said Ingo.
"Your move, Davros. White always goes first."

Chapter 43

Alenor had never seen a corpse before. She had never seen a body so devoid of humanity or eyes so blank and lifeless. The dead man was laid out on a slab in a small room at the back of the cells in the detention block that the Queen's Guard used to hold criminals awaiting the queen's justice. This was the first time she had been in this part of the barracks. The roughly dressed stone walls stank of stale urine and fear, which was only partly masked by the sharp smell of lye soap.

She was a little surprised that the smell of the mortuary or the sight of the cadaver didn't make her swoon. Wasn't that the appropriate thing for ladies of good breeding to do when confronted by something so brutal?

Alenor didn't know who the corpse was. The freshly dead body had been provided by the Brotherhood in exchange for concessions from the Queen's Guard that Alenor was sure she didn't want to know about. The man had been in his late thirties, she guessed. His hair was dark brown, his half-open, lifeless eyes an unusual shade of green, but other than that, there was nothing remarkable about him. He had died badly, though, obviously the victim of some terrible torment at the hands of his executioners. She wondered what he had done to run afoul of the Brotherhood.

"Who is he?" the Lion of Senet asked.

Alenor looked to Alexin for the answer.

"His name was Jules Stark," the captain informed him. "He was a petty thief, a gambler and a drug runner. We captured him during a raid on a dust den near the wharves."

Alenor had heard of dust dens. They were usually hidden in out-of-the-way places in the seedier parts of the city, and provided a haven for those who craved an illegal dose of poppy-dust, along with those who traded in it.

"And why do you think that this corpse would be of any interest to me?" Antonov asked.

"Because we found this on him, your highness," Alenor said, handing him a small envelope.

Antonov accepted it from her and examined the broken seal before opening it. He pulled out the folded sheet of parchment inside and took a few moments to read the contents of the letter, his expression betraying nothing. Alenor knew what the letter said. She had helped Alexin compose it. It had been quite a chore to come up with the right words—vague enough to make the letter appear genuine, yet specific enough to convey exactly what they wanted.

Antonov looked up at her. "You've read this?"

Alenor nodded. *Over and over,* she was tempted to say. "Yes, your highness."

"And what do *you* think it means?"

"I wasn't sure, your highness. That's why I ordered my guard to interrogate him."

Antonov looked down at the broken, battered corpse. "Your guard is as ham-fisted as they are incompetent, Alenor. They killed him."

"But not before we learned what we wanted to know, your highness," Alexin pointed out, looking a little offended.

"Which was?" Antonov prompted impatiently.

"Stark is Damitian. He'd just arrived in Kalarada when we apprehended him. It turns out he's been supplying poppy-dust to a select list of customers in Kalarada for years. Most of his clients were merchants, even a few palace functionaries. Some of the names we extracted from him were Senetian, your highness."

Antonov did not look pleased. "And the others?"

"Nobody really important. Except for one name."

"Do you have a particular taste for the dramatic, Captain, or are you trying to drag this out for as long as possible just to irritate me?"

"The name he gave was Neris Veran," Alenor blurted out, suddenly fearful for Alexin.

Antonov turned to look at her. "Neris Veran is dead."

"Not according to this man," Alexin said. "He claimed to know him; claimed that he'd seen him as recently as a few weeks ago. In Damita. According to Stark, he fled to Damita at the end of the War of Shadows and has been enjoying the protection of Prince Oscon ever since."

It was not an unreasonable scenario. Oscon of Damita had been the only ruler of means to side with Johan Thorn, although since being defeated on the battlefield, the old prince had retreated into exile, leaving his son Baston to rule his principality. Damita was still nominally an independent nation, but with Baston on the throne, it was hard to tell where Damita ended and Senet began.

"And you expect me to believe that this man was supplying Neris Veran with poppy-dust?"

Alenor shrugged helplessly, her innocence all the more convincing because she was genuinely afraid of what she had got herself involved in. "I don't know, your highness. I don't even know if the information is genuine."

"It might be a clever ruse by the pirates to throw me off the scent."

"Really?" she asked, suddenly feeling faint. *This is never going to work. He's going to realize this man has been dead for too long. He's going to know that he didn't die here under interrogation. Somebody probably saw them bringing in the body. He probably knows everything and is just toying with us, to see how deeply we're involved . . .*

"You've been duped, Alenor," Antonov announced suddenly.

"Your highness? I . . . I don't understand."

Antonov smiled at her indulgently. "Of course you don't understand, my dear. That's why you should have come to me as soon as you arrested this man, not let your bumbling Guardsmen handle it."

"Sire, we interrogated the man for hours," Alexin objected.

"And learned precisely what he wanted you to hear, Captain. Interrogation is an exact science, and I seriously doubt that any of your men has the experience to do it properly."

"But why would someone try to do such a thing?" she asked, her confusion quite genuine.

"You're to be married soon, Alenor. There are any number of people who'd like to prevent that from happening."

"But the letter—"

"A carefully worded plant designed to pique my interest. It's obviously not genuine. The grammar is far too exact, the language much too fluent, to be the work of a barely educated petty thief." Antonov looked down at the corpse again with a frown. "I suspect the intent was to make us think this man knew where Neris Veran was, in the belief that I would drop everything and go charging off to Damita to search for him."

"But what if the information is genuine?" she asked.

He shook his head. "Neris is dead, Alenor. For years Johan Thorn was able to distract me by making me think otherwise. This is simply proof that they have nobody with even a fraction of his wit to lead them now." Antonov laughed softly. He appeared genuinely amused. "As if I would fall for anything so clumsy."

"What should we do?"

Antonov smiled at her. "There's no need for you to worry about that, Alenor. I'll take care of it."

She nodded slowly and lowered her eyes so he could not see her fear. Fortunately, it made her look submissive, rather than deceitful. "I'm sorry I didn't bring this man to your attention sooner, your highness. I'll know next time."

"I'm sure you will. Come now; let's return to the palace. These gloomy dungeons are no place for a young lady."

Alenor nodded meekly and accepted the arm the Lion of Senet offered her. She kept her eyes fixed firmly on Antonov, afraid that if she caught Alexin's eye, she would betray them all.

Antonov had not believed them, but according to the message the Baenlanders had sent her, that didn't really matter. It was not actually Antonov this intrigue had been designed to trap. All she could do now was wait and let the seeds they had planted sprout in more fertile soil.

In fact, nobody would know if their ploy had been successful until Antonov had a chance to speak to Belagren.

Chapter 44

Tia had developed a theory about human behavior over a number of years, mostly based on her observations of Neris. As far as she could tell, the human brain had a finite capacity. You could only fit so much into one head and, according to her theory, high intelligence came at a price. A person's intelligence, she hypothesized, was in direct proportion to his common sense, and the more you had of one, then the less you seemed to have of the other.

She felt her theory had been totally vindicated when she emerged clean and contented from her bath, only to learn from the innkeeper that her "brother" had left a message saying he was going for a walk to have a closer look at Bollow's unique architecture.

Tia was quite willing to accept that, like her father, Dirk Provin had one of those odd minds that saw things nobody else could see. She had overheard enough of his conversations with Neris to know the two of them shared a love for something most people could not even comprehend (although in truth, it was the conversations she *had not* overhead that really worried her). Neris had tried to explain his fascination with numbers to her once. He had spoken of the elegance of mathematics, of the beauty and simplicity of something so pure that it could never be corrupted.

To Tia, he had sounded like a man in love.

But having the ability to calculate in your head how much the world weighed did not excuse one for acts of blind stupidity, which was what Tia considered Dirk's little excursion to be. A few hours before, he had been diving into alleys to avoid the Sundancers, and now he was off on a trip to see the sights. The sheer idiocy of it left her gasping.

What if he was recognized? What if he inadvertently ran afoul of the City Guard? Or worse, what if he was up to something? Suppose at this very moment he was betraying her? Perhaps, any minute now, the City Guard would come marching through that door to arrest her...

It's my fault, she realized. *I should never have let him out of my sight.*

"Your brother's back, miss," the innkeeper informed her, pointing to the entrance of the taproom. He was a heavyset man with a barrel chest and quick eye for the needs of his customers. Since she had inquired about her "brother's" whereabouts, he had been watching the door almost as closely as Tia.

Tia's head spun round to find Dirk standing in the doorway, looking around the room for her. She waved to get his attention. As soon as he caught sight of her, he headed across to the small table she had commandeered near the kitchen door.

"Where have you been, Little Antonov?" she hissed as soon he sat down on the stool opposite.

"I thought I'd visit the Lord of the Suns and ask him to send a message to the High Priestess informing her of our plans," he told her blandly, raising his hand in the direction of the innkeeper to indicate he wanted a drink.

Tia glared at him. "You just can't give me a straight answer, can you? You've always got some glib, sarcastic comeback."

"Well, what did you *think* I was doing, Tia?"

"I thought you were probably..." she hesitated and then shrugged, feeling a little sheepish, "...doing something like sending a message to the High Priestess informing her of our plans, actually."

Dirk smiled. "Well, there you go. I didn't let you down."

She sighed heavily. "Where did you *really* go, Dirk?"

"I went for a walk."

"We've just walked four hundred miles," she reminded him. "And we've another two hundred to go. Isn't that enough for you?"

"It's a different sort of walking. I like new places. I like getting a feel for different cities."

"We're supposed to be saving the world, Little Antonov, not broadening your horizons." She stopped while the innkeeper placed a foaming tankard in front of Dirk and then waited until he had returned to his counter before continuing. "Just because you're highborn and you missed out on your grand tour of the mainland when you turned eighteen, doesn't mean you can use this little expedition to make up for it. What you did was stupid."

"And to think I was hoping you'd be in a better mood once you'd had a bath," he remarked, taking a sip from his ale.

"Don't try making this my fault. My mood was just fine until I discovered you'd gone sightseeing."

"I'm sorry."

"You damn well should be," she agreed.

He was silent for a moment, looking suitably chastened. Then he reached into his pocket. "Would you forgive me if I gave you a present?"

His question stunned her. "You bought me a present? *Why?*"

Dirk placed a small pendant on the table, attached to a fine silver chain. She picked it up curiously and discovered it was a tiny bow and arrow, wrought of fine silver wire.

The necklace was exquisite, and he had probably wasted their last coin on it. "How much did this cost?"

"Not as much as you think."

"That's not an answer. Did you steal it?"

He smiled. "No."

"Do we have any money left?"

"Lots, actually."

Tia fingered the delicate bow for a moment, thinking she had never seen anything so pretty. Then she frowned. "What have you been up to, Dirk?"

"I discovered a delightful new game called Rithma. Turns out I'm quite good at it."

"You've been *gambling?*"

"Not really. Gambling implies taking a chance. I was pretty sure I could win, so it wasn't much of a gamble at all."

"Don't split hairs. How much did you win?" she asked suspiciously. "Exactly."

"One hundred and eighty-seven silver dorns," he told her.
"And the necklace."

Tia was speechless. That would buy more than a few supplies. For that money, they could hire a coach and four to drive
them to Omaxin. "I can't believe you'd do anything so damn
stupid! Suppose you'd lost?"

"I told you. I knew I could win so it wasn't really gambling." He held out his hand for the pendant. "If you don't want
it, I'll take the necklace and the money back."

Tia glared at him. "That's right. Go back to the game and
offer to return your winnings. Then they'll be *certain* not to remember you."

"Good point. I guess you'll just have to keep it."

He looked far too smug. He must have known there would
be no way to return it without causing a fuss.

"I don't understand why you thought *I'd* want this. I'm not
some silly girl with nothing better to do than preen herself in
front of a mirror all day. I don't wear jewelry."

"I doubt if wearing a simple necklace will cause you to start
swooning, Tia."

Tia got the feeling that somewhere behind those steel-gray
eyes he was laughing at her. "What else did you buy?" she
asked, deciding it might be safer to change the subject.

"Nothing yet. I thought we could go through the markets
tomorrow before we leave and replenish our supplies. And unless you expect me to work out everything with a stick in the
dirt, we need to buy some writing materials, too. Parchment
and ink, maybe some charcoal sticks."

"Now that we can afford to," she snapped, jiggling the tiny
bow and its chain in front of him.

"Look, if it annoys you that much, I'll get rid of it," he suggested. "I might be able to sell it..."

"No," she declared, slipping the chain into her pocket.
"You're not going to do anything of the kind. You've caused
enough trouble already. I'm not going to allow you to com-
pound the damage by trying to make it better."

Dirk took another sip of ale and made no further attempt

to argue about it, which Tia thought a little strange. She sometimes thought Dirk quarreled with her just because he could.

"Why don't you go take a bath? You stink."

He took a large swallow of the ale, and then nodded and climbed to his feet. "Good idea. You'll be here when I get back?"

"Unlike some people, I don't find it necessary to wander off sightseeing every time I enter a new city."

He smiled. "Maybe you should. Your horizons could do with rather a lot of broadening."

Dirk left the table before she could respond to that, so she settled for calling him a few choice names under her breath to vent her wrath. The innkeeper, seeing that she was alone again, hurried to her table to see if she wished to order more ale. She declined the offer, deciding to drink the remainder of Dirk's unfinished ale instead.

She drank determinedly, then took the chain with its tiny silver bow and arrow out of her pocket and fingered it thoughtfully. She had never owned a piece of jewelry before. In Mil, jewelry was something you stole and then fenced to the Brotherhood for whatever you could get for it.

It really was a pretty little thing. But it was frivolous and she could not believe Dirk had risked their last remaining coin to win it. With a snort of disgust for Dirk and his stupid present, she slipped the chain over her head and tucked the pendant inside her shirt. The little bow rested just above her breast and the silver was warm against her skin.

She would keep it there until she decided what to do with it.

Chapter 45

It was a mixed blessing being away from Avacas and the Hall of Shadows, the High Priestess mused. On one hand, she didn't like being out of touch with what was happening in the capital. On the other hand, all the events of import appeared to be happening around Antonov at the moment, and wherever he was, so she would be.

She was filled with a deep sense of satisfaction, now that Morna Provin was finally dead. For years she had privately fretted about the wisdom of letting that treacherous bitch live, but was helpless to do anything about it. In some bizarre pact that only men seemed prone to making, Antonov had given Wallin his word that Morna would remain unharmed while the duke lived, and so she had, for nigh on twenty years.

But it was over now. The Queen of Darkness was dead and good riddance to her.

Interesting, though, that someone had put an arrow through her left eye, putting an early end to what had been, up to that point, a very entertaining spectacle.

Antonov was certain Dirk Provin was responsible. She had scoffed at the suggestion until she had learned the fate of the *Calliope*. The destruction of Antonov's ship was a particularly exquisite form of revenge. It would take someone who knew Antonov well to understand what his ship meant to him. Perhaps it *was* Dirk who killed Morna, although to make such a shot under pressure was not a skill that she thought the boy owned. He was a scholar, not a warrior, and the bow and arrow was the weapon of the lower classes. If Dirk had been responsible, she doubted he actually loosed the arrow that killed Morna himself. He must have had an accomplice. Probably one of his Baenlander cohorts.

That Marqel had stumbled across such amazing intelligence regarding his whereabouts was a stroke of good fortune that was long overdue. It was a pity that the girl had let the half-wit return to his ship, but to arrest him on Nova meant involving the Queen's Guard, and once that happened, Kirsh would have learned of it and the boy would have been handed straight over to the Lion of Senet. While Belagren enjoyed a cordial relationship with Kirshov, his first loyalty was to his father. It would never have occurred to him that the High Priestess might want or need news of Dirk Provin even more than Antonov.

Belagren would have dearly loved to get her hands on Dirk. Or find Neris Veran. She was not particularly bothered which. She needed one of them. She needed someone to get through that damn Labyrinth.

The gate that had killed three of her people by showering them with acid had finally been cleared, only to reveal yet another barricade farther along the tunnel. How many of those damn things had Neris constructed? They had broken through twelve gates so far. Surely this was the last one?

The cost of keeping her people in Omaxin was draining her, the constant need to justify the expenditure to Antonov even more so. The Lion of Senet had agreed to fund the expedition when she was at the height of her power. But as the years dragged on, he began to question both the need and the cost of the venture.

Realizing she had just read the same sentence three times, Belagren threw down the letter she was holding in disgust. It was from Rudi Kalenkov, the Shadowdancer she had left in charge of the excavation in Omaxin.

Rudi was a small, ferrety little scholar with a good eye for organization, but the letter contained nothing but bad news. The engineers who had been examining the latest gate estimated that to dismantle it was going to cost a small fortune, and who knew how many lives. She had long ago given up thinking that anyone *other* than Neris could actually open it, unless, by some unforeseen miracle, she was able to find Dirk Provin, and then somehow convince him to aid her. Rudi needed workers brought in—stonemasons, laborers and the like—and they all expected to be housed, and fed and paid.

"Bad news?" Madalan inquired from the desk by the window, looking up from the more mundane dispatches from Avacas that Belagren could not be bothered with.

"Is it ever anything else from Omaxin?" she grumbled. The High Priestess walked to the window and looked down over the crashing ocean far below. "Why doesn't it get any easier, Madalan?"

"It's the price we're paying for embarking on this course of action with only half the information we needed," Madalan reminded her.

"We've Ella to blame for that," Belagren snapped.

Madalan didn't answer her. The High Priestess looked down at her aide with a frown. "You're not agreeing with me."

"I'm not disagreeing with you," Madalan pointed out.

"You think it's my fault?"

"I think we're all responsible, in part. The excitement of our discovery overruled prudence, I fear."

"You'll be fearing a damn sight more if something occurs that we haven't forecast," Belagren warned. "Goddess, do you realize that I wake every morning before the second sunrise, just to assure myself that it happens?"

"Worrying won't make the second sun rise," Madalan said, with infuriating logic. "The next Age of Shadows may not even happen in our lifetime."

"And you don't think I need to *know* that for certain?" she demanded. "You don't think that I would love nothing more than to go to Antonov tomorrow and assure him that his sacrifice was worth it? That in return for the life of his son the Goddess has assured me there'll not be another Age of Shadows for a thousand years?"

"Why not tell him that anyway?"

"Because with my luck the very next day the damn second sun will disappear again!"

"It's got to be worth consideration, though. I don't really understand all that stuff Neris told us, but I do recall that he drew a very big circle in the dirt. Presumably, the next Age of Shadows isn't due for a long time yet."

"I can't build a whole religion on a probability, Madalan."

"Not when sex, drugs and human sacrifices work so much better," the older woman agreed wryly.

Belagren turned on her savagely. "Don't say that! Not even in jest. You're the right hand of the High Priestess of the Shadowdancers! Do you realize what would happen if people thought *you* had no faith?"

"I have faith," Madalan assured her. "Mostly in your ability to turn every circumstance to your advantage. You'll find a way to deal with this, Belagren. You always do. Besides, you might end up finding the Provin boy. *If* Marqel's information is correct. Not that I trust a lot that comes out of the mouth of that sly little bitch."

Belagren smiled briefly. "But she's *our* sly little bitch. Actually, I think I'm starting to grow quite fond of her. Do you believe she had nothing to do with Caspona and Laleno dying?"

"Not for a minute," Madalan declared.

"Neither do I," the High Priestess agreed. "But she's covered her tracks well."

"A little too well for my liking," Madalan complained. "Be careful, Belagren. She could turn on us just as easily."

"Don't worry," Belagren assured her old friend. "I can handle one grasping little Dhevynian thief."

The assurance did not satisfy Madalan much, but before the other woman could answer, there was a knock at the door. Belagren impatiently called permission to enter.

"My lady?"

"Yes, Marqel?"

"There is a messenger here from the mainland. From the Lord of the Suns."

Belagren glanced at Madalan and rolled her eyes. "Just what I need! More trouble from that senile old fool in Bollow."

"It's not like Paige to send you anything," Madalan pointed out with a curious frown. "He can barely bring himself to speak your name."

"Shall I show him in, my lady?" Marqel asked.

"I suppose you'd better," she sighed.

Marqel returned a few minutes later with a young man of about twenty, wearing travel-stained leather trousers and a linen shirt, not the yellow robes of a Sundancer that she was expecting. The messenger bowed and handed over an envelope bearing the Lord of the Suns' seal. Belagren accepted it and looked at the young man curiously.

"You're not a Sundancer."

"No, my lady. I'm a courier. I usually work out of Bollow delivering messages between there and Talenburg."

"The Lord of the Suns employs couriers, now?" Madalan asked with a raised brow.

The young man shrugged. "I wouldn't know, my lady. I only know that I was paid to deliver this to the High Priestess as quickly as possible from Bollow."

"And is the Lord of the Suns expecting a reply?" Belagren asked.

"If he is, my lady, he didn't instruct me to wait for it."

Nodding thoughtfully, she dismissed the courier and broke the seal on the letter. She snapped the folded page open with a flick of her wrist, a little surprised to find it written in an unfamiliar hand. As she read the contents, the blood drained from her face. She was forced to sit down before she was halfway through it, feeling faint before she got to the end.

"My lady?" Marqel asked in concern.

"Get me wine, Marqel," she ordered, feeling light-headed. "A large one."

The young Shadowdancer hurried to obey. Madalan rose from her seat at the desk and walked across to Belagren.

"What's wrong?"

"Read it." Belagren was incapable of saying anything else. She thrust the letter at her old friend with a shaking hand.

Madalan read the letter, her eyes widening in shock. "This can't be genuine!"

"And if it is?" Belagren asked tonelessly.

"This is a trick! It has to be! Paige Halyn thought this up as some sort of desperate last-ditch attempt to discredit us!"

The High Priestess shook her head. "He's not capable of anything so inventive."

Marqel returned with the wine and handed it to the High Priestess. The girl was burning with curiosity, but was wise enough to say nothing. Belagren accepted the goblet and downed the entire contents in a swallow.

"Get me another," she ordered. "And find that messenger before he leaves the palace. I need to know how long ago he was dispatched from Bollow."

Marqel was smart enough not to question her orders. She

filled the wine glass again and left without so much as a hint of defiance. Perhaps she was finally learning her place.

"Belagren, there's an old saying, you know. If something seems too good to be true, then it probably is."

The High Priestess nodded. "Oh, don't worry, Madalan. I'm sure there's more to this than meets the eye."

"But—"

"But I can't ignore it. At worst, it means I will be able to give Antonov something he desperately wants."

"And at best?"

"At best, we are saved," the High Priestess told her aide, shaking with disbelief, almost too stunned to accept that, out of nowhere, a miracle had landed in her lap. "If this letter is genuine, we are saved."

"Perhaps," Madalan agreed doubtfully.

Marqel slipped back into the room and sketched a hasty curtsy. "Three weeks, my lady."

"What?"

"The courier, my lady. He left Bollow three weeks ago."

Madalan frowned. "That has to be some sort of record."

Belagren nodded. "Which means our young friend is already in Omaxin. Or so close to it that it scarcely matters."

"What are you going to do?" Madalan asked.

Belagren barely gave herself time to think about it. Time was the one thing she did not have.

"For now, I'm going to do as he asks, Madalan. I'm going to send a message by bird to Rudi today, and withdraw the Shadowdancers from Omaxin."

"And after that?"

"After that, as soon as this damn wedding is out of the way, I'm going to have a word with the new Regent of Dhevyn."

"Kirshov? Is it wise to involve him in this?"

"Not only wise, but essential, according to *that*," she said, pointing to the letter Madalan was holding. When her old friend seemed unconvinced, Belagren smiled and looked at Marqel, thinking of a day several years ago on Elcast, when a desperate young man had come to her for help to save a young thief from the lash.

"Don't worry about it, Madalan. Kirshov Latanya owes me a favor."

Chapter 46

The northernmost town in Senet, and the last real outpost of civilization before they reached the ruins in Omaxin, was the small town of Tawell. It took Dirk and Tia close to two weeks to cross the grasslands of northern Senet bordering Lake Ruska, which separated Omaxin from the ancient city of Bollow. Game was sparse and they were limited by what they could carry. Their meager supplies had dwindled alarmingly by the time they reached the village. Unless the departing Shadowdancers left their excess food stores behind in Omaxin, Dirk thought, they were going to get very hungry trying to discover when the next Age of Shadows was due.

The barony of Tawell actually belonged to Alenor D'Orlon. It had been given to her as a child by the Lion of Senet while she was living in Avacas, and had been administered by Antonov's people in her absence ever since. As far as Dirk was aware, Alenor had never laid eyes on the place.

Not that there was much to see. The township was small: little more than an inn, a blacksmith and a few scattered houses. The manor house was closer to the lake, several miles from the town. Dirk was not keen on stopping in the village, but Tia was becoming concerned about their supplies. It wasn't as if they couldn't afford it, she pointed out tartly. Dirk bore her stings stoically, thinking she would be far angrier if she knew what else he had done in Bollow.

"The whole purpose of coming all this way on foot was not to draw attention to ourselves," he pointed out, as Tia walked beside him on the road leading into the village.

"That's why you sneaked out of the inn in Bollow and made a name for yourself playing Rithma, was it? To be inconspicuous?"

"Bollow was different," Dirk objected. "For one thing, it was a city a hundred times bigger than this place. They probably forgot about me an hour after I left the Rithma tent. They'll remember us here in Tawell for months."

"No, they won't," Tia assured him confidently.

"How do you know that?"

"Because we're not the only strangers in town."

As they neared the outskirts of the village, Dirk discovered Tia was right. There were a large number of wagons parked haphazardly on the common, brightly painted, in a wild cacophony of colors. The people around the wagons barely glanced at the two strangers as they walked along the road, more interested in setting up their own camp.

"Who are they?" Dirk asked.

He had never seen wagons like these before, or people dressed so strangely. The men wore large, loose trousers gathered at the ankles and tucked into short leather boots. The women wore similar shirts to the men, but most of them wore skirts that looked as if they were made of dozens and dozens of scarves tucked into the brightly enameled belts they wore.

"Sidorians, I think," Tia told him.

Sidoria was, on paper at least, an independent nation, but its population was almost entirely nomadic. As they had few cities worth conquering, Antonov had left his northern neighbor largely untouched, preferring to dominate the more fruitful islands to the south of the mainland.

"I didn't think they strayed into Senet if they could avoid it," he remarked.

"Well, we're pretty far north. I suppose they have to trade with someone." She glanced at him with a hopeful smile. "I hear their food is pretty good."

Dirk shook his head. "Now who's trying to broaden her horizons?" he accused.

"I'm merely heeding your advice. You were the one who said they'd remember us in Tawell for months. The Sidorians, now, they're nomadic. They'll be gone in a few days, back across the border. It won't really matter what they remember about us, will it?"

She actually had a very good point, but Dirk was disinclined to admit it, just on principle. "They don't look like they'd welcome strangers."

"How would you know?"

"I don't," he admitted. "It's just a feeling I have."

"So you're a seer now as well as a genius?"

Before he could stop her, Tia turned off the road and walked over to the nearest wagon, where a young mother was tending three small children. Tia spoke to her at length, turning to point at Dirk at one point in the conversation. He had no idea what she was saying to the Sidorian woman, but both of them broke into gales of laughter, which—he was certain—was at his expense. A little after that, Tia called him over with a wave of her hand.

"This is Risilka," Tia told him as he approached the two women warily. "She's invited us to dinner with her family."

"We've no wish to put you to any trouble," he assured her, thinking Tia incredibly rude for forcing herself on these people.

"You'll be no trouble, Little Antonov," Risilka promised him with a smile. "My father likes to hear about what's happening in the south, and it's not often we meet people who've come from there recently. Tasha tells me you play Rithma, too."

"Tasha seems to have told you quite a bit," he remarked with a frown, thinking that at least she'd had the sense not to use their real names. But that was about all the sense she had shown.

"He claims he's quite good at it," Tia informed her new friend with a smirk in Dirk's direction. She was enjoying this.

"Well, my father will put him to the test. And while the men are making fools of themselves trying to pretend they have brains, I will teach you how to dance, Tasha."

"Thanks for the offer, but I don't need to know how to dance," Tia replied quickly, looking rather alarmed.

"Of course you do," Risilka scoffed. "How else are you going to catch a husband?"

"Risilka's right, Tasha," Dirk agreed with a perfectly straight face. "How else *are* you going to catch a husband?"

Tia glared at him. "Why don't you go play your games with the other boys, Little Antonov?"

"Come," Risilka ordered. "I'll introduce you to my father and my husband. Then Tasha and I can take care of women's business."

Dirk followed Risilka without another word, deciding against making any further comment when he caught the dangerous say-one-more-word-and-I'll-kill-you look that Tia gave him.

Risilka's father, Verril, was a slender, weatherbeaten man with the most impressive mustache Dirk had ever seen. It took up half his face and drooped down over his chin, almost brushing the front of his intricately embroidered shirt. Her husband was a bigger man with a mustache well on its way to rivaling her father's. All the men, in fact, sported spectacular mustaches. Dirk quickly discovered that impressive facial hair was a mark of manhood among the Sidorians, and his clean-shaven chin marked him as a callow boy.

Risilka left him in the care of the men, who had gathered under the shade of a large, open pavilion, where they smoked their long carved pipes, played Rithma and relaxed, while the women got the camp set up and prepared the food.

"So you come from Avacas?" Verril asked as Dirk took a seat on the cushions surrounding the large, gloriously carved Rithma board. Risilka's husband, Lokin, was staring at the board intently, as his opponent, whose name Dirk didn't catch, made his move. Dirk glanced at the board, thinking neither man had a hope of beating the other, the way they were playing.

Dirk turned back to Verril and nodded. "That's right."

"You look Dhevynian, not Senetian," the Sidorian remarked. "And if that girl is your sister, then I'm the Lion of Senet." His comment sparked a round of laughter from the other men in the tent.

Dirk smiled. "I wouldn't have thought you'd met so many Dhevynians that you could tell the difference."

"Don't confuse ignorance with stupidity, boy. Just because we don't live in stone houses and read books like your people doesn't make us fools. Are you running away from her father or her husband?"

"Something like that," Dirk agreed.

Verril laughed and slapped him on the back. "Young love, eh! I can remember when I was young and foolish. The trouble is you marry them, and they have children and then you get to be just another chore on their list."

"Perhaps I shouldn't marry her then," Dirk suggested, thinking never a more prophetic suggestion had been made in living history.

"Too late for that, boy!" Verril declared with a slight frown. "You can't take a bite out of the fruit and toss it away. Once you've tasted it, then you're honor bound to finish what you started."

Dirk was tempted to tell Verril that he had not actually tasted anything, nor was he ever likely to, given the way Tia felt about him, but he thought better of it. Let the nomads think they were lovers on the run. It really didn't matter.

"I'll keep that in mind," Dirk promised.

"Good lad," Verril said, slapping him on the back again. "Now, let's see if you really can play Rithma, eh?"

Tia was right about one thing: Sidorian food was delicious. It was spicy, sweet and hot, although Dirk decided not to inquire too closely about exactly what type of meat he was eating. He had heard stories as a child that Sidorians ate horses, dogs and even rats, and didn't want to spoil his enjoyment of the meal by learning that they were true.

The men ate separately from the women, but once the second sun had set and the children were put to bed in the wagons, everyone gathered near the pavilion. Several musicians picked up their instruments, which were mostly drums and small cymbals, and began play.

Tia came to sit beside Dirk on the ground as the other women went to join their husbands or fathers. One of the women began to dance around inside the circle of people, with small cymbals attached to her thumb and forefinger on each hand. The woman had long dark hair and wore her skirt low on her hips, which left her midriff bare. She seemed to be able to move every muscle in her body independently of the others, making her multicolored scarf skirt shimmer and shake in a manner Dirk found rather intriguing.

"You're gawping," Tia told him, sounding a little put out.

Dirk glanced at her. "Did Risilka teach *you* how to dance like that?"

"Even if she did, I'm never likely to do anything like that in public. It's obscene."

"Actually, it's fascinating. Do you realize the muscle control she must have to be able to move like that?"

"No, I don't. But you seem to have worked it out in record time."

Dirk smiled at her. "You know, Verril thinks we're lovers on the run from your father."

"Really?" Tia replied archly. "I told Risilka that you'd jumped ship in Tolace and were running back to our mother in the north because you were homesick."

"Did she believe you?"

Tia thought for a moment and then shook her head. "Now that I think about it, probably not. Do you think we should stay here tonight, or push on?"

"I'd like to keep moving, but I don't think we're going to be able to escape our hosts quite so easily without offending them. They seem friendly enough, but have you seen the size of the swords some of these fellows carry? I'm pretty sure they're not decorative. I wouldn't like to give the impression we don't appreciate their hospitality."

She nodded glumly in agreement. "I think you might be right."

"The food was good though," he conceded.

"We'll push on tomorrow then."

Dirk looked at her curiously. "Is something wrong?"

Tia shook her head. "Not really. It's just..."

"Just what?"

She shrugged, as if she couldn't really put her feelings into words. "I don't know. Maybe it's because we're here among the Sidorians. They're so...carefree, I suppose. They don't give a damn about what's going on in the rest of the world. They don't care about the Goddess, or being invaded, or what the Lion of Senet is up to. They just enjoy themselves and get on with their lives."

"We'll get on with our lives someday," he assured her, not sure if that was what she wanted to hear.

Tia smiled skeptically. "You think so?"

Dirk nodded. "I promise."

"You sound pretty certain," she replied with a frown. "What do you know that I don't?"

Dirk shrugged and did not reply.

That was one question better left unanswered.

Chapter 47

They reached Omaxin a week later, but veered off the road some three miles out of the ruins to avoid detection. They had been making their way painstakingly for most of the morning through the windswept hills that bordered the black lava flows of the ruins. Although the ground was fertile, the wind blew most of the topsoil away, leaving the windward side of the slopes barren and rocky. A stiff breeze swept across the lake and the sun beat down on them relentlessly. It was a dry heat that seemed to burn as they inhaled it. They both wore Sidorian scarves wrapped loosely around their heads and shoulders to protect themselves, and Tia's nose was still peeling from an earlier bout of sunburn.

"The Shadowdancers! They're leaving!"

Dirk scrambled up the slope on his belly beside Tia and

looked down over the ruined city of Omaxin. "You sound surprised."

"I'm not surprised," she replied. "I'm astonished. I can't believe such a stupid, dangerous and altogether far too complicated plan actually worked."

"You should have a little more faith in me, Tia."

"Based on what, exactly?" she asked.

Dirk didn't reply. He looked back over the caravan that was slowly wending its way south along the shore of the lake, his gray eyes the same color as the still water. And just as uninformative.

"Do you suppose it's a trick?" she asked when his silence began to irritate her.

He shrugged. "It's an awful lot of trouble to go to, just to pretend they're leaving. Anyway, why would they *want* to pretend? Who are they trying to fool? Did you tell them we were coming?"

"Did *you*?" she retorted.

Dirk smiled. "Actually, I might have mentioned it in that letter I sent to the High Priestess informing her of our plans…"

Tia pulled a face at him. "That joke is getting pretty tired, Dirk."

"Yet you always react the same way," he remarked.

"That's because deep down, I still wonder, every now and again, if you really *are* joking."

He rolled onto his back and looked at her. "One of these days, you're going to have to admit I really am on your side, you know."

"And I will," she promised. "As soon as you do something to prove it."

"Such as?"

Tia shrugged. "I don't know, Dirk. But it would have to be something fairly spectacular to convince me."

"I'll see what I can arrange."

"Don't bother," she told him. "I kind of like the idea that one day you'll turn out to be a traitor and I'll finally get to slit your throat."

Dirk shook his head at her, but he was smiling. "You really are quite disturbed, aren't you?"

"A fact that you would be wise not to forget," she agreed sagely.

Dirk shook his head wordlessly and slid back down the slope to where their packs rested against the base of one of the few trees that had managed to gain a foothold in the face of Omaxin's relentless winds. Tia watched him, reminding herself to be cautious. Dirk Provin was more dangerous like this, she thought, than when he was actually wielding a blade. There were even times when she forgot that she shouldn't trust him.

The longer she spent in his company, the more she had to remain on her guard, finally seeing what Reithan and Lexie and Mellie and all the others who had fallen under his spell had seen in him. It didn't make him trustworthy, but it made him *believable,* and that was the real danger. When Dirk Provin was being charming, he was too good to be true.

"Do you think we should wait before going down there?"

He nodded. "A full day at the very least."

"I thought you said they weren't pretending?"

"I said it was unlikely, not impossible. We'll wait a day or two, just to make sure they really have left the area."

"Fine," she agreed, picking up her bow. "In that case, I'm going to see what I can bag for dinner."

"You'll not find much out here," he warned.

"I'll find something," she assured him. "And when I do, you're cooking it."

"Considering your skills as a cook mostly involve the production of charcoal, I suppose I'd better." He stood up and dusted off his trousers before picking up his pack. "It's a pity Risilka didn't offer to teach you how to cook, rather than dance."

She pulled a face at him, but did not rise to the bait. It was no secret that she was the worst cook on Ranadon. It had only taken a few days on the road together for Dirk to volunteer to do most of the cooking, probably out of respect for his stomach. Fortunately for both of them, Dirk could usually turn out something edible, given the right ingredients.

"You just wait here and mind the packs," she ordered. "I'm going to find something to kill."

It took several hours before Tia snagged a scrawny rabbit that ducked in and out of the rocky crevasses in the foothills surrounding Omaxin. When she did finally manage to get an arrow off, she only grazed its shoulder, forcing her to track it for another hour until she spied it crawling into a small opening hidden in a narrow gap between two tall boulders. A small cascade ran down the rocks and behind them a slightly larger opening that hinted at a cave behind the surprisingly cool water. She had to breathe in and squeeze herself sideways past the waterfall to get to the warren, and then crawl on her hands and knees to reach the wounded creature. It was an awful lot of effort to go to for one measly rabbit, but she was determined not to return to Dirk without something to show for her afternoon's work. She could imagine the look of smug superiority on his face if she returned empty-handed.

"Gotcha!" she declared triumphantly as her hand latched onto a limp, furry paw. She pulled the rabbit free as it gave its last gasping breath.

When she returned to the place she had left Dirk, he was nowhere to be found and their packs were gone. Looking around at the empty landscape, a thousand thoughts swirled through her mind, the foremost of which was: *That rotten little bastard has gone looking through the ruins without me.*

"It took you all afternoon to bag one puny rabbit?"

She spun around to find Dirk slipping down the slope behind her, carrying their packs over one shoulder, a large piece of the parchment they had bought in Bollow in his left hand.

"Where have you been?"

"I got bored waiting, so I thought I'd start sketching a rough map of the ruins."

For some reason, his perfectly reasonable explanation annoyed her even more than the fact that he had not been waiting where she left him.

"I thought you didn't want to go down to the ruins yet?"

"I didn't. You get a much better view from up here in the foothills."

She tossed the rabbit at his feet. "You're cooking, remember."

Dirk dropped the packs to the ground and picked up the rabbit. He held it up for a moment and then looked at her curiously. "What did you do? Run him down *all* afternoon? He looks like he died of exhaustion, poor creature."

"Just cook the damn thing, Dirk."

He smiled at her irritation. She turned her back on him.

"Tia!"

As she turned, he tossed the waterskin to her. She caught it by reflex.

"We need water."

Tia trudged back toward the little waterfall, wondering why she put up with Dirk Provin. If she had any brains at all, she would never have agreed to come here. It was probably all for nothing, anyway. There was no guarantee Dirk could learn the secrets Neris had so carefully hidden away. In fact, a part of Tia rather hoped that he couldn't. And it had taken them so long to reach Omaxin. She was reluctant to remind Dirk of the fact, but she was sure that today was the day that Alenor D'Orlon was supposed to marry Kirshov Latanya. By now the damage was done. Dhevyn had a Senetian regent and a child queen too in love with her prince to understand that he was going to destroy her nation, one island at a time.

She reached the waterfall and splashed through the shallow puddle at its base, holding the skin in the stream of cool water while she berated herself for being so foolish as to agree to this ludicrous plan. Admittedly, Dirk had been reasonably tolerable company for most of the journey, although she had a niggling suspicion about what he had really been up to when he disappeared in Bollow for more than three hours. At least he had proved he could play Rithma, so she was inclined to believe his story about how he acquired the money—and that silly necklace. Risilka's father had been quite impressed by Dirk's skill at the game.

Even more annoyed that she was wasting her time fretting

about him, Tia reached her hand through the waterfall to see how large the cave behind it was. When she could not feel the back of the cave with her arm, she stuck her face through the sheet of water and her eyes lit up with amazement.

"Mushrooms!"

Mushrooms were a rare treat on Ranadon. They did not like the light or the heat of Ranadon's two suns, and she had only eaten them once before at an inn in Kalarada, where they had cost a small fortune but tasted like sautéed heaven. These were a faintly gold color, their thick undersides plump and greenish. Inside the small dark opening, the smell was dank, almost like potatoes left to rot. Grinning with delight, she stepped through the water into the cave and gathered as many of the rare treats as she could stuff in her shirt. She finished filling the waterskin and headed back to Dirk, dripping wet but in a considerably better mood than when she had left.

"I found these," she told Dirk as she came up behind him, fishing her unexpected haul out of her shirt.

Dirk was kneeling on the ground skinning the gaunt rabbit. He turned and examined the mushrooms warily. "How do you know they're edible?"

"Don't the poisonous ones have red spots or something?"

"How would I know?"

"I thought you knew everything."

He frowned. "I really don't think you should eat them unless you're sure they're safe."

"Don't be such an old woman, Dirk. They'll be delicious."

"Fine," he shrugged. "But if you die from eating these things, don't blame me."

"You could eat them first," she suggested. "That way I'll know if they're edible."

"*Good plan*. If they're poisonous, I die, and if they're not, you get your treat anyway."

She sighed happily. "I can't lose, can I?"

He rolled his eyes, but he did not seem particularly upset. "Go fetch some firewood while I finish skinning this poor excuse for a rodent."

"Will you cook the mushrooms?"

"I'll cook the mushrooms," he agreed. "But they're all yours. I have an aversion to eating unidentified and possibly deadly fungi."

"Your loss," she shrugged.

"And don't think I'm going to hold your head for you while you puke when they turn out to be poisonous," he called after her.

She smiled suddenly and looked back at him. "You know, Dirk Provin, sometimes you're a bigger girl than I am."

Chapter 48

It took Alenor's servants the best part of an hour to free her from the crystal-beaded wedding gown and prepare her to greet her new husband on her wedding night. The wedding had been a spectacular affair, as was the coronation that followed. Although it was an open secret that Rainan would abdicate on Alenor's sixteenth birthday, there were more than a few unhappy mutterings during the ceremony. Mostly, however, the Dhevynian nobles present at the coronation kept their opinions to themselves. The fact that the hall was lined with Senetian soldiers, who outnumbered the Queen's Guard three to one, aided them considerably in their efforts.

Kirsh paced the anteroom, bored senseless by the wait, wishing protocol had allowed him to stay at the reception for a while longer. Then again, he thought, maybe it was a good thing he wasn't there. Kirsh had a duty to perform and he was determined to do it well. He would not come to Alenor drunk or reeking of wine. In fact, he had quite deliberately remained sober, drinking only watered wine at the reception, careful how much he consumed. This was Alenor's first time, and he was going to make it as easy and as pleasurable for her as he possibly could.

Kirsh consciously put Marqel out of his thoughts. He was

married now, and while he fully intended to keep Marqel as his mistress, he would do it discreetly, so as not to offend his wife. He was confident that she was unaware of his relationship with the Shadowdancer. Alenor was not the type to remain silent when she had something to say, and Kirsh knew that if Alenor had any idea about Marqel, she would most *definitely* have something to say about it.

He had thought it a little odd that Alenor had invited Marqel to Kalarada, but decided it was merely a stroke of good fortune. Marqel had been responsible for his rescue in Nova, and Alenor was obviously very grateful. She must have forgotten that night of the ball in Avacas, when she and Dirk caught them in the woods in a position that could only be described as compromising. Anyway, he told himself, if Alenor thought he and Marqel were lovers, there was no way she would have allowed the Shadowdancer within a hundred miles of her island.

Kirsh was confident he could manage the responsibilities of a regent, a wife and a mistress. His father was the Lion of Senet after all, and had kept the High Priestess as his mistress all of Kirsh's life, as well as a string of other beauties that had come and gone through Avacas, their tenure so brief, their faces so uniformly beautiful and vague, that they had barely impacted on Kirsh at all.

"Your highness?"

Kirsh turned from his pacing to find Dorra standing at the door to the bedchamber, while an army of servants filed from the room carrying Alenor's dress.

"The queen is ready for you now."

It took Kirsh a moment to realize Dorra spoke of Alenor. The coronation had only been a few hours before. He was not used to the idea that she was a queen. He hurried to the door that Dorra held open for him.

"Good night, your highness," she said with a curtsy and a knowing smile, before closing it behind him.

Alenor was standing by the window, bathed in the red light of the first sun. She was dressed in a beautifully embroidered, almost transparent dressing gown and matching nightdress, probably unaware that the red sunlight outlined her slender frame through the sheer fabric in a rather enticing fashion.

She turned when she heard the door close, her expression pensive.

"Hello, Kirsh."

Kirsh discovered himself suddenly lost for words. He had known this girl for most of his life; known he would one day marry her for almost as long. Yet now that it was done—now he was here with Alenor as his bride—he discovered he had no idea what to say to her.

"You...you looked beautiful today," he stammered.

She smiled faintly. "I'm glad you thought it worth the effort. That dress weighed more than I do."

He walked over to the window and stood beside her. "How does it feel to be queen?"

"I don't know, Kirsh. How does it feel to be regent?"

He smiled. "Ask me in a few days when I have writer's cramp from signing proclamations all day."

She looked at him curiously. "Is that all you think being regent requires of you?"

"Don't start," he begged. "I've had enough lectures recently from my father about the responsibility of being Regent of Dhevyn."

"Did you listen to any of them?"

"Alenor, let's worry about ruling Dhevyn tomorrow. Tonight is for us."

"You mean to do your duty then?" she asked in an odd tone.

He took her hand and raised it to his lips. "It's the most agreeable duty I've had in a long time, Alenor."

She let him pull her close, let him kiss her, but she remained still in his arms. She did not kiss him back. He lifted his mouth from hers and looked at her curiously for a moment. "What's the matter?"

When she didn't answer him, he smiled. "Are you frightened?" he asked gently. "I won't hurt you, Allie."

"Won't you, Kirsh?" she said, searching his eyes for something.

"Of course not, silly," he promised, lowering his head to kiss her again.

She put her hands on his chest and gently pushed him away. "It's a pity you didn't decide that before you took Marqel as your mistress."

Kirsh stared at her, aghast. "Allie, I don't—"

"Don't bother lying to me, Kirsh. This is *my* palace. You've been serving in *my* guard. You honestly think I'm not aware of every single move you make? Goddess, you really are a fool."

She walked away from him, to the small table where her servants had laid out refreshments. She poured a cup of wine and sipped it before turning to look at him.

"Alenor, whatever you've heard...I know where my duty lies."

"Your duty?" she repeated bitterly. "How do you think that makes me feel, Kirsh? Knowing that you think of me as your *duty*?"

He threw his hands up in exasperation. "I didn't mean it like that."

"I worshipped you," she told him, her pain making him cringe with guilt. "I adored you. You were the only thing that made it bearable when your father took me away from my home. You were the only reason I could stand living under your father's roof. You were all I ever wanted."

"I know, but—"

He ducked hurriedly as she hurled the goblet at him. It shattered on the wall behind him, leaving a red stain on the delicately hand-painted wallpaper.

"That's what makes it so intolerable!" she cried. "I never hid my feelings. You knew how I felt! Yet you took up with that thief anyway!"

Kirsh thought he might die from the accusation in her eyes. "I never meant to hurt you, Alenor."

"And you *won't* hurt me, Kirsh," she announced with quiet determination, her sudden burst of fury now under control. "Never again."

He nodded, resigned to his fate. "I'll end it," he promised.

Alenor shrugged. "I don't really care whether you end it or not."

"What do you mean?"

"Have your whore, Kirshov Latanya. But don't think you can have me, too. I am not a *duty*. And I won't settle for the left-overs from some other woman's table."

He crossed the room to her, tried to take her in his arms.

"Don't touch me!" she ordered coldly.

"You can't be serious!"

"I've never been more serious about anything in my life," she informed him. "I am Queen of Dhevyn now, and I will put up with you as regent, because I have no choice. But don't think for one minute that you will *ever* spend a night in my bed. I will not lie there with my eyes closed thinking of Dhevyn while you do your *duty* thinking of Marqel."

"Your *duty* is to produce an heir!" he reminded her angrily.

"There will be no heir, Kirsh. Certainly not one of Latanya blood. How you explain that to your father is entirely up to you."

"You have no idea what you're doing!" he accused. "My father won't tolerate you defying him like this!"

"I *dare* you to go to him! I dare you to tell him that I won't let you into my bed because I'm jealous of your mistress." She laughed harshly, genuinely amused by the suggestion. "What do you think he's going to do, Kirsh? He won't be angry with me. He likes me. In fact, I spent most of my growing years do-ing my utmost to *make* the Lion of Senet like me. He'll be an-noyed at you, certainly, but he's not going to hurt you. You *know* what he'll do, don't you? He'll remove the problem. Your pre-cious Shadowdancer will simply disappear off the face of Ranadon. She'll probably wash up on the shore somewhere be-tween here and Avacas, a nameless, faceless, bloated corpse..."

"All right!" he yelled. "You've made your point."

"Don't take that tone with me," she said with icy dignity. "I am your queen."

"You're a spoiled, jealous, spiteful child!" he retorted. "And you're going to ruin everything to get even with me be-cause I committed the crime of falling in love with someone who loves me because of *me,* not because my father happens to be the Lion of Senet and I'm their only hope of holding on to their pathetic little kingdom!"

If his words hurt Alenor, he could not tell. Nor, at that moment, did he particularly care.

She shook her head sadly. "Do you really believe she'd love you if you weren't a prince, Kirsh? Are you so gullible that you think Marqel the Magnificent isn't in love with *what* you are, not *who* you are?"

"You have no idea what you're talking about."

"Perhaps not," she conceded. "And if you want to keep telling yourself that she loves you for any other reason than the wealth and power she thinks she'll acquire as your mistress, then you go right on believing it. My only concern is that I have made my position clear."

"As crystal," he agreed bitterly.

"Then get out," she ordered calmly. "Go spend the night with your whore."

Kirsh stared at her and realized he was looking at a stranger. He turned on his heel angrily and strode across the room, jerking the door open.

"Kirsh?"

He stopped and looked back at her.

"Do you remember that night in Avacas? That night of the ball?"

"What about it?"

"You'd have had her that night, if Dirk and I hadn't found you when we did."

"What's your point?"

"My point is, you should remember that Marqel went straight from your arms to Dirk's."

"That's not how it was! He raped her."

Alenor shook her head with a knowing smile. "You know that's a lie. That's why you got so mad at him, wasn't it? Because you knew, deep down, that the only way Dirk would lay a finger on Marqel was if she wanted it."

Kirsh found himself unable deny her.

"She used the Milk of the Goddess on him, Kirsh," Alenor

continued brutally. "She deliberately sought out Dirk Provin, drugged him and willingly gave herself to him within an hour of being with you. Some night, when you're lying in her arms imagining that she loves you, you might like to ask her why she did that."

Chapter 49

After they had eaten dinner, Dirk took his parchment and his stick of charcoal and clambered back up the slope to continue sketching out his map of the ruins in the red light of the second sun. Tia was in an odd mood: cheerful one moment, biting the next, so he thought it prudent to stay out of her way while she got over it. He had cooked her mushrooms for her, but had declined to try them himself. Something about the smell of them made him wary. Tia seemed to think they were delicious, though, and had even licked her plate clean.

Omaxin stretched out before him, a ghostly remnant of a once-great city hiding in the shadow of the magnificent, deadly mountain that had rained death on all those unfortunate enough to live within its reach. The volcano responsible for the city's destruction, Mount Probeus, its crater still smoking occasionally, stood some distance away, part of the range known as the Nurals. Dirk doubted it was planning to erupt anytime soon. He had lived near the unstable Tresna Sea on Elcast for long enough to know that an eruption was usually preceded by a series of tremors, and there had been no sign of anything like that since they had been in the north.

There was little to give any indication of how tall the ruined buildings of Omaxin had been before the eruption. The excavations of the Shadowdancers had been haphazard at best, and they were not here to study history, but to discover a secret. Most of their work seemed to center on an area off to the right, some half a mile from where Dirk lay, making his map. The lava flow that destroyed Omaxin must have been massive there. The molten rock had washed over that part of the city, leaving nothing but a featureless, windswept landscape in its wake. He could just make out a darker shadow in the rock face that indicated where the entrance to the Labyrinth lay.

"Dirk?"

He turned and glanced over his shoulder. Tia stood at the bottom of the slope looking up at him.

"Hmm?"

"What are you doing up there?"

"I told you. Making a map of the city."

"Did you want to see the dance Risilka taught me?"

"No," he retorted absently, turning back to his mapping. Then he spun round and stared down at her in astonishment. "*What* did you say?"

Tia smiled up at him seductively, her hands on her hips. Her shirt was unbuttoned to the waist, her bosom thrust forward. The tiny silver bow and arrow he had won in Bollow sat snuggled between her breasts "Ruins are boring...wouldn't you rather make a map of *me*?"

Dirk shoved his half-completed sketch aside and looked down on her with concern. "Are you all right, Tia?"

She began to climb up the slope toward him with a predatory gleam in her eye. "I've never felt better. Do you want to kiss me?" she asked.

"Now I *know* there's something wrong with you." Dirk scrambled backward as she neared him. "You look...unwell."

She did, too. Her pupils were dilated, her skin sheened with sweat and she was breathing hard, much harder than the short climb up the slope warranted.

"I feel wonderful," she sighed dreamily as she reached the top. She leaned into him and grabbed him on the backside. "Let's see how you feel."

"You're drunk!" he accused, jerking away from her. Where had she got the alcohol? Had she smuggled a bottle of *vod'kun* into her pack back in Bollow?

"I'm not drunk," she objected, rather drunkenly. With all the subtlety of an Avacas whore, she slid her arms around him and began to nuzzle his neck, just below his ear. "Kiss me, Dirk. Touch me. Let me feel you inside me. Let me—"

"Tia!" he cried in alarm, tearing her arms from his neck. "What's the matter with you?"

"Nothing that can't be cured by this," she giggled, reaching for his groin.

Dirk slapped her hand away. "Hey!"

"Are you shy, Dirk?" she teased. "Is that what it is?" She began to loosen her belt. "You don't have to be shy with me, you know..."

"Tia, do you even *know* what you're suggesting?"

After a fumbled attempt, she finally got her belt undone and pulled it free. Tia looked at it for a moment and then smiled mischievously. "Maybe Dirk's been a naughty boy? Maybe he needs a good spanking? Maybe he'd even like it?"

Panic stricken, Dirk backed away from her, trying to fathom her bizarre behavior. It was almost as if she had taken the Milk of the Goddess, but where she might have gotten hold of a dose of that vile substance out here in the middle of nowhere...

With a sudden rush of understanding, Dirk reached out, grabbed her by the arms and shook her, hard. "Tia, listen to me. This is not you talking. It's those damn mushrooms."

She shook him off and ran her tongue over her lips in a blatant invitation. "Don't be silly, mushrooms can't talk."

"They're not just any mushrooms," he tried to explain, pushing her away, and then stumbling backward as she began to pursue him with the relentless hunger of an animal in heat.

"You can't escape me, Dirk," she purred. "Now be a good boy and stop running away. Or am I going to have to tie you down?"

"Those mushrooms must have been Jaquison's Blight!" he yelled, scrambling out of reach. "That's what they make the Milk of the Goddess from!"

She had not heard a word he had said. Dirk guessed the effect of the mushrooms would not be as severe as the distilled and concentrated syrup that the Shadowdancers used at Landfall, but it was obviously bad enough. And Tia would have no control over what she was feeling. He knew that from experience. Nothing other than the need to sate her desire would be allowed to take root in her mind.

He glanced over his shoulder and realized that the only place he had to go was down the other side of the small hill toward the lake. Tia took advantage of his momentary distraction. The next thing he knew she was on him again, kissing him, rubbing her hips against him...and for one, foolish moment he let her. For one dangerous, insane instant, he actually contemplated giving her what she wanted...

Then common sense prevailed and he shoved her away. "Tia, if you do this, the only person you're going to hate more than me in the morning is yourself."

"I don't hate you, Dirk," she whispered, sliding her arms around him again, as her tongue flickered over his earlobe. "I could never hate you..."

"Oh, yes you could," he muttered feelingly, even though he realized by now that he might as well be talking to himself. He spared another glance over his shoulder at the lake.

"Don't tease me, Dirk," she begged. "Take me! Now... here..."

"By the lake," he suggested, in a desperate bid to distract her.

"What's wrong with here?" She was grabbing at his shirt, trying to tear it off him.

"The ground's too hard here," he told her. "It'll be much nicer down by the lake."

She giggled. "You want to do it in the water?"

"Even better," he agreed, peeling her arms from around his neck. He took her hand and she let him lead her down onto the marshy ground. Her skin was clammy and hot. A few feet from the lake she stopped dead and refused to go any farther.

"We're nearly there," he pointed out, tugging on her hand.

"I'm not taking another step until you kiss me. Here!" she added opening her shirt and pointing to her left nipple.

"But we're almost..."

"Not another step, Dirk Provin."

Reluctantly, he let her pull him to her and, with a great deal of trepidation, he did as she demanded. Moaning with desire, she grabbed him by the hair, pulled his head up and kissed him hungrily, grabbing his hand and placing it on her breast inside her open shirt. It took all his concentration to keep his mind on the task at hand. He forcibly turned her around with his free hand and then pulled away from her. Her eyes were wide, shining and filled with nothing but blank incomprehension.

"I'm sorry about this, Tia," he told her ruefully as he nuzzled her ear. "And there's nothing I'd like more than to give you what you want. But trust me; you'll thank me for this one day."

Then with all his might, Dirk pushed her into the chilly waters of Lake Ruska.

He dived in after her as she floundered in the water and pulled her head up. When she reacted by trying to kiss him again, he pushed her back under the water and held her there while she struggled. When she stopped fighting him, he pulled her clear of the water once more, and dragged her ashore, coughing and spluttering.

And then, despite the fact that he had sworn he would not do it, he held her head for her while she puked.

Dirk said nothing as he made breakfast; said nothing as he poured tea for both of them. He then sat on the opposite side of the fire, trying to pretend he didn't notice Tia scratching at the rash that had formed on her skin in the early hours of the morning. She stared determinedly into the flames and refused to meet his eye.

"This is driving me insane!" she muttered eventually, when the itching became unbearable. "And I think my head is going to explode." They were the first words she had spoken since he fished her out of the lake.

"It goes away," he told her. "You should be fine in an hour or two."

She did not acknowledge that he had spoken. In fact, she refused to look at him at all. They sat in silence for a long time.

"Last night..." Tia began, eventually. "Did I say anything...you know?..."

He shook his head. "No."

"Did I do anything? ..."

"No," he assured her.

"And we didn't? ..."

"No."

She met his eye for the first time. "Why not?"

"What do you mean, *why not*?"

"I don't remember much, Dirk, but I do recall that you could have had me any way you wanted me last night. I'm just wondering why you didn't."

"Maybe...because you would have knifed me the minute you woke up this morning?" he suggested with a faint smile in an attempt to lighten the mood.

A fleeting frown crossed her face. "I guess I'm just a little surprised. I wasn't expecting you to be so..."

"Honorable?" he asked.

"I suppose."

"Thanks a lot."

She scuffed at the ground with her boot for a moment, and then looked him in the eye. She was not a girl that flinched from much.

"Look...It was a stupid thing to do, all right? I should have listened to you about those mushrooms, and I'm sorry I got so...uncontrollable. But let's just put it behind us. We made it to Omaxin and now we have a job to do." She smiled thinly. "We have to save the world, remember?"

He nodded his agreement and climbed to his feet. "Let's go, then."

"Aren't we going to wait another day?"

He shrugged. "After the ruckus we made last night, if anybody is looking for us, they'll know we're here."

"And we're just going to put this unfortunate incident behind us, aren't we?" she confirmed, rising to her feet.

"Absolutely."

"In fact, there's probably no need to mention it ever again. To anybody. Ever."

"None at all," he agreed, turning away to check his pack so that she would not see his smile. "Unless..."

"Unless what?" she demanded suspiciously.

"Nothing," he replied, fighting to keep a straight face.

She glowered at him. "You miserable bastard! You're never going to let me forget this, are you?" She kicked dirt over the remains of their small fire and then pushed past him angrily, heading for the ruins. "I was right. I really *am* going to end up killing you one day."

Dirk watched her striding away, filled with a deep sense of regret. Before they left Omaxin, he knew, Tia would have plenty of reasons to want to see him dead.

And the least of them would be the night they almost spent together.

Chapter 50

Alenor's daily ride with her escort soon changed from being a good excuse to talk in private with Alexin to being essential to her sanity. Her responsibilities as queen left her little time for herself. The added burden of dealing with Kirsh, who was still furious at her for rejecting him, meant that the only peace she had—the only time she could be herself—was when she was out riding.

Alexin did not always ride with her. It would have been far too obvious if he had, and even if he was not her only link with the Baenlanders, she could not afford to give the impression that she was playing favorites among her guard.

Alexin was with her today, however, and they rode on ahead of the escort, Circael flying beneath her as if she had sprouted wings. When she finally reined in, there was no sign of her escort.

Alexin galloped up behind her with a scowl.

"If you get killed in a fall while I'm supposed to be protecting you, I'd have to fall on my sword, you know," he complained.

Alenor laughed, still exhilarated from the ride. "Then I shall try not to get killed, Alexin. Just for you."

He dismounted and walked over to her, offering her his hand. "That would probably make me feel better if I thought you meant it, your majesty."

Alexin helped her down and stepped back to allow her to look at the view. They were on the cliff path that wound down from the palace to a small rocky cove at the base of the cliffs. The Tresna Sea crashed against the rocks below them and a sliver of red sliced across the horizon as the first sun began to rise.

She studied the glorious sunrise in silence for a moment. "I hear Kirsh has been spending rather a lot of time training with the guard lately."

Alexin nodded. "He does seem a bit...aggravated. I had a short bout with him yesterday. For a while there, I thought he was really trying to kill me."

Alenor smiled. "I hear frustration will do that to you."

"Frustration?" Alexin asked in a puzzled voice.

"His Royal Highness, the Regent of Dhevyn, isn't finding married life quite what he imagined." She turned to face him. "I told him to go to hell, Alexin. He can have his Shadowdancer or he can have me. He can't have us both."

The captain frowned. "Was that wise, your majesty?"

"Probably not. But you've no idea how good it felt," she said. "And do you think you could stop calling me that?"

"Calling you what, your majesty?"

"Your *majesty*!" she said. "It makes me feel like I'm my mother."

"It wouldn't be appropriate..."

"It's not terribly appropriate that a captain of the Queen's Guard is plotting with the Baenlanders to bring down the Lion of Senet, either, Alexin, but that doesn't seem to bother you."

"It's not quite the same thing, Alenor."

She smiled. "There! That wasn't so difficult, was it?"

"Not difficult at all. But it's a dangerous habit to get into."

Alenor sighed. "I seem to have developed quite a taste for living dangerously, since I became queen."

"You handled yourself very well with Antonov," he told her. "I think you have quite a flair for intrigue."

"Really? I was shaking so hard I thought Antonov would know I was lying, just by looking at me."

"Well, it certainly set off a flurry of activity among the Senetians," Alexin remarked. "There've been so many birds flying back and forth between here and Avacas it's a wonder they don't collide with each other."

"I know. Belagren's been very busy. I've barely seen her. She sent Ella Geon and a few others back to Avacas the day after the wedding."

"I imagine Dirk will be close to Omaxin by now."

"Do you like Dirk, Alexin?"

The captain shrugged. "I don't know him well enough to say."

"Do you *trust* him?"

"Do you?"

"More than you know." She walked a little way along the path, and then glanced back at him. "If we ever manage to free Dhevyn, it will be Dirk who does it, you know. It won't be me."

"I think you underestimate your own determination, Alenor."

She shook her head. "It's nothing to do with determination. Johan Thorn was determined. So was my mother. Determination isn't enough."

"Aren't you afraid that if he does defeat Antonov, he'll want your throne in return?"

"Dirk doesn't want to be king."

"Are you sure of that?"

"Yes."

Alexin came to stand beside her on the cliff top. She glanced at him for a moment and then looked back at the rapidly reddening sky. "When I saw him on Grannon Rock, Dirk made me promise I'd trust him," she told the captain. "He made me promise I would keep my faith in him, no matter what happened in the future."

"An odd promise to ask for."

"I thought so, too," she agreed. "It makes me wonder what

he's really up to. That whole thing with the corpse and Antonov... I just have a feeling that we were doing what he asked, but not for the reason we think."

"Don't let it concern you, Alenor. You did what the Baenlanders needed you to do, and it appears to have been successful. Belagren has ordered her Shadowdancers out of Omaxin, and the Lion of Senet is preparing to head home, none the wiser that you were involved. You can't ask for much more than that."

"I could ask for a great many things, Alexin. I suspect most of them, however, are out of my reach."

"It will all work out in the end," he assured her with a smile.

"Now you sound like Rainan."

"Your mother's methods were not entirely without merit, Alenor."

"I suppose not," she agreed. "But you can't keep giving in to the Lion of Senet without it eventually becoming first a habit, then a way of life. That's why I took a stand with Kirsh. I may go down in history as the Virgin Queen of Dhevyn, but at least I have my pride."

Alexin looked her oddly, and then he smiled. "If it were up to me, your majesty, you'd not be the Virgin Queen for long."

Alenor blushed. "*Alexin!* That's a rather risqué suggestion from someone who not five minutes ago was suggesting it might be inappropriate to address me by name."

"I didn't mean to offend you..."

"I'm not offended," she assured him. "Actually, I think I'm flattered."

"Well, there you go then," he said with a grin. "A queen should have at least one courtier whose sole function is to flatter and beguile her."

"And what would be the function of the other fourscore courtiers I seem to have acquired since Antonov and Belagren arrived?"

"They would be the ones whose sole function is to remind you why we have to free Dhevyn," he replied, his grin fading.

"Oh, Alexin," she sighed. "I swear that at times, you're the only thing that keeps me sane."

"Which is a very sad state of affairs for a queen to be in," he remarked with a slight frown. "You really should have someone nearby whom you can trust."

"Who?" she sighed. "There's nobody I dare trust, Alexin. Except you and my mother, and I worry about her at times. She does all the wrong things for all the right reasons."

"I was actually thinking of your cousin in Bryton."

"Jacinta? She hates court life, Alexin. Mother invited her to Kalarada when I first returned home and she flatly refused to come."

"Perhaps if *you* ask her she might consider it," he suggested. "Jacinta and your mother differ somewhat in their views about Senet."

Alenor looked at him curiously. "You're not implying that Jacinta is in league with you and the Baenlanders, are you, Alexin?" She laughed suddenly. "Oh dear! Lady Sofia would curl up and die if she knew that!"

"As would *your* mother if she realized the same thing about you," he reminded her with a smile. "Please, Alenor. Send for her. I can't watch over you all the time."

"Are you sure that's the only reason you want her to come to Kalarada?" she asked curiously.

"What other reason would there be?"

"She's very pretty."

Alexin smiled. "She's also as sharp as a diamond blade, and passionately loyal to Dhevyn."

"All admirable qualities," Alenor agreed. "But you didn't answer my question."

"If you're asking me if I have designs on Jacinta D'Orlon," he said. "Then the answer is no. Even if I did, I'm only a second son. Jacinta's family would never consider me while Raban is unmarried. Besides, my heart belongs to someone much closer to home."

Before she could ask who his heart belonged to the sound of horses on the path behind them ended their conversation as the remainder of her escort rounded the bend, walking at a sedate pace. Alenor held out her hand to Alexin and he led her back to her horse. He gave her a leg up into the saddle and she gathered up her reins. The first sun had risen almost fully and the light had turned red.

"Thank you, Captain," she said.

He looked up at her curiously. "For what?"

"For being my friend."

He smiled at her, but did not say anything more as he swung into the saddle of his own mount and, with the rest of her escort, they turned and headed back toward Kalarada palace.

Chapter 51

Tia and Dirk explored the ruins for several days, mostly to assure themselves that they really were deserted. Tia was rather concerned at the haste with which the Shadowdancers had departed. They had left behind an amazing amount of gear. Pavilions, bedding, a tent full of food supplies, tools and even a milk goat were scattered through the abandoned camp. Dirk was of the opinion that the Shadowdancers' orders must have been to leave immediately, and that it had not been possible for them to take everything with them. Tia was not nearly as sure. There was something fishy about the whole setup; she just couldn't figure out what it was. To her, it looked as if they might return any minute.

"You want to tackle the Labyrinth this morning?" Dirk asked when she emerged yawning sleepily from the luxury of an abandoned Shadowdancer's tent she had claimed as her own. The upside of the Shadowdancers' hasty departure was that not only would they eat like kings while they were here, they had most of the creature comforts of a large expedition and none of the effort involved in getting them there.

"That's why we came, isn't it?"

She did not mean to snap at him, she just couldn't help it. Things were still very tense between them. Although Dirk had not mentioned it again, not since the morning after, Tia cringed every time she thought of that night she had eaten those damn mushrooms. He was thinking about it constantly, she was certain. And just because he had displayed a few shreds of honor by not taking advantage of her at the time, did not mean that he was not wondering about what it might have been like if he had...

"I said, we'd better take a few spare torches. It's going to be dark in there."

Tia started as she realized he had spoken to her. "What? Oh. Fine. Spare torches..."

He snapped his fingers in front of her face. "Hey! Tia! Wake up!"

She slapped his hand away impatiently. "Leave me alone! I'm awake!"

"Just checking," he shrugged. "Bring the waterskin, too."

She glared at him, and then picked up the torches and the skin. "When did I get promoted to pack mule?"

"About the same time you got demoted from insatiable seductress, I think," he replied with a smile.

Tia hurled the load she was carrying to the ground. "That's it! I've had enough of this!"

He sighed. "Just because you spend a good part of your day trying to invent new ways to torment *me,* doesn't mean I do the same to you. It was an accident, Tia. It wasn't your fault and you weren't responsible for what you said or what you did." He took a step closer to her and reached up to wipe away a tear from her cheek with his thumb. "And I swear, I will never tell anyone what happened. On one condition."

"What's that?"

He smiled. "That you admit it was kind of funny..."

She instinctively slapped his hand away.

Then she forced a smile, realizing that Dirk was offering her a way out. He was giving her a chance to laugh it off, to make a joke of it; to trivialize something that was potentially soul destroying.

He smiled at her as he picked up his own torch and

plunged it into the cooking fire to light it. "Are you still mad at me?"

Tia hefted the waterskin over her shoulder and turned for the well-worn path to the Labyrinth's entrance.

"I'll always be mad at you about something, Dirk Provin," she said over her shoulder. "You can count on it."

Dirk caught up with her at the dark gaping archway that was the entrance to the Labyrinth. They both stopped and stared up at the alien writing chiseled into the stone.

"What does it say?" Tia asked.

"I don't know. It's the same writing as the arches in Bollow, but I couldn't read that either. Did Neris ever mention what it said?"

"Not that I recall."

Dirk held the torch out in front of them as they stepped inside. The walls were smooth and slightly curved, etched faintly with symbols Tia did not have time to stop and examine. The darkness was oppressive, the temperature cool after the heat outside. About thirty feet into the tunnel, Tia stumbled into Dirk as they found the remains of a twisted doorway.

"This must have been Neris's first trap."

Dirk nodded silently as he helped her up and they stepped over the obstacle. They crossed several more ruined gateways, spaced about fifty feet apart. At one gate, they had to climb carefully over a huge granite slab. Dirk held up the torch and looked up at the hole in the ceiling from where the slab had fallen.

"I hope nobody was under that when it fell," he remarked.

They walked in silence for a time, the darkness closing in on Tia with smothering intensity as they made their way past the remains of the traps Neris had set in the Labyrinth. As they neared the remains of the seventh trap, they discovered a narrow bridge over the gaping hole in the floor. Tia glanced down as she crossed the rickety structure behind Dirk, wondering how far down it went. She could just see the faint glimmer of sharpened spikes poking up through the gloom.

Once past the collapsed floor, the hall curved, and what little daylight filtered into the tunnel disappeared. Tia unconsciously moved closer to Dirk and the security of the light he carried. She had never realized until this moment that she was afraid of the dark, probably because until now, she had never experienced true darkness.

The twelfth gate was little more than a hole in the wall and gave no hint as to what had been triggered when the Shadowdancers had forced it open. Tia stepped through, her pulse beginning to thump erratically as the darkness of the tunnel closed in on her.

"You know, strictly speaking," said Dirk, "this isn't a labyrinth at all."

"What do you mean?" she asked, suddenly glad that he had spoken. His voice helped drown out the pounding in her ears.

"A true labyrinth is a single path heading toward a goal at the center."

"Isn't that what this is?"

"Sort of. But this doesn't seem curved enough. It has a mouth, like a true labyrinth. But we should be walking a circuit. The walls are supposed to keep you on the path until you reach your goal in the middle of the labyrinth, which is actually only the halfway point, because then you still need to turn around and walk out."

"Fascinating, I'm sure," she agreed, rolling her eyes.

"All right," he admitted. "I'm being pedantic, I'll grant you that, but even though there's a bend in it, the path is too straight. This is just a tunnel, really. If it was a true lab— Wow!"

Tia bumped into Dirk as he stopped suddenly and held the torch high. The tunnel stopped abruptly. They were confronted by a solid wall constructed of polished granite, its surface mottled with golden flecks that spidered across the surface of the stone like the veins on an old drunkard's nose.

"You're supposed to be the second greatest mind on Ranadon and the best you can do is 'wow'?" she asked, trying to cover her nervousness with sarcasm.

He walked to the barricade blocking the way forward,

holding his torch even higher to get a better view. Into the wall were set six slightly raised blocks, laid out in a circular pattern. Each block was etched with a number, but as Dirk moved the torch along to light the whole wall, she could see no logical sequence to them.

"This is amazing!"

"So is Neris," she reminded him, reaching out to touch the wall. The granite was cold to the touch, hidden here in the darkness. "Or at least he was."

"How did he build this?" Dirk asked in awe, running his fingers over the number four hundred etched into one of the raised blocks.

"He didn't."

Dirk looked back at her in confusion.

"He designed it, but he didn't actually slave away for years dressing the stone and sliding every block into position himself. Belagren *sent* him here to Omaxin, remember. It was her idea to have Neris seal the caverns so that nobody else could discover their secret. She sent him up here with everything he needed— tools, laborers, craftsmen—the works. Do you think we'll be down here long?"

He glanced over his shoulder at her, looking rather amused. "You're not afraid of the dark, are you?"

"No...maybe..."

"Don't worry," he assured her. "We'll light the tunnel better when we come back." He turned back to stare at the wall. "What happened to the people who constructed the gates, do you suppose? Why didn't Belagren just ask one of *them* how to get through?"

"Rumor has it she tortured more than a dozen of them to death before she realized that knowing how to grind a spring doesn't make you a master clockmaker. Nobody but Neris ever really understood how it worked. Can you open it?"

"I don't know," he said, studying the wall closely.

"Well, if you do figure it out, just be *damn* sure you've got it right before you try it. The gate may be booby-trapped, remember. Get it wrong and you die—rather painfully, from what I saw on the way in."

"That's what I like about you, Tia. You always look on the bright side. What did Neris tell you about the gates, anyway?"

"Not a great deal."

He glanced over his shoulder at her. "Did I really bring you all this way because of your expert knowledge of the Labyrinth?"

"Hey, don't blame me. You're the one who assumed I knew something about it."

"Why do you suppose Paige Halyn sent Neris to Omaxin in the first place?" he asked, turning back to the wall in fascination.

"What do you mean?" But what she really wanted to ask was: "Why can't we discuss this outside?"

"Why Omaxin?" Dirk mused. "Why not the library in Nova? Or the cellars in Elcast, for that matter? Why *these* ruins? How did he know Neris would find the answer here?"

Tia shrugged. "Maybe it was a lucky guess. Or an unlucky guess, if you count what happened afterward."

"No. It doesn't make sense. The Lord of the Suns sent the only mathematical genius he had to a ruin in the middle of nowhere, when there were a score of other places he could have used his talents better. Belagren and the others were just along for the ride, really. Paige Halyn must have had a reason."

"Well, why don't we stop by his place on the way back through Bollow and ask him?" she suggested impatiently. *And can we please leave?*

"Maybe we should," he agreed thoughtfully.

Tia glared at his back. "I'll pretend you didn't say that. Can we go now?"

"Look at this."

With an exasperated curse, Tia stepped up beside him and looked up. He was pointing to an inscription chiseled into the stone above the numbers. It was not written in the ancient script of the ruins, but in the common tongue, which meant Neris had probably put it there.

" 'There is an eye that cannot see,' " she read in the flickering torchlight. " 'This is a place that must not be. But in the order of the making, patterns lurk there for the taking.'" She read it again and then glanced at Dirk. "What does it mean?"

"I was hoping you'd have some idea. He's your father."

Tia shrugged. "Well the first bit is pretty obvious. 'There is an eye that cannot see. This is a place that must not be.' He's referring to the Eye of the Labyrinth and the fact that Belagren wanted it destroyed."

"Really?" he asked in mock amazement. "And they say *I'm* the genius!"

She slapped at his arm impatiently. "All right! So even Eryk could have figured that out. But what does he mean by 'In the order of the making'? Do you think he's talking about the way the gate was made?"

"I've no idea."

Tia pointed to the numbers chiseled into the raised blocks. "Four, twenty-five, fifty, one fifty, two hundred, four hundred," she read. "What do you suppose the numbers are for?"

"That's the mechanism that works the gate, obviously." He pointed to a faint line running vertically down the center. The doors were fitted together so neatly that she had not even noticed the seam the first time she looked at the wall. The craftsmanship of the stonemasons who had constructed the gate was impressive. "Of course, the trick is going to be finding the right sequence to open it."

Tia nodded and took the torch from Dirk's hand. "Then you'd better get to work, hadn't you? I'm going back outside."

He seemed amused by her apprehension. "There's nothing in here that can hurt you, Tia."

"Fine. You stay here and play Lord of the Shadows. I need sunlight."

He studied her closely for a moment, perhaps realizing how oppressed by the darkness she was really feeling, and then nodded. "We'll go back outside for now. I need to get something to write these numbers on anyway."

"Let's go, then," she agreed, turning toward the entrance. When Dirk did not follow her immediately, she turned back to him. "*Now,* Dirk! It'll still be there when you get back."

With a great deal of reluctance, Dirk turned his back on

the gate and, in a surprising show of understanding, he wordlessly offered her his hand.

She took it without question, her fear of the dark outweighing any other feeling she might have for him at that moment and hand in hand, they walked back through the Labyrinth into the light.

Chapter 52

Rather to her surprise, Alenor's cousin, Jacinta D'Orlon, accepted her invitation to join her at court and arrived from Bryton not long after Alenor wrote to her, on a shabby-looking trader named the *Orlando*. She arrived without pomp or ceremony, presenting herself at the palace unannounced and demanding to see the queen. Alenor was delighted to see her cousin again.

Jacinta favored the D'Orlon side of the family. She was taller than Alenor, with rich, dark brown hair and eyes that seemed to change color with her mood, framed by thick dark lashes. At nineteen, she was something of a disgrace to the D'Orlon family, in that she had, to Alenor's knowledge, refused at least five potential husbands presented for her approval. She ran the risk of becoming an old maid if she was not married before she was twenty, a circumstance that appeared not to bother her in the slightest, but was driving her mother to distraction.

Jacinta embraced her warmly, and then held the queen at arm's length for a moment and examined her critically.

"My, aren't you all grown up now, little cousin!" she exclaimed with a smile. "Good thing you're wearing that crown or I'd never have recognized you."

Alenor self-consciously snatched the crown from her head and dropped it on the side table. "I've been with the council," she explained. "I don't wear it all the time."

"I should hope not!" Jacinta laughed. Then she turned to

Dorra, who was watching the reunion with interest. "You can go now, my lady. Alenor and I have lots of catching up to do."

"Your majesty?" Dorra asked, looking at Alenor. She was not going to let Jacinta order her about.

"You may go, Dorra."

The lady-in-waiting bowed and walked from the room, clearly displeased that she was no longer required.

"Goddess, Allie! This place is crawling with Senetians! Why do you put up with them?"

"I have little choice in the matter, I'm afraid," she admitted. "But let's not talk about them. Tell me everything you've been up to!"

Jacinta took a seat and smiled at her. "Let me see, what have I been up to? Well, I told my mother that I wouldn't marry Lord Birkoff from Tolace if he was the last man on Ranadon, which rather upset her plans for a big wedding at Landfall. Can you imagine *me* married to a Senetian? So then I applied to the university on Nova and got accepted, until they found out I wasn't really a boy from Lakeside. Mother nearly had apoplexy when she found out. The worst thing was that they offered that wretched little brother of mine a place, and the only reason he got in was because I did all the work for him. When your letter arrived I was tossing up between running away to sea and just killing myself to relieve the tedium."

Alenor laughed. "If you've been causing so much trouble, I'm surprised Lady Sofia let you come."

"I reminded her of how much more likely it would be that I'd find a suitable husband at court," Jacinta told her with a wink.

"I'm so glad you're here," Alenor sighed, as she sat beside Jacinta on the settee, surprised at how much she had missed having someone to confide in.

"The feeling is mutual, little cousin," Jacinta assured her. "My mother's next plan was to introduce me to that slimy little turncoat Baston of Damita, so you've probably saved me from a fate worse than death. I'm yours to command, your majesty."

"Will you stay, Jacinta? Will you be my lady-in-waiting?"

"What's the dreaded Lady Dorra going to have to say about that?"

"I don't really care. I'm the Queen of Dhevyn now. I can have all the ladies-in-waiting I want."

"Then I accept. On one condition."

"Name it."

"That you introduce me to all those big handsome Guardsmen you have lurking around the palace."

Alenor laughed. "I thought you weren't looking for a husband?"

"I'm not, Alenor. But just because I don't want to buy anything doesn't mean I can't browse around the store."

Impulsively, Alenor hugged her. "I wish you'd come sooner. It's going to be so nice to have a real friend around."

Jacinta studied her curiously. "I would have thought with you being a newlywed, you'd be too busy with your husband to want any other friends intruding, Allie."

Very little got past Jacinta D'Orlon, Alenor thought. Alexin was not just flattering her when he said that she was as sharp as a diamond blade.

"Can I tell you something, Jacinta? You must promise to keep it a secret. It's worth more than my life if it got out."

Jacinta's smile faded. "What's wrong?"

She lowered her eyes, and her voice to ensure they were not overheard. "I've never been with Kirsh. For that matter, I've never been with anyone. Kirsh has a mistress. She's a Shadowdancer. I told him he couldn't have us both."

"Good for you."

"You're not angry with me?"

"Of course not! I'd have done exactly the same thing."

"Alexin said it was a foolish thing to do."

"He's a man. What would he know?"

Alenor smiled faintly. "He said you're in league with the Baenlanders, too."

"Then he has a big mouth."

"Are you?"

"I'd be admitting to treason if I answered that, Alenor."

"So you are," she concluded. "Good. So am I."

Jacinta stared at the queen for a moment and then shook her head. "I think it's a good thing you did send for me, Alenor. By the sound of things, you're swimming way out of your depth."

"You don't know the half of it," Alenor sighed.

"Then I think you'd better tell me," her cousin said. "I can't help you if I don't know what's going on around here."

If Alenor had any lingering doubts about the wisdom of sending for Jacinta, they evaporated completely a few days later, the first time her cousin met Marqel. By then, Jacinta knew everything that was going on, including the identity of Kirsh's paramour.

She had been a little concerned that Jacinta might do or say something that would inadvertently betray her. Marqel still believed that Alenor had no idea about her affair with Kirsh, and it would be courting disaster to let the Shadowdancer even suspect that Alenor knew the truth. But when she met the Shadowdancer for the first time, Jacinta greeted her warmly and immediately engaged Marqel in a conversation about the comparative benefits of lavender oil and jasmine oil. Jacinta had studied herb lore for a time. Jacinta had studied just about everything at one stage or another, Alenor was convinced. She was an intelligent young woman, doomed to a future as the wife of a nobleman because she had the misfortune to be born a female and was related by marriage to the Dhevynian royal family. As she watched Jacinta and Marqel talking, she smiled wistfully, thinking it was a pity she could not introduce her to Dirk. He would have liked Jacinta.

"Your majesty?"

"Yes, Dorra?" she replied, turning to glance over her shoulder at her senior lady-in-waiting, who had been more than a little put out since Jacinta's arrival.

"Are you expecting his highness this evening?"

Jacinta's head jerked up at the question. "Honestly, Lady Dorra! What sort of thing is that to ask our queen? Look at her, you've made her blush!"

"I simply wish to know if I should turn down both sides of the bed, Lady Jacinta," Dorra responded testily. "It's a perfectly reasonable question."

"It's a terrible question!" Jacinta declared. "I think the queen deserves at least a modicum of privacy, don't you? I certainly don't think it's any of our business how often Prince Kirshov spends his night in her bed, and I'm appalled that you would embarrass Alenor by asking her such a thing so publicly. Don't you agree, Lady Marqel?"

Not surprisingly, Marqel was firmly on Jacinta's side. "I believe you're right, Lady Jacinta," she nodded, obviously warming to Alenor's new lady-in-waiting. "The queen and her consort deserve our protection, not our questions."

"Well said, Lady Marqel! I can see you and I are going to get along very well."

Alenor really did blush this time, but mostly because she could not believe that Jacinta would so blatantly ridicule Marqel and Dorra, and that neither of them had the faintest idea that she was doing it.

"I think, my lady, that if the queen and her beloved wish to spend the night together, between the two of them they can work out how to turn down the sheets."

Dorra glared at Jacinta. "Perhaps, when you've been at court a little longer, you will learn that some things can never be private, my lady. The sleeping arrangements of the queen is one of them."

"Then we must deal with the matter discreetly, my lady, not ask about it as if we're farmers checking to see if the bull is in the mating paddock."

"What do you suggest, my lady?"

"I suggest, my lady, that neither you nor I should concern ourselves with such matters. Perhaps the Lady Marqel would be so kind as to keep an eye on things? She is Prince Kirshov's spiritual adviser, is she not? I'm sure she'd be happy to inform us if she feels there is anything to be concerned about."

"More than happy," Marqel agreed willingly.

Alenor thought she'd burst from trying to hold in her laughter.

Faced with Jacinta's logic and Marqel's support, there was little Dorra could do.

"As you wish," she muttered, and left the room, slamming the door behind her.

Jacinta sighed heavily. "Oh dear, I think I've upset her. Would you follow her, Marqel, and see that's she's not too distraught?"

Having just been made responsible for reporting Kirsh's sleeping habits, which mostly involved visiting Marqel's room, the Shadowdancer was positively gloating over the prospect. And she was obviously feeling very kindly disposed toward Jacinta.

"Of course, my lady."

Marqel bowed and left the room after Dorra. Jacinta turned to Alenor with a grin.

"Well, that's taken care of that awkward little situation, don't you think?"

"Oh, Jacinta!" she laughed. "You're terrible! How could you *do* that?"

"I've had a lot of practice perfecting righteous indignation," she said. "Every time my mother trotted out a new hopeful, actually. But don't get too comfortable with the arrangement. Sooner or later, somebody's going to start asking questions, Allie. Particularly when you fail to produce an heir."

"I'll deal with that when they do," she shrugged, her amusement fading in the face of the harsh reality of her situation.

"Well, I suppose we can think of something by then," Jacinta said, coming to sit on the couch beside her. "I admire your bravery, though."

"What bravery?"

"Putting up with Marqel in your entourage. If it was up to me, I'd slap that little Shadowslut into the middle of next week."

"You mustn't call her that!"

"Why not? It's what she is. It's what they all are."

"I know. But the High Priestess is staying here in the palace. If she heard you saying that, you'd be..."

"A lot sillier than I look," Jacinta finished for her with a smile. "Don't worry, Allie. I can bow and scrape and say my prayers to the Goddess with the best of them. *Better* than a lot of them, probably. I've actually *read* the *Book of Ranadon*."

Chapter 53

The High Priestess waited for several days after Antonov left Kalarada before she sent a request to the new regent for an audience. She wanted to give him time to settle into his new role as both ruler and husband. Not that Kirsh was required to do much in either role. He was a figurehead almost as powerless as his new wife. Antonov had arranged it so that there was little damage either of them could do, while giving the impression to the rest of Dhevyn that they were doing something useful.

Belagren thought Antonov was making a big mistake with Kirshov. The boy was not nearly so easily controlled as Antonov believed, nor so dedicated to his father's cause as the Lion of Senet imagined. Belagren had watched Kirsh grow up, and she knew, even better than his father, that he wanted to leave his own mark on the world, and that fulfilling his father's dreams of global conquest was not actually the way he planned to do it. She understood what it was like for him to be the son of a man as powerful as Antonov, particularly a second son, whose role was essentially that of a spare heir.

She also suspected that Kirshov Latanya was not nearly as keen as his father to see Dirk Provin caught and brought back to Avacas.

There were two reasons for this that she knew of. The first was his friendship with Dirk, which Belagren suspected still lingered in the back of Kirsh's mind and made him reluctant to wish ill on his old companion. The other reason was simple jealousy. Antonov was quite infatuated with the idea that he could turn Johan Thorn's bastard into his disciple; that he could place the true heir of Dhevyn on the throne, confident in the knowledge that the boy belonged to him, body and soul.

That was never going to happen, of course and, after Dirk burned the *Calliope,* even Antonov's patience was starting to fray. But while Antonov harbored his fantasy, Kirshov grew increasingly reluctant about the idea. In truth, Belagren did not blame him. Antonov's plan had room for only one king of Dhevyn, and to place Dirk on the throne would mean unseating Kirshov.

It was typical of Antonov that he would so blindly believe in his son's loyalty that he would imagine he could attempt such a thing without considering that there might be adverse consequences.

To her mind, the Lion of Senet had misjudged his son quite badly; however, as it suited her own purposes at the moment, she did not point it out to him. Right now, Antonov's obsession with Dirk Provin had placed Kirsh right where she wanted him, and she intended to make full use of it. The High Priestess's only concern was securing the future for herself and her Church. She actually didn't give two figs about the next King of Dhevyn. She didn't care if he was a Latanya or the son of some goatherd they picked at random off the streets.

Madalan announced Kirsh a few minutes earlier than their arranged time, which was a good sign. Perhaps the boy needed someone to talk to. She amended the thought as Kirsh crossed the room and bowed politely. He was a boy no longer. He was a man, and Antonov should remember that if he expected to control him.

"I hope I haven't inconvenienced you by arriving early, my lady."

"Of course not, Kirsh," she assured him, indicating that he could sit. "I'm actually flattered that you chose to visit me. Now that you're regent, I suppose, by rights, I should have come to you."

Kirsh rolled his eyes. "I was glad of the excuse to escape, actually. Do you think the Dhevynians are plotting to destroy me by smothering me with trivia?"

Belagren smiled. "I wouldn't discount the possibility. How's Alenor dealing with it all?"

"Like a little trouper," he remarked sourly. "She's loving

every minute of it. The more trivial and idiotic the problem the better for her. She's got a new playmate, too. Her cousin, Jacinta D'Orlon."

"Of Bryton?"

Kirsh nodded. "*There's* a woman I'd like to see roasting on a Landfall fire. She pokes her nose into everything."

"I hear Jacinta D'Orlon refused a very generous offer from Lord Birkoff recently."

"Then Birkoff should consider himself a lucky man."

Belagren smiled sympathetically. "Well, Alenor doesn't have many close friends. You must allow her some."

"She can have all the friends she wants," Kirsh shrugged. "It's overeducated, opinionated, condescending relations that I have a problem with. Her mother is just as bad. Rainan questions every decision I make. For someone who's supposed to be retired, she's awfully nosy about what's going on."

"It must be difficult for her," Belagren agreed. "Would you like some tea?" She poured him a cup without waiting for him to answer.

"Well, if she doesn't get off my back, she'll find herself banished to the other side of the island to enjoy her retirement out of my way," he warned, accepting the tea from her. Belagren smiled. *Oh, Anton, how foolish you are not to realize the potential in your own son. You should forget Dirk and concentrate on Kirsh.*

"Has it been any easier since your father returned to Avacas?" she inquired as she poured a cup for herself. She was not really thirsty, but she knew well the value of the mundane social niceties. They smoothed the way for much more important things, and gave the whole meeting an air of cozy familiarity.

Kirsh shrugged and sipped his tea. "It's just one less person looking over my shoulder. And it's not as if I can actually *do* anything, like declare war on Sidoria or something equally absurd. There are so many aides and secretaries running around the palace, I could disappear for a month, and I doubt anyone would notice that I was missing."

She smiled sympathetically. "Why don't you?"

"Disappear for a month? Don't tempt me."

Belagren put down her teacup and clasped her hands in her

lap. She studied him closely for a moment. "Suppose I asked you to do something for me, Kirshov? Something that would require you to leave Kalarada for a while? Would you do it?"

Kirsh's eyes narrowed suspiciously. "I might. It would depend on what it was that you wanted me to do."

"What I want, Kirsh," she said, watching him carefully, "is for you to go and get Dirk Provin for me."

Kirsh stared at her silently. Warily. She was going to have to explain this very carefully if she wanted to keep him on her side.

"About a month ago, I received a letter from Dirk," she continued. "In it, he expressed his desire to return to Avacas, but not in the role your father has in mind for him. He wants to join the Shadowdancers."

"Why?"

"I think he's sick of being on the run. The death of his mother has affected him badly, and he now fears for his brother and his brother's wife. I believe he's afraid Antonov will continue to destroy those closest to him unless he is convinced Dirk is out of his reach. You know as well as I that Dirk wants no part of your father's plans to elevate him to the throne of Dhevyn. The Shadowdancers offer him the only chance he has of avoiding that fate. And your father, of all people, cannot deny him the opportunity to serve the Goddess."

"It doesn't sound like Dirk," Kirsh said doubtfully.

"It's been more than two years since you saw him last, Kirsh. He's had a price on his head, he's been hunted and pursued, and his mother has been executed. You've no way of telling how that has influenced his thinking."

"But why me?" Kirsh asked, still not convinced. "If you know where he is, why not just send a detail to collect him? For that matter, why doesn't he just surrender himself?"

She smiled understandingly. "Dirk is distrustful of all things Senetian, Kirshov, particularly since he burned your father's ship. In his letter, he specifically asked that you come for him. Perhaps he feels he can trust you not to run a sword through him at first sight."

"Then he's wrong," Kirsh snarled. "After what he did to Marqel, I'd just as soon see him dead."

Belagren frowned. *Damn that girl.* "Kirshov, while I do not for a moment condone what he did to my Shadowdancer, I feel Marqel may hold some responsibility in the matter. She did drug him with the Milk of the Goddess, after all."

The prince didn't look happy to be reminded of that. "That doesn't excuse what he did."

"No, but neither does it warrant killing him, my dear. If anything, Dirk's worst crime is showing a distinct lack of good judgment in his dealings with Marqel." She raised a brow in his direction. "A sin the casual observer might consider *you* guilty of also."

He seemed neither surprised nor concerned that Belagren knew of his affair with Marqel. "He murdered Johan Thorn. Have you forgiven him that, too?"

I was right. This boy really does have a good head on his shoulders when he decides to use it. "The Goddess believes in true repentance, Kirshov, otherwise we would all be denied her blessing. Help me apprehend Dirk and if I discover that he's lied to us, trust me, even your father won't be able to devise a punishment more terrible than my wrath. But if he's genuine in his desire to seek sanctuary in the arms of the Goddess, if he truly means it when he says that he wishes nothing more than to spend the rest of his life in study and prayer, then I can do no less than provide him with the opportunity."

Kirsh thought about it for a moment, and then nodded slowly. "Where is he?"

"Omaxin. I believe he wanted to do some soul searching in that most holy of shrines before taking up service with the Goddess. He's waiting for us there."

"When did you want to leave?"

"As soon as possible. I will arrange an escort of my own people to meet us in Paislee. For obvious reasons, I wish to involve neither the Queen's Guard nor your father until we have ascertained how genuine Dirk is in his desire to embrace the Goddess."

"My father knows nothing about this?"

She shook her head. "I thought it wiser not to involve him at this stage. He will be...disappointed...when he learns that

Dirk wishes to take up service with the Goddess rather than him."

"Are you sure it's wise not to inform him? He'll be furious when he finds out that you knew where Dirk was and said nothing to him. He won't be too thrilled with me for aiding you, either."

Belagren met Kirsh's eye evenly. This was the moment she would find out how well she had judged this young man.

"Do you intend to wait on your father's pleasure for the rest of your days, Kirshov? Is every move you make as Regent of Dhevyn going to be dictated by your father?"

Kirsh hesitated before answering, and then he shook his head. "No."

"Then you'll aid me in this?"

"Gladly, my lady."

"Thank you, Kirshov," she replied, graciously. "I was certain that I could count on you. More tea?"

Chapter 54

News that Kirsh was leaving Kalarada with the High Priestess for some undisclosed destination reached Alenor through her Senetian lady-in-waiting. Dorra inadvertently let it slip while Jacinta was fixing Alenor's hair only hours before he was due to depart. It concerned her greatly that Kirsh could make such travel arrangements without her knowledge. It was testament to how little she was actually involved in governing her own country.

Alenor confronted Kirsh in his rooms as he was dressing. She barged in without knocking and stood before him, her hands on her hips, her eyes blazing. Kirsh took one look at her and ordered his manservant from the room.

"So, were you actually planning to tell me that you were leaving?" she asked as soon as they were alone. "Or was I supposed to just notice that you were missing from the dinner table this evening?"

He met her anger calmly. "Well, you'd hardly notice I was missing from your bed, would you?"

His reply shocked her. It was unlike Kirsh to be so blunt. Or so cruel. "Is that why you're going away? Because I wounded your pride?"

"Not that it's any of your business, but I'm assisting the High Priestess with something very important."

"And the Goddess knows what the High Priestess of the Shadowdancers wants is far more important than you staying here to govern the nation you so recently accepted as your regency," she remarked scathingly.

"Dhevyn doesn't need me, Alenor," he shrugged. "You know it as well as I do. Neither of us has any real power."

"And so you think that justifies you abandoning your position to go chasing off to Goddess-knows-where with Belagren?"

"I might as well be doing something useful. I'm not needed here." He looked at her pointedly. "Not for anything."

"Is Marqel going with you?"

"Yes."

His admission hurt Alenor more than she thought it would. *He doesn't even try to hide it anymore.* That she only had herself to blame for the current state of affairs did little to console her.

"And what is to happen to Dhevyn in your absence?"

"I've made arrangements. Dhevyn will continue to function quite smoothly without me. And I can be contacted through the Shadowdancers in Avacas in the unlikely event that anything important happens while I'm gone."

"Does your father know about this?"

Kirsh frowned. "I am Regent of Dhevyn, Alenor. I am not answerable to my father."

She laughed bitterly. "That's got to be the most optimistic statement I've ever heard!" When Kirsh did not respond Alenor shook her head in amazement. "Goddess! You haven't told him, have you? He'll be furious when he finds out."

"It's not your place to tell him, Alenor. I will deal with my father. You need do nothing more than stay here in Kalarada and enjoy yourself. Your kingdom will continue to be administered efficiently by my people while I'm gone. Take the opportunity to relax a little. Go riding with the guard more often. You have been a little overwrought of late."

"Don't you dare treat me like a child!"

"You *are* a child," he reminded her harshly. "A fact you proved the day we married. And might I remind you that you will remain a child until your eighteenth birthday. Until that time, you won't question me, or interfere with how I choose to govern Dhevyn. Is that clear?"

The change in him took her by surprise. It was Belagren's influence, no doubt. He would never have dared defy his father like this without the High Priestess supporting him.

"Where are you going?"

"That's none of your concern."

"How long will you be away?"

"I'm not sure."

"What am I supposed to tell people?"

"Whatever you want."

She wanted to scream at him in frustration. "You can't just up and leave like this, Kirsh!"

"Actually, Alenor, I can. And now, if you don't mind, I have to finish getting ready." He turned his back on her and walked back into his dressing room. When he emerged a few moments later, he was shrugging on his jacket. He looked up, and seemed surprised to find her still standing there. His eyes were cold. "Was there anything else?"

Alenor wanted to cry. She wanted to roll back time. She wanted things back the way they were, when she loved Kirsh and thought that he loved her. She wanted to make it better but knew that she never could. Things had deteriorated too far for it ever to be truly right between them. They were barely even friends now.

"I must know where you're going," she insisted. "When your father finds out about this—and you can be certain that he will—I must be able to convince him that I knew about and approved your departure. He'll get suspicious otherwise."

Kirsh was silent for a moment, considering her words, and then he nodded slowly. "You're right. It would look better for both of us that way."

"Where are you going, Kirsh?"

"Omaxin," he told her, the news slicing through her like a sword dipped in acid. "The High Priestess and I are going to Omaxin."

Alenor managed to keep her composure for the next few hours. She even rode down to the wharf to see Kirsh off with Dorra and Jacinta, maintaining the fiction that the young Queen of Dhevyn and her prince consort were happily married and deeply in love. Kirsh climbed down from the open carriage and turned to kiss her good-bye, mostly for the benefit of the onlookers who had gathered to watch. She turned her face at the last minute so his kiss landed on her cheek. As she looked up, she saw Marqel standing on the deck of the High Priestess's ship watching them. She was too far away to see the expression on the Shadowdancer's face, but she could feel the other girl's eyes boring into her.

"Be careful, Kirsh," Alenor said.

He looked surprised. "I will."

"Have a good journey."

He nodded and turned away, heading for the ship. Alenor watched him climb the gangway, watched him greet the High Priestess and then walk over to stand next to Marqel as the sailors began to get the ship under way. He said something to Marqel that made her laugh, and then he turned and walked aft to speak to the captain.

"We shouldn't sit here baking in this sun," Dorra warned. "It will ruin your complexion."

"Nobody wants a freckled queen," Jacinta added wryly, with a wink at Alenor. There had been no time to explain to Jacinta what had gone on, but her cousin could sense something was wrong.

Alenor tore her gaze from the ship and looked at her companions. "You're right. We should get going. Take us to the barracks, Hugo!"

The coachman turned the open carriage around and headed back toward the palace through the city. Alenor smiled and waved to the people lining the streets as they went.

"The barracks, your majesty?" Dorra asked with a raised brow.

"One of the mares foaled yesterday, Dorra," she explained. "She had a splendid colt, I hear. Alexin promised to show him to me."

Dorra sighed heavily. "Your majesty, I really think it's time you outgrew this childish fascination you have with horses."

"But he's only a day old! He'll be so cute!" she declared, hoping she sounded like the child Dorra obviously thought she was. "Don't you want to see him, too?"

"Not at all, your majesty. I can't think of anything worse than standing around a smelly stable getting all misty-eyed about a beast of burden."

"We can return to the palace in the carriage, then," Jacinta suggested. "Alenor can have them saddle Circael and she can ride back to the palace after she's seen the new baby."

"That's a splendid idea! Is that all right with you, Dorra?"

The Senetian woman let out another long-suffering sigh, but she did not object to Jacinta's arrangements. With relief, Alenor settled back into the soft leather upholstery, her eyes fixed on the road ahead, deliberately not even glancing in the direction of the Queen's Guard who flanked the carriage.

Only a little while now, she told herself. *You can hold it in a little while longer.*

Alexin had not been part of the guard to escort Kirshov and the queen to the docks, but he came out to greet her as soon as he learned that the queen had arrived at the barracks. She allowed Dargin Otmar, the guard's master-at-arms, to hand her down from the carriage, issued orders to take Dorra and Jacinta back to the palace and then turned to look at Alexin. He must have seen the desperation in her eyes, but he gave no outward sign of it.

"This is a singular honor, your majesty," the master-at-arms told her as the carriage turned through the gates back toward the palace. "To what do we owe this unexpected visit?"

"Alexin informs me you have a new recruit, my lord."

Dargin turned to Alexin in confusion. "New recruit?"

"I promised to show her majesty Sunchaser's new colt," he explained.

"Ah!" the big man laughed, sounding a little relieved. "You should have sent word on ahead, your majesty. But if you'd like to wait for a moment, I will have the stables readied..."

"Please, there's really no need," she assured him. "I'm not so squeamish that I can't handle the smell of a bit of manure. Will you show me, Alexin?"

"Of course, your majesty."

Alexin led the way to the stables as Alenor forced herself to smile in acknowledgment of the numerous salutes she received as they passed the other Guardsmen. Alexin offered her his arm and led her past the lunging yard to the small stables reserved for the mounts that required isolation from the rest of the herd. As they stepped into the cool dimness of the stalls, Alexin glanced around to ensure they were alone, and then turned to her with concern.

"What's wrong?" he asked.

Alenor suddenly discovered she was crying. "We've got trouble, Alexin. Big trouble."

"What sort of trouble?"

"Belagren and Kirsh are going to Omaxin."

Alexin was silent for a moment. "Do you know why?"

She sniffed as she shook her head. "Kirsh just said he had something important to do. It's a coincidence, isn't it? There's no way they could know..."

"Shh!" Alexin warned, glancing around nervously. "I'll get a message to Reithan," he promised in a low voice. "But I'm afraid there's no way to warn...anyone else."

"But if they find him there..."

"Dirk's a smart boy, Alenor. I'm sure he'll be able to manage something."

"I'm so scared, Alexin," she admitted with a sob. "I nearly died when Kirsh told me where he was going. It was all I could do not to burst into tears right then. I'm no good at this. I can't even lie convincingly."

Alexin smiled at her, and then—somewhat hesitantly—he put his arm around her, as if sensing her need for comfort. "You're doing just fine, Alenor," he assured her softly.

She let him hold her for a moment, just relishing the feel of his embrace. Then she suddenly realized what would happen if anybody chanced upon them in such a compromising position.

"I'm sorry," she said, stepping away from him. "I shouldn't risk your life just because I'm a coward." She wiped her eyes, sniffed back the rest of her tears and squared her shoulders with determination. "You'd better show me this colt, Captain, or people will start to think we're doing something improper. Do I look like I've been crying?"

"Yes," he told her with a small smile. "But your love of horses is becoming quite legendary around here. Nobody will think it odd that you cried with happiness of the birth of a foal."

"And you'll get a message to . . . our friends?"

"The first chance I get."

"What would I do without you?" she asked, with a wan smile.

"Let's go look at this colt before someone sees us like this and you get to find out," he suggested.

Chapter 55

"Dirk!"

Tia's voice echoed eerily off the smooth curved walls of the Labyrinth. There was a quiver in her voice that he only ever heard when she entered the darkness.

"I'm down here by the gate!" he called back, resisting the temptation to add: "Where else would I be?"

The flare of light from her torch appeared a few moments before Tia did.

"You're spending far too much time in this damn tunnel," Tia complained as she stepped into view. "Are you any closer to figuring it out?"

Dirk shuffled the notes he had made around, and then shrugged. "I'm guessing that I have to hit each of the six numbers in sequence."

"We figured that out the day we found it," she reminded him. "What's taking so long?"

"Well, there are six different numbers I can choose to hit first. After I've chosen the first one, I've then got five different numbers to choose from and so on until I have only one choice for the last number. Fortunately, there are only six numbers and they're all different, so assuming I only have to hit each number once, there are only seven hundred and twenty possible combinations. All I have to do now is work out which one of those seven hundred and twenty possible combinations isn't going to kill me."

"You can't ever give a simple answer to anything, can you?" she sighed. "How long is it going to take?"

"Forever, unless I can figure out what Neris meant by that stupid verse."

"Well then, you need a break," she declared. "Maybe if you forget about it for a while, the solution will come to you."

He shook his head doubtfully. "Numbers are logical, Tia. I *know* there's a sequence here somewhere and it makes perfectly good sense. The trouble is Neris would have realized that any mathematician with half a brain could eventually work it out, too, no matter how obtuse. Whatever he chose it'll be something different. Something unique. Something that only he knew about."

"Maybe you'll think better on a full stomach."

He glanced up from his notes. "That hint was about as subtle as a lava flow."

"I found these!" she announced proudly, producing two speckled eggs from behind her back. "We can have blincakes."

"What you really mean is we can have blincakes if *I* cook them."

"Naturally. I'd just ruin them if I made them."

"Do we have everything we need?"

She smiled. "The previous tenants were very thoughtful. They left enough to feed us for months, if need be."

"Goddess! I hope it doesn't come to that!"

"So you *will* cook them?"

He nodded. She was in a remarkably good mood, no doubt because she had spent the day scouring the lake shore for eggs, rather than looking over his shoulder in the darkness of the Labyrinth. Every time Tia came in here, she grew more and more apprehensive. It was odd to discover Tia was afraid of the dark. Until she had entered the Labyrinth that first time, Dirk had been quite convinced Tia Veran was not afraid of anything.

"You're not as obsessed about blincakes as Neris, are you?"

She laughed. "No. You can make them any way you want. I can't taste the difference."

"Neris can," he told her with a shake of his head. "I made them for him once and didn't mix the ingredients in the right order. He threw the whole batch out and made me do it all over again until I'd memorized the recipe *and* gotten it all in the right order. And then he spent the rest of the day telling me how stupid I was."

"I think he's done that to everybody who's tried to cook for him."

Dirk stood up and stretched his arms above his head. He had been crouching over his notes, trying to puzzle out the sequence for the best part of three weeks now. His muscles were protesting their forced idleness, and his mind was starting to feel like scrambled eggs. He was glad Tia had come to drag him out of the tunnel. And he was looking forward to the blincakes, even if he did have to cook them himself.

"I'll go chase up Nellie," she offered. "You're going to need milk."

Nellie was the name Tia had given to the she-goat the Shadowdancers had left behind. Tia had adopted the abandoned creature as a pet, and it followed her everywhere—until she tried to milk it. If Tia even *thought* about tying Nellie up, with some indefinable animal sixth sense, the goat would vanish into the ruins, and it sometimes took hours to find her again.

"Good luck."

With a legitimate excuse to escape the darkness, she headed off to find the recalcitrant goat. Dirk picked up his torch and made his way back through the Labyrinth, squinting as he stepped outside into the light, surprised to see a smudge of red on the eastern horizon. He had not realized how late it was.

Dirk tossed the torch into the sand near the entrance, and then headed to the tent where the supplies left behind by the Shadowdancers were stored. He was glad he had thought of demanding that sufficient food and shelter was left for him and Tia, and it was a good sign that Belagren had done as he asked—or rather, demanded. He had not left much doubt about his intentions if she did not do exactly as he wanted.

As he gathered up the ingredients he needed, he tried to calculate how long they had been here in Omaxin or, more specifically, how long it was since they had left Bollow. He had lost track of the days, so engrossed was he in the problem of the gate. He wondered how much time they had left.

Dirk realized he should probably warn Tia about what he had done. He should have told her about the letter to Belagren while they were still in Bollow. Instead, he let her think he was joking. Of course, she would never believe the truth, he was certain of that, and his silence would do nothing but make him look even more guilty when the time came...

Maybe she was better off not knowing. Too many people had died because of him already. He would not allow the toll to climb any higher. He certainly wasn't going to endanger Tia if he could avoid it.

And that was the problem. He truly did not want to hurt her, but he *needed* her to be upset. The more outraged Tia was when she learned the truth, the more credibility he would gain in the eyes of the High Priestess.

Several months of living in close proximity with Tia Veran had changed his opinion of her somewhat. She was still annoying, temperamental and stubborn, but she was also intelligent (which was hardly surprising, given who her father was), resourceful and extremely independent...and when she kissed him...

Dirk pushed *that* thought away, hastily. It was going to be bad enough when Tia discovered he had betrayed her.

I've been down in the tunnel on my own way *too long* . . .

"Have you seen Nellie?" Tia asked, poking her head through the tent flap.

Dirk jumped with fright at her unexpected appearance. "What? No, I haven't."

"Damn that goat! I swear she can read my mind."

"Try down near the lake," he suggested.

She looked at him quizzically. "Are you all right?"

"I'm fine. Why do you ask?"

"Because you were just sitting in here, staring off into space. I had to call you three times before you answered me."

"I was thinking about the gate," he told her with a shrug. It was a perfectly acceptable excuse.

"Well, get your mind off the gate and onto the blincakes, boyo," she ordered. "It took me all day to find those damn eggs, and if you botch them up, I'll probably have to disembowel you or something."

He frowned. "You really do have an unhealthy obsession with causing me grievous bodily harm, don't you?"

She grinned at him. "I thought it was one of my more endearing traits."

"Not from where I'm sitting."

"Don't be such a baby. How long will they take?"

"The blincakes? That depends on how long it takes you to milk that goat."

"Do you remember the recipe?"

Dirk rolled his eyes. "Two cups of flour, a teaspoon of salt, three quarters of a cup of milk, an egg, an eighth of a cup of lard and a quarter of a cup of treacle. In that order. I remember it very well. Neris made sure of it. He even made me measure out the cups of flour in teaspoons."

Tia smiled, remembering Neris doing the same thing to her. "Fifty teaspoons to a cup. I learned to count measuring out the ingredients for Neris's damn blincakes."

"I'm not surprised," Dirk agreed. "He called it the beautiful simplicity of numbers. Do you think he did *anything* without breaking it down to a mathematical equation?"

Before she could answer him, the baleful bleating of a goat clearly echoed through the ruins. Tia cocked her head to one side, trying to determine the direction of the sound. "I swear that beast is taunting me," she muttered.

The bleating came again, even closer this time.

"Sounds like it's coming from over near the corral," Dirk suggested. "Do you want a hand catching her?"

"And let that slot-eyed little bitch think she has me beaten? Not a chance. You just take care of the cooking, Dirk, and I'll take care of that damn goat."

Chapter 56

The blincakes were delicious, and there were enough so that they were able to have the leftovers for breakfast the following morning. By the time the second sun had risen fully they had eaten their fill, and Dirk was drinking the last of his tea before disappearing back into the gloom of the Labyrinth again to puzzle out Neris's gate.

"You know, you're going to make someone a very good wife someday," Tia told him, as she licked her fingers appreciatively. Dirk really was quite handy to have around at times, when it came down to it. "Reithan's always trying to convince me I should learn to cook properly. He says I'll never catch a husband otherwise."

Dirk smiled. "I rather imagine if you ever decide to catch a husband, Tia, you'll run the poor sod down, club him over the head and drag him back to your cave by the ankles."

Her eyes flashed angrily for a moment, then she laughed as she realized he was joking. It had taken a long time, but she had finally reached the point where he could make such a comment and not get throttled for it.

"I'll have you know there are any number of young men in Mil who would gladly allow me to 'drag them back to my cave by their ankles,' as you so poetically put it."

"A few months at sea will do that to a man, I hear," he remarked with a grin.

"I'm in too good a mood to let you irritate me today, Dirk Provin." She sighed contentedly and settled back into a more comfortable position. "Since you did such a good job of making the blincakes, I've decided to be nice to you all day and ignore your infantile and pathetic attempts at humor."

Dirk suddenly leaned forward and stared at her. "What did you say?"

"I said your jokes are infantile and pathetic."

"No! Not that bit! The other bit!"

She shrugged, rather puzzled by his sudden excitement. "I said I'd decided to be nice to you today. Surely it's not that rare an occurrence that you need to get so worked up about it."

"For making the blincakes!" he finished for her excitedly. "Of *course*!"

Tia looked at him blankly.

"That's it!" he cried, jumping to his feet. "'But in the order of the making, patterns lurk there for the taking.' That's the sequence!"

She shook her head in bewilderment. "What are you *talking* about?"

"Come on!" he urged. "I'll show you."

He turned and ran for the entrance to the Labyrinth without waiting to see if she was following. He got three steps inside before he realized he had forgotten a torch in his haste and turned around, almost colliding with Tia, who'd had the presence of mind to light one first before attempting to enter the darkness. He grabbed her wrist and dragged her forward. He was too excited to wait for her to pick her way carefully through the gloom.

"Slow down!" she demanded as he pulled her along. "You're going to trip us both up!"

"Don't be such a girl," he retorted impatiently.

She muttered a curse, but she kept up as he ran toward

Neris's gate. When they reached it, he dropped to his knees among the scattered notes he had made and pulled out a fresh sheet and a stick of charcoal. She stared at him, wondering if all the time he had spent in the darkness had finally sent him over the edge. There was a fine line between genius and madness. She knew that for a fact.

"What's Neris's recipe for blincakes?"

"Are you *serious*?"

"Very." Dirk laughed suddenly. "No wonder Neris spent all day telling me I was stupid. He wasn't talking about making blincakes. He was talking about the fact that he'd told me how to open the gate and I was too thick to realize it."

"Dirk," Tia said patiently, as if she was talking to Neris in one of his more eccentric moments. "Please don't tell me that you think the secret to opening this gate is the recipe for blincakes."

"Sort of."

"That's insane."

"So is Neris." He looked up at her and smiled. "It's not as crazy as it sounds, trust me. I'll show you. It's two cups of flour, right? And a teaspoon of salt, three quarters of a cup of milk, an egg, an eighth of a cup of lard and a quarter of a cup of treacle. In that order. He's adamant about it."

"*So?*" she prompted impatiently.

Dirk scratched out the series of numbers on the sheet he found and then held it up for her. "See!"

She stared at it uncomprehendingly.

"Look!" he explained impatiently, reading the figures to her. "Two, one-fiftieth, three-quarters, one, one-eighth, and one-quarter, assuming that one cup equals fifty teaspoons. Multiply them by two hundred and you get four hundred, four, one fifty, two hundred, twenty-five and fifty. It's the ratio of the ingredients to each other! Four hundred to four to one fifty to two hundred to twenty-five to fifty." He pointed at the wall where the same numbers were chiseled into the raised stones. "There's no secret mathematical sequence there! It's the recipe for blincakes!"

"I think you've spent way too much time down here alone in the dark, Dirk."

He laughed as he climbed to his feet. "Do you remember I asked you once what you were hoping for? That I'd find a way through the Labyrinth or die trying? You said either one would do."

"I remember," she agreed, a little uncertain as to why he would bring that up now.

"Well, you're about to get your wish."

"Dirk! *No!*" she cried as he turned to face the wall. "If you're wrong it will kill us!"

"Then stand back," he suggested.

Before she had a chance to protest any further, Dirk depressed the first stone. It slipped into the wall smoothly and silently. He waited for a moment, and when death did not rain down on top of him, he depressed the stone marked with the number four.

"So far so good."

"This is suicide!" Tia muttered behind him as he depressed the third stone, but she made no attempt to stop him.

"This is why we came," he reminded her, reaching up for the two hundred. The fourth stone slid into place as smoothly as the others had.

There was still no indication that he had triggered any deadly traps, but neither had the gate made any sound, or done anything to indicate that his idea was working. He depressed the fifth block with a reasonable amount of confidence. Tia was fairly certain by now that if he was wrong, they would not find out about it until Dirk pressed the last number.

His hand hovering over the sixth stone, Dirk hesitated for a fraction of a second. Tia's heart was racing as he pushed it, unconsciously cringing as he did. She was half expecting the wall to come crashing down on top of him, or the floor to open up and swallow them both.

"Nothing happened," Tia said.

"I'm still alive," he pointed out.

"But it didn't open."

"That's because it's a lock," he told her. He glanced over his shoulder at her and smiled. "What were you expecting? That the wall would magically swing open with a fanfare of trumpets as soon as I was done?"

"Actually, I was expecting to see you engulfed in a ball of flame, or something equally gruesome," she admitted. "But trumpets would have been nice a touch. Do you think it's unlocked now?"

"Let's find out."

Dirk turned to the wall and pushed on the left side with all his might—and almost landed on his face when the gate swung smoothly open.

Recovering his balance, Dirk glanced at her as Tia moved up beside him. He did not seem surprised when she slipped her hand into his and held it tightly. Dirk took the torch from her and held it high as they cautiously stepped into the absolute blackness beyond the gate.

Chapter 57

Although the darkness was complete, Tia knew they were no longer in a tunnel. The air felt different; it smelled slightly musty and there was an indefinable feeling of vast space around them. Dirk's torch cast a circle of flickering light that did nothing to penetrate the gloom.

Beyond it there was nothing but blackness.

As Dirk led her into the darkness her heart began to race. Despite the fact that Tia knew they were in a large cavern, the feeling of claustrophobia was overwhelming. She gripped Dirk's hand even tighter and could feel her palms sweating. The only sound was the *tap-tap-tap* of their sandals on the smooth floor, the hissing of the sputtering torch and the sound of her increasingly ragged breathing.

"This place must be huge," Dirk breathed in awe. He didn't sound frightened. He sounded full of wonder and delight.

"Let's go get...some more torches and find out...later," she suggested.

He glanced at her in concern. "Are you all right?"

"I'm fine," she lied. She was trembling so hard she thought her teeth might start to rattle.

"Look at the floor," Dirk said.

She glanced down. By their feet was a thick gold line that curved away into the blackness. Still holding her hand, Dirk followed the line until they came to the end, where it curved back in the opposite direction. In the center, where the two curved lines were at their widest, was a large golden circle.

"The Eye of the Labyrinth," she whispered. Tia was not sure why she was whispering. It just seemed appropriate. "It's set into the floor."

Dirk held the torch higher. The stone was a creamy color, flecked with darker particles that glittered in the firelight. What they could see of the Eye was inlaid into the polished ignimbrite in gold with a precision that Tia had not thought possible.

"It must be a decoration of some sort," Dirk speculated, raising the torch higher to make the most of the small amount of light. "Perhaps this cavern was part of a temple."

"Why do you think that?"

"Maybe the Eye held some sort of religious significance for the ancient residents of Omaxin—in the same way that the suns hold significance in our time. Stay here," he ordered, shaking Tia's hand from his.

"Don't you dare leave me!" she cried in panic.

"I'm not going far. I just want to pace this out..."

"No! You can come back later and build a bonfire in here for all I care, but you're not leaving me here standing in the dark while you go off exploring."

He turned to her with a reassuring smile. "There's nothing to be afraid of."

"I'm not afraid!" she snapped. "I'm terrified. I feel like this whole damn building is about to come down on top of me."

"It's stood for thousands of years, Tia. Why would it choose now to collapse on us? That's illogical."

"Shove your logic, Dirk Provin!" she exclaimed. "I just don't like it, all right? I don't need a reason and you can't talk me out of it. Now can we go? I'll come back when you've got the place lit up like the second sun is shining in here."

Dirk looked at her oddly for a moment, and then, with no warning, he tossed the torch back toward the door, plunging them into darkness.

"What are you *doing*?" she yelled, her heart beating so fast she was sure it would explode out of her chest. Panic welled up inside her as their only light sputtered and died on the floor out of reach.

Tia wanted to scream. She felt rather than saw Dirk in front of her. He took both her hands in his and held them tightly. He must have felt her trembling, must have known how terrified she was.

"Tia!" he said sharply. "Listen to me! Nothing can hurt you! Darkness is just the absence of light. There are no monsters lurking in the shadows and the building is *not* going to fall down and crush us."

She was panting heavily, her breath coming in ragged gasps. "Get me...out of here...Dirk...I can't breathe..."

"Yes, you can," he commanded. "Now take a deep breath and close your eyes."

She did as he ordered, unable to tell the difference between her eyes being open and closed.

"Breathe," he commanded.

She took a few ragged breaths and then forced herself to breathe deeper. "Don't let me go..."

"I won't let you go. Breathe."

"We'll never get out of here," she sobbed as she recovered enough breath to speak coherently. "The torch has gone out and we don't know where the door is..."

"Open your eyes."

She did as he asked, but she could not notice any discernable difference.

"Now look to your left."

"I can't see anything!" she cried in panic. "I swear if I ever get out of here I'm going to kill you for this..."

"Of course you are," he agreed soothingly. "Now do as I say."

"But I don't see anything!"

"You're not looking. Give your eyes time to adjust. You can make out the door if you look closely. There's enough light filtering in from the tunnel to see the outline. It's faint, but it's there."

Tia wiped her eyes, not realizing that she had been crying. She looked hard in the direction Dirk indicated, and after a few moments she began to make out a slightly lighter patch in the blackness.

"Can you see it?"

She nodded, then realized he would not see the movement. "Sort of."

"So there's no reason to panic, is there? You're not trapped. You can find your way out of here anytime you want."

His hands relaxed their hold. She instinctively gripped them tighter. "Don't you even think of letting me go!"

"I won't." There was a smile in his voice.

"And don't laugh at me, either."

"I wouldn't dream of it."

"Why are you doing this to me?"

"Because I need your help, Tia. You're no good to me in here if I can't get you past the door."

"You selfish bastard."

"I know," he sighed. "You can add it to the long list of reasons you already have to despise me."

She wished she could see his face. There was something in his voice that sounded almost like...regret.

"What do you mean by that?"

"Nothing. It doesn't matter."

"Dirk?" Tia reached out in the darkness to where she thought his face might be. She felt his cheek, rough and stubbled under her hand. He hadn't shaved for days, so engrossed had he been in the problem of the gate.

Then Dirk turned his face slightly and kissed her palm.

It did not surprise her as much as it should have. What did surprise her was that she didn't pull away. She just stood there, surrounded by a darkness so complete and smothering that even as close as she was, she could not see his face.

She felt his breath on her cheek before she felt his lips. When he kissed her, her heart began pounding in terror, but she didn't know if it was the oppressive blackness, or the fact that she was letting him, that caused her panic attack. Her senses seemed amplified in the absence of any other stimuli. The only thing she could hear was her own ragged breathing; the only thing she could feel was Dirk's kiss. He was deceptively strong, and his embrace felt like an extension of the darkness. It somehow made the deprivation of her other senses bearable. Without thinking of the consequences, she slid her arms around his neck and he pulled her even closer. The darkness pressed in on her until there was nothing left for her to comprehend but the fact that she was kissing Dirk Provin as if there was nothing else in the world that mattered more.

"Don't let me go," she breathed softly after a time.

She could feel his smile against her lips. "It'd be nice to think you meant that because you actually *wanted* me to hold you, rather than because you're terrified of the dark."

She stayed in his arms, hiding from the darkness. "Why did you kiss me?"

"You're not armed."

"Are you actually capable of answering a question like a normal person?"

"Apparently not. Are you all right now?"

She shook her head. "I'm dreaming, aren't I? This is a nightmare."

"Do I often kiss you in your nightmares?" he asked curiously.

"All the time."

"Did you want me to stop?" he breathed into her ear, sending a shiver down her spine.

She leaned back in his arms and searched the darkness, trying to see his face, hoping to read what was in those disconcerting metal-gray eyes. Her sight had adjusted to the gloom, but not enough to see him clearly.

"Is that why you brought me in here? To kiss me?"

"You mean, did I pretend to suddenly figure out Neris's sequence so I could open the gate just to lure you into the darkness, scare the sunlight out of you then have you throw yourself at me out of gratitude? You vastly overestimate my powers of planning and organization, Tia."

"Now you're making fun of me."

"Well, you do sort of invite it, you know…"

"Will you get me the hell out of here if I kiss you again?"

"If you want me to."

I must be crazy to let this happen, she thought as she closed her eyes. Then Dirk kissed her again and right at that moment, she discovered she didn't really care.

They stayed up late that night, gathering together every torch they could find to take back into the cavern tomorrow so that they could get a better look at the Eye. Dirk was more animated than she had ever seen him, which peeved Tia a little when she realized that he was just as excited about what they might discover in the cavern as he was about what had happened between them.

Exactly *what* had happened between them had her a little confused. Once they were back out in the red light of the first sun, it seemed almost surreal. Had Dirk really kissed her like that? *And more important, why didn't I just knee him in the groin and run like hell?*

"Is there any more oil in the tent?" Dirk asked. He was kneeling by the mountain of equipment he was readying for tomorrow's expedition into the cavern.

"I'll check," she offered absently, glad of the excuse to be doing something. Every time she looked at him she didn't see the Dirk she knew and despised, she saw nothing but the darkness and…*Oh for the Goddess's sake! Get a grip on yourself, girl!*

EYE OF THE LABYRINTH

"If there's no oil left, look around and see if there's anything else flammable we can use," he called after her.

She raised her arm to acknowledge that she had heard him and made her way to the supply tent. Halfway there, Nellie appeared, trotting alongside her like a faithful dog.

"What do you think I should do, old girl?" she asked the goat.

Nellie stared up at her with her coin-slot eyes and said nothing. Tia fetched the last of the lamp oil from the tent and returned to Dirk. He took it from her and added it to the pile, then stood up and nodded with satisfaction.

"That's just about everything we need."

She looked at the pile doubtfully. "A packhorse wouldn't go astray."

"It'll take a few trips to move it all inside," he shrugged. "But that doesn't really matter. I'm all done here now. I'm going to try to get some sleep. We've got a long day ahead of us tomorrow."

"Good night, Dirk."

He turned and headed for his tent without another word, patting Nellie absently on the head as he passed her. Tia watched him leave then turned for her own tent. She bent down to lift the flap, and then muttered a curse and dropped it back into place.

"Let's get something straight," she announced, marching into Dirk's tent without warning.

He spun around in stunned surprise to find her barging in on him halfway through taking off his shirt.

"I'm not going to spend days, weeks, maybe even months playing games with you, Dirk Provin. Either there's something going on between us or there isn't. If there's not, then tell me now, so I know. If there is, then let's cut out the nonsense and do something about it."

Dirk stared at her, speechless for the first time since she had met him.

"*Well?*"

"Just like that?" he managed, eventually. "Let's *do* something about it? What exactly did you have in mind?"

"What do you *think* I have in mind, you idiot?" she snapped. "Goddess! You really are thick, aren't you?"

"You haven't been eating mushrooms again, have you?" he asked.

Suddenly, Tia's bravado deserted her. She blushed a deep shade of crimson. "You promised you'd never mention that again." Tia turned to leave, realizing that she had just made the biggest mistake of her life. And an even bigger fool of herself.

"I might, if you ever stopped throwing yourself at me," he said.

Tia's first reaction was to turn around and slap him but he caught her wrist as she raised it to strike him and gently pulled her closer.

"Let's agree on something," he suggested as he put his arms around her. "You stop trying to cause me grievous bodily harm, and I won't make any further references to your ferocious behavior while under the influence of hallucinogenic mushrooms."

Filled with uncertainty, Tia thought about his offer for a moment and then nodded. It was impossible to tell what he was thinking. His eyes gave away nothing.

"Sounds fair," she agreed.

A lot more hesitantly than she had barged into his tent, she kissed him, a little cautiously at first, afraid she had imagined what it felt like in the darkness. She was not sure, but it felt like part desire, part hunger and part terror.

"You do realize, don't you," he remarked a few moments later, "that you're probably the most unromantic female on the whole of Ranadon?"

Tia opened her eyes and smiled. "This from the man who tried to scare me to death before seducing me? That's a bit rich."

"Just so long as you remember whose idea this was in the morning. I've a feeling your second thoughts might be quite fatal."

"Dirk, just shut up and get on with it, will you?" she said as she began to undo the remaining buttons on his shirt. "Goddess! Why couldn't I have found somebody who doesn't talk so much?"

He laughed softly as he slipped the shirt from his shoulders. "You used to complain that I didn't talk enough."

"There's a time and place for everything, Dirk," she told him, impatiently.

He kissed her again, the urgency between them putting an end to further conversation. At some point, her shirt was tossed across the tent. Their trousers and sandals presented something of a hindrance, but somehow they managed to get rid of them without too much difficulty. They stumbled backward in their haste and fell onto the narrow camp bed, which creaked alarmingly under their combined weight.

Tia laughed at the sound as she lay back on the bunk. Dirk bent to kiss her again, and then he stopped suddenly when he spied the necklace he had given her in Bollow nestled between her breasts. With his finger, he lightly traced the V-shaped line on her skin where she was tanned and freckled from long hours in the sun in an open-necked shirt. Then gently, he picked up the little silver bow and arrow. He looked at her curiously. "You're still wearing it."

"And you thought I was unromantic."

With a smile, Dirk let the pendant drop. Tia closed her eyes as she felt his tongue trailing down between her breasts toward her navel. She arched her back with a cry that was caught somewhere between terror and delight and after that, she did not think about much at all, for a long, long time.

Chapter 58

When Tia woke the next morning she was alone, and all the doubts and fears that she had pushed away the night before came crashing down on her like a falling building. She sat up and glanced around. Her clothes were strewn across the tent where they had thrown them in their haste last night, like a silent reprimand.

Dirk's clothes were gone.

She scrambled off the narrow pallet and hurriedly gathered up her things, cursing all the while under her breath as she got dressed. She emerged into the sunlight to find the fire smoking and the pile of equipment they had gathered the night before missing. Dirk was already in the Labyrinth.

Grabbing one of the few torches left behind, she lit it from the fire and headed off toward the Labyrinth with a purposeful stride. Tia rehearsed what she was going to say, over and over, but it didn't seem to make much sense.

It'll sound better when I say it out loud, she decided as she stepped into the darkness. Things always sounded better when you said them out loud.

When Tia stepped through the last gate into the hall, she stopped suddenly, her eyes wide with wonder. Dirk had been busy. There was a line of torches that stretched away into the distance, slicing the gloom like a sword-cut made of warm yellow light. The ceiling was lost in the gloom, but the golden Eye in the floor reflected the flames unevenly, giving the impression that it was winking at her. The few walls that she could see were covered with elaborate illustrations of circles within circles. There were pictures of creatures she had never seen, so real it was as if they had been captured and stored in miniature behind glass. There were images of cities she was sure could never have existed and, strangest of all, every ten feet or so, a large opaque window was set into the wall, though on closer inspection, it was obvious that even before the eruption, there would have been only solid rock behind them.

Momentarily forgetting why she had come, she walked to the wall on her right and held the torch up for a closer look.

"Now who's gawping like a country boy on his first trip out of his village?" Dirk asked from behind her.

She squealed with fright at the unexpected voice. "Don't sneak up on me like that!" she cried as she spun around to face him.

"I'm sorry," he said, relieving her of the torch she was waving wildly between them. "I didn't mean to frighten you. Isn't this place amazing?"

She stared at him in bewilderment. "Is that all you can say?"

He looked at her with a puzzled expression. "I suppose, if you really want, I could think up a more colorful adjective..."

She punched his arm impatiently. "I meant about us! About...what happened..."

"Ah..." he said warily. "That."

"What do you mean...ah...*that*?"

Dirk regarded her cautiously, and then he nodded in understanding. "I'm sorry."

"Why are you apologizing?"

He sighed. "I realize you've probably come down here to run a blade through me. But you don't have to worry. It won't happen again."

"What are you talking about?"

"It's just...well, I mean there's no future for us really, is there? And it's not even as if you like me all that much, and..." He turned away from her, making it impossible to see his face and guess what he was really feeling.

"So it meant nothing to you?" she said to his retreating back.

He did not answer her. He began to walk away.

"Don't you dare just turn your back on me!"

Dirk turned and retraced the few steps between them cautiously, his eyes the color of dull metal, his mood impossible to fathom in the uncertain torchlight. "It was a mistake, Tia. Look at us. You're already angry at me."

"Well, that's not my fault," she retorted uncomfortably. "And I'm not angry. It's just I woke up and you were gone..."

"So you're mad at me because I'm an early riser?"

She searched his face for some hint of what he truly felt, but as usual, she had no idea if he was dying a little inside or laughing at her. "I am making such a mess of this, aren't I?"

He appeared to consider the matter for a moment, and then nodded. "Pretty much."

"Kiss me, Dirk."

"Why?"

"Do you need a reason?"

He searched her face doubtfully. "Are you sure about this, Tia?"

In reply, she slid her arms around his neck. He tossed the flickering torch aside and kissed her hesitantly, as if expecting her to pull away. Tia closed her eyes as his doubt gave way. His arms tightened around her, and she found herself pushed up against the wall, all her fears and doubts forgotten...

"Wow!"

She opened her eyes with a languid smile, not sure what she had done to provoke such an exclamation of awe. But Dirk wasn't even looking at her. He was staring at the wall behind her.

"Look at this!" he exclaimed excitedly, moving her aside and reaching for the discarded torch.

"Dirk..."

"This is it! This is how Neris must have worked out when the Age of Shadows would end!"

She stared at him. "But what about?..."

He was tracing his finger over the mural that, to Tia, looked like nothing more than a whole lot of circles. "He used to draw these circles all the time. This must be the orbit of the two suns of Ranadon."

A part of Tia was delighted that he had made such an important discovery, but mostly she was irritated by the way he had cast passion aside for something so...inanimate.

"How can you tell what those circles mean?" she asked, a little petulantly. "More to the point, how did you manage to work it out while you were supposed to be kissing me?"

He glanced at her with a grin. "You must inspire me to great leaps of intuitive reasoning. Like Neris and the poppy-dust."

"Poppy-dust destroyed Neris," she reminded him, not sure she liked the idea of being compared to a dangerous narcotic.

"Then it's a better analogy than I realized," he chuckled.

Tia rolled her eyes, realizing the futility of arguing with him. "Do you really think this mural is what we're looking for?"

Dirk moved a little to the left, holding the torch high, tracing the incomprehensible series of diagrams carved into the stone. Then he stopped suddenly and scooped up a handful of shattered stone that lay at the base of the wall and held it up for her examination with a wry smile.

"Behold! The secrets of the second sun of Ranadon," he said.

"How can you tell?"

Dirk pointed to the wall where he was standing. Tia moved closer to get a better look. The diagrams suddenly stopped, shattered by a gaping hole in the mural. On the floor beneath the hole lay a pile of cracked stone. It looked as if some-one had quite deliberately defaced the wall at that point with a sledgehammer.

"This is it. All the phases of the first and second suns," he explained, pointing to the series of carvings. "And I'll bet you all the pumice in the Tresna Sea that the ruined section was the part we needed to work out when the next Age of Shadows is due."

"How can you be so certain?"

"Because this wall wasn't damaged by accident." Dirk suddenly chuckled softly. "Your father has a wicked sense of humor."

"Care to let me in on the joke?"

"Don't you see? The whole Labyrinth...the traps he set... everything he did to keep Belagren out of here...It doesn't matter. None of it matters..."

"Why?"

"Because there's nothing here for Belagren to find."

"You mean Neris destroyed it?"

Dirk nodded. "I have a bad feeling that I could work on these diagrams for the rest of my life and never learn what Neris knows."

Tia smiled at the delicious irony. "So Belagren spent half a lifetime trying to get into this cavern and it's useless." Then her face creased into a frown as another, less pleasant thought oc-curred to her. "That doesn't help us much, either, Dirk."

"Maybe," he shrugged. "I won't know for certain until I've

had time to study it closely. But I'll wager there's little useful information here."

"So it's all been a waste of time," she concluded.

"Maybe not," he shrugged. "There's a lot to study..."

Tia shook her head. "I don't know why I was worried about you. I mean, it's not as if we're ever going to actually spend any time together ever again, now that you've got this place to play in."

He tore his gaze away from the wall long enough to smile at her. "Jealous?"

"Of a wall? I think maybe I am."

"You can come and distract me every now and then," he offered.

"I have a bad feeling you're not that easily distracted, Dirk." Tia sighed, thinking of a kiss that ended with Dirk getting excited about an ancient mural.

He didn't answer her. He was too busy studying the damn wall.

Chapter 59

Alenor got an unexpected break from Dorra's constant surveillance about a week after Kirsh's departure for Omaxin. Since her husband had left Kalarada, her lady-in-waiting had been particularly vigilant, and had even insisted on accompanying her on her daily ride with the guard. Even Jacinta had not been able to deter her. But thanks to a meal of spoiled shellfish, Dorra and two dozen or more members of the palace staff were trapped in their rooms, looking miserable and pale, not daring to venture too far from the garderobes.

Most of the victims were Senetian. Shellfish was considered a delicacy of Senet, a dish the Dhevynians had never really embraced. There were lots of recriminations, of course, and angry mutterings about the stupidity of the Dhevynian palace chefs—

at whose feet the Senetians firmly laid the blame for their illness. The mood in the palace was quietly buoyant, as not only the queen, but most of her staff, suddenly found themselves free of Senetian interference, even if only for a few days.

Alexin came to visit her as soon as he heard of the epidemic. For once, Alenor did not have to justify his admittance or find an excuse to be alone with him. Dimitri Bayel simply announced him and left.

"Dimitri seems rather jovial this morning," Alexin remarked, as the Lord Seneschal closed the door on his way out. "I swear he almost whistled on the way here."

"Almost every Senetian in the palace is bent over the garderobes this morning," Jacinta told him happily. "I really must speak to the cooks. It was such a good idea to serve shellfish at dinner last night."

"I'd be careful if I were you, Lady Jacinta," he warned with a smile. "They might start to think we're deliberately trying to poison them."

"The idea does have a certain morbid attraction," she admitted. She put aside her tapestry and rose to her feet. "But for now, I'm going to make the most of this little piece of unexpected sunshine. If you'll excuse me, your majesty, I have a few things I'd like to take care of."

"Of course, Jacinta," said Alenor. "I'll be all right here with Alexin."

"Yes, well, if he tries to take advantage of you...just be quiet about it, will you? Dorra's got a dreadful headache and I'd hate for her to be unduly disturbed."

A little embarrassed, Alenor smiled as Jacinta let herself out of the room, but her good humor faded as all the other problems she currently faced suddenly seemed to crowd in on her.

"You've been much happier since Jacinta arrived," Alexin noted.

"She's wonderful. She bullies Dorra unmercifully, though. I'm sure they'll come to blows one day."

"If they do, my money's on Jacinta."

"So is mine," she agreed. "Have you been able to get a message to...the others?"

"That's why I'm here," he told her. "A certain cousin of mine is here in Kalarada at present. He arrived yesterday. I thought you might want to meet with him."

"Reithan is *here*?" she gasped.

Alexin nodded. "And with most of your Senetian watch-dogs incapacitated, there'll never be a safer time to speak with him."

"When does he want to meet?"

"Now," Alexin said. "He'll be gone by first sunrise tonight."

"I'll have someone saddle my horse."

"Already taken care of, your majesty," he said, offering her his hand. "I took the liberty of informing Lord Bayel that you would be visiting the barracks again this morning to see the colt."

She smiled at him as she placed her hand in his. "You're getting a little bit ahead of yourself, aren't you, Alexin?"

"Just taking advantage of the situation, your majesty."

"I'm not sure I should be happy that you're taking advantage of me," she said lightly, but when she looked at Alexin, suddenly he was not smiling anymore.

"It would be very easy to take advantage of you, Alenor."

There was something odd in his tone. Something that Alenor suspected shouldn't be in the voice of a Guardsman ad-dressing his queen. She found she could not meet his eye. "You think I'm a silly girl playing at being queen, don't you?"

He still had hold of her hand. Gently, he pulled her closer, and lifted her chin with his finger, forcing her to look at him. "I think you're the most courageous person I know. And I'm not the only one who thinks you're going to become the best queen Dhevyn's had in a living memory. Ask Jacinta if you don't be-lieve me."

She searched his face for some hint that he was simply flat-tering her. "But I'm so frightened all the time..."

"But you still do what you have to, Alenor. That's what makes you brave. Any fool can plunge ahead fearlessly when they're too stupid to realize the risk. But when you know what's at stake, when you realize the danger and you do it anyway, because it has to be done, that's true courage."

"Then why does it feel so scary?"

"So you can tell when you're being brave. Otherwise, how would you know?"

She smiled. "Now you're teasing me."

He was still holding her close, much too close for comfort. Alenor suddenly became very aware of him. He was so much taller than she was so that when she lowered her eyes she found herself looking at his lips, which made her think of that day in Nova when she had kissed him...

"We should get going," Alexin suggested, as if he knew the dangerous direction her thoughts were heading.

She took a step back from him, trying to regain her composure. "Yes," she agreed, a little unsteadily. "We should."

Reithan was waiting for them in the barracks. When they reached the stall where Sunchaser and her colt were stabled, she discovered the Baenlander squatting by the foal, petting it with a smile. The stables were sharp with the smell of manure, but Alenor hardly noticed it. Her heart was racing, as it always did when she was courting danger. She reminded herself of what Alexin had told her. *I'm scared witless, so that must mean I'm being brave.* The thought did not actually help very much at all.

"I didn't think sailors liked horses," she remarked as she stopped by the railing, hoping she sounded calm and confident. "Or that they allowed wanted men to lurk about the stables of the Queen's Guard."

Reithan stood up from the foal and turned to look at her. "We've more friends in the guard than you know, your majesty."

She glanced at Alexin for a moment, then turned back to Reithan. "I'm beginning to realize that. Is it safe for us to talk here?"

Alexin nodded. "The Lord Marshal is away visiting his daughter on Bryton, so Dargin's in charge at the moment. Tael

Gordonov took the bulk of the guard out on patrol this morning. Those that are left can be trusted."

Somewhat reassured by Alexin's words, she turned to Reithan. "You've heard about Kirsh and the High Priestess?"

"Alexin told me. Did your husband say *why* they were going to Omaxin?" the pirate asked.

"I had to drag even that much out of him. Can you get a message to Dirk?"

Reithan shook his head helplessly. "There's no way to contact him or Tia, I'm afraid."

The news just seemed to be getting worse and worse. "Tia? You mean Tia Veran? Neris's daughter? She's with Dirk in Omaxin? But that's terrible! Antonov wants to get his hands on her almost as much as he wants you."

"It seems awfully coincidental that the High Priestess suddenly decided to visit Omaxin now," Alexin remarked. "She hasn't been back to the ruins since before Johan was captured."

Reithan obviously agreed with him. "Did Kirshov give no hint about the reason?"

"He just said he had to aid the High Priestess in something very important."

"Capturing Dirk Provin and Tia Veran sits nicely under the heading 'something very important,'" Alexin pointed out.

"But how could the High Priestess know where they are?" Alenor asked. "Who else knows about it?"

"Other than you and Alexin, your majesty, only a few of our people know where Dirk and Tia went, and I'm certain the information didn't come from one of us."

"Are you implying that *I'm* to blame?"

The Baenlander shrugged uncomfortably. "I don't mean to imply that you might have deliberately betrayed us, your majesty, but pillow talk can be dangerous."

Alenor was shocked by what he was suggesting. "You think *I* betrayed Dirk's whereabouts in the throes of passion with my husband?" she spluttered in disbelief.

"It's been known to happen..."

"It wasn't Alenor," Alexin announced in a tone that ended any further discussion on the subject. Reithan looked at his cousin curiously for a moment, and then nodded, accepting Alexin at his word.

"Then perhaps this is just a horrible coincidence," Reithan shrugged. "That doesn't make it any less dangerous for Dirk and Tia, though."

"What are we going to do?" Alenor heard herself asking the question and wondered when the Queen of Dhevyn and the Baenlanders had become "we."

"I think I'll head for Avacas," Reithan said. "I've got contacts there who might know what's going on. Or the Brotherhood could help."

"Are you sure?" Alenor asked doubtfully. "Kirsh didn't even tell his father what he was doing."

Both men looked at her in surprise. "The Lion of Senet doesn't know that the Regent of Dhevyn left for Omaxin with the High Priestess?"

Alenor shook her head. "Kirsh was quite put out when I suggested that his father should be told about it."

"This gets stranger and stranger," Reithan said with a frown.

"Captain!" a voice called urgently. Alenor jumped nervously at the call, certain they had been discovered.

Alexin turned to look over his shoulder at the Guardsman who hailed him. With a sigh of relief, Alenor recognized the young man as one of the guards who frequently made up her escort when she was out riding.

"What is it, Pavel?"

"Tael and the patrol are heading back, sir. Dargin said to tell you that you've got about ten minutes."

Alexin nodded and turned back to Reithan and Alenor, as the Guardsman slipped away silently.

"You'd better get out of here," he warned Reithan.

"I'll try to get a message to you from Avacas if I learn anything useful," he promised. "But I've a feeling there's not much I can do."

"Be careful," Alenor said.

Reithan smiled at her as he climbed through the rails of the stall. "I'm always careful, your majesty. It's sort of a job requirement in my line of work."

When Reithan was gone, Alexin opened the stall for Alenor. In the distance, they could hear the jingle of tack and the clattering of hooves in the cobbled yard as Tael Gordonov's patrol returned to the barracks. She held out her hand and the colt made its way unsteadily to her. Alenor fell to her knees and put her arms around his slender neck. For a moment, she closed her eyes and hugged the foal, breathing in the horsey smell of him, and then she looked up at Alexin.

"I thought of what to name him," she said. "Nadyezhda."

"Nadyezhda?"

"It's from the old language," she explained. "It means hope."

Chapter 60

The Lord of the Suns had little choice but to suffer Belagren and her party as his guests when they arrived in Bollow, mostly because Kirshov Latanya was leading her guard. Not for anything would Paige Halyn risk offending the Lion of Senet's favorite son. The High Priestess felt no guilt about arriving so unexpectedly. The Lord of the Suns' residence was huge. It was manned by a small army of servants, and it could easily accommodate her escort and the large number of retainers Belagren had in attendance.

The official residence of the Lord of the Suns' was several miles outside Bollow, on the shores of Lake Ruska. The house was built of alternating blocks of dark granite and creamy ignimbrite, which gave it an odd, checkered appearance. Four onion-domed spires marked the cardinal points of the house, which was as ancient and elegantly designed as the nearby city.

It sat in the center of a beautifully manicured park, complete with peacocks roaming the lawns and long-necked swans gliding smoothly across the glassy surface of the lake.

Once they were installed in their rooms, Belagren sent for Madalan and settled down in the Lord of the Suns' drawing room to wait for her. The trip from Kalarada had been rushed; the ride from Paislee forced; and she was glad of the chance to rest before tackling the most onerous part of their journey: the last two hundred miles to Omaxin.

They had taken the long way, swinging around Avacas, as she did not wish to confront Antonov until this was done. Belagren worried constantly that he would send someone to investigate why his son had abandoned his post as regent in Dhevyn for an unexpected pilgrimage to Omaxin.

"Old Paige really does quite well for himself out here in the backwaters, doesn't he?" Madalan remarked as she slid the doors shut behind her. The drawing room, like the rest of the house, was tastefully decorated with pieces that came from all over the world. The rugs were Sidorian, the elegant blackwood sideboard from distant Galina. Even the landscaped murals that covered the walls had a distinctly Damitian flavor.

Belagren stood by the window, watching the first sunrise stain the lake red as it crept over the horizon. She glanced over her shoulder at Madalan with a brief smile.

"He's not as big a fool as we like to think. He knows he can't do anything about us, so he's hunkered down here in Bollow for the past two decades and feathered his nest very nicely."

"You should have gotten rid of him years ago," Madalan suggested with a frown.

Belagren shook her head. "And risk getting a Lord of the Suns in his place who has a spine? Paige Halyn suits me just fine, Madalan."

"And when he dies? He's an old man."

"Then I will take his place. I will be the Lady of the Suns *and* the High Priestess of the Shadowdancers."

"How do you plan to manage that? The Lord of the Suns designates his own successor."

"He'll do as I tell him, or his brother will be gracing the next

Landfall Feast on Elcast as the main sacrifice. Why do you think I've left that limping fool on Elcast undisturbed all these years?"

"Once again, you appear to have thought of everything," Madalan agreed. "What did you want to see me about?"

"I want you to go back to Avacas," Belagren said, turning to face her. "With this new development, I believe it's time we did something about the heir to Senet."

"Is that wise? Kirsh has only been married for a couple of months. Won't it appear a bit odd if Misha suddenly dies?"

"He needn't die immediately, but he needs to take another turn for the worse; bad enough that he has to be moved to the Hospice at Tolace to recover, I think."

Madalan did not seem to agree. "Do we really need to get rid of him? By all accounts he was becoming quite confident in his role as the heir to Senet while his father was away. He's a lot more astute than his brother, even with his...problems."

"All the more reason to dispose of him. The last thing we need is an heir to Senet who we can't anticipate or control. No, Misha must go to Tolace and word must get around that he may not recover this time. I don't want him dying in the palace, and I certainly don't want to risk Antonov suspecting anything."

"Then why not just send Ella a message?"

"And commit my instructions to paper? Surely you jest?"

Madalan raised a brow with a faint smile. "That would be rather foolish, wouldn't it? Shall I take Marqel back with me, or have you decided to let her stay with Kirshov?"

"She can stay for the time being. She's being very cooperative at the moment, and Kirsh is genuinely fond of her. Besides, I'd rather have that dangerous little mischief-maker where I can keep an eye on her."

Madalan nodded, but before she could reply, there was a knock at the door. Annoyed at the interruption, the High Priestess called permission to enter, determined to have the fool who dared disturb her lashed to within an inch of his life.

"I see you've made yourself at home," remarked the Lord of the Suns as he stepped into the room. Belagren bit back the furious retort she was planning and smiled graciously.

"Your generosity and hospitality are most appreciated, my lord."

"You make it sound as if I had a choice in the matter, my lady."

Paige moved stiffly to the sideboard and poured himself a small glass of wine. He did not offer his guests refreshment, but Belagren decided to let the insult pass. *Have your petty victories, old man. I will win in the end.*

"Actually, your unexpected visit gives me an opportunity to speak with you on a rather important matter," he said, turning back to face her. "I was planning to write you, but perhaps it's better if I tell you face to face."

"You intrigue me, my lord."

"Do I?" he asked absently. "I don't mean to."

"What did you wish to discuss?"

"The matter of my successor." He moved across the room and took a seat opposite her, lowering himself into the chair cautiously, as if he was in great pain. *Madalan was right. He really is an old man.*

"Odd that you should bring that up," she remarked. "Madalan and I were just discussing it."

The old man smiled. She wished she could read him better, but the long beard that obscured half his face made it difficult to see his expression. Belagren had always distrusted men with beards. She thought they were hiding something.

"Well, if you've plans to tell me who I should name, I fear you're about a week too late. My will is already sealed in the Tabernacle of the Temple in Bollow."

Although she gave no outward sign of her irritation, Belagren could have slapped the old fool. She knew the traditions that bound the Church as well as any Sundancer. Once the Lord of the Suns' will had been locked away in the tabernacle, it could not be tampered with. If there was even the slightest hint that it had been, then the will was void and the appointment of the next Lord of the Suns was done by election. That was something she could not risk.

"Might I inquire as to the identity of your successor?"

"It's not you," he told her with a certain degree of malice.

"Then who?"

He took another sip from his glass, deliberately drawing out the silence. Then he looked at Madalan. "It's you."

"Me?" Madalan gasped in surprise.

The old man shrugged. "Consider it my last great act of defiance. I know that in reality there's no way I can stop you, Belagren, and the truth is, I long ago lost the will for the fight— about the time I watched you convince a once decent and devout young man to slit his baby son's throat simply to further your own ambitions, actually."

"But why *Madalan?*"

"She is your right hand, isn't she? That makes her close enough to you that you won't challenge my decision, but I still manage to deny you the one thing you've never had, which is my title. It's petty, I know, but I'm an old man and I'm dying. I should be allowed my little luxuries."

Belagren stared at the Lord of the Suns, quite astonished that he had had the wit to think of such a thing. He was right, of course. With Madalan elevated to Lady of the Suns, her closest confidante would become head of the Church. It in no way hampered the High Priestess's power, but it denied her the one thing that had always been out of her reach.

"And if I decide to challenge it?"

"I'll be dead, Belagren. I won't be in a position to care."

"It's a masterful stroke, my lord," she admitted begrudgingly. "You're not renowned for your political savvy. It's a pity for you that you didn't develop such a skill sooner."

"But rather lucky for you though, eh?"

She could not tolerate him looking so smug. "You said you were dying. Do you have any idea when we can expect this happy event?"

"In the fullness of time, Belagren. Don't rush me. I'll die when I'm good and ready." He finished his wine, placed the empty glass on the side table and painfully climbed to his feet. "And before you start arranging any accidents for me, just remember that my will is only valid if I die of natural causes. If there is even a hint of foul play, the new Lord or Lady of the Suns must be elected by the members of the Church. You may want to do the numbers, my lady. Your Shadowdancers are highly visible, but there are a lot of Sundancers still out there. Old men and women like me, who remember what it was like to worship the Goddess the way she truly should be worshipped, without death or Landfall bastards, without rope tattoos or foul potions. Every out-of-the-way town and remote village in Senet, and quite a few in Dhevyn, even as far away as Damita—all the places you never think to send your people because they aren't important enough for you—have Sundancers who remember the old ways and who will be called on to vote. I'll let you work out the odds for yourself. As for me, I'm content that I've slowed you down a little."

"You sound like a bitter old man," she accused.

"That's probably because I *am* a bitter old man," the Lord of the Suns agreed.

"You can't blame me for your own shortcomings, my lord," Belagren said.

He squinted at her accusingly. "But I do blame you, Belagren. I had such plans once, before the Age of Shadows. I was going to leave a legacy behind me that would help Ranadon, not plunge it into barbarism. Do you know what I really wanted to do as Lord of the Suns?"

Both women shook their heads.

"I wanted to educate people," he told them. "I wanted to set up schools. I wanted my Sundancers to do more than just worship the Goddess. I wanted them to become teachers. Instead, thanks to you and your lies and your Shadowdancers, I was barely able to keep the Sundancers intact. You drained us of our resources and our will, Belagren. You have made ignorance and narrow-mindedness into virtues. When I die, your right hand will assume my title and that will be the end of it." He shuffled painfully across the room to the door, turning to look at her before he opened it. "You're going to Omaxin to collect the Provin boy?"

She nodded warily. Belagren was not pleased that Dirk had involved the Lord of the Suns in this.

Paige Halyn shook his head sorrowfully. "Your ability to corrupt others never ceases to amaze me, Belagren. I hope you don't live to regret offering that young man asylum. He's more dangerous to you than poor Neris ever was, but I doubt you've the wit to realize it." He slid the doors open then hesitated and looked back at her again with a malicious smile.

"Actually, that's not true," he said. "I hope you *do* live to regret it. Badly."

Chapter 61

With the return of the Lion of Senet to Avacas, Misha's role in ruling Senet was significantly curbed. Lord Palinov stopped sending him reports, and he had not seen the Palace Seneschal or the Prefect of Avacas in more than three weeks. Boredom had quickly replaced Misha's feeling of being a contributing member of the royal family.

His father seemed pleased with what Misha had done in his absence, even congratulating him on his solution for the Talenburg levee wall dilemma. But after a brief meeting to bring his father up to date—in which Palinov did most of the talking and gave the impression Misha had done little but sign whatever was put in front of him—he had barely seen his father at all. He certainly had not been invited to continue to offer his opinion about how Senet should be governed.

Although Misha was disappointed, he was not surprised. Like most able-bodied men, Antonov equated physical disability with stupidity. He had actually seemed mildly astonished that Misha had coped as well as he did, but he made no suggestion that Misha might like to sit in on his daily meetings with Palinov, or that his eldest son might want to be kept up to date on the Talenburg situation, even though he was the one who had engineered such an acceptable solution.

Misha was, effectively, sent back to his rooms to quietly rot, out of sight and out of mind.

"Is everything all right, Misha?" Ella asked with some concern as she let herself into his room. He was sitting by the fireplace staring at his chessboard, trying to remember a game he'd had with Dirk once, when the young man had beaten him in about eight moves. Misha could not, for the life of him, remember how he had done it.

"I'm as well as can be expected under the circumstances," he replied, a little bitterly. They said that about the Crippled Prince a lot: "as well as can be expected under the circumstances." "Why do you ask?"

"I've been gone for hours. You've not moved a muscle. I swear you're still staring at the same chess piece you were studying before I left."

"There's little else to do," he reminded her sourly. "Where have you been?"

"The Hall of Shadows. Madalan arrived back from Bollow today."

"What was she doing in Bollow?" he asked, out of a desperate need for conversation, more than any real interest in the movements of the Shadowdancers.

"She didn't say," Ella shrugged. "Can I get you a rug? Something to drink, perhaps? You look a little pale."

"I feel no worse than usual," he assured her. "Nor any better, for that matter."

"Still, I might have Yuri drop by later and check on you. We don't want you coming down with anything. You've not the strength to fight off a serious illness."

"Or the wit to do anything useful, it seems."

She looked at him curiously. "You're not still brooding over the fact that now your father's back, your assistance is no longer required, are you? It's been nearly a month since he returned, Misha."

"Has it only been a month? It feels like a year."

"It's not like you to brood."

"Maybe I'll take up brooding as my new hobby," he suggested. "Then they could call me the Brooding Prince, rather than the Crippled Prince."

Ella smiled. "It's not like you to wallow in self-pity, either."

"I have to do something to pass the time."

She walked across the room and placed her hand on his

forehead with a slight frown. "Are you sure you're feeling well? You seem to have a slight temperature."

"I'm not sickening for something, Ella," he insisted, jerking his head away from her touch. "I'm just bored, that's all."

"Perhaps," she agreed doubtfully. "I think I'll have Yuri check you over all the same."

"Whatever," he sighed, thinking she would not let go of this until he agreed. Ella could be as tenacious as a terrier with a bone when she set her mind on something.

By the following morning, Misha was feeling much worse. Even his tonic did little to revive him. He felt weak and shaky, and after he threw up his breakfast, even the thought of food began to repulse him.

Yuri Daranski, the Shadowdancers' physician, called in to check on him after he refused lunch, tut-tutted meaningfully over the prince, and then took Ella into the other room to discuss his condition. Misha was rarely consulted about either his illness or the treatment required, so he thought nothing odd about it. He was feeling too ill to care much, anyway.

By the evening of the next day, Misha's fits began again, but this time it was not an isolated occurrence. He had three of them during the night. By the following morning, what little strength he had to start with had been sapped by the constant convulsions. His skin felt as if it had been dragged through the palace laundries, beaten for a time over a washboard, wrung out and then tossed over his skeleton to dry.

Ella was by his side constantly, her expression concerned, as she urged him to be strong, feeding him the tonic that had always helped him so much in the past, and that now appeared to be useless. He saw Yuri two or three times a day, but the physician was helpless. The fits grew more frequent and more savage, until Misha was certain each time he saw the warning, dancing white lights before his eyes that the next fit would be the one that killed him.

Misha's condition deteriorated so rapidly that finally even his father became concerned. Antonov visited him just as the second sun was setting five days after he had fallen ill. Misha had just had another fit, and Ella and Olena Borne were cleaning him up. As the fits became more intense, he quite often lost control of his bladder. This last fit had been the worst one yet. He had lost control of his bowels, too, while he was unconscious.

Antonov gagged as he stepped into the room, took one look at his son, and then turned to Ella. Misha feigned unconsciousness. He still had enough wit left to be humiliated that his father should see him in such a desperate state. It was easier for both of them if Antonov did not have to meet his eye.

"How long has he been like this?"

"Nearly a week now, your highness. He seems to be going from bad to worse."

"Can't you do anything for him?"

"Nothing we have tried is working. I fear this may be the beginning of the end."

"You mean he's dying?" Antonov asked bluntly.

"If we can't get him to keep any food down, then if the fits don't kill him, starvation and dehydration certainly will," she confirmed in a voice filled with regret.

So they think I'm dying.

"Surely there must be something you can do?"

"We've tried every remedy known to us, your highness, and even a few dubious herbal cures, but nothing seems to make a difference." Ella hesitated for a moment, and then, with a touching tone, she added, "You may have to prepare yourself for the worst."

His father was silent for a long time.

"There is something we might try, to ease his suffering, if nothing else," Ella suggested tentatively.

"What?"

"We could move him to the Hospice at Tolace. They are far better equipped to deal with the terminally ill, your highness, and maybe one of the physicians there has some knowledge that might help the prince recover."

"Will he survive the journey?"

Ever the pragmatist, aren't you, Father?

"It can be done in stages, sire, so as not to distress him further. I really feel it is the only thing left to us."

"You're assuming he'll not recover," Antonov remarked with all the emotion of a man discussing putting down a wounded horse.

"He's never been strong, your highness," Ella reminded him gently. "You've always known that it was a possibility that Misha's weakness would eventually be his undoing."

"The bad blood comes from his mother's side of the family," Antonov told her. "The Damitian Royal House is notoriously inbred."

It's so much easier to blame Analee, isn't it, Father? You can't bear the thought that my weakness is in any way attributable to you.

"You're sure there's nothing you can do for him here?" The Lion of Senet sounded a little uncertain.

"We'd have done it already if there was, your highness."

There was another long pause as Antonov thought about it.

"Send him to Tolace, then," he agreed finally. "Make whatever arrangements you must to see that he survives the trip, and once he gets there I want regular reports regarding his improvement. Or lack of it."

"His fate will be as the Goddess wills it, your highness," Ella told him.

"I've given her one son already, my lady," the Lion of Senet replied bitterly. "She's getting a little greedy, don't you think?"

The comment almost shocked Misha into betraying the fact that he was conscious and had heard every word of the exchange.

It was the closest his father had ever come to admitting that he loved him.

Chapter 62

Tia snuggled closer to Dirk when she felt him stirring, not wanting to leave the comfort of his arms. Her head was resting on his chest as she listened to his heart beating, thinking it strange that she should find such comfort in it. Not so long ago, nothing would have made her happier than the thought that Dirk's heart had *stopped* beating...

After several awkward nights making do with the narrow camp bed, they had tossed it out of the tent and made up a bed on the ground, which proved much more comfortable and practical. Tia had given up trying to work out the whys and wherefores; given up trying to rationalize away her confusion. It seemed enough, at the moment, to just let it happen.

"You awake?" Dirk asked softly.

"Not really," she murmured.

"We should be getting up. It's well past second sunrise."

"Why don't you take the day off?" she suggested sleepily.

"And do what all day?"

She looked up at him with a sleepy grin.

He laughed. "I can't *believe* you mean that, Tia."

"It's your fault. I was a nice girl until I met you." She sighed and snuggled into his arms again. "I wonder what Lexie would have to say about this?"

"She'd probably tell you I'm a nice boy."

"She did, actually." Tia looked up at him curiously, comfortable enough with Dirk now to ask something that had puzzled her for months. "Why did you tell her?"

"Why did I tell who, what?"

"Lexie. About Johan."

"I'm not sure," he said after a moment's thoughtful silence. "I just knew I couldn't go on living under her roof pretending everything was fine. It seemed like the right thing to do."

"She's forgiven you."

"Have you?" he asked.

Tia didn't answer immediately, not even certain in her own mind how she felt about it any longer. Nothing was the same now; everything she had previously thought was true had been thrown into doubt. "I think I forgave you the night Morna died."

"I'm sorry I asked you to do that."

"I'm sorry you *had* to ask."

He held her close for a moment and then he smiled. "We're a mawkish pair this morning, aren't we?"

She sighed heavily. "What *are* we going to do when we get back to Mil?"

He hesitated before answering. "Do we have to worry about that now? We're a long way away from discovering anything of value in the cavern."

He was right about that much. "But we've been here so long already. We can't stay up here forever."

"That's true," he agreed. "That's why we really should get back into the cavern today. I've barely even begun to make sense of it."

"I forgot how single-minded you can be," she groaned. "You're as bad as Neris sometimes."

"You're the only person I've ever met who can make intelligence sound like a curse."

"Where I come from it is a curse," she reminded him. "It gets you into all sorts of trouble."

When he didn't answer, she looked up at him and frowned. He had an odd expression on his face, as if she had caught him in an unguarded moment.

Dirk was like that. No matter how open he seemed, she could not avoid feeling there was a part of him that he always kept locked away from her. It worried her a little, but she tried not to dwell on it. There was so much to be forgiven, or at least put behind them, before they could even think of the future. For now, Tia had to content herself with the knowledge that whatever had happened between them these past sixteen days had radically altered everything she believed about Dirk Provin, and that so far, the change had been for the better.

"What's the matter?" he asked, sensing something was wrong.

"Nothing, really. I was just thinking about us. About how strange it all is."

"*Strange?* There you go, getting all romantic on me again."

She smiled. "You know what I mean. Is this real, Dirk? Or is this just the inevitable result of two people spending way too much time alone out here in the wilderness? Would this have happened if we'd stayed in Mil?"

"Does it matter?"

She sat up and looked at him thoughtfully. "I think it does. Do you love me, Dirk?"

He pushed himself up on one elbow. His expression was serious, his eyes as unreadable as ever. "Do you trust me, Tia?" he asked in reply.

"I hate the way you always answer a question with a question. What's trusting you got to do with it?"

"Trust is everything."

"Then I trust you..."

"You shouldn't," he warned suddenly, throwing back the covers. He climbed over the bedding, stood up and began to get dressed.

Tia stared up at him with concern. "What do you mean by that?"

He continued dressing and didn't answer her.

"Tell me, Dirk," she insisted.

He turned to face her as he tucked in his shirt and forced a smile. "Nothing, really. Forget it."

She searched his face for some indication that he was hiding something from her. But Dirk could tell her the second sun had disappeared and she wouldn't know he was lying until she looked over her shoulder and saw it shining in the sky behind him.

"Then don't say things like that. It scares me."

"I think I'll go and work in the cavern for a while."

"What about breakfast?"

"I'm not hungry."

He smiled at her, but it seemed artificial, and when he left the tent, she lay down again and stared at the canvas roof for long time, unable to avoid the feeling that Dirk had quite deliberately avoided the question about whether or not he loved her.

Tia went hunting after breakfast, feeling the need for both the exercise and the solitude. Dirk's odd comment about not trusting him still bothered her. She could not imagine why he would say such a thing, particularly as he'd spent much of the past two years trying to convince everyone in the Baenlands that he *could* be trusted.

She had become familiar with the lie of the land around Omaxin, and had found quite a few game trails in the foothills, and she now followed one that she had discovered on her last foray, but had not had time to investigate. The trail took her quite high above the ruins, and she stopped when she reached a small ledge to look down over the city. It was hard to appreciate the size of the place walking among the fallen buildings, but up here, she got a sense of how vast the city had been. It must have housed tens of thousands of people before it was destroyed. She glanced up at the smoking peak of Mount Probeus. Had they all died in the eruption, or had the lava been slow enough to let them flee the death trap their city had become?

Before she could wonder about the answer, she caught a glint of something to the south. Curious, she shaded her eyes with her arm and studied the landscape. Then she saw it again, the distinct flash of sunlight on metal. When she realized what it meant, Tia swore under her breath and abandoned her quest for game. She slung her bow over her shoulder, turned and sprinted back toward the ruins.

Even at a run, it took a long time to get back the camp. She had not realized how far she had wandered from the ruins. By the time she reached the entrance to the Labyrinth, she could clearly hear the jingle of tack and the sound of the advancing horsemen.

"Dirk!" she cried, running through the tunnel toward the cavern. She barely even noticed the darkness. "Dirk!"

"What's wrong?" he asked, emerging through the gate at the sound of her panicked cry.

"Riders!"

He did not react immediately.

"Did you hear me?" she asked. "There's a troop of riders heading this way! We have to get out of here!"

He nodded slowly and reached for her hand. "Tia—"

"They're almost on us!"

He pulled her close and kissed her, hard and hungrily. Then he held her face between his hands and closed his eyes, touching his forehead to hers for a moment.

"I'm so sorry, Tia," he whispered in a voice choked with regret.

He let her go and turned toward the entrance of the Labyrinth without looking back. Tia watched him leave with a feeling of dread. There was something poignant and terribly final in the way he had spoken; the way he had kissed her.

She followed him slowly, stopping in the shadows as he emerged into the light.

The horsemen had reached the Labyrinth and were milling about outside. The rider in the lead, on a huge, impatient gray stallion, was Kirshov Latanya. Just behind him, on a much more sedate mount, rode the High Priestess Belagren. The other riders consisted of their escort and a score of Shadowdancers.

The Regent of Dhevyn dismounted when he spied Dirk and drew his sword. The two men faced each other for a tense moment before either of them spoke.

"Kirsh."

"Dirk."

Dirk glanced at the sword and shook his head. "Put it away, Kirsh. Even if I was planning to fight you, I wouldn't be stupid enough to face someone as well trained as you with a naked blade."

Kirshov Latanya sheathed his blade with some reluctance, as the High Priestess dismounted and walked up beside the prince, pulling off her riding gloves.

"My lady."

She glanced over Dirk's shoulder at the Labyrinth for a moment, then met his eye.

"Did you open it?"

Dirk nodded. "As I said I would."

Tia bit back a cry of despair as she realized what she was witnessing.

Belagren's eyes lit up with excitement and she turned to

Kirshov. "Tell your people to make camp. I want my Shadow-dancers to get to work immediately."

Kirsh nodded, turned back to the rest of the troop and began issuing orders. Dirk remained standing in front of the Labyrinth facing the High Priestess.

"You promised me something else, Dirk. I don't see her."

"She's here."

"No!" Tia cried in an agonized whisper. *"No, no, no . . ."*

"Does she know about your plans to join the Shadow-dancers?" Belagren asked.

Dirk glanced over his shoulder into the darkness, where he must have known Tia was listening to every word. "I imagine she does by now."

It was the way he spoke, as much as his words, that sliced her to ribbons. It was that same bland, toneless voice he used the night he killed Johan. He was betraying her, with no hint of emotion, not a shred of conscience or regret. Even worse was the realization that this was no chance meeting. Dirk had obviously arranged it. He really was the traitor in their midst who, until recently—until she had been blinded by her own stupidity—she had always feared he was.

Tears of rage and betrayal and humiliation that she had allowed herself to think for a moment that he loved her—or that she loved him—blurred her vision as she slipped her bow from her shoulder. Her hands were shaking so hard she could barely nock the arrow. Tears coursed silently down her cheeks, dampening the fletching as she drew back the string.

"Is she likely to cause trouble?" Belagren asked Dirk.

He turned his gaze back to the High Priestess and shook his head. "She'll be no trouble at all," he said, as she let the arrow fly with a wordless cry of anguish.

Chaos erupted outside as the arrow took Dirk in the back, knocking him to the ground. Tia let the bow slip from her hand and fell to her knees, crying too hard to see if the wound was fatal.

PART FOUR

BETRAYAL

Chapter 63

Dirk winced as Belagren stood over him, while one of her Shadowdancers treated his wounded shoulder. The young physician seemed competent enough, and the wound was a clean one. He wasn't sure if Tia had deliberately missed, but he was grateful that the arrow had only passed through the muscle and flesh of his left shoulder and missed both the bone and any vital organs. He shouldn't complain, he supposed. He had wanted Tia to appear upset when she learned of his treachery. It just had not occurred to him that she might be armed, or that her wrath might prove so potentially fatal.

I couldn't have staged a more convincing scene if I'd planned it.

The tent flap opened and Kirsh ducked his head as he entered. He looked at Dirk with a frown. "You're lucky your girlfriend is such a lousy marksman," he remarked.

Dirk glanced up at Kirsh, gritting his teeth as the physician tugged on the stitches a little harder than he needed to. He said nothing. Tia's safety lay not in his protection, but in his indifference.

Belagren turned to Kirsh. "What have you done with her?"

"She's in one of the tents under guard. I had to tie her up, I'm afraid. She stabbed one man and bit another when they tried to disarm her."

"Perhaps, when we're done here, you should talk to her, Dirk," Belagren suggested. "It'll be much easier on everyone if you can convince her to behave in a civilized manner."

"I think I'm the last person on Ranadon she wants to speak to at the moment."

Kirsh nodded in agreement. "She was quite upset when she learned she hadn't killed you."

Dirk glanced at Kirsh and wondered what he was really thinking. Was he also sorry that Tia had missed his heart, or was he simply disgusted that Dirk had turned traitor to his own people? It was hard to tell with Kirsh. He prized honor almost above life itself, and by no stretch of the imagination could he describe what Dirk was doing as honorable.

The physician tied off the last stitch and made Dirk hold out his left arm so he could bandage it. When he was done, he gathered up his instruments and turned to the High Priestess. "If he keeps it clean, the wound should heal well enough."

"Thank you, Stefan. You may leave us now."

The Shadowdancer bowed to the High Priestess and the prince and left the tent.

"If you would excuse us, Kirshov, I'd like to speak to Dirk alone."

Kirsh nodded and left without another word. His mood worried Dirk a little. It was unlike Kirsh to be so cold and aloof.

"He thinks you're a traitor," Belagren remarked, noticing his frown.

"I am a traitor," he shrugged, a movement he immediately regretted when a sharp pain shot through his shoulder. "What did you tell him to get him here?"

"The same thing I've been telling his father since the Age of Shadows. Omaxin is a holy shine and the cavern is the Goddess's Temple. Only in there can one hear her voice clearly."

"It never ceases to amaze me how normally reasonable, intelligent people can rationalize away the most illogical arguments, all in the name of their faith."

"It would be unwise for you to express such sentiments if you're to convince Antonov you are genuine in *your* desire to embrace the Goddess."

He smiled sourly as he gingerly pulled his bloodstained shirt over his bandaged shoulder. "*You* have to convince him, Belagren, not me. I could just as easily go to him and tell him what I know."

"He wouldn't believe you."

"He will," Dirk disagreed with a grimace as he raised his arm to get it in the sleeve. "I can *prove* you're a charlatan. I wonder what Antonov would do to you if he ever discovered the depth of your deception?"

She began pacing the small floor space in the tent. "Don't

think you can frighten me, boy, just because you figured out how to open that gate."

"You *should* be frightened of me, Belagren," he warned, biting back the wave of agony that washed over him from his efforts to get dressed. "You should lie awake at night for fear of me." He wondered if the fact that he was pale and sweating with pain somehow robbed the threat of substance.

"Then why don't I just have Kirshov kill you now?" she suggested. "He would, you know. He's still mad at you because he thinks you raped Marqel."

"So have him kill me. All it means is that I'll be dead and you'll be no better off than you are now. Actually, it'll be worse than that, because now you *know* something is going to happen and you won't have a clue what it is or when it will occur. You made a huge mistake being so accurate about the return of the second sun, you know. Now Antonov expects the Goddess to be that specific every time."

"You hinted at this important celestial event in your letter. I've kept my end of the bargain. What is it? And when will it happen?"

"You haven't even begun to keep up your end, Belagren."

"What more do you want? My protection? You'll have that as a Shadowdancer."

"I'm not wearing those ridiculous red robes, and I'm not joining your disgusting little cult as a glorified whore, so you can send me off every Landfall to screw the brains out of some disaffected noblewoman who thinks watching a man burn alive is the best way of worshipping her Goddess."

"That was never my intention, Dirk," she assured him. "You would be permitted to study, of course. Now that we have access to the cavern again, there is so much to be learned..."

"I'm not staying in Omaxin, either. I'm sick of being stuck out here in the wilderness. Your Shadowdancers can copy down the information in the cavern and I can work from their notes. I've discovered I like my creature comforts. I want to go back to Avacas."

"That could be dangerous. Antonov is rather peeved at you at the moment."

Dirk smiled suddenly. "I wish I could have seen the look on his face when he saw the *Calliope* in flames."

"That was a very mean-spirited thing to do, Dirk."

"Burning my mother alive wasn't exactly an act of kindness."

Belagren sighed. "You're not making this any easier on either of us."

"I'm not trying to, Belagren. We have a business deal. Don't insult my intelligence by pretending it will ever be anything more than that. You know I don't believe in you *or* your imaginary Goddess. And that's just fine, because if I did, I'd be of no use to you. I want to be safe, and I want a title with enough power behind it to ensure that I *stay* safe. Give me what I want and I'll keep you in power, and the next chapter you write in the *Book of Ranadon* will do nothing but sing your praises. Cross me, and believe me, I'll take you down when I fall."

She stopped pacing for a moment and looked down at him. "I'm interested in why you chose to side with me, Dirk. If you're so keen on securing power for yourself, why not simply surrender to Antonov? He'll make you a king."

"Have you taken a close look at what's happened to the past few kings and queens of Dhevyn?" he asked with a bitter laugh. "I'm safer in Senet, I think."

"Your cynicism astounds me. The boy we took from Elcast was never so cold or calculating."

"The boy you took from Elcast no longer exists. He died the day the Butcher of Elcast was born."

The explanation seemed to satisfy her. "You said you wanted a title. Did you have one in mind, or am I supposed to arrange for someone to lose his estates so that you can be kept in the manner to which you appear to have become accustomed?"

"I want to be your right hand," he told her.

Belagren was horrified. "Out of the question!"

"Fine. I'll just wait until we get to Avacas and have a nice long chat with my Uncle Antonov, shall I?"

She shook her head. "Better men than you have tried to shake his faith, Dirk Provin. Antonov won't listen to your heresy."

"Better, undoubtedly, but not smarter." He met her eye evenly. "You've no idea who you're dealing with, Belagren. If you think you can manipulate me the way you did Neris, you're sadly mistaken. I'm not some besotted fool hanging out for his next dose of poppy-dust. The *only* thing you can give me—that I want or need—is protection from Antonov Latanya. In return, I'll give you the information you need to keep fooling him and the rest of your pathetic followers into believing that you really are the Voice of the Goddess. Beyond that, I want nothing more but to be left alone."

"But to make you my right hand? How would I explain such a thing?"

"That's not my problem," he said. "But if you want to know when the eclipse is due, you'd better find a way."

"Is that what you were hinting at in your letter?" she demanded, seizing on his apparent slip. "There's going to be an eclipse? When? When is it?"

"Soon enough that you'll be able to reassure Antonov that the Goddess is still talking to you."

"How do I know you're telling me the truth?" she asked suspiciously. "You've not had long enough in the cavern to work out something like that."

"I didn't work it out. Neris told me about it."

"Did he also happen to mention when the next Age of Shadows is due?"

Dirk smiled. "We'll discuss that when I'm sitting at the right hand of the High Priestess of the Shadowdancers."

She looked at him thoughtfully. "I have Neris's daughter. I might not even need you."

"Don't waste your time hoping she knows anything worthwhile," Dirk scoffed. "She's useless. Johan raised her, not Neris. She barely even acknowledges that her father still lives. If you can call the state he's in 'living.' He's completely insane, and so lost in the poppy-dust he can barely string a coherent sentence together."

"Yet you claim he had the wit to tell you of the eclipse."

"I spent two years as an outcast in that damn hellhole in

Mil, Belagren. I had plenty of time to piece together his ramblings."

"Does Tia Veran know of the eclipse?"

He shook his head and discovered that was nearly as painful as shrugging. "Her only value to you will be the Lion of Senet's gratitude when you hand her over to him. Let Antonov find out for himself that she's not worth anything to anyone."

Belagren studied him closely for a moment. "And what exactly is her value to *you,* I wonder?"

"Tia Veran just shot me in the back," he reminded her with cold indifference. "I'm not particularly interested in what you do to her."

Belagren couldn't tell if he was lying, and it frustrated her. "You've lost quite a bit of blood. You should rest," she advised. "Tomorrow we'll inspect the cavern, and you can tell my people what you want them to do." She turned for the tent flap, then glanced over her shoulder at him. "You'd better be worth the trouble you're causing me, Dirk Provin."

"I've just thought of the title I want."

"What is it?" she snapped.

"The Lord of the Shadows," he said. "I want to be known as the Lord of the Shadows."

Chapter 64

For nearly a week, Tia remained a prisoner in the tent she had so recently shared with Dirk, and the bitter reminder of her own foolishness did little to improve her temperament. She did not see him in that time. All she saw was the Shadowdancer responsible for delivering her meals, and the silhouettes of the guards who surrounded her tent.

She had heard Dirk's voice on a number of occasions, and each time he was talking to the High Priestess, issuing orders about the information he wanted collected from the cavern.

Dirk apparently had no intention of staying here in Omaxin to learn the secret of the Age of Shadows. He sounded like he was arranging for an army of Belagren's lackeys to do the legwork, leaving him free to puzzle over the problem in the luxury and comfort awaiting him in Avacas.

His treachery was staggering, but in hindsight, all the hints were there. That she had ignored them just made the torment worse. Oh, he'd been clever about it. So clever that he had not bothered trying to hide what he was doing. He had told her what he intended when they were still in Tolace, she realized. He had said then that the smart thing to do would be to surrender and return to Avacas. And how often on the journey here had he told her that he had betrayed her to the High Priestess, and let her think he was joking? When she thought about it, he had not actually lied to her much at all. She had been duped willingly, assuming that if Dirk really meant what he said, the last thing he would do was admit it openly.

Painful though it was to admit it, Tia began to appreciate how dangerous Dirk Provin really was. He was not just a boy with a good head for numbers; he was a political animal with an intelligence and level of cunning that few could match. *How could such evil, such cruelty, reside in the heart of any child born of a great man like Johan Thorn?* For the first time since Dirk had killed him, Tia was glad Johan was dead. She was glad he wasn't alive to witness what his son had become.

The sense of betrayal she felt was so overwhelming it made her feel physically ill. It did little to ease her suffering to realize that she was not the only one he had fooled. For two years she had watched him seduce the people around her into believing that he was nothing more than a victim of circumstances beyond his control. He had fooled Reithan into trusting him by helping them escape Avacas. He was probably laughing to himself as he made his heart-rending confession to Lexie and Porl about the torment he was suffering after he had killed Johan. Mellie was a willing victim. Such perfidy was incomprehensible to a child. Even Neris had fallen for him, his mind so hungry for stimulus that he would have believed anything Dirk told him, just for a chance to share ideas with someone who understood what he was talking about.

One by one, he had conquered them all, until there was only Tia left who doubted him. So he had brought her out here into the wilderness, and eventually worn her down, too. Only he was not content just to make her believe in him. He had to go that one step further.

He had made her think she loved him.

She was his crowning achievement, the proof that he was invincible. How he must have laughed at her. How he must have delighted in the chase. How triumphant he must have felt the night she came to his tent and threw herself at him like an Avacas whore...

How can I break it to Reithan and Porl? How do I tell Lexie? Or Mellie? How can I possibly tell them what he's done? These questions, she decided in the end, were moot. The High Priestess appeared to have little interest in her. Tia was to be delivered to Avacas and handed over to the Lion of Senet. The chances were good that she would never see her friends again, anyway. It would be someone else's responsibility to destroy their illusions about Johan Thorn's ignoble son.

She learned of her fate from a young Shadowdancer named Marqel, who delivered her meals twice a day, and who had gone out of her way to ensure that Tia was comfortable. She was a stunning young woman with long wheat-colored hair and a rope tattoo on her left arm. Somewhat to Tia's surprise, she was Dhevynian, not Senetian. Tia assumed that was the reason the girl appeared to be so solicitous of her comfort. It was Marqel who had asked Prince Kirshov to remove the ropes that bound her. And it was Marqel who told her about the letter Dirk sent from Bollow, offering his cooperation and Tia Veran, in return for the High Priestess's protection.

"Did you see the letter?" Tia had asked, recalling Dirk's words when he had returned to the tavern after he disappeared in Bollow. *I thought I'd visit the Lord of the Suns and ask him to send a message to the High Priestess informing her of our plans.* How confident he was! The cocky little bastard had actually told her what he had done and she had just assumed he was kidding...

Marqel nodded. "It was very specific. He said that if the High Priestess removed her people from Omaxin, so that he could have unhindered access to it, he would wait for her here. He said he had knowledge of an event that would consolidate the power of the Church for generations to come."

So that whole elaborate ruse in Kalarada with Alenor was for our benefit, not Belagren's, Tia realized. *He was planning this long before we reached Bollow, possibly even while we were still on Grannon Rock.*

Poor Alenor. What would she do when she learned of Dirk's treachery? And what event was he referring to? She was certain he had not discovered anything useful in Omaxin yet. Anyway, he had sent the letter from Bollow. If he knew something was going to happen, he must have known about it long before now. Even as far back as Mil...*Neris,* she realized with a sigh. *We all believed Dirk when he said Neris had told him nothing useful, and the whole time he was pumping my father for information for the High Priestess. And it's my fault,* she told herself savagely. *I was the one who thought he might be able to get Neris to open up.*

"What else did the letter say?"

"He said he wanted to join the Shadowdancers. And that you were with him. He asked for the reward on you."

Tia shook her head, still unable to quite grasp the depth of his duplicity.

"I'm sorry, Tia. This news must pain you greatly."

"I'm sorry, too," Tia agreed. "Sorry I didn't kill him when I had the chance."

The Shadowdancer smiled. "If it's any consolation, he appears to be in a great deal of pain."

"Good."

Marqel patted her hand sympathetically. "I understand how you feel, Tia."

"No, you don't," she accused, shaking off the unwanted comfort. "You're one of them."

"Because of a twist of fate—not anything I deliberately set

out to do. You must trust me when I tell you that I share your hatred for Dirk Provin."

Marqel spoke with a surprising amount of venom, and Tia found herself believing her. Something Dirk said to her once suddenly leapt to mind—something about the Shadowdancer who had accused him of rape being Dhevynian, not Senetian.

"Are you the one he—"

Marqel lowered her eyes that were suddenly filled with pain. "Yes."

"Dirk said you lied about it."

"He's the one who lied about it. If you don't believe me, ask Prince Kirshov. He saw me after it happened. He can tell you of the injuries I suffered at Dirk Provin's hands."

"And now he's going to join you."

Marqel shrugged philosophically. "I'm not in a position to question the decisions of the High Priestess. No doubt she has her reasons for accepting him." Then the Shadowdancer smiled suddenly. "Cheer up, Tia. Things mightn't be as bad as they seem."

Tia held up her left hand, with its partly missing finger. "That's what happened the last time I met the Lion of Senet, Marqel. Somehow, I don't think I'll be quite so lucky next time."

"I wish there was more I could do to help you," Marqel said.

"Kill Dirk Provin the first chance you get."

Marqel met her eye and smiled. "Gladly."

After Marqel left the tent, Tia crawled into the bed she had shared with Dirk and curled herself into a miserable ball. She lay there for a long time. She did not cry. Tia had cried all the tears over Dirk Provin she intended to.

On impulse, she reached inside her shirt for the tiny bow and arrow she still wore around her neck. Tia fingered the pendant idly, wondering why she hadn't torn it off and thrown it away...*Because it reminds me of him,* she realized. *Until they burn me at the stake I will wear this damn thing to remind me to trust my instincts next time.*

Suddenly, Tia knew what she had to do. She was, in part, responsible for this. She had brought Dirk to Mil; introduced him to Neris. She was even willing to admit that she had ignored her own doubts because she *wanted* to believe that somehow, Johan's son might prove to be the savior Johan turned out not to be.

Tia threw back the covers and sat up decisively, slipping the necklace back into her shirt. It was time to stop moping about like a girl. Time to stop feeling sorry for herself.

And there was not going to be a "next time," if she didn't start making plans to escape.

Chapter 65

They stayed in Omaxin for nearly two weeks before Belagren was satisfied that her people had everything under control. Marqel continued to tend the prisoner, Tia Veran, while Dirk issued orders like a little general, instructing the Shadowdancers who were to remain behind about what he needed them to do in order for him to continue his work back in Avacas.

Belagren was pathetically solicitous of his needs, and Marqel began to wonder if there was *anything* she would deny him. Although she had lied to Tia and told her that she had seen the letter Dirk sent to the High Priestess from Bollow, she only knew part of what it contained, gleaned from the conversations she had overheard between Belagren and Madalan. But whatever Dirk had hinted at in his letter, it was sufficiently important that the High Priestess was prepared to do just about anything Dirk asked in order to secure his cooperation. She and Rudi Kalenkov followed Dirk around the cavern like faithful puppies, taking notes, asking questions and nodding agreement to everything he demanded.

Kirsh grew increasingly irritated by the delay, anxious to return to Avacas and get back to his duties as regent in Kalarada. When he questioned why they were taking so long,

Belagren gave him her well-practiced answer about the cavern being the Temple of the Goddess, and how important it was to understand the ancient writings that might reveal her will. When Kirsh bluntly asked why, if the Goddess spoke to Belagren directly, it was necessary to read what had been written down previously, she had almost choked.

"The Goddess doesn't like to repeat herself," Dirk had replied, saving Belagren from having to think up a convincing excuse.

"What do you mean?"

Dirk waved his arm to encompass the hall. They had lit every corner of it now, revealing a massive chamber, easily four times the size of the ballroom at Avacas Palace. The walls were made of the same creamy stone as the floor, and every inch was decorated with either script or diagrams that made no sense at all to Marqel. The Eye of the Labyrinth glared up at them from the floor with its unblinking stare. Marqel noticed that, almost unconsciously, the Shadowdancers working in the cavern walked around it, rather than risk stepping on it, as if it had a life of its own.

"The Goddess has spoken to others in the past," Dirk explained. "The ancient residents of Omaxin wrote down her words. Now it's up to us to figure out what she told them, so we don't make the same mistakes they did."

"And you can make sense of this gibberish?" the prince asked doubtfully.

With his right hand, Dirk pointed to a line of incomprehensible squiggles chiseled into the wall behind them. His left arm was still in a sling.

"It says, 'Do not question me.'"

Kirsh nodded slowly. "Very well, but can you work any faster? We really should be heading back to Avacas."

"Another day should see us ready to leave, your highness," Belagren assured him.

Once Kirsh had left the hall, Belagren turned to Dirk in amazement. "You can read the ancient script?"

"Of course I can't. I've no idea what it says."

"But you said—" Belagren began, and then she smiled at him with something akin to admiration. "That was very slick."

EYE OF THE LABYRINTH

"It's what you're paying me for, Belagren," Dirk pointed out coldly, before turning back to Rudi to continue issuing the orders he had been dictating before Kirsh so rudely interrupted him.

In between watching Tia Veran, Marqel did her best to make sure the reason Kirsh wanted to return to Kalarada was not because he was missing his wife.

They never spoke about Alenor. It was almost as if she did not exist. Kirsh had spent his wedding night doing his duty, but almost every night since then, it was Marqel, not Alenor, who had shared his bed. It amused her to think that Alenor was so timid, so frigid, that Kirsh could not bear to be with her. Even more amusing was that the little queen smiled warmly at Marqel whenever they met in the palace, with no inkling that her beloved husband was cheating on her. Jacinta's suggestion that she report any irregularities in Kirsh's sleeping habits had given her the perfect excuse to cover for him. She was quite fond of Jacinta D'Orlon, thinking her an even bigger fool than Alenor.

Initially, Marqel had resented the chore of being Tia Veran's jailer, but after a few days the task began to entertain her greatly. On principle, she warmed to anyone who hated Dirk, and Tia's hatred ran so deep that she made Marqel feel positively congenial toward him.

It was the stupid girl's own fault, of course. Any idiot should know not to get involved with someone like Dirk Provin, and if Tia was idiot enough to actually fall in love with him, then she deserved everything she got. Marqel took a certain perverse pleasure in sympathizing with Tia. She delighted in dropping little snippets of information, confirming how badly Tia had been duped; positively relished the hurt and pain in the other girl's eyes when she gave her details of his treachery.

It gave her something to do.

When their column finally headed out of the ruins in the direction of Avacas, it was a considerably smaller party than the one that had ridden into Omaxin. Rudi and the Shadowdancers who had left the ruins several months previously to give Dirk a chance at the gate remained behind to continue their work. Their task now was to document everything they could in the cavern, and send the information on to Dirk in Avacas, so that he could duplicate Neris Veran's work and learn when the next Age of Shadows was due.

Marqel rode with Tia for the most part, strengthening the poor girl's impression that she actually cared what happened to her. Several days in Tia's company, however, with her black looks and even darker moods, began to wear on Marqel. After they stopped for lunch five days south of Omaxin, she re-mounted her horse and rode up to where Kirsh sat at the head of the column, giving the signal to move out.

Unfortunately, she had to ride past Dirk to reach Kirsh. He looked at her for a moment and then glanced at the prince.

"You appear to have done rather nicely for yourself," he re-marked. "From worthless thief to mistress of the Regent of Dhevyn in less than three years."

"Kirsh won't always be the Regent of Dhevyn," the scorn in his voice prompted her to reply, as she slowed her horse to match the pace of his mount.

"True," Dirk agreed. He rode with both reins in his right hand. Although he had dispensed with the sling, he still didn't have the full use of his shoulder. "When Alenor comes of age, he'll be demoted to prince consort."

"That's not what I meant!" she snapped without thinking.

He glanced at her curiously. "Then what did you mean, Marqel?"

She looked away, horrified to realize how close she had come to giving away Belagren's plans for Misha. "You're just jealous."

"Of you? You must be joking."

"You're jealous of the power I have now."

Dirk smiled skeptically. "What power? You're riding in Kirsh's wake, Marqel. You have none of your own."

"Power is power, whichever way you get it."

"You think so? Would you like me to show you real power?"

"How?"

He glanced over his shoulder at the High Priestess. "Suppose I tell Belagren *I* want you. Suppose I demand that you give up Kirsh and whore yourself for me instead?"

"Kirsh would never allow it."

"It isn't in Kirsh's power to do anything about it. You're a Shadowdancer. You're answerable to the High Priestess, not him. If she chose to end your affair, you'd be able to do nothing to stop it. Nor would Kirsh even try to defy her. He's not going to throw away the regency of Dhevyn for you."

"Belagren needs Kirsh."

"The High Priestess needs me more than your lover right now, Marqel. She'd risk offending him to find out what I know."

"You don't know what you're talking about."

"Perhaps not," he conceded. "Let's call Belagren over and ask her, shall we? Would you care to take odds on who has the most power then?"

For a moment she was afraid he actually meant to do it. "You wouldn't dare!"

"I'd dare it, Marqel," he warned. "You're just fortunate that I'd happen to prefer sleeping in a scorpion's nest to sharing a bed with you."

She smiled at him smugly. "Insult me all you want. You can't hurt me anymore, Dirk Provin."

"I don't recall hurting you a first time," he pointed out.

"Kirsh thinks you did."

"And haven't you made the most of that little piece of artful fiction?"

"You're such a hypocrite, accusing me of being a liar. Look what you've done. You've murdered, lied, cheated..."

"You left out rape," he said, and then he looked at her pointedly. "Ah, but that's right, I never *actually* raped you, did I? That was something you and Belagren thought up afterward."

"It doesn't matter. Everyone believes you did. I've even convinced your little friend what a monster you are."

"Who? Tia? She wouldn't have taken much convincing."

"She's in love with you, did you know? She won't admit it, but you can tell her heart is breaking. Or at least she *was* in love with you. Until you sold her out." Marqel's eyes narrowed as she watched him, trying to gauge his reaction.

"She *thought* she was," Dirk agreed with an indifferent shrug. "Being in love is something you women like to pretend, to avoid facing the painful truth when you're acting like sluts. You're guilty of exactly the same thing, Marqel. Do you imagine you're in love with Kirsh? Doesn't that somehow make it more tolerable, to think you're sleeping with him out of genuine feeling, and not because Belagren likes the idea that through you, she's got the Regent of Dhevyn by the balls?"

"You're a callous little prick, aren't you?"

"And one with the power to ruin you if I choose," he reminded her.

"You know, when I heard you were coming back, I thought you must have changed," she laughed scornfully. "But you haven't. You're still the same arrogant, conceited fool who tried to teach me how to read. You've been away a long time, Dirk. Things have changed. You don't understand anything."

"I understand this much, Marqel. I have my own plans. I don't particularly care what you do or who you do it with. Just don't get in my way."

Something in his tone of voice convinced Marqel that Dirk, in his present mood, was not someone to be trifled with. She stared at him for a moment, wondering if she should warn the High Priestess. Then she realized that it wouldn't matter if she did. Belagren was convinced Dirk was the answer to all her prayers, and he was going out of his way to prove to her that he was.

Without another word, she urged her horse forward and cantered ahead to ride with Kirsh.

Dirk Provin was not her problem.

Chapter 66

The simple task of escorting the High Priestess back to Avacas was something Kirsh could have done in his sleep. What made the task so onerous was the fact that Dirk Provin was the reason for this journey. Much as he would have liked to learn what Dirk had been up to these past few years, the knowledge that he was escorting the man who had hurt the woman Kirsh loved, the man who might replace him in his father's affections, made it far too difficult.

He had not spoken to Dirk much, too angry with him to indulge in idle conversation. Why, after all this time, Dirk had decided to return to Avacas, was something Kirsh would have very much liked to have known. He didn't believe that Dirk had suddenly discovered the Goddess or his vocation with the Shadowdancers, and was a little concerned that the High Priestess did believe it. A few months before, Dirk had burned the *Calliope* to the waterline in revenge for his mother's death. It was totally illogical to assume that he now wanted to embrace the same Goddess to whom his mother had been sacrificed.

"Your highness?"

Kirsh turned to the man who had hailed him. He was one of Belagren's guard, normally stationed at the Hall of Shadows, and had been called away to escort the High Priestess's party north. He was a tall, competent sort of fellow, or least Kirsh assumed he was. The journey to Omaxin and back had required little more of her guard than that they watch over one reasonably well-behaved prisoner, look alert and help set up camp each evening.

"Yes, Teric?"

"The camp is ready, sire."

"Then inform the High Priestess that she can take her rest. Have you set the watch?" There was not really a need for it, so close to Avacas, but the habits drilled into him in the Queen's Guard were hard to shake.

"Yes, your highness."

Kirsh nodded. "Carry on, Captain."

Teric saluted and turned back to the camp. Kirsh remained where he was standing, some distance from the campsite, on a slight rise that looked out over the lush hills separating them from Avacas. It was still early. There was no hint yet of the first sunrise. Tomorrow they would head into the passes and be home within a few days. Kirsh still thought of Avacas as home, and the way things were going with Alenor, he probably always would.

He heard footsteps behind him and sighed, wondering what Teric had forgotten to tell him now. That man was efficient, but he was painfully conscious of Kirsh's rank, and felt the need to report every minor detail for the prince's approval.

"What now?" he asked, glancing over his shoulder. It was not Teric who approached, but Dirk. "Oh, it's you."

Dirk walked up beside him and stopped to look out over the view that Kirsh was pretending to admire. "Can we talk, Kirsh?"

"I've got nothing to say to you, Dirk."

"Then will you listen to me?"

"Listen to your miserable excuses? Thanks, but I've got better things to do." He turned and began to walk along the small ridge away from the camp.

"Why are you so angry at me?" Dirk asked curiously. "Because I left? Or because I came back?"

Kirsh stopped and looked back at him. "That you even have to *ask* proves you have no honor at all."

Dirk shrugged. "Just because what I'm doing isn't honorable in your eyes, doesn't mean it's wrong."

"Actually, Dirk, that's exactly what it means. I don't know what you're playing at. All I know is that in order to save your own neck, you've betrayed the people who gave you shelter."

"They're *your* enemies, too, Kirsh. I would have thought you'd be grateful."

"One doesn't have to be on the same side to have honor."

Dirk sighed, as if he couldn't be bothered arguing. "Look, I didn't come here to get into an argument with you about my honor. Or lack of. I came here to call on yours."

Kirsh looked at him with a puzzled frown. "What are you talking about?"

"You owe me a favor."

Kirsh looked away at the reminder, wishing he had never challenged Dirk to that stupid race up the stairs of Elcast Keep when they were boys. "What can I give you that you can't get from Belagren? Or my father?"

"I want you to let Tia go. I want you to help her get out of Senet."

Kirsh stared at Dirk suspiciously. "Why?"

"Because . . . perhaps I'm not entirely without honor."

Kirsh snorted contemptuously at the suggestion.

"What I did to her was despicable," Dirk admitted. "I'm feeling guilty. And it's not as if she knows anything worthwhile. It just seems a shame to let Barin Welacin amuse himself with her for weeks on end, simply to find out she knows nothing I wouldn't have volunteered anyway."

"The depth of your descent into ignominy is staggering, Dirk."

The insult appeared not to bother him. "Will you do it?"

"To repay the favor I owe you, you would have me betray the High Priestess and my father. Does it amuse you to demand that I stoop to your level?"

"That's *your* moral dilemma, Kirsh, not mine. You owe me a favor. Whatever is in your power to grant me. Well, this *is* in your power to grant and, once it's done, the debt between us is canceled."

"And how am I supposed to do this thing? I assume that if you've decided I have the power to grant this favor, you've also worked out how it might be accomplished?"

Dirk nodded. "Your biggest hurdle will be getting Tia to believe that you want to help her. But I wouldn't worry too much about her taking advantage of the opportunity once she realizes it's there. If I know Tia, she's probably already stolen a spoon, and is secretly sharpening it on a stone each night, ready to slit the throat of the first guard who falls asleep on his watch."

Kirsh looked at Dirk, trying to reconcile the intelligent, thoughtful boy he had known with the calculating, heartless young man who stood before him.

"If I do this thing, then I am no longer obligated to you?"

"You never need speak to me again if that's what you want," Dirk agreed, apparently unconcerned by the loss of Kirsh's friendship.

He nodded slowly. "What do you want me to do?"

"She needs to get away before we reach Avacas. It will be too late and too difficult once Barin has a hold of her. She'll need a horse and supplies to see her to the coast, and you have to ensure that she gets away cleanly. It will be hard enough for Tia on the run, without your thugs hunting her down."

"I find it a little odd that you seem so concerned for her welfare. If she means so much to you, why betray her in the first place?"

"Call me a sentimental fool," Dirk replied flippantly.

"I can think of many things I'd like to call you. Sentimental isn't one of them."

"And one other thing," Dirk added, ignoring Kirsh's censure. "This is between you and me. You're not to involve anyone else, especially not Marqel."

"But I'll need her assistance . . ."

"Find a way to do it without her, Kirsh. I don't want that bitch to know anything about this."

Kirsh bristled at the insult. "You will not speak about Marqel in such a manner."

"She's using you. You know that, don't you?"

"What I know is that you're in no position to judge me."

Dirk was silent for a moment, and then he shrugged. "Whatever. Just make certain neither Marqel nor Tia knows that I'm involved. If you want to tell your mistress *you're* letting Tia escape, be my guest."

"You don't want Tia to know either?"

"It'll be better for her if she thinks you're acting on your own. Besides, she despises me. I don't want to confuse her by doing something noble."

Dirk's attitude was beyond Kirsh's comprehension. "I don't understand you anymore, Dirk."

"I don't think you ever understood me in the first place, Kirsh."

"I'm only just beginning to appreciate how *little* I knew you. I'm almost afraid to imagine what you're planning to do when you get to Avacas."

"I don't want to be King of Dhevyn, Kirsh, if that's what concerns you. Even if I wanted the job, I'd never do anything to hurt Alenor."

"Then why did you come back?"

"Twelve men died the day your father made me into the Butcher of Elcast," he replied bitterly. "I killed Johan Thorn on his damn terrace, and then I had to beg somebody to kill my own mother to end her suffering. Running away didn't work. My mother died because your father was trying to drive me out into the open. You know it as well as I do. I'm Johan Thorn's bastard, Kirsh, not his heir. At least among the Shadowdancers, with Belagren's help, I have some hope of convincing your father I have no interest in the plans he has for me. Maybe then the killing might stop."

"So, for the noblest of reasons, you have chosen the most ignoble path," he concluded. "Surely you could have found a better way?"

"You mean a more *honorable* way? What do you think I should have done, Kirsh? Go charging into Avacas armed with nothing more than my trusty sword and my noble heart, hoping they would win the day for me? I'm sorry to disappoint you, but I come from a long line of realists. It just doesn't work that way."

"You've made yourself into an outcast."

"I was an outcast from the day the world found out who sired me. It's merely the degree that's changed."

Kirsh shook his head, still not able to understand how a man could do what Dirk had done, even for good reason, and still live with himself.

"I'll see Tia Veran gets away," he agreed reluctantly. "And I won't let her know you were instrumental in organizing her escape. Beyond that, I want nothing more to do with you."

Kirsh walked past him, heading back toward the camp, his heart heavy with the weight of the favor he owed Dirk.

"How's Alenor?" Dirk asked his retreating back.

He stopped warily and looked back at Dirk. "She's fine. Why?"

"Does she know about Marqel?"

"Mind your own damn business."

His cousin smiled at him knowingly. "Next time, before you raise your flag on the high moral ground, take a good long look at your own behavior, Kirsh."

"Don't you dare compare what you've done to my actions," he snarled. "And don't even *think* about interfering. Alenor is my *wife,* and what happens between us is our concern and nobody else's. Stay away from her. And from Marqel. If I find you doing anything to harm, or even upset, either one of them, I'll kill you."

"Would you really kill me over that thief?" Dirk asked curiously.

"Without a moment's hesitation."

Dirk nodded, as if he accepted Kirsh's word on the matter. "You've no more honor than I have, Kirsh."

Kirsh was a little surprised to realize that he meant exactly what he threatened. He would kill Dirk, given half a chance. The most painful thing, however, was realizing that he *wanted* to kill Dirk, not because he had hurt Marqel; or even because he might hurt Alenor.

Kirsh wanted to kill him because he was right.

Chapter 67

They were past Talenburg and only two days out of Avacas, the camp just stirring in anticipation of the second sunrise, when Tia received a visit from Kirshov Latanya.

She had only met him once before, in the palace at Avacas, when she had tried to help Prince Misha during a fit. He had yelled at her that day, thinking she had somehow contributed to his brother's condition, so her first impressions of him had not been good. Neither did it help that he was the spitting image of his father, or that he had been Dirk's closest friend in Avacas.

Unfamiliar voices outside her tent woke her, and she scrambled to her feet, as the newly crowned Regent of Dhevyn ducked under the tent flap and then straightened up and glanced around her bare accommodation. Like his father, he was a big man; his fair hair almost brushed the canvas roof. Prince Kirshov stared at her for a moment before he spoke. He seemed extremely uncomfortable.

"We'll be in Avacas the day after tomorrow," he announced.

Tia nodded silently, not sure if she was expected to comment.

"When we get there," he continued, "the High Priestess plans to turn you over to my father."

"Marqel told me."

"It won't be pleasant for you."

"I imagine not," she replied guardedly, wondering where he was going with this.

"You've been treated very poorly."

"Actually, your highness, I've been treated quite well. Marqel has been very considerate of my comfort."

"I meant by Dirk."

Tia's expression darkened. "Don't even speak his name in my presence."

Kirsh nodded in understanding, which surprised her. "In this, I am on your side. I find his conduct in this matter quite repellent." Kirshov seemed to be having some difficulty getting out what he had come to say, and she was curious to find out what he wanted.

"I can do nothing to stop him betraying your people, Tia."

"I wouldn't have expected you to care."

"Perhaps I don't," he agreed. "But you are currently within my sphere of influence, which means that in some small way I can hinder Dirk's plans."

Tia took a step backward warily. *He's going to kill me,* she realized with a start. *He wants to foil Dirk's plans, so he's going to kill me . . .*

Kirsh reached down into his boot and withdrew a long, slender, but unremarkable dagger. Tia took another step back, but there was not much farther she could go, and she would never escape him in the close confines of the tent. She considered screaming, but realized it was pointless. The only people who would hear her cries for help were his men, and even if they wanted to object, nobody was going to stop Kirshov Latanya from doing exactly what he pleased, even if that included murder. Kirsh tossed the knife into the air and caught it deftly by the blade between his thumb and forefinger.

And then offered it to her, hilt first.

She stared at the knife uncomprehendingly.

"Take it!" he urged.

"Why?" she asked cautiously. "So you can claim you killed me in self-defense?"

His expression was puzzled for a moment, until he realized what she was assuming. "I didn't come here to kill you. I'm letting you escape."

"Why would you do that?"

"I told you. To confound Dirk."

She shook her head in disbelief. "This is a trap. You've probably got a whole squad out there waiting to hunt me down for a bit of sport."

"For pity's sake, woman! Take the damn knife!" he snapped impatiently. "I've arranged for us to stop and give thanks to the Goddess for a safe journey when the first sun rises tonight, so, for a short time, everyone will be involved in their prayers and there'll only be one guard on your tent. I'll leave a horse saddled and equipped with enough supplies to see you to the coast, but after that, you're on your own. You can cut your way out through the back of the tent. I'll try to stall Marqel bringing your dinner for as long as I can to give you time to get away. When you leave, don't go south. Double around behind us and ride in our wake. That way I can concentrate the search for you toward Avacas, and you should be able to avoid detection until we reach the city."

"You've really thought this through, haven't you?" she remarked, reaching for the blade. Even if it was a trap, she reasoned, she still had a better chance armed and out in the open than here in the camp.

"Trust me, I've thought of little else recently."

"I don't suppose you can arrange for me to get my bow back?" she asked.

"I can't promise it, but I'll see what I can do." He turned to leave, bending down to pass through the tent flap.

"Thank you."

"I'm not doing this for you, Tia Veran," he said, and then he was gone, leaving her staring after him thoughtfully, unconsciously turning the blade over and over in her hands.

The day dragged for Tia, and the knife Kirshov had slipped her burned like a hot brand in the side of her boot. She rode in her usual place near the back of the column, occasionally catching sight of Dirk ahead of her as he rode next to Belagren. She spent much of the day amusing herself by calculating how hard and how far she would have to throw the knife to hit him, and exactly where she would have to aim to make sure she killed him this time. It was a pointless exercise. She would barely get the blade clear of her boot before somebody noticed what she was doing. Anyway, it was much more important that she escape.

Somebody had to warn the others in Mil about Dirk's betrayal.

Once she was clear of the camp, Tia planned to avoid Avacas altogether, thinking that if Kirshov's assistance *was* a trap, she would be better off away from the city. She would make her way to Tolace, she had decided. There was a Brotherhood man there that she knew, one she was fairly certain Dirk had no knowledge of. Boris Farlo would know where the *Makuan* or the *Orlando* was, perhaps even the *Wanderer*. And he would provide her with a safe house until she could get out of Senet.

Faced with the prospect of escape, Tia's mood improved considerably. She had shaken off much of her earlier self-pity, and provided she didn't let herself dwell on the last few weeks she had spent in Omaxin, she discovered she was more than capable of decisive action. This situation just had to be dealt with, she decided. Dirk's treachery was always a possibility, and they had not survived in Mil for as long as they had by being foolish. Dirk probably didn't know enough about navigation to have learned the tricky channels of the delta that led into Mil in the time he had been among them, and even if he did, forewarned, they could evacuate the village and move everyone up into the caves.

And that was the key. Forewarning. Tia had to remain alive long enough to warn her people in the Baenlands. And if that meant letting Dirk Provin live a little longer, then so be it.

And the next time I try to kill you, you deceitful, devious, double-crossing bastard, she swore silently to his back, *I won't miss.*

They stopped early that night to allow the escort time to set up the camp before the first sunrise. The campsite was well used by travelers on the road, with a large grassy area bordered by a small stream, which provided fresh water for the horses.

Once it was erected, Tia was escorted to her tent and, as Kirshov Latanya had promised, left with only one guard in attendance, while the rest of the party gathered on the lush grass down by the stream to wait for the first sunrise. As the first hint of red began to stain the sky, Tia could hear Belagren's voice raised in prayer, then the massed voices of her small congregation as they responded.

She wasted no time slicing a long cut in the canvas wall of the tent, wincing as the fabric ripped loudly, certain it could be heard all over the campsite. As soon as the slit was large enough for her to squeeze through, she slipped outside and ran, in a crouch, to the trees where the horses were tethered. Tia ran down the line of horses, looking for the mount Kirshov had promised, glancing constantly over her shoulder at the sky. The red light of the first sun was creeping slowly in from the east. She did not have much time.

The horse at the very end of the line was still saddled and

laden with two saddlebags and a bedroll. She slipped the hobbles from the horse's forelegs and grabbed the bridle, leading it toward the concealment of the treeline.

Once she had reached the trees, she stopped and checked the horse. It was an ordinary-looking chestnut, with one white sock, but it looked sound and seemed docile enough. Still fearing a trap, she checked the girth strap closely, then lowered the stirrups a notch, before swinging into the saddle.

Bending low over the horse's neck, Tia wound her way through the trees away from the camp, heading north, back toward Talenburg.

As the night reddened, and there was no sign of pursuit, she allowed herself to relax a little and ponder the strange turn of events that had turned Dirk Provin into her enemy and Kirshov Latanya into her friend.

Chapter 68

How could you let this happen?" the High Priestess angrily demanded of Kirsh when he reported the escape of Tia Veran.

"I think you underestimated the resourcefulness of your prisoner," Dirk remarked, taking a sip of his wine. He had been sharing a glass of wine with Belagren, while the High Priestess did her level best to extract the information regarding the eclipse from him, when Kirsh arrived to announce the loss of their prisoner. Dirk had told Belagren nothing yet, and refused to elaborate until he was confirmed in his new role as her right hand. His usefulness to Belagren would diminish somewhat once she had that information, and he intended to extract full value from it.

"Then why didn't you *warn* us about her resourcefulness?" Belagren snapped at him.

"You didn't ask."

The High Priestess muttered a very unladylike curse and turned back to Kirsh. "Have you sent out search parties to look for her?"

"Of course," he informed her. "But there's a lot of ground to cover. We'll be lucky to find her."

She nodded absently. "Do what you must," she said dismissively.

Kirsh bowed and left the tent. Belagren turned to Dirk. "What am I supposed to tell Antonov?"

"Don't tell him anything," Dirk suggested. "He doesn't know you were holding Tia Veran prisoner, and if you don't tell him about it, then there's nothing for him to get upset about."

"You lie very easily, don't you?"

He raised his glass in her direction. "I stand humbled in the presence of the master."

"You'll push me too far one day, young man."

Her warning didn't bother him. In fact he quite enjoyed needling her. "It's not a matter of lying. It's a matter of not complicating the truth. Antonov is going to be in enough of a flap when he learns that I'm back. You don't need to add to the general confusion by telling him you had Tia and then lost her." He took another sip of his wine. "Didn't Kirsh say she escaped while we were giving thanks to the Goddess? Maybe it was the Goddess's *will* that she escaped," he added with a smile. "You know what a fickle old cow she can be."

"You seem rather amused by this turn of events. Did you have anything to do with it?" she asked suspiciously.

"Yes, that *must* be the answer," he agreed. "I went to Kirsh and asked him very nicely to let her go, and so of course, he did."

"You do know that I will kill you if you cross me?" she asked.

Dirk shrugged. "For that threat to mean anything, Belagren, I would have to care."

Torn between returning to Avacas or losing several days searching for Tia, Belagren ordered Kirsh to abandon the search later the next morning. They broke camp after an early lunch, and pushed on well after the first sunrise to make up for the time they had lost trying to locate their escaped prisoner. Belagren was in a foul mood. She had been hoping to ease Antonov's aggravation over Dirk by giving him Tia to amuse himself with. Now she had to find another way to soothe him, and her options were limited.

Dirk found her dilemma rather entertaining, and it gave him hope that he might just manage to get away with this. What had Tia said in Omaxin? "I can't believe such a stupid, dangerous, and altogether far too complicated plan actually worked." She had not been referring to this particular plot, but her sentiments were very fitting.

He went out of his way not to think about Tia, because when he did, he spent a great deal of time in mental self-flagellation. When he told Kirsh he did not want to confuse Tia by doing something noble, he spoke the truth. To have let things escalate as they had was stupid, dangerous and selfish. And cruel. He could have turned her away. He *should* have turned her away. The false hope he had allowed Tia for the short time they had been lovers was never going to last. He had known that as far back as Grannon Rock.

It didn't help that he knew she was out there somewhere, armed and angry, wanting nothing more than his extermination. She could be trailing them now, waiting for a chance at a clear shot. And she would not miss this time. Tia was very good, and the distress that had ruined her aim the last time was well under control by now, replaced with cold determination. Dirk rode with his back muscles clenched in anticipation of the arrow he half expected to thump into him every time the trees closed in on the road, or they passed an outcropping of rocks that offered an assassin a good perch.

"The High Priestess wants to go straight to the palace when we get to Avacas," Kirsh informed him as he trotted up beside Dirk.

"No point in delaying it, I suppose," Dirk agreed. "Will we get there today, or are you planning to stop for the night again?"

"We're going to push on," Kirsh said. "We should reach Avacas later tonight."

They rode in silence for a while, Dirk's eyes anxiously scanning the ridges of the low mountain passes they traveled through. He was sweating, but suspected it had little to do with the heat from the second sun.

"Feeling a little nervous?" Kirsh asked, guessing the reason for his skittishness.

"A little," he conceded.

"The cost of treachery is rather high, isn't it?"

Dirk looked at Kirsh in annoyance. The Senetian prince's moral superiority was beginning to irritate him. "Up there with the cost of adultery, I suppose."

Kirsh glared at him wordlessly and then kicked his horse into a canter toward the head of the column.

It was going to be a very long day, Dirk decided.

It was late when they reached Avacas, but early enough that most of the taverns were still open. As they pushed through the city toward the palace, Dirk looked around, thinking Avacas had changed little in the two and a half years since he had seen it last. If Bollow was a faded but elegant old lady, then Avacas was her loud, brash offspring. It was crowded and dirty and vibrant; the hub of civilization on this world and arrogantly aware of the fact.

They saw the spires of the palace long before they reached it, and the sight brought back a rush of memories for Dirk, most of them unwanted. For the first time since he had decided on this perilous course of action, he began to have serious doubts about his ability to see it through. How would he feel standing on the terrace where he had killed Johan? Or walking the paths of the palace gardens where Marqel had gotten the better of him?

I'm insane, he decided. *Completely, utterly and certifiably insane to think I can pull this off.*

The palace gates swung open at their approach. Dirk wasn't sure if it was because the Palace Guard recognized Kirsh and Belagren, or if word had already reached them that the High Priestess and the Regent of Dhevyn approached. They dismounted in front of the wide granite steps, and grooms swarmed over their tired mounts. Kirsh dismissed the escort and, with Dirk, Belagren and Marqel, headed into the palace.

It was late enough that any dinner guests at the palace had already departed for the evening. A shocked servant, tripping over his own tongue at the unexpected appearance of such notable guests, informed them that the Lion of Senet was in his private sitting room. Kirsh led the way, his footfalls muffled by the thick carpet runner. Dirk glanced at the small group, thinking they were a sorry lot, tired and travel stained. Belagren must be truly concerned if she would prefer to let Antonov see her in such a state, rather than risk taking the time to freshen up before confronting him.

Kirsh knocked on the doors to Antonov's private sitting room and opened them without waiting for an answer.

Dirk had played this scene over and over in his mind a thousand times, so he was taken completely by surprise when Kirsh stopped just inside the door and gasped. The Queen of Dhevyn and the Lion of Senet were sitting opposite each other in comfortable armchairs near the unlit fireplace, apparently enjoying a cozy nightcap.

"Alenor! What are you doing here?"

Antonov rose to his feet and turned to face them. Other than a little more silver in his golden hair, a few more lines on his well-formed face, he had changed little since Dirk had seen him last. If Antonov was surprised by their sudden arrival, he did not let it show.

"What did you expect, Kirsh?" the Lion of Senet asked sternly. "You take off without warning, leaving your bride of a few weeks all alone in Kalarada. Although I see now," he added, glancing over Kirsh's shoulder at Dirk, "that you may have had good reason." He looked at Belagren and smiled slowly. "I was planning to take you to task also, my lady, for encouraging Kirsh's impulsiveness, but perhaps I should reward you instead."

"We need to talk, Anton," the High Priestess replied.

"That we do," Antonov agreed. Then he finally turned his full attention to Dirk.

"Dirk."

"Your highness."

"I notice you're not wearing chains. Can I assume that you've returned to Avacas willingly?"

"Yes, sir."

Antonov scowled at him. "You burned my ship."

"You burned my mother."

For a tense moment he did not reply, and then suddenly the Lion of Senet smiled warmly. "You've not learned any respect, I see. Still, we can talk about it later and you can tell me everything you've been up to. This is proving to be a wonderful evening." He walked to where Kirsh and Dirk were standing, his expression almost blissful. Antonov placed one hand on Kirsh's shoulder and the other on Dirk's. "The Goddess is truly smiling on me. Not only do I have my son and young Dirk back where they belong, I'm going to be a grandfather."

Kirsh visibly paled. *"What?"*

Antonov laughed delightedly. "You're a bit of a scoundrel, Kirsh, seeding an heir and then running off to let poor Alenor deal with it on her own."

Dirk looked at Alenor. She was still sitting silently by the fireplace, her hands clasped demurely in her lap, her eyes downcast.

"Goddess! Boy! You look like you've been poleaxed!" Antonov chuckled.

"I don't understand ..." Kirsh muttered in confusion.

"Do I have to spell it out for you, son? Alenor's pregnant! You're going to be a father!"

Antonov was right, Dirk thought. Kirsh did look as if he had been poleaxed. He glanced at Alenor again. She raised her eyes and met his, her expression guarded. Dirk turned and glanced over his shoulder at Marqel, who stood silently and inconspicuously just behind the High Priestess. The look on her face was one of absolute hatred, and he saw that it was directed not at him, but at Alenor.

"Come, all of you," Antonov urged. "Let's have a drink to celebrate!"

"We really must talk, Anton," Belagren insisted.

"Later, Belagren," Anton told her as he turned and led Kirsh and Dirk into the sitting room. "We can talk as much as you want later."

Chapter 69

Whose child is it?" Kirsh demanded as soon as he and Alenor were alone in her suite on the fourth floor.

They had spent a tense hour smiling and trying to look like a happy couple for Antonov's benefit, while Kirsh fumed and Alenor was torn by the joint trauma of anticipating Kirsh's reaction to her condition and the shocking and totally unexpected appearance of Dirk Provin.

That Dirk had betrayed the Baenlanders was bad enough; that he could destroy her with a few well-chosen words made it infinitely worse. She had thought that Kirsh learning she was pregnant was the worst thing that could happen to her.

Dirk's appearance forced her to rethink that assumption.

Oddly enough, it gave her strength. Dirk could attest to the fact that she had been conspiring with the enemies of the Lion of Senet to destroy him. In light of that, the mere fact that she was carrying another man's child seemed quite insignificant. Alenor walked to the settee and sat down, before she looked up and calmly met Kirsh's gaze.

"Why yours, of course, dearest," she replied with a venomously sweet smile.

"We both know that's not possible."

"Isn't it?" she asked innocently. "And why would that be?"

Kirsh glared at her, his fury growing with each breath he took. "I'll find out who it is, Alenor. And then I'll kill him."

"So it's perfectly all right for you to take a lover, but when I do it, suddenly it's a capital crime. I'll tell you what, Kirsh, why don't I confess everything and then you can have my lover put to death...right alongside Marqel at the next Landfall Feast. Sort of a matched set thing..."

"Stop it!" he snapped.

"Surely you're not suggesting that *you* should be allowed to keep your lover, but mine has to die?"

"You're the Queen of Dhevyn, Alenor!"

"And you're her regent. What's your point?"

"My point is, you're carrying another man's bastard!"

"No, I'm not, Kirsh," she told him firmly. "As far as the rest of the world is concerned, and *particularly* as far as your father is concerned, I am carrying *your* child. If you repeat your allegation outside this room, I will go straight to your father and tell him I took a lover because you were too busy with your mistress to be with me. Regardless of what he does to me, it should see the end of Marqel rather smartly, don't you think?"

She knew she was right. That Kirsh had allowed this to happen would infuriate his father. And as far as Antonov was concerned—it would be all Kirsh's fault. She had gone to great pains to give the impression that she was far too ingenuous to do anything so calculating. But did Kirsh love Marqel enough to allow her to get away with such a threat? Alenor was counting on the fact that he did.

"You're insane if you think I'll let you pass off another man's child as mine."

She smiled cheerfully. "Look on the bright side. Now I'm in such a delicate condition, nobody will expect you to spend time in my bed. You can go play with your Shadowdancer all you want for the next few months."

"And after that?"

"You'll be a doting father," she predicted confidently. "If it's a boy, do you think we should call him Antonov, after your father?"

"Just tell me who it is!" he demanded.

Alenor made a great show of thinking about it. "Hmm... let me think...nope! It's no use. There were just so many of them," she sighed airily. "I couldn't even begin to guess who the father is."

"I'm glad you think this is funny, Alenor."

"Well it is, rather," she pointed out. "I mean, if Marqel announced she was pregnant, nobody would raise an eyebrow over it. The child would be born and raised a royal bastard, and probably do very nicely for himself, with a title or some diplomatic post of importance to make him feel wanted. Why should my child be treated any differently?"

"Because you're a queen."

"Oh, so you noticed that, did you?"

Kirsh swore savagely as a knock sounded at the door. He crossed the room and jerked it open to find Dirk standing outside, flanked by two guards. Dirk would be allowed nowhere unescorted until he had spoken to Antonov.

"What the hell do you want?"

"Alenor sent a message asking to see me."

Kirsh stood back to let him enter. "Come on in," he said scathingly. "The queen apparently enjoys the company of other men in her rooms late at night."

Dirk stepped into the room giving Kirsh a puzzled look, as the guards took positions on either side of the door outside.

Kirsh glared at Alenor angrily. "This isn't over," he snarled, and then he left, slamming the door heavily behind him.

Dirk looked at Alenor curiously. "All is not well in paradise?"

She smiled faintly, hoping she looked much calmer than she felt. "Don't worry about Kirsh. The shock of impending fatherhood seems to have rattled him a bit."

Dirk stared at her doubtfully for a moment but he seemed to accept her explanation.

"I think I was more flabbergasted than Antonov when I saw you walk into that room this evening," she added. "What are you doing here, Dirk?"

"Betraying everyone I know."

"It certainly seems that way."

He took the seat opposite her. He looked tired, she thought.

And much older than his nineteen years. The strain of his treachery had visibly marked him. "I asked you to trust me, Alenor. No matter what."

"That's a pretty tall order in light of your present situation, Dirk. What are you really up to?"

"I can't tell you."

"Can't or won't?"

"Won't," he conceded. "If I go down, Allie, I'm not going to take you with me."

"Don't you think that's for me to decide?"

"Not in this case."

She shook her head, certain he had no concept of the danger he was in. "The Baenlanders are going to want you dead. And there's no telling what Antonov will do."

"I know."

"Don't you care?"

He shrugged. "I'm trying very hard not to care. It's easier that way."

She hesitated for a moment, before asking, "Is taking my throne part of your plans?"

Dirk shook his head with a smile. "I'm joining the Shadowdancers. As Belagren's right hand, no less. I'm to be known as the Lord of the Shadows."

Alenor stared at him in shock. "How did you? ... Oh, Goddess, Dirk, what are you *doing*?"

"Probably digging myself into a hole I'll never be able to climb out of," he predicted. "But I have a plan of sorts. I just hope I live long enough to see it through."

"That's not very likely," she warned. "There are going be a lot of people who are seriously angry with you. And some of them are closer than you realize," she added, thinking of Alexin's reaction when he learned of what Dirk had done. What would he do? What would Alexin's brother, Raban, do, back on Grannon Rock? Dirk could betray the whole Seranov family's involvement with the Baenlanders. Her own safety seemed irrelevant when she realized the number of people who were threatened by Dirk's sudden decision to return to Avacas.

"Then do me a favor and warn them off."

"I'm not at all certain that I should," she said with a frown. "For all I know, you're simply telling me you have a plan, just so I *will* warn them off, making me complicit in your treachery and leaving you free to enjoy the fruits of your betrayal."

"If you believe that, Alenor, then you don't trust me at all."

She sighed heavily. "I don't believe it, Dirk. But I can't see how I can convince anyone that you truly haven't betrayed us." *Not if I'm really not convinced myself,* she added silently.

"I don't want you to convince anyone of anything. It's safer for everyone, me included, if they believe I'm a traitor. Just carry on as usual." He smiled thinly, adding, "And if you hear of anyone plotting to assassinate me, ask them not to."

"And what reason should I give?"

He shrugged. "Tell them you like my smile."

Alenor shook her head doubtfully. "I don't know how you can joke about this."

"It's easier to deal with than blind terror, which is probably what I should be feeling."

She held out her hands to him. He took them in his and moved to sit beside her on the settee. "Just promise me it will all work out in the end, Dirk."

"I promise."

"Just like that?"

"I'm a good liar. A very good liar, actually. I can even fool myself on occasion."

She searched his face for some sign of what he was really thinking. Every instinct she owned told her that Dirk was still her friend, while everything he had done recently screamed the opposite.

"You took my advice and went to Omaxin. Did you have any luck?"

"Yes and no. I got through the Labyrinth."

She was not surprised. "Were you able to learn when the next Age of Shadows is due?"

"It's early days yet," he told her with a noncommittal shrug.

She shook her head, consumed by doubt and fear, for

herself as much as her cousin. "I hope you know what you're doing, Dirk."

"Trust me," he said.

And against all reason, Alenor realized that she did.

Chapter 70

The following day, Dirk found himself called to his most arduous test yet—that of facing the Lion of Senet. When he was admitted to Antonov's study, the prince was sitting behind his gilded desk, bathed in the sunlight that the desk was so carefully positioned to catch.

"Come in, Dirk. And close the door."

Dirk did as Antonov ordered and then stood in front of the desk, waiting for the prince to say something. Like his first meeting with Antonov, Dirk had tried to envisage this conversation a thousand times over, but he suspected it would end up being nothing like he imagined.

"The High Priestess informs me that you wish to join the Shadowdancers."

"Yes, sir."

"She says you've had something of an epiphany."

"I suppose you could call it that."

Antonov leaned back in his chair and scowled. "What I *should* do, you ungrateful little pup, is hang you."

"For what crime, exactly?" Dirk asked. "Killing Johan Thorn? You were planning to do that yourself. Raping a Shadowdancer, perhaps? You know as well as I do how flimsy that accusation is."

"How about conspiring with the enemies of Senet?" Antonov suggested. "Piracy? Drug running? The wanton and criminal destruction of the *Calliope*? Goddess knows what else you have been up to lately."

"Mostly I was trying to avoid you, sir."

That comment gave Antonov pause, and then he asked thoughtfully, "Are you so afraid of me, Dirk?"

"The only thing I'm afraid of is that you won't believe me when I tell you that I have no interest in your plans for me. I don't want to be Johan's heir. I wish I'd never heard of him." In that, Dirk was admitting an indisputable truth. His whole life had begun to fall apart the day Johan Thorn arrived on Elcast.

"So now you wish to be a Shadowdancer? Is that out of a genuine desire to serve the Goddess, or a convenient way of avoiding me?"

"If you remember, your highness, the reason I left Elcast in the first place was to join the Shadowdancers. It was you who decided to delay my admittance to their ranks."

"At your mother's request," Antonov reminded him.

"If I recall, sir, it was Wallin Provin who negotiated that arrangement. My mother never wanted me to leave Elcast at all."

Antonov nodded slowly. "What were you doing in Omaxin?"

This was where the danger lay, Dirk knew. He must walk a fine line between the truth and his carefully constructed lies.

"After my mother was sacrificed to the Goddess, I was pretty angry..."

"I noticed," Antonov noted with a frown.

"I decided to confront her head on. I wanted to know how a Goddess who teaches love and forgiveness could condone such torment."

"So you sought the answers in Omaxin?"

"It's where the High Priestess first heard the Voice of the Goddess," Dirk reminded him, using Antonov's faith to strengthen his argument. "I figured that would be the best place to confront her."

The Lion of Senet nodded slowly, Dirk's logic making perfect sense to a man who believed so wholeheartedly in the infallibility of the High Priestess that he had murdered his own son at her behest in the belief that the Goddess had willed it.

"What happened in Omaxin that wrought this remarkable change in you?"

"Nothing much, at first. When I got there, I discovered the tunnel into the temple had been blocked."

"Yes, I know," said Antonov. "Among the more pernicious

things that Neris Veran did was to deny the High Priestess access to the most holy place on Ranadon."

"I was there for weeks, trying to figure out how to get into the temple, and was on the verge of giving up when it suddenly came to me..."

"What happened?"

Dirk nodded. "It was indescribable, sir," he said, hoping that if he claimed it could not be described, Antonov would not demand a detailed description. "It was as if I'd been visited by the Goddess. I didn't hear her words exactly, but at that moment, I felt her presence. I just walked into the Labyrinth and opened the gate."

Antonov studied him thoughtfully. He was quite blinded by his beliefs, but Antonov Latanya was neither stupid nor easily fooled. That he had been duped about his Goddess for so long was more a testament to Belagren's skill than a slight on the Lion of Senet's character. He *had* to believe that Dirk was genuine in his desire to join the Shadowdancers. If he was not convinced, his threat to hang Dirk remained a very real possibility.

"Do you now claim to speak to the Goddess?"

Dirk shook his head. "That is the privilege of the High Priestess, sire. But I can understand some of the writings in the temple. I've asked the High Priestess if I can be allowed to study and translate them."

The dilemma Dirk's revelation posed for Antonov was considerable. He was torn between his faith and his political interests.

"She also tells me that your position is unique."

"Sir?"

"The High Priestess says that this gift you have been given by the Goddess to understand her writings requires special consideration. She tells me that you are to be made Lord of the Shadows."

Dirk fought down a smile. He had not been very serious about the title when he suggested it, and was a little surprised that Belagren had granted it to him. *Lord of the Shadows.* That was the title Tia had scathingly applied to him for enjoying the dark challenge of the Labyrinth. It was quite fitting, actually.

"I only hope I can do the title justice, your highness."

"If I decide to let you keep it," Antonov snorted. "Belagren says you've been with the Baenlanders all this time."

"Yes, sir."

"What can you tell me about them?"

"Anything you want to know," he offered.

"Can you get my ships through the delta?"

"Except that," he amended. "I only sailed it two or three times the whole time I was there." The lie came easily to him.

"Then what intelligence you *do* have is probably useless."

"I returned because I felt the Goddess calling to me, your highness, not to provide you with information to destroy your enemies."

"You might like to rethink your position on that, Dirk. The Baenlanders are *your* enemies now."

"I know that, and truly, sir, if I could give you the information you need I would, if only to prove my loyalty."

Antonov watched him closely, studying every move he made—every twitching finger, every blink of his eyes—looking for some indication that he was lying. Dirk was watching Antonov just as closely, trying to determine if he had been found out.

"To let you off, after what you've done, would set a very bad precedent," Antonov said. "To allow your crimes to go unpunished because you've had a moment of clarity would be asking for trouble. I can imagine every miscreant from here to Sidoria suddenly deciding the Goddess is calling them the moment they get caught."

Dirk allowed himself a small smile at the thought. "I can see your dilemma, your highness."

"And yet, the translation of the Goddess's work is an important task. I suppose I could send you back to Omaxin."

Dirk did not answer him, certain that he knew Antonov well enough to know that it was not a serious suggestion. Antonov would want him near, on the off chance Dirk might have a change of heart.

"Or I could keep you here in Avacas, under house arrest. That would leave you free to do the Goddess's work and still send a message to the world that criminals cannot hide behind her skirts."

"I will honor whatever you decide, your highness," Dirk informed him with a degree of resignation. There was no point in trying to appear meek or humble. Antonov would not believe that for an instant.

"You're damn right you will, boy," Antonov agreed. "I'm tempted to hand you over to Barin for a week or two, anyway, just to remind you of your fate, should you decide to run away again."

"I'm done with running away," Dirk assured him. The truth was always easier than a lie.

"I'm still at a loss as to what drove you to it in the first place."

Antonov's arrogance was a never-ending source of amazement to Dirk. That he could not understand what had forced Dirk to flee Avacas the morning after Johan Thorn's killing was almost laughable.

Don't you understand? he wanted to yell at him. *You drove me to kill my own father. You made me the Butcher of Elcast! You tried to mold me into an image of yourself, for no better reason than the chance to gloat in the face of the man who had the appallingly bad manners to object when you invaded his country.*

"I was confused," he shrugged, letting no hint of what he truly felt reflect in his eyes.

"And now?"

"I see things much more clearly."

Antonov still looked doubtful. "Were it not for the fact that the High Priestess believes you are genuine in your desire to serve the Goddess, I'd have you put to death in a heartbeat. You do understand that, don't you?"

"Yes, sir."

"Belagren is not so easily fooled, I think, that you would be able to lie about such a thing to her and get away with it."

"No, sir."

The Lion of Senet glared at him, perhaps detecting a hint of insolence in his docile compliance. "You will remain here in the palace," Antonov decreed. "You will be under house arrest. You will be guarded at all times and will not be permitted to leave the palace grounds without my express permission. Is that clear?"

"Yes, sir."

"Furthermore, you will undertake such studies as the High

Priestess deems necessary to translate the inscriptions from Omaxin, and you will report to me at least once a week on your progress. If I decide you are not applying yourself with sufficient enthusiasm, I will arrange to have Barin Welacin brought in, and the Prefect can point out to you the error of your ways."

"Yes, sir."

"You will also, before you begin your studies for the High Priestess, document everything you know about the Baenlands. I don't care if you think it's useful or irrelevant. That will be for me to decide. I want maps, defenses, a layout of their fortress, escape routes...everything you remember. I also want a list of names. I want to know who shelters them, who aids them, and who is dealing with them behind my back."

"Yes, sir."

Antonov nodded in satisfaction. "Then we understand each other, Dirk."

You don't even begin to understand me, Antonov Latanya. "Yes, sir."

"In that case, you may go."

Dirk bowed and turned for the door, his heart pounding with relief that he had got off so lightly. More importantly, Antonov had done exactly what Dirk was hoping he would do. There was hope yet.

"One other thing, Dirk," Antonov added.

He turned back to face the prince. "Sir?"

"Neris Veran. Is he alive?"

Dirk shook his head. "I hear he died some years back from an overdose of poppy-dust."

"So you never met him?"

"No, sir."

"Pity."

"Why is that, your highness?" Dirk asked, a little concerned by the inquiry. Antonov's question about Neris had caught him off guard.

"It would have been a salutary lesson for you to meet Neris Veran, Dirk. Then you could have seen, firsthand, the vengeance the Goddess is capable of wreaking when her very existence is questioned."

"I no longer question her existence, your highness." *What would you do, I wonder, if you learned that I am the voice of your deity?* "In fact," Dirk added with moving sincerity, "I realize now that the Goddess resides within me."

Antonov smiled, pleased by Dirk's profession of faith.

"Welcome home, Dirk," he said.

Chapter 71

The last thing Marqel was expecting to discover on her return to Avacas was that the Queen of Dhevyn was pregnant. How could that turgid little cow have conceived so quickly? By her estimation, Kirsh had slept with his wife less than a handful of times since they married, and he certainly never laid a hand on her before that day. At this rate, Alenor would breed like a damn rabbit, and there'd be a dozen heirs running around Dhevyn and Senet in as many years.

It did not help Marqel's mood that Kirsh had hovered solicitously by his wife's side, and that the two of them had smiled and carried on like a pair of young lovers all evening. Even though she was quite sure Kirsh was acting for his father's benefit, Marqel was still unsure about Alenor. How that girl could be so thick not to realize what was going on totally escaped Marqel. It must be something about the way they raised noblewomen, she concluded. They were such vapid, useless creatures that they couldn't see past their own stuck-up little noses.

Kirsh did not seek her out that night, so the following morning she presented herself to the High Priestess to find out what Belagren wanted her to do. Marqel had a bad feeling that she would be sent back to the Hall of Shadows, the High Priestess having decided that, with Alenor pregnant, Marqel's presence was no longer required.

Then it occurred to her that she did have another reason to stay in the palace. With her hand raised to knock on the door of

Belagren's room, she hesitated, and then, with a smug little smile, headed down the hall and knocked on the door of Prince Misha's room instead.

When she didn't receive an immediate reply, she waited, and then knocked again. When silence still met her knock, she opened the door and poked her head through.

"Hello?"

There was still no answer. Glancing up and down the hall to make certain she was unobserved, Marqel slipped inside.

Misha's suite was immaculately clean and, more important, it was tidy. The prince lived in these rooms and rarely ventured outside, but even with servants running after him all day, when he was here, the inevitable clutter and chattels of daily living gave the rooms a lived-in feeling.

There was not a book out of place, not so much a chair askew. Tellingly, Misha's chess set was put away on the table under the window, the pieces lined up at either end of the board patiently waiting for a new game. He was gone, but where, she could not imagine. He was too weak to leave the palace, even for a short holiday, and Ella Geon would never have countenanced him going off alone.

She was still trying to puzzle it out when the door opened fully. Marqel spun around guiltily only to find it was just one of the laundry maids who changed the towels and sheets on the fourth floor. She was a buxom blonde and palace gossip had it that she was would sleep with any man in Avacas for the price of a meal and a few good ales.

"Sorry, my lady. I saw the door open..."

"Emalia, isn't it?"

"Yes, my lady."

"Where is Prince Misha?"

"He's gone, my lady."

"I can see that," she snapped. "*Where* has he gone?"

"To Tolace, my lady. To the Hospice."

"Why?"

"The prince took quite poorly, ma'am. Real sick, he was. Lady Ella thought the sea air might do him good."

We're on the coast here, she thought, *that's not the reason.*

"You said he was poorly? What did you mean? What was wrong with him?"

"Can't rightly say, ma'am," Emalia shrugged. "I mean, he's never been a well lad, everyone knows that, but since Prince Kirshov got married he just seemed to go downhill. He always used to say hello when I changed his towels, but it got so that he hardly said a word no more. He just lay there, all listless and weak. Lady Ella was real worried about him."

Lady Ella was probably responsible, Marqel decided with interest.

"When did he leave for Tolace?"

"A while back now, my lady. After Lady Madalan came back to Avacas—that was more than two months ago now—he just seemed to go from bad to worse, poor pet. Then Lady Ella and Master Daranski had this big meeting with Prince Antonov and they told him that the prince might do better at the Hospice, so they packed him off to Tolace. An' then, just when it looked like being quiet for a while, the little queen turns up from Kalarada unexpectedly. Not that I mind, though. We all sort of missed her after she left. You get used to having people around, you know? And she was such a sweetie as a child. Real well mannered, you know? Just like you think a little princess ought to be..."

"Oh do stop babbling, you stupid girl!" Marqel snapped, even though Emalia was probably five years her senior. "Did you hear anybody say what was wrong with the prince exactly?"

"I'm not privy to that sort of thing, my lady."

"You seem to be privy to everything else," Marqel remarked. "Including what Lady Ella and Master Daranski said to Prince Antonov in a private meeting. Or did they invite you along so they'd have a permanent record of the conversation?"

The girl appeared too stupid to realize that Marqel was insulting her. "Why would they do that, my lady?"

Marqel muttered a curse. "Be off with you! Shouldn't you be scrubbing floors or something?"

Emalia squared her shoulders, looking quite offended. "I'm the fourth-floor laundry maid. I don't do floors!"

"Then go and do...whatever it is that you do."

Emalia dropped a brief, barely respectful curtsy, made even more insolent by the scowl she wore. "As my lady commands."

The maid turned and left the room, leaving Marqel alone to ponder the strange turn of events that had removed Misha from the palace. Ella Geon was still in Avacas, but that did not mean she wasn't responsible for Misha's deteriorating health. In fact, it could simply mean that she wanted to distance herself from him, in case his condition proved fatal.

The thought that Misha might die gave her pause. If his decline was on the orders of the High Priestess, then he might well be dead within a matter of weeks. Marqel knew of no order to finally terminate Misha, but that didn't mean it hadn't been spoken. In fact, it was more than likely she wouldn't know of it. One did not issue orders to eliminate the heir to the throne of Senet where one was likely to be overheard . . .

So Misha might die soon, she thought. *Damn!*

That did not suit Marqel at all. In fact, little had happened lately that did. She thought she had things under control when Alenor invited her to Kalarada, and she was installed as Kirsh's mistress. The future looked even rosier when he invited her to Omaxin and left his frigid little wife behind. But then Dirk Provin turned up, and now Alenor was here in Avacas, and pregnant, and being fussed over like a prized brood mare.

If Misha were to die now, before Marqel could conceive a child by Kirsh, then no child of hers would ever be considered a potential heir. In all likelihood, she would be made to get rid of it. Everything hinged on being the firstborn, she knew. Boy or girl, legitimate or not, the child born first to any future king was always important.

And that stupid bitch's child would be born before the next Landfall Feast.

That Marqel had not conceived a child was not for lack of trying on her part. She had taken all the herbs she knew of that were supposed to increase a woman's fertility. She had even fed Kirsh a concoction once, telling him it would ease a headache, just in case the problem was his. Obviously it was not. If Alenor had conceived so quickly then Kirsh's seed must be sound.

Perhaps the problem was hers? Perhaps the herbs Kalleen

made her drink each night to stop her conceiving had a lasting effect. Perhaps after that time on Derex, when the herbs had not worked and she had fallen pregnant at the tender age of thirteen, and Kalleen had taken her to that sleazy old herb man in the shop behind the tannery and made her drink that foul stuff to get rid of it...Perhaps that had done something to her? She remembered thinking at the time, as she lay on the narrow bunk in the wagon she shared with Lanatyne, screaming in agony, that the stuff they had given her seemed designed not just to get rid of the baby, but to disembowel her in the process.

For the first time, Marqel was forced to confront the possibility that perhaps she *couldn't* have a baby. All the men she had been with since then, from the nameless old men who wanted her to call them "Daddy," to the countless sailors from the *Calliope* in Elcast, even Dirk Provin and then Kirshov...None of them had gotten her with child, which was something of a miracle in itself.

Marqel cursed savagely. She did not mind the thought that she could not have children in general, but it annoyed her intensely that she might not be able to cement her position by giving birth to a royal bastard.

And that pious, waspish little princess gets bedded twice and suddenly she's with child. It's just not fair!

Well, Marqel decided, *if I can't give Kirsh his firstborn, then neither will Alenor.*

For Marqel, things like that were quite easily taken care of.

She knocked on the door of Alenor's suite later that evening, once she was sure the queen had retired. Lady Dorra, the suspicious, dark-eyed, lady-in-waiting that Antonov had chosen several years ago to watch over Alenor, admitted her with a frown. Marqel was certain she knew about her and Kirsh, but Dorra's job was to watch over the little queen, not worry about what the Queen's consort did when he was not with his wife. She might not approve, but neither did she really care.

"I thought the queen might like some peppermint tea," Marqel explained, raising the tray she carried a little. "She looked a bit pale at dinner."

Dorra stood back to let her enter. "She's just getting ready to retire. I'll ask her."

"Is the Lady Jacinta not here?"

"She stayed in Kalarada," Dorra told her. "Just put it there."

Marqel carried the tray into the room and placed it on the table in front of the settee. "I thought it might help her sleep. A good night's sleep is very important in her condition."

The lady-in-waiting picked up the cup, sniffing the sweet-smelling steam rising off the drink appreciatively. Peppermint was such a wonderful condiment. It masked the taste of so many things.

"Make sure she drinks it all," Marqel advised.

She watched Dorra take the cup into the other room with a concerned smile. When Dorra emerged a little while later, she volunteered to take the empty cup down to the kitchens, to save Dorra the trouble of summoning a servant. As she left the suite, Marqel wished the lady-in-waiting a good night's sleep.

And then humming to herself, she took the tray back to the kitchens to wash the cup and remove any trace of the poison.

Chapter 72

The pain woke Alenor in the middle of the night. The red sun was high overhead when she suddenly sat up in bed as a violent pain ripped through her abdomen. Gasping with the shock of it, she doubled over, wondering what had caused such a thing. She had not eaten anything odd at dinner, and could not think what would cause her such discomfort. She was still wondering about it when another pain ripped through her like a butcher's knife.

She cried out in terror as much as pain, but it was followed almost immediately by another contraction, even worse than the previous one.

This time she screamed.

Her screams brought Dorra running into the room. Alenor

toppled sideways on the bed, her knees drawn up under her chin as wave after wave of agony tore through her.

"Your majesty?" Dorra inquired with some concern.

"Help me..." It was all she could manage. The pain cleaved through her again, and she had only the breath left to cry out. Dorra hurried to her side and pulled back the tangled sheets.

"Goddess!" she exclaimed in shock.

Alenor glanced down. The bed was stained bright red as the blood gushed from between her legs. "Dorra!" she cried in panic. "What's *happening*?"

"Stay right there, your majesty," the lady-in-waiting ordered, as if Alenor had any choice in the matter.

She cried out again as the pain seemed to grow worse with each pounding thump of her heart. Dorra ran from the room, leaving Alenor alone, sobbing and frightened. Somewhere, amid the torment, she realized she was losing her baby. Perhaps there really was a Goddess. *Perhaps I'm being punished...*

"Your majesty! Alenor!"

Choking back her sobs, Alenor wiped her eyes. The physician Yuri Daranski hurried into her room and stood over her for a moment with a concerned frown. Then he pulled back the sheets, took one look at the bright blood spilling from her womb and turned to Dorra decisively.

"We have to stop the bleeding," he said. "Get her on her back."

They tried to move her, but Alenor screamed, too afraid to unclench her knees. The pain slashed through her in waves, as if someone was standing over her with an invisible sword, slicing the unborn child from her womb. She was trembling and cold, as if her fingers and toes had been dipped in ice.

"Alenor!" Yuri said sharply. "You must let us help you!"

"But it *hurts*..." she sobbed uncomprehendingly. "Oh, Goddess! It hurts so much..."

"Then let us help you, your majesty," he urged. When his pleas received no response he looked up at Dorra. "Find the Shadowdancers. I think both Ella Geon and Olena Borne are in the palace tonight. I will need their assistance."

Dorra fled the room at a run and Yuri turned his attention back to Alenor.

"Tell me where it hurts exactly," he said.

She tried to answer him, but the only thing she could manage was a sobbing moan. *Oh dear Goddess! Make it go away!*

"I need you to lie on your back, Alenor," Yuri explained soothingly, trying once again to get her to move. "I know it's painful, but if we're to save your baby, we must stop the bleeding."

"I can't..." she moaned. "Just make it stop...*please*..."

"I can only make the pain go away if you help me to help *you*."

Alenor wanted to help him. She wanted to make it stop, but she just could not bring herself to unclench muscles that had tightened in terror. Somewhere through the pain she heard more voices. She was dimly aware of Ella and Olena arriving.

"Get me towels, sheets, anything!" Yuri ordered urgently. "She's hemorrhaging badly. We must try to stem the flow. And we must get her onto her back. It will put pressure on the abdominal vena cava and help slow the bleeding."

She protested weakly as Ella and Yuri forced her onto her back, no longer having the strength to fight both the pain and the physicians trying to help her.

"Do you have any lavender oil?" Yuri asked Ella.

"Of course," the Shadowdancer told him. "But it will do little to ease such intense pain. Poppy-dust would be more effective..."

"No!" Yuri told her emphatically. "I'll not risk her child by giving her anything so strong."

"It's patently clear that she's lost the child, Yuri," Ella pointed out with callous disregard for Alenor's feelings. "Our concern now should simply be for the queen's comfort."

Alenor whimpered, and tried to roll onto her side.

"Stay where you are, Alenor," Yuri insisted, placing a firm but gentle hand on her shoulder. "It will all be over soon."

Olena hurried back into the room carrying a pile of fresh towels. Yuri grabbed one from her, rolled it into a tight cylinder, and then Ella held her legs apart while he held it in place. The indignity of her position seemed minor compared to her pain.

"She needs ergot," Ella suggested. "A few grains will help stop the bleeding..."

"No!" Yuri said. "Not until I'm certain what has brought this on."

"I've some clary sage mixed with jasmine and geranium we can use to massage her abdomen," Olena offered. "It might help the womb to contract and slow the bleeding."

"Get it," Yuri ordered, turning to Olena. "And get a servant in here to darken this room. I want as little light as possible. And then get the kitchens to prepare several pitchers of sugared water. We need to keep her fluids up."

Olena rushed off again to do as Yuri ordered. Alenor glanced down through her tears to find Dorra standing at the foot of the bed.

"Will she live?" her lady-in-waiting asked.

"If we can stop the bleeding," Yuri replied. "Where is Kirshov? Her husband should be here."

"I'll find him. Should I wake Prince Antonov?"

Yuri hesitated for a moment, and then he nodded. "Perhaps you should."

With a terrified sob, Alenor clutched at his arm. "Am I dying, Master Daranski?"

"Of course not, your majesty," he told her comfortingly. "You're just having a little problem keeping the baby, that's all. Just hang on a little longer, my dear. Olena has gone to fetch something for the pain, and then we'll massage your belly with some special oils, which will ease it even more."

Olena returned a few moments later with the oils Yuri needed. He took them from her and then returned to Alenor's bedside. "I want you to open your mouth, Alenor. This won't hurt. I just want to put a few drops of lavender oil under your tongue. It will help the pain."

She did as he asked, the lavender tasting sharp and strange as he dropped it carefully into her mouth. He handed the small vial back to Olena, and then took the clary sage oil from her. "Massage this into her abdomen. It will be painful at first, and she may fight you, but don't stop."

Olena nodded and moved to the bed. She tipped some of the oil onto her hand and then lifted Alenor's nightdress and began to rub her belly. Far from relaxing her spasms, the oil seemed to encourage them to contract. She screamed, but the Shadowdancer ignored her protests.

"I've not seen a spontaneous abortion this violent before," Yuri remarked to Ella with a frown.

"Are you suggesting this *wasn't* spontaneous?" Ella asked in surprise.

"She displays all the symptoms of ergot poisoning."

"Which is why you don't want to give her any more," Ella concluded with a nod of understanding. "It might not slow the bleeding, it might kill her."

The physician shrugged. "If she was the daughter of a minor baron and this was six weeks after Landfall, I'd not hesitate to diagnose an abortifacient. But this is the Queen of Dhevyn."

Alenor fought through the agony to listen to the conversation. She gasped in horror. "I...I didn't...I *swear*! I didn't take anything..."

Ella looked down at her. "Nobody is suggesting you did, your majesty. Are you feeling any better?"

She nodded weakly as she realized that the lavender had taken a slight edge off the pain. Or perhaps the worst was over. She found she didn't care. Alenor just wanted to curl up into a ball and die. She was frightened and in pain. She wanted her mother. She wanted to be held and cuddled and told that everything would be all right.

But instead she was here in Avacas Palace, with nobody she trusted and nobody she loved, except...

Alenor forced herself not to name him, even in her thoughts. She wanted so badly for him to come to her, to hold her and make everything better, but even in her agony, Alenor had the wit not to call out his name. If she was going to call for anybody, she must call for her husband. To name another man might prove fatal for both of them.

"What in the name of the Goddess is going on?" Antonov's voice boomed from the next room. The doors flew open and he strode into her bedroom, barefoot and bare-chested, dressed only in the trousers he had hurriedly thrown on in answer to Dorra's summons.

"The queen is hemorrhaging, your highness, however, we should have it under control soon."

"Has she lost the baby?"

Yuri glanced down at Alenor for a moment and then nodded sadly. "Most likely."

I'm being punished, Alenor sobbed silently. *This is what I get for thinking I could be happy...*

"Alenor?"

She felt Antonov's weight on the mattress as he sat down beside her, felt his hand gently brush the hair from her forehead.

"You mustn't cry, my dear," he told her gently. "You're young and strong. There'll be plenty of other babies for you and Kirsh."

"I'm so sorry..." she sobbed in a voice barely more than an agonized whisper. He didn't understand what she was apologizing for, but that didn't matter. Maybe, if she was truly sorry, the pain might stop...

"Now, now, you mustn't blame yourself, Alenor. These things happen." Antonov turned to Yuri. "She is to get whatever she needs to make her well."

"Of course, your highness."

He turned back to Alenor with a warm smile. "See? Master Daranski will make everything better."

"I'm sorry to cause such a fuss..."

"Nonsense. You're a queen, Alenor. Queens are allowed to cause a fuss." He patted her hand in a fatherly manner, but his sympathetic smile faded as he rose to his feet, and turned to look at the others in the room.

"And now," he said, in an icy tone, "would someone like to tell me where the hell my son is?"

Chapter 73

Y ou're drunk," Antonov accused Kirsh when he was escorted into his father's study by the guard sent into the city to look for him. They had found him in a tavern near the wharves where the Regent of Dhevyn was making himself very popular by footing the bill for everyone in the taproom. Kirsh hated to drink alone.

He smiled. "Tired and a little confused, maybe..."

"You should have been here. With your wife."

"Alenor seems to get along very nicely without me," he remarked. It was the closest he dared come to admitting the truth about his relationship with her. He was not so drunk or foolish that he would let the truth slip. Angry, certainly, but not so foolish as that.

"While you were out making every tavern owner in Avacas between here and the docks a wealthy man, your wife was having a miscarriage."

The news sobered Kirsh considerably. "Is she all right?"

"She lost the baby, Kirshov. And you should have been there. Not whoring around town."

"I wasn't..." he began, and then he thought better of trying to defend himself. "I'm sorry."

"She almost died."

"But she'll be all right, won't she?" He was a little surprised to find himself genuinely concerned for her. The news that the child she carried, the child that belonged to some nameless man he would dearly like to kill, was now lost, had not really sunk in.

"Eventually. She was calling for you."

Kirsh found that hard to believe, but he could hardly admit it to his father. "I'll go to her."

"Not in that state you won't," Antonov decreed, looking him up and down with disdain. "You're filthy and you stink like a cheap whore. Get cleaned up first, and then you may visit with her. And you'll damn well stay with her until she's well again. I didn't waste the last few years trying to convince the Dhevynians that you and Alenor were truly in love, just so you could ruin everything because you're too damn thoughtless to be with your wife when she needs you."

Kirsh opened his mouth to defend himself, but realized that anything he said would just make things worse. "Yes, sir."

He turned to leave, but Antonov called him back.

"Kirsh?"

"Sir?"

"Send the Shadowdancer away."

"Marqel's got nothing to do with this...quite the opposite. Alenor likes her. She was the one who invited Marqel to Kalarada."

"Which means at least you're being discreet," Antonov conceded. "But your wife needs you at the moment more than your mistress does. It won't hurt you to put her aside until Alenor's recovered. And you're lucky I didn't find you with Marqel tonight while Alenor was bleeding to death, or I'd have taken care of her myself."

"I can handle it, Father."

Antonov studied him thoughtfully for a moment and then nodded. "See that you do handle it, Kirsh. Alenor must recover and bear another heir as soon as possible."

"I hardly think you need an heir from Alenor and me now that you've got Dirk Provin back," Kirsh retorted bitterly. Perhaps he was drunk enough to say something truly stupid after all.

Antonov's expression darkened. "Just do what you're supposed to be doing, Kirsh, and let me worry about Dirk Provin."

"I hope *you* can handle *him*," Kirsh said, and then turned and left the room before his father could take him to task for his insolence.

Freshly bathed and dressed in clean clothes, and certainly feeling much more sober than when he confronted his father, Kirsh was let into Alenor's room just on second sunrise. He was shocked when he saw her. The darkened room was hushed and reeked of lavender. She looked tiny and pale against the sheets, her eyes puffy and red from crying. As Dorra stood back to let him into the bedroom, Olena was heading out carrying an armload of blood-soaked sheets. The amount of blood startled him. Could you lose that much and still live?

Yuri Daranski looked up when he heard Kirsh enter, his face a portrait of stern disapproval. "You're here," he remarked unnecessarily.

"I'd like to be alone with my wife," Kirsh announced.

The physician nodded and, with Ella and Dorra, he silently

left the room. Kirsh crossed the rug to the bed, his earlier anger fading a little in the face of Alenor's obvious distress.

She turned to look at him as he approached, her eyes welling up with tears. "You must be pleased."

"I never would have wished such a thing on you, Allie," he said, sitting on the bed beside her.

"Well, at least you'll be spared the shame of having to raise another man's bastard."

"My father said you nearly died."

"I wish I had," she whispered, as the tears spilled onto her cheeks.

He took her hand in his and held it for a moment. Despite what had happened between them recently, he felt for her, although he had to admit he was feeling relief as much as sympathy.

"Allie, you didn't...I mean, this *was* an accident, wasn't it?"

"You think *I* did this?"

"Not really," he admitted. "I just couldn't help but wonder."

"I wanted this baby, Kirsh."

"Even though it wasn't mine?"

"Especially because it wasn't yours."

He found himself unable to meet her accusing gaze.

"How did we ever get into such a mess, Allie?"

She did not answer him.

"Is there anything I can do?" he asked. "Anyone I can... get for you, perhaps?"

She smiled thinly. "Nice try."

"I didn't mean it like that."

"Not consciously, perhaps. But if I had the wit not to call for him when I thought I was dying, Kirsh, I've certainly got enough sense not to tell you who it is now."

"We can't go on like this, Alenor," he sighed with a shake of his head.

She wiped her eyes and looked away. "You chose this course, Kirsh, not I."

That was one argument he was not prepared to get into right now. "We'll have to stay here in Avacas until you've recovered enough to travel," he told her, looking for a safer subject.

She shrugged apathetically. "It makes no difference. Your father has enough people running my kingdom that they hardly need you or me there."

"I'll see to it you have everything you need."

"Your father's already done that."

"Is there *anything* I can do?"

"You can go to hell," she told him, and then she turned her face away and refused to speak to him further.

Marqel was waiting for him in his rooms when he returned, and he held her wordlessly for a long time, unable to confide, even to her, what was wrong. She kissed him after a time and then searched his face for some hint of what he truly felt.

"I'm so sorry, Kirsh," she said. "You must be so disappointed that Alenor was too weak to carry the child past the first few months."

"It's tragic," he agreed.

"Shouldn't you be with her now?"

"I've been to see her. She's still upset. I don't think she wants to know me right now."

"She'll get over that."

"I doubt it," he muttered.

Marqel looked at him curiously. "Is something wrong, Kirsh?"

He shook his head. "It's been a long night."

"And I shouldn't stay," she added, surprising him with her intuitiveness. "Your wife has just had a miscarriage, my love. It wouldn't look too good if word got around the palace that you consoled yourself that same night in the arms of your mistress."

Kirsh glanced at the window. The second sun was almost fully risen. "It's not night any longer."

"I should still leave. I'll come back later, when things aren't so...fraught."

He smiled at her understanding. "I love you."

"I know you do."

"I wish..." he stopped the thought from even forming in

his mind. What he wished for could never be, and it served no useful purpose to hope that it might.

"You wish what?"

"Nothing."

"It'll all work out for the best, Kirsh," Marqel assured him. "Just you wait and see."

Kirsh kissed her again and then let her go. As she slipped from the room, he wondered where she got her confidence from. Perhaps it had something to do with being a Shadow-dancer. Maybe it was her faith in the Goddess that made her so certain that things would fall into place as she willed them.

Right now, Kirsh could feel the start of a tremendous hangover beginning to form, and all he wanted to do was crawl into bed, pull the covers over his head and sleep it off.

Maybe, when he awoke, he thought wistfully, he wouldn't be married to a woman he didn't love, in love with a woman he could never marry, pretending to grieve the loss of a child he had fervently wished was dead.

And that was the hardest thing to deal with, Kirsh realized. Before losing himself in the taverns of Avacas, he had stopped for a moment in the Goddess's temple that his father had built in the grounds of the palace.

He had prayed—begged, almost—that she would make the problem go away.

It seemed the Goddess had answered his prayers, but for some reason, it didn't do anything to ease the guilt he felt for asking.

Chapter 74

Tia reached Tolace some ten days after she escaped the High Priestess's convoy. They were ten days of hiding and living off the land, of dodging other travelers and trying to look inconspicuous whenever she could not avoid them. Fortunately,

Kirshov Latanya had kept his word, and provided her with enough food that she was able to go for days without having to hunt. He had also, she discovered with delight, returned her bow and quiver of arrows, which she found hidden in the bedroll.

She was still at a loss to explain the Senetian prince's behavior, even after days of doing little else but think about it. It was suspiciously out of character, from what she knew of him, and she was certain the Lion of Senet would be furious to learn that Tia Veran had once again slipped through his fingers. All she could conclude in the end was that he really meant it when he said he thought Dirk's actions were repellent, and with some sort of honor-twisted logic, had decided to let her go, in an attempt to redress the injustice.

It was raining when she finally reached the outskirts of Tolace, with its long Hospice wall and its tall granite cliffs. The rain was warm, however, and it didn't really slow her down much. She had decided it was safe enough to use the road, this far south of Avacas, and had covered the last ten miles in half the time it had taken her to cover the previous five.

The market was winding down for the evening when she trotted into town. It was past first sunrise and the heavy rain clouds were bloody and oppressive in the light of the red sun. Most of the stallholders beneath the wall had closed up for the evening, the rain driving away the few customers who ventured out this late in the day.

Boris Farlo, the Brotherhood man she knew in Tolace, had a small shop opposite the Hospice wall, which sold a large variety of woven baskets that his wife and five daughters made in a small workshop out the back of his shop. The wares were expertly crafted, ranging from small wicker baskets useful for little more than storing trinkets to the huge trunks favored by the nobility for traveling. *And the odd dead body,* Tia speculated, thinking of the cheerful little man's other occupation. His goods were renowned for their craftsmanship, and were shipped all over Senet and Dhevyn, which made the harmless-looking little Senetian basketmaker very valuable to an organization whose prime function was smuggling.

It was almost closing time when she dismounted outside a
shop selling flowers some way down the street. She walked past
the basket shop twice, as casually as she could manage, waiting until the last customer had left before she stepped inside. It was clut-
tered with all manner of wickerwork, and she had to duck under
some of the baskets hanging from the ceiling as she neared the
counter. Boris looked up, with his best new-customer smile, which
changed to a much more genuine smile when he recognized her.

"Tasha!"

Tia rarely used her own name in Senet, and certainly not
since there had been a price on her head. Boris probably knew it
was not her real name; he might even know her true identity,
but they kept up the fiction that he did not. He was a short man,
with a well-rounded belly, the result, no doubt, of his wife trying to teach five daughters how to cook.

"Hello, Boris."

"This is a surprise! I wasn't expecting to see you!"

What he really meant was there were no Baenlander ships
in port at the moment. Tia had thought that would be too much
to hope for. Life rarely worked out so neatly.

"I'm just passing through," she explained. "I need somewhere to stay until I can get a message to my brother." The
"brother" she referred to was Reithan. Had she said "father,"
Boris would have known she meant Porl Isingrin. Her "uncle"
was Dal Falstov, the captain of the *Orlando*.

Boris nodded. "Somewhere discreet?" he asked knowingly.

"The discreeter the better," she agreed, wondering if there
was such a word.

"Why don't you go out back and say hello to Gilda and the
girls? As soon as I close up the shop, we can have a nice long
chat and you can tell me what you need."

Boris's wife Gilda was like a female version of her husband:
short, round and jolly, although Tia knew that she was just as
highly placed as her husband in the Brotherhood, and far more
dangerous when crossed. There was a story that Tia had heard
once, claiming Gilda Farlo had castrated an amorous sailor

with her trimming knife when he tried to get fresh with one of her daughters. Tia didn't know if the story was true, and decided it probably wasn't prudent to ask.

The kitchen was full of the smell of boiling cabbages and beets, as Gilda ordered her small army of daughters around the kitchen like a little general. She offered to help, but Gilda would have none of it, insisting that Tia get out of her wet clothes and sit by the fire to dry off, even though it was quite warm and the fire did little more than make her sweat.

Boris came through from the shop about a half an hour later, as Tia was sitting in front of the stove, wearing a borrowed skirt and blouse that belonged to Caterina Farlo, who was at least three sizes bigger and a head shorter than Tia.

"Now we can talk," he announced, taking a seat at the scrubbed wooden table with a sigh of relief. He lifted his feet up and without being asked, the youngest girl—a chubby blonde about fourteen—hurried over with a footstool and placed it under his feet.

"Tea, Mother!" he ordered cheerfully.

"On the way," Gilda assured him, a few moments before placing a steaming cup in front of him. "Would you like some tea, Tasha?"

"No thanks, Gilda. I'm fine." Given the opportunity, Tia knew from her past visits to this house, Gilda would pour tea down her throat endlessly, until she was all but drowning in it.

"So when did you slip into Senet?" Boris asked, taking an appreciative sip from his cup.

"Just after Landfall," she explained, seeing no point in lying to him. He would have known the *Makuan* was in Senetian waters then, anyway, and rather ironically, for a bunch of criminals with no discernable morals, the Brotherhood had a very dim view of liars.

"And now you need to get *out* of Senet?" he guessed.

"The sooner the better," she agreed. "Do you know where any of our ships are at the moment?"

"The *Orlando*'s tied up in Paislee, so that would be the closest. I've not seen the *Wanderer* for a while, and the last I heard the *Makuan* was in Derex."

"Then I should head for Paislee," she suggested.

Boris shook his head. "It's a long way to Paislee, lass, and she could easily sail before you get there. It'll be quicker if I send a message to our people by bird, and they can let Dal Falstov know you're here. He can then decide whether he wants to pick you up here or have you meet him somewhere safer."

"Somewhere safer?"

"Tolace is crawling with the Lion of Senet's Guard at the moment," Gilda informed her.

"Why?" Tia asked cautiously. *Surely they're not here looking for me already?*

"Misha Latanya has been brought to the Hospice," Boris explained. "There's talk that he's dying."

"Dying?" she asked in surprise. *How could he be dying?* Tia wondered. He was just another poppy-dust addict, and they were either lost in the dust or dead from it. There was no middle ground.

"Aye," Gilda agreed. "It's a sad state of affairs. I hear he's quite an amiable young man."

"He is," Tia confirmed absently.

Gilda and Boris both looked at her in surprise. "You know him?"

"I met him once," she told them, silently cursing her loose tongue. "I'm surprised to hear he's dying, though. Did you hear what was wrong with him?"

"Not really," Gilda shrugged. "It's just one of those unfortunate things, I suppose. Some people are just born with weak blood."

Weak blood, my arse, Tia thought skeptically. *Weak-willed is more like it.*

"Why don't you visit with him while you're here?" Gilda suggested brightly.

"Pardon?" Tia gasped.

Boris chuckled. "Don't listen to Mother, Tasha, she's teasing. What she means is that we have a safe house in the grounds of the Hospice. You can stay there until we hear from the *Orlando.*"

"In the *grounds* of the Hospice?" she repeated doubtfully. "I thought you said it was crawling with Antonov's guard."

"Which is what makes it so safe," Gilda explained. "The last place they look for people hiding from them is right under their noses."

"Never fear, Tasha," Boris assured her. "We'll not see you come to any harm. Unless, of course, you don't like Mother's cooking, in which case she'll probably whack you over the head with her spoon, tie you up and hand you over to the guard herself."

They all laughed. The five Farlo daughters pushed and jostled each other good-naturedly as they took their places at the table. Gilda hefted the heavy cauldron of borscht onto the table and began to dole it out into large, glazed pottery bowls.

Tia took her place at the table and joined in the laughter warily, not entirely certain that Boris was joking.

Chapter 75

It was almost a week after Alenor's miscarriage before Dirk was able to see her, and when he did, he was shocked by her appearance. Always a small girl, she now seemed so thin and fragile that a stiff wind might blow her away. He stepped into the room as Dorra announced him, leaving his ever-faithful escort waiting in the hall. He looked at Alenor with concern. The room was dim, the windows covered to keep out the bright light of the second sun, and the air was heavy with the scent of rose petals that smoldered in a small dish by the bed. Alenor sat propped up on a mountain of pillows, her pale face almost as white as the silk sheets she lay on.

"Dirk!" Alenor said with a weak smile as Dorra closed the doors and stood in front of them like a sentinel.

"How are you?"

"Feeling a little better," she assured him. She looked past him to her lady-in-waiting. "Could you arrange some tea, Dorra? And when Captain Seranov gets here, send him straight in."

"Your majesty, it's not appropriate for you to be alone with…"

"Oh, Dorra," she sighed. "Dirk is my cousin, and we've already had numerous discussions about the captain of my guard."

"Very well, your majesty," Dorra agreed with a great deal of reluctance. She opened the doors behind her and headed into the other room, pointedly leaving them open.

Dirk walked to the bed and sat down, taking Alenor's hand in his. It was so small, so thin, he was afraid it might crumble in his grasp if he held it too tightly.

"I spoke to Yuri. He says you're coming along nicely."

"Master Daranski would probably say that even if I was gasping my dying breath."

Dirk smiled. "Well, at least you haven't lost your sense of humor."

"But I lost my baby." She sounded so small and frightened.

"There'll be others," he lied, with an encouraging smile. "A miscarriage is just nature's way of telling you that this child wasn't meant to be."

Dirk felt a little guilty for the lie. Yuri had told him the damage to Alenor's womb was severe. It was unlikely that she would ever carry another child. That news worried Dirk a great deal, and not only for the effect such knowledge might have on Alenor. If Antonov suspected that Alenor could no longer bear him the heir to Dhevyn he so desperately wanted, then his only alternative heir was Dirk. He had begged Yuri to keep his suspicions to himself for Alenor's sake, hoping that Yuri would not realize Dirk had another reason for being so considerate of his cousin's delicate state of mind.

"Nature is very perceptive," Alenor remarked in an odd voice, turning her head away to avoid meeting his eye.

Dorra bustled into the room carrying a tray with two steaming cups of tea. She offered the tray to Dirk, who lifted the cups and placed them on the side table beside the bed.

"Will there be anything else, your majesty?"

"Her majesty will call you if she needs anything," Dirk answered for the queen.

Dorra glared at him, but Dirk's position was too ambiguous for her to challenge him confidently. "As you wish, my lord." She curtsied politely and left the room, but did not close the doors behind her.

"Alenor?"

When she looked back at him, her eyes were filled with tears. "I'm being punished, aren't I?" she asked in a small voice.

"What are you talking about, silly? Punished for what?"

She glanced past Dirk into the other room to check on Dorra's whereabouts before she answered. "It wasn't Kirsh's baby, Dirk," she whispered.

He did not respond immediately. In fact, he was quite numb with the shock of her revelation. "Did Kirsh know?" he asked cautiously, in a low voice.

She nodded. "I've never been with him, Dirk. Not even on our wedding night. He was furious when he found out I was pregnant."

Furious was probably an understatement, he thought. Then something else Yuri said to him when he inquired after Alenor began to make sense. "Who else knew?"

"Nobody."

"Are you sure about that? What about the baby's father?"

"Well, of course he knew."

"And do you trust him?"

"As much as I trust you."

He was silent for a moment, debating how much he should tell her. He purposely did not dwell on the implications of her news. That Alenor had spurned Kirsh and taken a lover was something he was not quite ready to deal with just yet. "Alenor, do you know that Yuri suspects your miscarriage wasn't an accident?"

"I remember him saying something like that the night it happened." She suddenly clutched at his hand. Her grip was disturbingly weak. "Oh Goddess, Dirk! You don't think I took something deliberately, do you? I didn't try to get rid of it, I swear!"

"But maybe somebody else did," he suggested.

"Who would do such a thing? Kirsh was the only one who

knew the truth, and I don't care what you say, he would never do anything so dreadful."

He nodded in agreement. "Kirsh would go to his father and tell him everything before he killed an innocent child, even one that wasn't born yet."

"Then who could have done such a thing?"

"What about your faithful watchdog?"

"Dorra? I don't think so. If she suspected anything, Antonov would know about it, and I wouldn't be lying here having my every whim catered to. I'd be in a dungeon having a long and painful chat with Barin Welacin."

He thought for a moment, and then it came to him. The one person in Avacas he was certain was capable of such a heinous act, and more important, had the knowledge of and access to the herbs required to induce an abortion. Someone with plenty of reason to not want Alenor to carry her child to term, regardless of who the father might be. He did not share his thoughts with Alenor, however. There were other, better ways to deal with the author of this tragedy. And, for Alenor's sake, it would be better if she did not suspect who had been responsible. He didn't think she was so good an actress that she would not betray herself if he told her of his suspicions.

"You must be more careful, Alenor."

"*I* should be more careful?" she asked archly. "That's rather ironic, coming from you." She stopped speaking suddenly and looked over his shoulder at the door. Dorra was standing there, glaring at them suspiciously. "Yes, Dorra?"

"Captain Seranov is here, your majesty," her lady-in-waiting announced.

"Send him in, please," she ordered, with a hint of the old Alenor behind her frail command. "And close the doors, would you? The light is hurting my eyes."

Dorra admitted Alexin and with a disapproving scowl, closing the doors behind him as Alenor had asked.

Dirk rose to his feet, partly out of politeness, and partly out of a strong sense of self-preservation. The captain of Alenor's guard looked very smart in his blue-and-silver uniform, but he was also rather conspicuously armed, and Dirk could well imagine how Alexin felt about the news that Dirk Provin was now the Lord of the Shadows and the right hand of the High Priestess of the Shadowdancers.

"What's *he* doing here?" Alexin asked coldly, stopping just inside the closed doors with his hand resting on the hilt of his sword.

"We need all the powerful friends we can get, my love," Alenor told him. "Would you watch the door, Dirk?"

She held out her hands to Alexin, and he hurried to her bed, taking her in his arms and holding her silently.

Dirk was rendered almost speechless by the depth of their lunacy. "You're a pair of damn fools!"

They clung to each other desperately for a moment. Dirk realized that this was probably the first chance they'd had to be alone since her miscarriage. Alexin let Alenor go and turned to face him, his hand reaching for the sword.

"No, Alexin," Alenor commanded. "Dirk won't betray us."

"He's betrayed everybody else he's had anything to do with lately," Alexin snarled. "Why not you or me?"

"You're still permitted to walk freely through the Lion of Senet's palace armed with a sword, Alexin," Dirk pointed out. "Do you think that likely if I'd betrayed what I know about you and your family?"

"Is that a threat?"

"More a blindingly obvious fact."

"Your very presence in this room is an insult," Alexin spat in disgust.

"You're a fine one to talk," Dirk accused. "Alenor nearly died because of your carelessness. You have an interesting way of interpreting *your* oath to protect your queen, Captain."

"Stop it, Dirk!" Alenor ordered. "This is just as much my fault as Alexin's."

He was not entirely unsympathetic to her plight. *How lost and lonely must you have been to turn to Alexin for comfort?* But it did not excuse such stupidity. Even if Alenor was too naive to realize the risk, Alexin certainly should have known better.

He shook his head in disbelief. "Have the two of you *any* idea of the danger you're courting?"

"It wasn't like we planned anything," Alenor said defensively. "It just...happened."

"Then make it *un*happen, Alenor. Now. Send him back to Kalarada. For Alexin's sake as much as your own. Kirsh will kill him if he finds out, and Antonov will destroy you."

"I'm not afraid to face Kirshov Latanya," Alexin declared with quiet determination.

"You should be, you fool!" Dirk snapped in annoyance. "Because while you're busy defending your honor, the Lion of Senet will be back on Kalarada disbanding the Queen's Guard for treason and replacing it with his own."

His words silenced both of them. Neither Alenor nor Alexin had apparently given any thought to the consequences of their affair, beyond what they felt for each other.

What a mess we've all made of our lives, he thought.

"Dirk, please don't be mad at me," she said, begging for his understanding. "You've no idea what it was like on Kalarada. Kirsh spent all his time doting on his mistress, and then up and disappeared on me for months. I have nobody I can trust except Alexin and Jacinta. Antonov's spies watch every move I make..."

"Who's Jacinta?"

"My cousin. I left her in Kalarada to keep on eye things while I was in Avacas."

"Jacinta *D'Orlon*?" he asked, having heard the name mentioned in palace gossip. She was quite notorious, actually, which was how Dirk had heard of her. "Is this the same Jacinta D'Orlon who told Lord Birkoff that she'd rather marry the male of another species than share his bed?" He rolled his eyes in despair. "Now there's someone you can *obviously* rely on for tact and good judgment."

Alenor managed a weak smile. "She never told me she said that..."

"How in the name of the Goddess did you manage this without being caught?" he asked in astonishment.

"We were careful," Alexin told him.

"Not careful enough," Dirk retorted.

"When I discovered I was pregnant, we decided I should come to Avacas," Alenor explained. "Jacinta thought that if I could tell Antonov before Kirsh got back, then he'd assume that it was Kirsh's child and then Kirsh wouldn't be able to deny it."

"That was a pretty big gamble, Alenor. You beat us here by less than a day."

"But it worked," she shrugged. "Will you help us, Dirk?"

"Help you how?"

"You could use your influence to get some of the Senetians out of Kalarada," Alexin suggested.

"Why should I? So you two can indulge your affair in ignorant bliss while the world falls to pieces around you?"

"That's not fair, Dirk," Alenor said, quite hurt by his lack of sympathy.

"Very little in this world is, Allie."

"You're wasting your time, Alenor," Alexin advised. "He's not going to help anybody but himself. All you've done by confiding in him is made the danger worse."

"I won't betray you," Dirk promised. "I've got problems enough of my own without buying into yours. But that doesn't mean I don't think what you're doing is stupid and dangerous."

"You don't care that *Kirsh* has a mistress."

"Antonov won't kill Kirsh for taking a lover, Alenor."

"But now that you're back and he has an alternative heir to Dhevyn, he'd destroy Alenor without hesitation if he learned she had taken one," Alexin concluded, convincing Dirk that maybe the captain was not quite as dense as he first thought.

"Get out of Avacas," Dirk said to Alexin. "Today, if possible."

"I won't send him away, Dirk."

"You must, Alenor," he insisted. "Besides, I need him to get a message to Reithan for me," he added, turning to face the captain.

"What could you possibly have to say that the Baenlanders would want to hear?"

Dirk took a deep breath before he answered the question, certain beyond doubt that his next words would provoke a reaction.

"I'm going to tell Antonov how to get through the delta," he informed Alexin calmly. "You'll need to warn him so they can evacuate Mil."

PART FIVE

A
LITTLE
TASTE
OF THE
SHADOWS

Chapter 76

The safe house in the grounds of the Hospice in Tolace was far more luxurious than Tia was expecting. It was designed to accommodate members of the nobility recovering from whatever it was that members of the nobility were prone to suffer from. That was, Tia guessed, anything from a mild cold to a galloping dose of the pox.

She was installed in the house under the name of Lady Natasha Orlando (Gilda's idea of a joke), sent to the Hospice to recover from a broken heart. Gilda posed as a hired chaperone so she could later deny any involvement with Tia if anything went wrong. She had concocted some fabulous tale about Lady Natasha being abandoned by a heartless cad on the eve of her wedding in some province in northern Senet Tia had never heard of. The basketmaker's wife had then taken the Shadowdancer who was arranging her admittance aside, and suggested that they keep the poor girl away from sharp implements, poisons and anything else with which she might do herself harm.

Doing her best to look brokenhearted (not a difficult task under the circumstances), Tia had been shown the small cottage where she was to rest and recuperate until she recovered—or the *Orlando* arrived to collect her—and then left to her own devices. The Shadowdancers who staffed the Hospice seemed to be of the opinion that the care of the Lion of Senet's heir took precedence over the broken heart of one not very important noblewoman, who should probably just pull herself together and get over it.

The only downside of the arrangement was that she was required to forgo her usual comfortable trousers and shirt and dress like a lady. Gilda managed to find her two skirts and several embroidered blouses of surprisingly good quality—no doubt they were stolen—and she made Tia hide her other garments and her weapons among the four wicker trunks she sent along with her, to give the impression that Lady Natasha actually had some luggage. No noblewoman traveled without piles of luggage, Gilda explained, so Tia arrived at the Hospice with one almost-empty trunk that held her few possessions and three larger ones stuffed with rags.

Once she was settled into her cottage, Tia spent several days just enjoying the chance to rest. Her meals were delivered by silent servants wheeling small carts along the gravel paths to the various cottages within the high protective wall. The food was excellent and she was largely left alone. It gave her plenty of time to recover from the strain of the past few weeks, far too much time to berate herself for being a fool, and not nearly enough time to prepare for the future.

The Hospice gardens were beautiful. They were a complex network of narrow graveled paths that wound through the cottages and often ended in surprising little grottos with tinkling fountains, or carefully tended flowerbeds that bloomed with different flowers depending on whether the second or the first sun was overhead. Never one for sitting still for long, Tia explored the gardens for hours, staying away from the main buildings where most of the Shadowdancers worked and the poorer patients were treated, and avoiding the discreet little cottages that housed the other, more distinguished patients.

It was on one of her forays through the gardens, some three days after her arrival, that Tia stumbled across Misha Latanya.

The prince was sitting on a garden seat, wrapped in several rugs, beside a small fountain that splashed over an elaborately carved representation of the twin suns of Ranadon. She wandered into the grotto and did not realize at first that she was not alone. The garden seat was set in an alcove cut into the tall hedge surrounding the graveled clearing, and Misha sat huddled so deeply in his blankets that she didn't notice he was there.

He must have moved, or made a sound—Tia wasn't sure—but something caused her to turn around. She stared at him in shock. The prince was almost unrecognizable. He was wasted and thin, his eyes hollow sockets set deep into his head. He trembled constantly, and a small bead of spittle sat on the corner of his mouth, as if he could not stop himself from drooling.

"I'm sorry," she mumbled, turning to leave. She lowered her eyes, praying that he would not recognize her.

"*Tia?*" His voice was weak and understandably surprised.

She debated denying it, or simply running away, but either action might pique his curiosity. Even if Misha Latanya was in no condition to chase her down, he had a whole guard here in Tolace who were, and were probably within shouting distance even now. She glanced around, wondering where they were. It seemed odd to leave the prince alone in such a state.

"I sent them all away," he explained, guessing the reason for her nervous look as she scanned the bushes. "I wanted to be alone."

With a resigned sigh, Tia walked over to the garden seat and sat down beside him.

"You look awful."

He smiled wanly. "I don't feel all that wonderful, either."

"What are you doing here?"

"I'm more interested in what you're doing here," he replied. "The last I heard you'd fled back to the Baenlands." He smiled for a moment, although it was obviously an effort. "I must say, I wasn't all that surprised to learn that you were Neris Veran's daughter. And I missed you after you left. Emalia would never discuss politics with me. She's hopeless at chess, too."

Tia smiled. "Sorry about that. But given a choice between running away and staying around so that Barin Welacin could chop me up one finger at a time, running away seemed the better idea."

He reached a trembling hand through the blankets he had drawn so tightly around himself and picked up her hand with its missing little finger. "I can't believe my father stood back and watched while Barin did that to you."

"He ordered it," she told him flatly.

Misha nodded reluctantly. "It's easy to turn a blind eye to what goes on when you're unwell. I was stunned to learn that you were Ella's daughter, though. She never speaks of you."

"I don't waste much breath on her, either."

"And Dirk? Have you news of him?"

Tia frowned. "Dirk Provin is back in Avacas enjoying the

patronage of your father and the High Priestess. He's doing very nicely for himself."

Misha looked truly surprised. "He came back?"

"Not until he'd learned enough about the Baenlands to make sure that he had plenty to tell the Lion of Senet," she said bitterly. "Speaking of which, why haven't you called your guard? Shouldn't you have me arrested or something?"

He shook his head. "I've no interest in seeing you lose the rest of your fingers, or worse. The war you're fighting is against Senet, not me."

"You *are* Senet, Misha. You're the heir to the throne."

He held up his trembling hand for her to see. "Look at me, Tia. I'll be lucky to live until the next Landfall Feast. I'll not inherit anything."

His assumption that he was dying annoyed Tia for some reason. "Well, whose fault is that?" she snapped.

Misha looked at her curiously. "You think I *want* to be like this?"

"Well, you did have a choice. I mean you have wealth, power, everything you could ever want..."

"What are you talking about?"

"Poppy-dust, Misha," she told him, a little exasperated by his lack of understanding. "You didn't have to take the damn poppy-dust."

The prince stared at her with blank incomprehension. "You think I'm an addict?"

"I don't think, Misha. I know it for a fact. I could never understand why someone like you would feel the need—"

"You're mistaken, Tia," he cut in, quite offended by the suggestion. "I've never taken poppy-dust in my life."

She shrugged off his denial. "You can lie to yourself, your highness, but there's no point lying to me. I grew up watching a man slowly destroy himself with the dust, and trust me, I know the symptoms. And if you want my opinion, that's all that's wrong with you now. You're not dying. You're just not getting enough poppy-dust and you *think* it's killing you."

Misha shook his head. "You're mistaken."

"Whatever," she replied indifferently. "It's your life."

He seemed truly rattled by her diagnosis. "Tia, why would I do such a thing?"

"I don't know. Maybe you were bored."

"Bored?" he asked, looking wounded. "Is that what you think of me? That I'm just some idle rich fool with nothing better to do than to waste his life taking poppy-dust?"

"It happens."

"You're wrong, Tia. Completely and utterly wrong."

"Like I said, it's your life." She heard footsteps on the gravel and rose to her feet. "I'd better get out of here. You might be feeling magnanimous toward me, but I doubt your guard thinks the same way."

"Take care, Tia."

She nodded and slipped through a small gap in the hedge as a Shadowdancer rounded the path.

"Are you all right, your highness? I thought I heard voices."

"Can we go inside now please?" he asked. His voice was shaky and uncertain.

"Of course," the Shadowdancer agreed. "I'll have someone carry you back."

Tia did not hear the rest of the conversation. She headed back through the gardens to her own little cottage, hoping that today might be the day that Gilda came to visit with a message from Dal Falstov telling her that the *Orlando* was on its way to Tolace to collect her. And wondering why Misha Latanya sounded so surprised when she accused him of being a poppy-dust addict.

Chapter 77

Marqel's reason for staying in the palace grew less and less credible every day. With Misha gone to the Hospice in Tolace, Ella had no need for her assistance, and in any case, she had been replaced long ago by two other acolytes that Belagren had sent to the palace to replace Laleno and Caspona after their untimely deaths.

Antonov was extremely concerned about Alenor, or at least he appeared to be. Marqel was of the opinion that the Lion of Senet's distress over his daughter-in-law's condition had more to do with his plans for a Senetian heir to the Dhevynian throne than any real concern for the little queen. The whole palace knew the current mood of the Lion of Senet, so, like everyone else, she tiptoed around him, which included not doing anything to remind him that she was Kirsh's mistress.

As for Kirsh—he had not been to her room in days.

Ironically, the only place she found she could make herself useful was in caring for Alenor, a task she found rather laughable, given that she had caused the ailing queen's current problems. Alenor was such a fragile little thing. It was taking her a long time to recover from the ergot that Marqel had slipped into her peppermint tea. Treating Alenor also gave her an excuse to see Kirshov, who spent a great deal of time with his wife, even though it was patently clear to everyone that Alenor neither wanted nor welcomed his company.

The queen's other most frequent visitors were the captain of the Dhevynian Queen's Guard and Dirk Provin.

Marqel dismissed Alexin Seranov as insignificant. Although he was obviously concerned for his queen, he bothered her on a daily basis (sometimes several times a day) with reports of the most inconsequential things. Alenor—to her credit—bore the interruptions with a remarkable amount of stoicism. Marqel frequently offered to turn him away, but the little queen would smile wanly and insist that she must keep up appearances, and if that meant listening to an endless list of reports from the captain of her guard, then so be it.

Dirk Provin was a different matter entirely. If anybody suspected her as the culprit behind what had happened to the queen (and the rumors were rife in the palace that Alenor's miscarriage had not been an accident), then it was probably Dirk, but he had said nothing to her. Marqel was inclined to think he believed the official line, which was that the Queen of Dhevyn had suffered a tragic miscarriage, but that she was recovering well and would soon produce another heir.

The truth was somewhat less rosy. Alenor had lost a massive amount of blood, and it was going to take a long time for her to recover fully. There was also a good chance she would never have another child, a happy circumstance that Marqel had not really planned on. It seemed only fitting, really. In light of that, she positively enjoyed helping care for the little queen.

When she had arrived that morning, Dirk was with Alenor. She knew he was in the room, even before she opened the door. He was still under house arrest, and the guards assigned to watch his every move stood at either side of the doors to the queen's suite, waiting patiently for him to finish his visit.

When Marqel entered the bedroom, Dirk was sitting on the bed talking to Alenor. Dorra had eased her rules somewhat when it came to Dirk, mostly because he was the only one who seemed to be able to get Alenor to perk up a little. Kirsh's presence was awkward (Alenor probably blamed him, or something equally silly), Antonov made her nervous, and everyone else seemed to irritate her.

The queen was sitting up in bed, propped up on a mountain of pillows, petting a tiny gray kitten that Dirk was teasing with a piece of string.

"Look, Marqel," Alenor said as she looked up. "Dirk brought me a present."

Marqel had little time for cats. They were too independent and gave too little in return for the food you wasted on them. "She's beautiful. What are you going to call her?"

"I don't know," Alenor said. "Could you think of a name?"

"I'm not very good at that sort of thing, your majesty. Why doesn't the Lord of the Shadows think up a name?"

"Most of the names I thought up, Alenor doesn't like," Dirk said. "I suggested Stoppit."

"That's only because you want to make a fool out of me, yelling 'Stop it, Stoppit!' whenever it does something naughty," Alenor laughed. She was quite animated this morning. This was the best Marqel had seen her since she had lost the baby.

"What do you think, Dorra?" Alenor asked, as the lady-in-waiting came into the room carrying a vase of fresh roses.

"I think you shouldn't have that cat on the bed, your majesty," Dorra grumbled. "I also think it's far too early for you to be entertaining visitors."

Dirk rose from the bed and smiled winningly at Dorra. "I was just leaving, my lady. And so was Marqel."

"I was?" she asked in surprise.

"I have need of your assistance, my lady, and as Alenor will be busy trying to think up a name for her new friend for some time, I'm sure you can be spared."

Marqel was immediately suspicious. She could think of no reason at all why Dirk would need her help, and a million reasons why he wouldn't. But on the off chance whatever he wanted would keep her here in the palace, she nodded her agreement.

"I'll see you later, Alenor." He walked to the door and beckoned Marqel to follow, smiling at Dorra on the way out.

His ever-present guard fell in behind them as they left the queen's suite and headed down the hall to Dirk's room, where the taciturn soldiers took up station either side of his door as Dirk opened it for Marqel.

She knew she had made a big mistake when she heard Dirk locking the door behind him as soon as they were inside.

"What are you doing?"

"Sit down," he ordered, his pleasant demeanor of a few moments ago a distant memory.

"You lay one finger on me, Dirk Provin, and I'll scream like a banshee."

He looked at her for a moment and then laughed. "You are deluded beyond belief if you think that's why I brought you here."

"Then why *did* you bring me here?"

Dirk walked across to the window and looked down over the lawns for a moment before he turned to face her. "I told you to sit down."

"I don't have to do what you tell me."

"You'd better get into the habit, Marqel, if we're to do business together."

His words startled her into compliance. She crossed the room and took a seat on the couch, sitting on the edge.

"I have a proposition for you."

"What sort of proposition?" she asked dubiously.

"Well, for a start, you're going to end your affair with Kirsh."

She smiled. "Because you decree it? I don't think so."

"I think you will," he assured her. "And what's more, you will never go near Alenor or Kirsh again."

"And how do you intend to make me?"

"Because if you don't, I will go to Antonov and tell him you were the one who aborted his grandchild."

Marqel froze for a fraction of a second, before attempting to laugh off the allegation. "That's ridiculous! Prince Antonov would never believe it!"

Dirk had not missed her hesitation. "I can *make* him believe it, Marqel. You can bet your life on it. In fact, you *will* be betting your life on it."

He could, too, she knew. But she was also certain that Kirshov would never believe it of her, and that gave her a measure of protection Dirk Provin could do nothing to undermine. "And *that's* your proposition? Give up Kirsh and leave your little queen alone or you'll tell on me? If that's all you brought me here for, you can shove your empty threats, Dirk Provin," she announced rising to her feet. "I don't need you."

She turned on her heel and walked to the door.

"Why settle for half, when you can have it all, Marqel?"

Marqel stopped and looked back at him curiously. "What do you mean?"

Dirk leaned against the windowsill and crossed his arms. His smile was sly and far too smug. "Why settle for the boy when you can have the man?"

His questions made no sense. "What are you talking about?"

"Power, Marqel. If you do exactly as I say, I'll give you all the power you want. More than you ever dreamed of."

Now he had really piqued her interest. "How?"

"I'll make you High Priestess," he said.

Marqel stared at him in shock. "But you hate me!"

"That's precisely why I've chosen *you*, Marqel," he agreed. "I despise you and everyone from Avacas to Elcast knows it. There would never be the slightest suspicion that we're in league with each other."

That made sense, but there was bound to be more to it. "That's not a good enough reason to offer me something as powerful as the High Priestess's job."

"My other reason is far more practical," he admitted. "I *have* something on you, Marqel. Given a choice in the matter, I probably wouldn't deal with a murderous, psychopathic little whore such as yourself, but honorable people rarely do things you can blackmail them with, so I find myself forced to work with whatever comes to hand."

His reasoning made perfect sense to a girl raised amid criminals and whores. And she was certainly not going to dismiss such an offer out of hand, even if that offer came from such a dubious source as Dirk Provin.

"But how can you make me High Priestess?"

"Quite easily. The Goddess will start talking to you, not Belagren."

"You'll tell *me* what you were going to tell the High Priestess?" she gasped, realizing immediately the value of what Dirk was offering her.

"How long do you think Belagren will be able to hold on to the position of High Priestess if she's fallen out of favor with the Goddess?"

It was almost too good to be true. It probably *was* too good to be true.

"You'll tell me when this eclipse thing is coming?" Marqel actually had no idea what an eclipse was. She just knew that one was coming, and that Dirk Provin was the only one who knew when.

He shook his head. "The eclipse is months away. I need you to do this sooner. I'll give you something else to tell Antonov."

"Like what? How can I prove the Goddess speaks to me if I don't know about the eclipse?"

"All in good time, Marqel. Do we have a deal?"

"How do I know I can trust you?"

"You don't. All you can count on is that for reasons I have no intention of explaining, I want Belagren brought down, and I'm offering you the chance to take her place."

"What happens if I say no?" she asked. "I could leave here now, go straight to Belagren or Kirsh, and tell them what you've offered me."

"Do it," he shrugged, unconcerned. "Because when I leave here I'm going to meet with the Lion of Senet. If either Kirsh or Belagren comes bursting into his study full of righteous indignation, I promise you, before they get their first sentence out, Antonov Latanya will know who was responsible for the death of his unborn grandchild."

She thought about it for a moment and then nodded. "What do I tell Kirsh?"

"Nothing. He'll get over it."

"He loves me."

"More fool him."

She sat back down on the couch and considered the offer thoughtfully. "I would have to become Antonov's mistress?"

"More than likely. He has a thing for sleeping with the Voice of the Goddess. He thinks it's one of the perks of being the Shadow Slayer. And even if he's reluctant, I'm sure, with your skills, you can make him see things your way."

"But he's old."

"Then maybe he'll let you call him Daddy."

Marqel glared at him. She had forgotten he was there on Elcast that day in the Hall when she had been tried by Antonov and questioned about where she had acquired her ill-gotten gains. Dirk would never let her forget her humble beginnings. But despite that, Marqel could see possibilities in the offer. Possibilities that she was certain that even Dirk had not thought of.

Possibilities that she did not intend to share with him, either.

"What about Belagren? She's going to be furious. Suppose she tries to have me killed?"

"I'll take care of the High Priestess."

"Will you kill her?"

"No."

"Why not?"

"Because I choose not to."

She nodded slowly, thinking that if Dirk was too spineless to do something about the High Priestess, she could take care of that minor detail herself.

"And I suppose I get to be High Priestess on the condition that I do exactly as you say?"

"That goes without saying."

"So I get to be only as powerful as you allow," she complained. "Where's the fun in that?"

"You're going to be High Priestess of the Shadowdancers and mistress of the most powerful man in the world, Marqel. What more do you want?"

"What's in it for you?"

"I will be the Lord of the Shadows, your right hand. You can have all the fun you want—within reason—while I'll take care of all the boring little administrative details involved in running the show, which you have neither the interest nor the wit to deal with. That way we both get what we want."

"And what about Paige Halyn? Doesn't the Lord of the Suns have a say in who should be High Priestess?"

"If the Lord of the Suns had any power over Belagren, don't you think he'd have used it by now? He won't be a problem."

She nodded, thinking that it must be true.

"So we have a deal?"

"We have a deal," she agreed. "What do I tell Antonov the Goddess has told me?"

"You're going to tell him how to get through the delta into Mil."

Marqel was truly surprised, although what he offered frightened her a little. There seemed to be no limit to what Dirk Provin was willing to do, no end to those he was prepared to betray, to get what he wanted.

It would do well to remember that, she thought.

"Just one other thing we need to be clear on, before we pro-

ceed," he added, walking from the window to take the arm-
chair opposite her.

"What's that?"

He smiled knowingly and it chilled her to the core.

"I don't drink peppermint tea," he said.

Chapter 78

The day after Tia met with Prince Misha, Gilda came to
visit her with the news that the *Orlando* was coming for
her. Dal Falstov would have a longboat off the same secluded
beach where she had been dropped off with Dirk, at second
sunrise in two days. Giddy with relief, Tia spent the rest of the
day pacing her small cottage until she thought the walls would
close in on her, and then she went for a walk in the gardens.

She avoided the grotto where she had met Misha, sticking
to the more secluded paths closer to the wall. Now that she
knew she was going home, all her earlier doubts and fears began to plague her. *How do I tell them?* she asked herself over and
over. *What do I tell them?* Tia glanced up at the second sun as she
walked, wondering why it had not appeared to move. Time was
dragging, and it seemed to go slower and slower now that rescue was at hand.

When she arrived back at her cottage just on first sunrise
she found it surrounded by the Lion of Senet's personal guard.

Her first impulse was to flee, but they had already seen her,
and there was a small chance she could bluff her way through
this. If Misha had betrayed her and informed his guard who she
really was, then there was no hope for her. She would never
make it out of the Hospice grounds. But if he had not, there
might still be a chance she could convince them she really was
Lady Natasha Orlando.

There was nothing hostile in their demeanor as she moved
toward the cottage warily. The officer in charge actually saluted

her politely as she approached, and the guard standing near the door held it open for her. Filled with trepidation, she stepped into the small living room of the cottage, to find Misha Latanya sitting by the fire, which had been lit in her absence.

He looked up as she entered and smiled. His eyes were bright, and he was much more animated than he had been the last time she saw him.

"Lady Natasha! How nice to see you again. I was certain it was you I spied yesterday taking a turn in the gardens. How long has it been since I saw you last in Avacas? It must be two years at least, surely?"

Tia nodded cautiously, realizing that Misha spoke for the benefit of the Shadowdancer who accompanied him. "It must be that long, I suppose, your highness."

Misha looked over his shoulder at the Shadowdancer and smiled triumphantly. "There, Sonja, didn't I tell you Lady Natasha and I were old friends? You may leave us now. I'll call you if I need you. My guard will see me back to my quarters when I'm done."

The red-robed woman looked uncertain, but she was not about to deny the crown prince when he seemed so certain. She bowed and left the cottage, closing the door behind her.

Once they were alone, Misha smiled at Tia rather smugly.

"How did you find me?"

"I have every person in this place at my beck and call, Tia. It wasn't hard."

"You look a lot better today."

"I feel better. I took your advice."

"What advice?" She could recall telling him off, but not giving him any advice.

"I've taken poppy-dust. I demanded it, in fact, which caused something of a stir."

"You took it deliberately?"

"I did. And lo and behold, my symptoms disappeared! I've stopped shaking. I feel more alert than I have for weeks. I can eat without throwing it back up again. I haven't had a fit all day. You were right. I'm an addict."

"You hardly needed me to point that out, your highness," she said, taking the seat opposite him.

"Actually, Tia, I did."

"You would have admitted it to yourself eventually."

"That's not what I mean. I swear, Tia, until today, I have never knowingly taken a grain of poppy-dust in my life."

She didn't say anything. Neris had days like this, too, when he decided none of it was his fault. Addicts were like that.

Misha sensed her skepticism. "I know you probably think I'm just trying to fool myself..."

"I believe that *you* believe it," she agreed, which was as far as she was willing to pander to his self-delusion.

Misha leaned forward, his expression so earnest, so genuine, that she almost felt sorry for him. "I speak the truth, Tia. If I'm an addict, it's not because of anything I did. It's because somebody deliberately set out to make me one."

She stared at him, staggered by what he was suggesting. Then she remembered that this young man had been in the care of Ella Geon for most of his life, and suddenly she did not doubt him.

"I believe you," she said.

He looked very relieved. "I was afraid you wouldn't. I was afraid you'd think I was merely suffering from some drug-induced delusion."

"When do you think it started?"

"A long time ago. I can't seem to remember a time when Ella wasn't making me take her 'tonic.' There's nothing else I've ever taken regularly enough for it to have the same effect."

"And when you took this tonic you always felt better?"

"Much better. Every time."

"Why?" she asked curiously. She was not referring to why the tonic worked, and Misha seemed to understand that.

"I've been asking myself the same question, over and over," he admitted.

Tia began to feel genuinely sorry for him. It must be something of a shock to realize that you'd been systematically poisoned for over half your life by the people you trusted most.

"Do you think your father?..."

Misha shrugged. "I don't think so, but I can't be certain. Kirsh was always his favorite. But he always professed an extreme abhorrence for poppy-dust addicts. It's a bit hard to imagine him condoning my addiction."

"Maybe that just made him turn a blind eye," Tia said thoughtfully. "Belagren had to have been in on it, if Ella was involved."

"But why would the High Priestess wish me ill? What reason could she have for wanting to harm me? I've never done anything to her."

"What happens if you die?"

"You mean the succession? It goes to Kirsh, of course."

"And who is your brother now married to?"

"Alenor..." He slumped in the chair a little. "The Queen of Dhevyn."

"Seems pretty cut and dried to me, your highness."

"I can't believe it."

"Miss your next dose of poppy-dust," she suggested. "That should convince you."

He sighed and leaned back in his chair. "I thought I was going mad. Part of the reason I came here was so that you would sit there and laugh at me. I was hoping you'd tell me I was insane to imagine such a plot could exist."

"You're speaking to the daughter of a man who was destroyed just as deliberately as you've been, Misha," she pointed out. "Not only do I know such plots can exist, I'm living proof of one. You don't need to convince me that Ella Geon turned you into a poppy-dust addict. Nobody would raise an eyebrow when you died at a tragically young age and your younger, more pliable brother—who also happens to be the Regent of Dhevyn—is forced to step up and take your place."

He was silent as the implications of his plight settled on him like a weight being slowly lowered onto his shoulders. "What should I do?" he asked.

"Why are you asking me? You hardly even know me."

"Which, oddly enough, makes you one of the few people I can trust. How do I know how many people are involved in this? How high does it go? Have I been sent here to Tolace to die? Is every Shadowdancer I meet part of the plot? Are my guard guarding me, or waiting on orders to end my life? Once you begin wondering about it, the suspicion never seems to end."

"If I was in your place, I'd run like hell," she told him.

He smiled sadly. "It's a nice thought, but where would I run to, Tia? Where is there anyplace on this world that is beyond the influence of my father and the High Priestess?"

Tia hesitated for a moment before she answered him

"There's always Mil," she said.

Chapter 79

The decision to leave Senet was surprisingly easy for Misha, given that the alternative would more than likely mean his death. After he left Tia's cottage, he could think of little else, trying to decide if his sudden wish to flee was out of a genuine need to save his own life, simply a desire to relieve his boredom, or merely the drug-induced delusions of a pathetic addict.

Accepting that he was addicted to poppy-dust had also been something of a shock, but Misha was far too familiar with the feeling of relief and well-being that flooded his mind and body after he had taken Ella's tonic to question the assertion once he had consciously taken poppy-dust. There was simply no difference. His trembling stopped, his mind cleared, his fear of having another convulsion began to abate. The reasons for his addiction were another matter entirely, but he chose not to dwell on them for the time being.

There would be time enough later to wonder why this had been done to him. Time enough later to do something about it.

Getting out of the Hospice and down to the beach to meet Tia's pirate friends should have been a fairly straightforward exercise.

Smuggling out the Crown Prince of Senet rather complicated matters.

Misha was guarded closely and attended almost constantly by the Shadowdancers charged with his care. Getting free of them for long enough to get out of the Hospice grounds was not going to be easy. Tia decided not to tell the people who were aiding her (she refused to mention their names) the identity of her unexpected traveling companion, just that she had met an old friend in the Hospice who needed to get out of Senet nearly as much as Tia did.

The plan they devised in the end was quite simple. They needed a diversion, which Tia promised to arrange, that would distract the guards long enough for Misha to slip out of his room. He slept alone, which was fortunate, and because he was safe in the grounds of the Hospice, his escort made themselves comfortable in the front room of the cottage each night, and did not worry too much about patrolling the grounds outside.

"You'd better take another dose of poppy-dust before we leave," Tia had advised as they made their plans to escape in the privacy of her small cottage. "The last thing I need is you collapsing on me before we get out of the grounds of the Hospice."

Misha lay on his bed, waiting for her to come for him, going over the plan in his head for the thousandth time, his mind unnaturally alert from the dust. It was about two hours before the second sunrise, and the sleeping Hospice lay quiet in the light of the red sun. He suffered more than a few doubts about the wisdom of placing his fate in the hands of Tia Veran as he waited. He did not really know her. Didn't know if she genuinely wanted to help him, or if she would simply take this opportunity he was so recklessly handing her, and bend it to her own purposes.

Does it matter? he wondered. *If I stay, I will surely die, either by deliberate intent or accidental overdose.*

He didn't know if Tia wished him harm, but he was certain beyond doubt that someone in Senet did—someone with sufficient power and the ill-will to arrange for him to be systematically destroyed by poppy-dust.

It was dangerous to trust Tia, Misha knew. But it would be fatal to trust the people he had known and depended on all his life.

Finally, when he was sure she was not coming for him, he heard a rattle against his window, and then a painfully loud creak as Tia opened it.

"All clear?" she whispered, poking her head through.

"They think I'm asleep," he whispered back.

Tia climbed nimbly through the window and hurried to the door, walking so lightly that her feet made no sound on the rug. She was dressed like a boy, in leather trousers and a well-worn linen shirt, and had a bow slung over her shoulder, a quiver of arrows at her hip. Poking out of her boot was the hilt of a dagger that bore the rampant lion of Latanya engraved in its hilt. He decided not to ask how she had acquired it.

Placing her ear against the wood, Tia listened for a moment to satisfy herself that they would not be disturbed, checked that the door was locked, and then came back to the bed, looking down at him with a frown.

"Can you walk at all?" she asked softly.

"A little. And not far."

"Well, you've wasted away to nothing, so I should be able to carry you if I have to," she told him.

As it was, she had to half drag, half carry him to the window. She propped him on the sill and looked at him closely. Misha tried not to let her see the pain he was in, or the effort it cost him to hold himself upright.

"Are you sure you want to do this, your highness?"

"I'm sure."

Apparently satisfied that he would not change his mind and raise the alarm, Tia nodded and then whistled softly into the red night. A moment later a small, rotund man with a cheerful demeanor appeared beneath the window. Without a word, he helped Tia get Misha through the window, then the two of them carried him to a small cart the fat little man had waiting for them. She shoved Misha none too gently into the cart, and then jumped in after him, pulling a pile of loose sacks

over them, as her accomplice climbed into the driver's seat and
clucked his horse forward, away from the cottage.

Tia's diversion was worthy of Dirk Provin. As they wound
slowly along the graveled paths of the Hospice toward the gate,
Misha looked toward the storeroom, where, the previous day,
he had noticed a load of wicker baskets destined for use in the
Hospice laundry being delivered. Unaccountably, it burst into
flames. Shouts of alarm suddenly filled the air, as the flames
hungrily ate the wicker and threatened to spread to the nearby
buildings.

Tia pushed the sacks back a little to see what was happening.

"How did you make *that* happen?" Misha whispered, as
several Shadowdancers hurried past them toward the fire, paying no attention at all to the cart or its occupants.

"I have friends," she shrugged. "It's one of those things
you're better off not knowing about."

He glanced back at the driver for a moment and then
smiled at Tia. "The local basketmaker will be happy. The Hospice will have to purchase another load of baskets to replace
those destroyed in the fire."

Tia did not confirm or deny his suspicions, but she did
smile. "Quite a profitable exercise all round."

"We're coming to the gate," the driver hissed. "Get down."

Tia rearranged the sacks to conceal them as Misha felt the
wagon coming to a halt.

"Bit of excitement going on back there," the jolly fat man
chuckled to the gateman.

"Aye," the man agreed. "Did you find the basket you were
looking for?"

"I did, thank you, Gustav. It was good of you to let me in so
late. I found it in the kitchens ready to be used as onion storage.
Good thing I didn't wait until second sunrise to go looking for it."

"Well, I'd not like to cross Mistress Gilda either, my
friend."

The driver laughed. "It's a wise man who understands that.
I'm just happy that I can go home now and not get my head
caved in with a rolling pin. How was I supposed to know the

damn thing was a special order? It looked just like all the others to me."

"Well, you get along now," the gateman advised. "And give my regards to Mistress Gilda."

"I will," he promised, as he clucked at the horse and it began to move slowly off.

After a while, Tia threw back the suffocating sacks with a grin. The horse clip-clopped steadily along and the world around them seemed quiet. There was no sound of pursuit, just the distant cries coming from the burning Hospice.

"We made it," she announced.

Misha nodded, but found his heart racing too hard to answer her. He had never done anything so daring. Or so dangerous.

The fat little man in the driver's seat turned back to smile at her. "Aye, Tasha, we made it. Now get back under those sacks until we're clear of the town."

"I can't thank you enough for your help, Boris."

"Yes, you can," the little man chuckled. "Just wait until you get my bill."

Chapter 80

The longboat was right where Dal Falstov had promised, crewed by several familiar faces and Grigor Orneo, the *Orlando*'s first mate. He was a big man, with a broad girth and a foul mouth. Tia didn't know him all that well, but right now he was the best thing she had ever laid eyes on.

"Are you all right?" he asked as she ran down the beach toward them.

"I'm fine. But my friend needs help."

With a wave of his arm, Grigor dispatched two of the

sailors to aid Misha down to the boat. Boris turned his cart around and was headed back to town before they had the long-boat into the water. The sailors pulled hard against the under-tow to get them out to the *Orlando,* which was anchored offshore. Misha sat in the bow, his eyes bright from a combina-tion of poppy-dust and what was, Tia realized, probably the biggest adventure of his life.

What am I doing? she wondered. *First I bring Dirk Provin to Mil, now I'm bringing home the Lion of Senet's heir! Will I never learn?*

It took three of the sailors to help Misha up to the *Orlando,* and he was looking quite queasy by the time they finally got him aboard. Tia clambered nimbly up the rope ladder behind them, and the other sailors began to winch the longboat up.

"Get her under way, Grigor," Dal Falstov ordered as soon the longboat was secure. He turned to Tia and added, "I don't like hanging around the coast off Senet without a good excuse."

Dal was a small, dapper man, with dark hair and warm brown eyes, who enjoyed playing the part of the gentleman trader, even though the vast majority of his goods were ac-quired though theft. In many respects, he was the antithesis of Porl Isingrin, who was scarred and abrupt, and actually looked like a pirate. They were both good men, though, and she trusted Dal Falstov with the same confidence that she had in the cap-tain of the *Makuan*.

"We need to head back to Mil," Tia told him.

He shook his head. "Sorry, lass, but you're lucky I even risked this detour to come get you. We're headed for Bryton. We'll get you home eventually, but I'm afraid we'll have to take the long way round."

"No, it's you who doesn't understand, Captain," she in-sisted. "We must head straight for the Baenlands."

"Why?"

"Dirk Provin has betrayed us."

"Aye, I heard a rumor to that effect in Paislee. He seemed like such a nice lad, too."

Tia rolled her eyes, but decided not to argue with the cap-tain. She pointed to Misha, who was sitting on the deck, where

the sailors had dropped him. He was still too weak to stand un-
aided on solid ground. He had no chance of keeping his feet on
the heaving deck of a ship. "He's the other reason."

"Who is he?"

"Misha Latanya."

Dal studied the prince for a moment and then treated Tia
to a baleful glare. "You've kidnapped the Crown Prince of
Senet."

It was not so much a question as a bald statement of fact.
Tia had not actually thought of it like that, though. Kidnapping
sounded so... bad.

"I suppose..."

Dal stared at her for a moment longer and cursed. "Let's turn
this bitch around, lads!" he bellowed. "We're heading back to Mil."

When Mil finally came into view several days later, Tia was relieved to discover that the *Makuan* was anchored in the muddy
waters of the delta, although she could see no sign of the *Wanderer*.

Dal Falstov navigated the tricky channels of the delta with
skill. Tia knew the route through the delta—barely—but she
had never tried it on her own. *Did Dirk know it, too?* she wondered, as they tacked yet again, while Dal Falstov bellowed instructions to his men. *And if he does know the route, has he already
told the Lion of Senet about it? Are they already preparing their in-
vasion fleet? How much time do we have?*

Dal finally gave the order to heave to, once they reached the
calmer waters of the bay. Tia was already helping Misha into
the longboat, before the anchor had been dropped.

The prince's condition had changed little during the voyage. Dal had a supply of poppy-dust aboard, destined for Bryton, so they were able to keep him fairly stable; Tia just wasn't
sure what she was supposed to do with him now. Misha was appalled by his addiction, and kept wanting to refuse the poppy-
dust, but Tia could not afford for him to go into withdrawal
now. Even assuming he could eventually wean himself off the
drug, it would be a long, painful process that she was not quali-
fied to supervise.

"So, that's Mil," Misha remarked as the sailors dug their oars into the water and they left the *Orlando* behind. His eyes were bright with the false well-being of the poppy-dust. He had just taken another dose, so, for the next couple of hours at least, he would be quite alert and rational.

"Not what you were expecting?" Dal Falstov asked from the stern. The captain had left the *Orlando* in Grigor's care. There were other, more pressing matters to be seen to at the moment, than the relatively simple task of securing his ship.

"After all the stories I've heard about this place, I was expecting some huge black fortress with massive defenses, and reinforced towers and smoking gargoyles."

Tia smiled. "Legends and rumors can be rather useful at times."

Misha scanned the small village with interest. "You couldn't defend this place against attack for more than a few minutes."

"We know," Tia agreed. "That's why it's so useful that everybody thinks we have a huge black fortress with massive defenses, and reinforced towers and smoking gargoyles."

They beached the boat a few minutes later. There were several people waiting for them, wondering what had made the *Orlando* return so early. Dal sent one of the boys who came to meet them for Petra, the herb woman, to take care of Misha. When she arrived sometime later, she was leaning on the arm of an old man that Tia recognized as the man they had helped escape Elcast the night Morna Provin died.

"Master Helgin!" Misha declared in surprise when he saw the old physician. "What are you doing here?"

"Exactly the question I was about to ask you, your highness."

"Take care of him," Dal ordered the physician. "We'll work out what to do with him later."

Master Helgin nodded and led the way back down the beach toward the village, as Misha was carried between two sailors.

As Tia watched the prince being taken away, Porl Isingrin slipped down the black dunes toward them.

"Tia!"

"Hello, Captain," she said as she turned to face him.

"Goddess! When we heard the news, we feared the worst. How did you get away?"

"It's a long story."

"Well, you can tell us up at the house. Lexie's waiting for you."

"Is Reithan here?"

"He will be soon. The lookout just spotted the *Wanderer* entering the delta."

"Then we'd best get ready," she warned. "We've got big trouble coming."

Chapter 81

Dirk was wary of any summons to attend the Lion of Senet, particularly when it was delivered without warning, and required his presence on the terrace outside Antonov's study. He had killed Johan Thorn on that terrace, and had no desire to revisit it in this lifetime.

Antonov was alone when Dirk arrived, sitting on the low marble balustrade, staring up at the night sky that was streaked with red, as if some giant animal had clawed a savage opening through the clouds.

"The beauty of the Goddess is everywhere we look," Antonov remarked when he heard Dirk behind him. Then he turned to look at him. "Do you remember this place?"

"Very well."

When Dirk offered no further comment, Antonov glanced at the paving, in the general direction of where Johan's body had fallen. "They've never been able to completely remove the stain from the tiles."

"I'm sorry. Perhaps the next time I kill someone for you, I can do it without making quite so much mess."

"Don't take that tone with me, boy."

"You sent for me, your highness?" Dirk replied. He wasn't

going to stand here and reminisce with Antonov. Not when it involved the killing of his own father.

Antonov remained seated, but turned on the balustrade until he was facing Dirk. "I wanted to speak to you about Alenor."

Dirk was instantly on his guard. "Wouldn't you be better served talking to Kirsh? He's married to her."

"But you're her friend, Dirk. You two have always been close. And I know you visit her frequently. How does she seem to you?"

"I'm not sure if I understand what you mean, sire."

"Does she seem happy to you?"

"She just lost her baby, and almost lost her life, your highness. It's a bit much to expect her to be jumping for joy just yet."

"I understand that, Dirk. It's just she seems so...morose. She will barely speak to Kirshov, and my presence helps little. And the rumor that her miscarriage wasn't an accident refuses to go away."

Antonov sounded genuinely concerned. Was he afraid for Alenor, or merely impatient that she was not getting over her loss quickly enough? He was unashamedly impatient for an heir.

"Who would want to harm Alenor or her child?" Dirk asked, without giving any hint that he knew the answer.

"If I didn't know better, I might think you were responsible," Antonov replied, watching his reaction to the accusation carefully.

"*Me?*"

"You probably know enough herb lore to produce a concoction that would rid her of a child, and if Alenor dies without an heir, like it or not, you are the only other living Thorn besides Rainan."

"If I wanted Alenor's throne, your highness, all I need do is ask you for it."

The Lion of Senet smiled. "Which is why I'm certain you had nothing to do with it. Still, the rumors concern me. As does her obvious depression."

"Maybe she's just homesick," Dirk suggested, thinking that he might be able to do one small thing to aid Alenor. "That lady-in-waiting you have watching over her is worse than a drill sergeant. Perhaps if you allowed her own people to care for her, she might start to perk up a little."

"Lady Dorra has done an excellent job with Alenor," Antonov disagreed.

"Not if someone managed to slip Alenor an abortifacient, she hasn't," Dirk retorted.

Antonov was silent for a moment. He apparently had not thought of that. "Are you suggesting that it was Dorra?"

"Not at all. I'm simply suggesting that Dorra works for you, your highness, not for Alenor. Her first and only consideration is what you require of her. Alenor is merely a job to her. Get rid of the woman. Let Alenor send for some of her own friends from Kalarada until she's well enough to return home. Unless you think she's plotting against you, or you suspect she has a lover stashed away in the garderobe, there's no need to watch her so closely. It can't be easy for her—or Kirsh—to have someone constantly looking over their shoulders, especially during such a trying time as this."

"Perhaps you're right," Antonov conceded thoughtfully.

They were interrupted by Barin Welacin before Dirk could aid Alenor further. The Prefect of Avacas stepped out onto the terrace from the study and glanced at Dirk curiously, before bowing to Antonov.

"I'm sorry to disturb you, your highness," he said, his mild-mannered, pleasant face creased with concern. "I've just received news from Tolace that I thought you would want to hear."

"Is it Misha?" Antonov asked, with a certain degree of resignation. Dirk wondered if this was finally the news that Misha had died, which everyone seemed to be quietly expecting to be delivered at any moment.

"He's not dead, your highness," Barin hurried to assure him. "At least not that we're aware. He's missing."

"What do you mean he's missing?" Antonov snapped. "How can he be *missing*?"

"There was a fire in Tolace, your highness. Deliberately lit, it was discovered afterward. The fire was in one of the storage rooms of the Hospice, and far from your son's accommodation.

He was never in any danger from the flames. Afterward, however, there were only two people unaccounted for. One of them was Prince Misha."

"And the other?"

"A Lady Natasha Orlando," Barin told him. "From the duchy of Grissony in northern Senet."

"Grissony? I've never heard of it."

"That's because it doesn't exist, your highness."

"Then who was she?"

"Tia Veran," Dirk said, not bothering to hide his smile.

Both Antonov and Barin Welacin looked at him.

"The Orlando name is a new twist," he explained, "but she always goes by the name Natasha when she's in Senet. If Misha is missing, your highness, the first place I'd be looking, if I were you, is the Baenlands."

"Are you suggesting the Baenlanders have kidnapped my son?"

"Well, they've tried everything else they can think of to get at you."

Antonov was silent for a moment, and then he turned to Barin. "Fetch Kirshov, and the High Priestess. And Palinov, too."

"I'll leave you then, sire, to deal with this..."

"The hell you will," Antonov snorted. "You'll stay right where you are, Dirk Provin. You're the only person I have who has any reliable knowledge of these Baenlanders. It's time to prove that you really are genuine in your desire to serve me and the Goddess."

The High Priestess was the last to arrive, as she had returned to the Hall of Shadows and it took some time to get a message to her. She took a seat on the terrace beside Antonov, and listened carefully as Barin explained all that had happened, adding in the intelligence that Dirk had provided about the identity of Lady Natasha Orlando.

"Tia Veran?" Kirsh asked with concern. "How can you be certain it was her?"

Dirk thought he looked more than a little guilty. Since it was Kirsh that allowed her to escape, he was probably blaming himself for this. Or if not himself, then Dirk.

"It's the sort of thing Tia would do," Dirk informed them.

"Do you know this girl well, then?"

Dirk shrugged. "Reasonably."

"Then where would she have taken him?" Barin asked.

"The Baenlands, of course," he replied, his tone leaving no doubt about how stupid he thought the question was. "Where else would they go?"

"And you are certain you don't know the way through the delta?" Antonov asked him, watching him closely.

"I swear by the Goddess, your highness," Dirk lied smoothly, his face open and honest, his whole demeanor radiating sincerity. "I cannot tell you the way through the Spakan River delta."

"Then we'll have to find somebody who does," Kirsh said, giving Dirk an accusing look.

"Anton, have you considered waiting until you receive a ransom demand?" Belagren suggested. "Perhaps the best way to deal with this is to wait until they contact us, and we find out what they want."

"I will not deal with those pirates," Antonov declared. "I don't care if all they want is two sacks of flour and a milk goat. I will not trade with them."

"Even if it means saving Misha's life?" Dirk asked curiously.

"Even if it means that," the Lion of Senet agreed harshly.

"The High Priestess's suggestion does have merit, your highness," Palinov ventured. "I mean, we all know how sick the prince is. There is no guarantee he will survive long in the care of the Baenlanders. Perhaps we should simply take a 'wait-and-see' approach?"

"You're suggesting I simply leave my son to die, Palinov?"

"It's a harsh way to put it, your highness, but yes, that's exactly what I'm suggesting."

Antonov did not immediately dismiss the suggestion out of hand. Kirsh, however, exploded with fury at the idea.

"Absolutely not!" he cried. "How dare you sit there and suggest that we leave my brother to die in the hands of those barbarians!"

"Settle down, Kirsh," Antonov warned. "We must consider every possibility here, even the unpalatable ones." Then he turned to Dirk. "What do you recommend we do, Dirk?"

"It's not really my business, your highness."

"I'm making it your business, Dirk. You know these people. What are they likely to do with Misha?"

"They won't kill him," he assured them. "At least, not deliberately. They may ask for a ransom, they may even insist you withdraw from Dhevyn."

"They must know that will never happen, no matter what they threaten."

"The more sensible ones will understand, but Tia's more passionate about her cause than most. She won't give Misha up for anything insubstantial."

"It doesn't matter what the ransom is," Antonov repeated. "I will not pay it."

"Then your only option is to launch a rescue mission," Dirk advised. "If you won't deal with them, then all you can do is go in and get Misha out yourselves."

"But we don't know the way through the delta," Kirsh reminded him.

"Then you should pray to the Goddess for guidance," Dirk replied. "Because I don't see any other way for you to rescue Misha from Mil."

Chapter 82

If Marqel had detested being taught to read by Dirk Provin, then being forced to memorize the complex instructions for sailing through the Spakan River delta was infinitely worse. Dirk refused to write them down, making her come to his room each evening to learn the next part, but only after he was satisfied that she remembered the previous night's instruction without error.

She knew why he was doing it. He did not trust her, and by giving her the instructions piecemeal, he was preventing her from taking any action until he decided it was time. So she struggled to remember the landmarks and the turns, all the while cursing him for his attention to detail.

After nearly two weeks, Marqel had learned all but the last few instructions to Dirk's satisfaction. She stood in the center of his room and repeated them back to him in a bored voice, then glared at him.

"Satisfied?"

"It'll do. Although I hope you're planning to put a little more enthusiasm into it when you speak with Antonov."

"How am I supposed to do this, anyway?" she asked. "Just go up to him and say, 'Excuse me, your highness, but I was chatting to the Goddess the other day and she told me how to get through the delta'?"

Dirk allowed himself a brief smile. "I think we can be a little more subtle than that. Can you cry on cue?" Then he laughed at his own foolishness. "Of course you can," he scoffed, answering his own question. "You can magically make bruises appear, too, as I recall."

"You want me to cry?"

"Being spoken to by the Goddess is a singular honor. You're going to be very moved by the experience. And humbled, although that might be asking a bit much of you."

"I can be anything you want."

Dirk looked at her disdainfully. "There's a line I'll wager you've used a lot."

"Jealous?"

"I thought we'd established how little I desire you, Marqel."

"Do you really?" she asked curiously. In Marqel's world there was nothing she could not achieve, nothing that was out of her reach, if only she was prepared to use her body to get it. It seemed unbelievable that Dirk Provin was not driven—at least in part—by the fact that she had chosen Kirsh over him. She stepped closer to him and smiled. "Is that why you chose *me* to do this thing?"

He shook his head at her in disgust. "You're unbelievable."

"You ought to know," she reminded him, close enough now to reach out and take his hand in hers. He did not resist as she placed his hand on her breast and pressed it close.

"Don't you remember what it was like, Dirk?" she whispered.

He nodded wordlessly, his hand sliding up until he was caressing her throat.

"I remember," he said softly. Then his hand began to tighten around her windpipe. His metal-gray eyes bored into hers and suddenly she was afraid. "Now here's something for you to remember. If you *ever* try something like this on me again, you *will* speak to the Goddess, Marqel. In person."

He let her go with a shove. She staggered backward, gasping for air.

"You could have just said no!" she accused, rubbing her neck where he had gripped her.

"You seem to respond so much better to threats," he remarked in a conversational tone. "Let's go over it one more time."

"Why?"

"Because I said so."

Still rubbing her neck with a petulant scowl, Marqel did as he ordered.

Marqel knew she wasn't as clever as Dirk Provin, but she was not as stupid as he assumed. By the following evening, he had told her enough of his plan that she could judge its merits and flaws for herself.

Mostly, she didn't have a problem with it. The only point on which she vehemently disagreed with Dirk was the fate of the High Priestess. Dirk wanted to see her humiliated. He wanted to glory in Belagren's shame when she realized he had double-crossed her.

Marqel considered that an indulgence they could not afford. More specifically, an indulgence *she* could not afford. It was all right for Dirk Provin. He was protected by the knowledge he had about the upcoming eclipse, so Belagren would not dare harm him, but she could have Marqel's life snuffed out in a moment.

Marqel did not actually dislike Belagren enough to care much whether or not she got to witness her disgrace and humiliation. All Marqel was concerned about was that she would be out of the way. Besides, it would be much more poetic—not to mention dramatic—if, on the same night the Goddess chose Marqel as her voice, the former holder of that salubrious position was taken to the Goddess's bosom to sit at her right hand ... or wherever she damn well wanted to sit.

Making her own modification to Dirk's plan was easy.

Belagren suspected nothing. Marqel had stayed in the palace at Dirk's request because he had found countless menial and useless tasks for her to undertake as his assistant. If the High Priestess thought it odd, she made no comment about it. If anything, the contempt with which Dirk always treated Marqel probably made Belagren think he was doing it out of spite, which she would understand and, in her current mood, probably tolerate indefinitely.

Kirsh had been to her several times, but his visits had been quick, furtive and ultimately unsatisfying. Marqel found herself being critical of things that had always amused her in the past. Habits she thought were endearing suddenly irritated her.

Dirk was right. Why settle for the boy when you could have the man?

With growing excitement, Marqel looked forward to the day she would reveal her new gift to Antonov. She was sick of sneaking around. She wanted to be openly acknowledged as somebody important, somebody of substance. That was never going to happen while Kirsh was married to Alenor, she realized now. His father, on the other hand, was powerful enough that he could (and frequently did) flaunt any mistress he chose, and nobody dared say a word.

Marqel was still smiling over the shining future ahead of her as she walked up the hall toward Dirk's room. When she reached it, and noticed the absence of his ever-present guard, she cursed. It was not like him to miss their evening sessions, and they only had a few weeks left before Dirk judged the time was right to put their plan into action. She always thought of it as "their" plan, particularly since she had made a few modifications to suit herself.

"Where is Lord Provin?" she asked a servant who was carrying a tray down the hall in the direction of Alenor's room.

"He's with Prince Antonov, I think, my lady. The High Priestess just got back from the Hall of Shadows, and I know Prince Kirshov was called to meet him downstairs."

Marqel nodded and dismissed the girl with a wave of her hand, wondering what had forced such a meeting this late. Belagren split her time between the palace and the Hall of Shadows, but she had returned to the Hall only yesterday, with the intention of staying there for some time. Marqel had not expected her back so soon.

That she was still excluded from such important meetings simply drove home the need to do something to change her status. *Before too long,* she promised herself, *there won't be an important decision made in Senet that I'm not a party to.*

Marqel headed back to her room, and then, on impulse, changed direction and headed downstairs to the kitchens. She would make a pot of peppermint tea, a habit she had gone to great pains to establish, so that nobody would work out that Marqel's sudden craving for peppermint always coincided with somebody else dying.

Besides, nothing traveled faster than a rumor, and whatever was going on in Prince Antonov's study might well be the subject of discussion in the kitchens.

Several pots of tea later, Marqel returned to her room, still none the wiser about what was going on in Antonov's study. It had not been a wasted evening, though. She had been carefully cultivating the friendship of several assistant cooks, whose cooperation she would need the next time she wanted to prepare a pot of tea that was not quite as innocuous as the one she had shared with them this evening.

Marqel was brushing out her long blond hair when a

knock sounded at her door. She wondered if Kirsh had decided to risk coming to her, and debated feigning sleep. She didn't want to see Kirsh. All he did was remind her of what she would soon have, which made his presence more irksome than welcome. But if it was Kirsh, she might find out what had happened to necessitate the return of the High Priestess.

Putting down the brush, Marqel walked to the door, surprised to find not Kirshov, but one of Dirk's guards standing outside.

"The Lord of the Shadows wishes to see you, my lady," he told her politely.

"Now?"

"Yes, my lady."

Marqel muttered a curse and turned for her shawl before following the guard back upstairs to the fourth floor. She was getting a little fed up with Dirk and his arrogant assumption that he could order her around like a bonded slave. She intended to tell him so, too.

She never got a chance.

"There's been a change of plan," Dirk informed her as soon as the guard closed the door behind her. "You're going to have your visit from the Goddess tomorrow."

"Tomorrow!" she gasped. "Why?"

"The Baenlanders have kidnapped Misha from Tolace. If ever Antonov is going to believe that the Goddess is talking to you, and not Belagren, it is now, when you give him the information he needs to rescue his son."

Chapter 83

Lexie, Porl Isingrin, Dal Falstov and Tia Veran gathered on the veranda of Johan's house a little while after the second sun had set. Lexie had greeted her with a warm hug. Tia met her gaze evenly, and shrugged off her foster-mother's embrace.

Lexie knew her too well to be fooled, and there were things about this tale she was about to relate that she did not want anyone to know.

"Should we wait for Reithan?" Tia asked.

Porl shook his head. "I've got someone waiting for him down on the beach. He'll be here soon. What happened?"

Tia took a deep breath and told them.

She told them about the long trek north, of Dirk's comments in Tolace about surrendering, about his disappearance in Bollow. She told them of the Shadowdancers' departure from Omaxin, and how Dirk had used Neris's blincakes recipe to open the gate, which brought a smile to everyone's face.

She told them about the High Priestess's arrival, and without so much as a tremble in her voice, how she had tried to kill Dirk, but had missed hitting anything vital. And then she told them of the trip back to Avacas, of Kirshov Latanya's strange offer to let her escape, and of how she met up with Misha in Tolace.

What she did not tell them was anything about eating mushrooms or that, for a short, blissfully happy and ultimately painful time, she had fancied herself in love with Dirk Provin.

"How much damage can he actually do?" Porl asked when she had finished her tale.

"A fair bit," Dal suggested. "He went out with Reithan in the *Wanderer* a number of times. You had him on the *Makuan,* and he sailed on the *Orlando* twice. Even if he doesn't know his way through the delta, he knows names, faces and, even worse, some of our contacts in the Brotherhood. The Goddess knows what *they'll* do if they think we've crossed them."

"But we haven't crossed them," Tia objected. "Dirk has."

"The Brotherhood won't see the distinction," Porl warned.

"Did he give *any* indication of his intentions, Tia?" Lexie asked. She had been shattered to hear about Dirk, and was still having trouble coming to terms with the fact that Johan's son had betrayed them.

Tia shook her head. "Not really. But then again, he did... sort of. He kept telling me that he'd written to the High Priestess, but I thought he was joking."

"He seemed so...sincere."

"Aye," Porl agreed. "We should have listened to Tia. She never trusted him."

"Well, it's too late now to punish ourselves over what might have been," Dal reminded them. "What we need to do is decide how we're going to deal with it."

"Where's the little bastard now?" Porl snarled.

"He's in Avacas," Reithan announced, walking onto the veranda. "He's been awarded the title of Lord of the Shadows and has been appointed the right hand of the High Priestess."

"You were in *Avacas*?" Lexie gasped.

Reithan nodded as he took the seat beside her. "I was in Kalarada when I heard that the High Priestess was heading for Omaxin, so I headed for Avacas. I was about to leave when I heard that Dirk had been captured. I stayed in Avacas looking for you, actually," he told Tia. "The same day Dirk returned to the city, Alexin arrived with Alenor. I managed to arrange a meeting with him. It doesn't look good."

"We were just trying to decide how much he can tell Antonov."

"A lot."

"How can we be sure about that?" Lexie asked, still hoping for the best.

"Because he sent me a message, Mother, *telling* me he was going to tell Antonov anything he wanted to know."

They all stared at him.

"He's making no secret about what he has planned. He told Alexin to tell us we had about a month before he would reveal the route through the delta, and if we were planning to evacuate Mil, then we should do it before then."

"Why, that arrogant little—" Porl began, too angry to finish the sentence.

"But does he even *know* the route through the delta?" Tia asked hopefully. "I mean, it's pretty tricky. It takes years to learn it."

"He knows," Reithan assured them. "He's as smart as Neris, and he grew up on an island surrounded by boats. Dirk's a pretty competent sailor, actually. He probably had the route memorized the first time we brought him through."

"I can't believe he fooled us all so completely," Dal Falstov said with a shake of his head. "Except for young Tia, here, we all thought he could be trusted."

"I don't think he deliberately came here with the intention of betraying us," Lexie speculated.

"Lexie!" Tia cried in disbelief. "What *more* does he have to do to convince you he's a traitor?"

"I'm not denying that he's betrayed us, Tia. I'm simply saying that he didn't have to warn us of his intentions. Nor did he have to wait."

"Maybe he's simply bragging," Porl suggested. "Gloating over the fact that he could bring us down. Maybe the sadistic little prick thinks it'll be more fun if we have to sweat on it for a while."

"Does it matter?" Tia snapped. "Whatever his intentions, he's turned on us."

"According to Alexin," Reithan told them, "if he's suffering any torment over what he's done, he's certainly not letting it show."

"How long do we have?" Dal asked.

"I met with Alexin about two weeks ago and headed straight back here as soon I spoke to him. If we had a month then, we've only a couple of weeks now, before he tells, and another week or two for Antonov to get a fleet organized, and a couple more weeks after that for them to get here."

"So in six weeks we're done for," Tia concluded.

"Six weeks is plenty of time," Lexie assured them. "We can evacuate everyone safely long before then."

"To where, Lexie?" Tia demanded. "These people live here because they have nowhere else to go."

"Some of them will have families in Dhevyn who can shelter them. The rest will have to move inland. We can shelter in the caves for a time."

"A very short time," Dal warned. "Tia's right, my lady. Our options are very limited."

"They're limited by only one thing," Tia declared. "Dirk Provin."

"What are you suggesting?" Porl asked.

"We kill him. Before he can betray us."

Her suggestion was met with a round of silent, considered looks. Only Lexie closed her eyes, as if the option was too painful to consider.

"How?" Reithan shrugged. "He's in the palace in Avacas. He's guarded constantly. You won't get near him."

"I can get near him," she promised.

"But can you kill him, Tia?" Dal asked thoughtfully. "Have you got it in you to make the killing stroke?"

"Where Dirk Provin is concerned," she told them with quiet certainty, "absolutely."

Lexie gave her a worried look, but said nothing.

"If we leave today, we can get back to Avacas in about ten days," Reithan calculated.

"That's cutting it awfully fine," Porl warned. "If you don't get there before he talks, killing Dirk Provin, no matter how satisfying it might be, becomes an unnecessary risk."

"Then ask the Brotherhood to do it," Dal suggested. "We can contact them by bird today." He laughed humorlessly. "I'd like to see that little bastard dodge a professional assassin."

"That will cost a fortune!" Lexie gasped.

"If it saves Mil, it'll be worth every dorn," Dal replied.

"Let's do both," Tia suggested. "Send them a message asking them to take out Dirk Provin if he's still alive two weeks from now. In the meantime, Reithan and I can go back to Avacas and try to get to him ourselves. If we fail, then paying the Brotherhood to do it will be more than worth it."

"Aren't you all forgetting that we have a bargaining chip, here?" Lexie asked.

"You mean Prince Misha?"

"Surely there's room here for negotiating a settlement?"

"What's Misha Latanya got to do with this?" Reithan asked, a little confused.

"Tia kidnapped him," Dal told him, and then he turned back to the others. "The man's been systematically poisoned over a long time. That's not the sort of thing you do to a prince you have great future plans for."

Reithan stared at Tia in shock. "You *kidnapped* Misha Latanya?" he hissed as Dal was speaking.

"Sort of..."

"And even if he was the Lion of Senet's favorite son," Dal continued, "Antonov will still not deal with us. He'd rather see his son die, I suspect, than negotiate with his enemies."

"And suppose we stop Antonov this time?" Porl added. "It doesn't solve the problem of Dirk Provin knowing the way through the delta, and being at liberty to divulge the information any time the mood takes him."

"We should contact the Brotherhood," Lexie decided sadly. "It will be expensive, but I'd rather pay them than risk any more lives in Avacas, when they could be more use here, helping to evacuate the settlement."

Tia stared at her, quite disappointed that she was to be robbed of her chance at vengeance. "I could do it, Lexie," she insisted. "I *could* kill him."

"I know you could, Tia," Lexie replied. "That's what worries me."

Chapter 84

The news about Dirk Provin betraying the Baenlanders was all over the *Orlando,* even before the ship docked in Mil. Eryk learned of it from his shipmates and promptly got into a fistfight with Owen Hantze, the carpenter's apprentice, when he tried to defend his former master. He had denied the accusation vehemently, certain Dirk would never do such a thing, but the rumors would not go away, no matter how many fights Eryk got into.

What made it even worse was that it appeared to be Tia who was the source of the rumors. Eryk could not believe that she would spread such horrible gossip about Dirk, so he decided to confront her himself and find out if it was true. If she admitted to being the guilty party, he intended to make her take back the dreadful things she was saying about him. That way, the world would be back to the way it should be, and all this frightening stuff about Dirk being a traitor would go away.

When he finally climbed out of the longboat and stepped onto the black sand of Mil, he looked up at the tall stilted house overlooking the bay, wondering if Tia was up there still. He could see a number of figures gathered on the veranda, but could not make out exactly who they were.

"Hey!" Grigor snapped at him, noticing the direction of his gaze. "Don't even think about it, lad."

Eryk looked at the mate in confusion. "What do you mean?"

"You know you're not allowed up near Johan's house anymore."

"But I don't want to see Mellie. I want to speak to Tia!" Actually, that was not quite true. Eryk would have given his right leg to see Mellie again, but he knew how foolish it would be to attempt it. Everyone in Mil was fiercely protective of Johan's daughter, as Eryk had discovered to his peril when he had tried to kiss her.

"Why didn't you speak to her while she was on board the *Orlando,*" Grigor asked, "instead of waiting until we landed and you had an excuse to go up to the house?"

"I never got a chance!" he protested. "Please, thir...I mean, sir, it's really, really important."

Grigor stared at him for a moment, as if debating how sincere he was, and then he nodded. "I'll see she gets a message that you want to see her, lad. That's the best I can do. But if I catch you within a half-mile of Johan's house, I'll skin you alive myself. Understand?"

"Yes, sir! Thank you."

Grigor stalked off toward the village, leaving Eryk staring up at the house, wondering if Tia was up there, even now, spreading her dreadful lies about Dirk.

It was much later that evening before Tia appeared at the entrance to the longhouse. The village women were still sorting through the haul off the *Makuan,* although there had been little from the *Orlando* to add to the pile. Usually, they were away for much longer, and did not head home until the ship was full of contraband, lifted mostly from the holds of the Senetian traders who plied the shipping lanes between Dhevyn and Senet near the treacherous rocks off Daven Isle.

Assuming Tia had come to see him, Eryk ran to the door. "You got my message!"

Tia had been glancing around the longhouse, looking for someone. She seemed a little surprised that Eryk had accosted her.

"What message?"

"The one Grigor gave you. The one that said I had to see you."

Not finding whoever she was looking for, Tia turned her full attention to Eryk.

"Why did you want to see me?"

"You have to thop...I mean...stop saying those things about Lord Dirk, Tia. Everyone thinks he's really bad now, and if you would only tell them what really happened..."

His voice trailed off as Tia's expression darkened. "I've not said a word about Dirk that isn't true, Eryk."

He shook his head, determined not to believe it. "It can't be..."

Tia suddenly seemed to take pity on him. "Come outside, Eryk. I think you and I need to talk."

Eryk followed Tia out onto the veranda, and then took a seat beside her on the top step of the longhouse. She had an odd look on her face, almost as if she was hurt, but he could see no sign of injury on her.

"Eryk, Dirk has gone back to Avacas," she explained slowly, to make certain he understood. "He wasn't captured, or tortured, or made to do it by anyone else. He wrote to the High Priestess and asked if he could join the Shadowdancers."

"But you were going to help him rescue Lady Morna! And when you couldn't, you saved Master Helgin and then you went to Tolace. You were his friend, Tia! What did you do?"

Tia looked at him in astonishment. "What did *I* do? Not a damn thing except trust him, Eryk, when I should have known better. I know it wouldn't matter to you if another Age of Shadows came round tomorrow, because you think the sun shines out of Dirk's arse anyway, but your precious Lord Dirk betrayed everyone in Mil. Including you."

"I don't believe it."

"That's not my problem, Eryk," Tia shrugged unsympathetically. "What's done is done. Trying to pretend it isn't real won't make it go away."

"You did something," Eryk insisted. "You did something bad to him and made him run away."

Tia sighed and climbed to her feet. She looked down at him with a shake of her head. "You believe whatever you want, Eryk. I'm done talking about it. To you or anyone else."

Later that night, as he lay on his bunk in the narrow bungalow where most of the single men slept when they were in port, Eryk thought over everything he had heard since Tia had returned. It had all been bad news, but Eryk still refused to believe that Dirk was in any way responsible for any of it.

He felt so alone and friendless in Mil with Dirk gone. Any access to Mellie was denied him now, and the other sailors on the *Orlando* treated him with disdain. They never actually said anything, but they all knew what had happened at the Troitsa Festival. And then Tia started saying all that stuff about Dirk being a traitor, and things got even worse because everyone knew that Dirk was his friend, too, and they now looked at Eryk as if he was tarred with the same brush.

His cheeks wet, Eryk turned his face to the wall, in case somebody came by and saw him sniveling like a baby. He fervently wished that he knew what to do. Dirk was not here to advise him. He wasn't allowed to see Mellie, and Eleska Arrowsmith had walked past him in the longhouse, deliberately turning away from him as he tried to greet her. He had no friends among the crew of either the *Makuan* or the *Orlando*. As for Tia, she had become Dirk's enemy and, in Eryk's simple mind, that made her his enemy as well.

Desperately unhappy, Eryk tried to think what Dirk

would do. He was smart. He was brave, too. He always knew the right thing to say, the best thing to do. If he had gone back to Avacas, then he must have had a really good reason, and Tia was just too pig-headed to admit it.

Marqel was in Avacas, too, he remembered. She had been so nice to him in Nova, and had shown him things he had never dreamed of. Not that her instruction would be of any use if he could not even get to talk to Mellie...

As he lay awake thinking about it, Eryk slowly came to a decision. He had only one true friend in the world and that was Dirk Provin. Whatever Dirk was doing now, whatever he had done in the past, it was all because he was smarter than everyone else and nobody understood him. Tia was wrong. They were all wrong. And Eryk intended to prove it.

He sniffed back his tears. The *Orlando* would sail again soon, and when it did, he decided, he would take all his meager possessions with him. At some point they were bound to call in to a Senetian port.

And when they did, Eryk would walk off the ship and not look back.

After that, Eryk drifted off to sleep and dreamed of Mellie. In his dream, Mellie loved him and nobody tried to keep them apart. Then the dream changed suddenly, and they took her away from him again. He searched for her, wandering through barren streets and deserted buildings he did not recognize, calling her name, but try as he might, he could not find her. He caught a movement over his shoulder, a shadow that passed just out of sight. He called out to it, but it flittered away like a wisp of insubstantial mist. He headed back through the deserted buildings again, through the abandoned streets, which began to close in on him, and then he realized he was running through the bunkhouse in Mil and the shadow was just ahead, tantalizingly out of reach...

He woke with a start and glanced around the bunkhouse, but there was nobody there, except the other sailors from the *Orlando* and the *Makuan* who did not have homes to go to.

Their soft snores filled the air with a gentle buzz, as if the room was full of midges. He missed the silence of the goat hut; missed the solitude. It was only since he had been surrounded by all these sailors that he had truly begun to feel alone.

Eryk lay back again with a sigh, his heart pounding from his nightmare. He had been having a lot of them lately—ever since Dirk had gone away. But they would be over soon, he promised himself. Soon he would have no more nightmares, and everything would be back the way it was supposed to be, because he was going to find Dirk Provin.

Eryk was going to Avacas to join his only friend.

Chapter 85

Although Dorra seemed intent on keeping her bedridden until the next Age of Shadows, Alenor finally convinced Yuri Daranski that she would regain her strength much faster if she was allowed to get out of bed.

The physician relented unhappily, and Alenor began to take short walks along the wide halls of the Avacas palace, always with a Shadowdancer—either Olena or one of the acolytes—to keep an eye on her. Alenor resented the escort at first; or at least until the first time she ventured out of her room. She was horrified to discover that even after a short distance, she was feeling light-headed and nauseous, and had to be helped back to her bed. But slowly the walks grew longer, and she began to hold out some hope that she might eventually recover from this ordeal.

She tried not to think of the child she had lost. It did no good to wonder if it had been a boy or a girl. Nothing was gained by trying to imagine who the child might have favored. Would it have been dark-haired and brown-eyed, a true Thorn in both looks and nature? Or would it have inherited Alexin's blond hair and fair coloring?

Alenor forced herself to stop dwelling on it, concentrating instead on placing one foot in front of the other, as she walked back along the hall, her footfalls silent on the thick carpet runner. She was returning from her latest excursion, a walk that had made it all the way to the top of the stairs and back again. She could see the door to her room ahead of her.

Just a few more steps, she told herself proudly.

Then she glanced up the hall and spied Marqel, dressed in her nightdress and wrapped in a shawl, slipping into Dirk's room. She stopped for a moment, wondering why Marqel would be visiting him so late.

For that matter, why was Marqel visiting Dirk at all?

"Are you feeling ill, your majesty?" the acolyte, Ilga, asked with concern. She was a Landfall bastard and a Shadowdancer, like Marqel, but much more likable. Like all Belagren's people, she was a beautiful girl, with glossy dark hair and a waist that seemed too small to contain the organs in her body that should have been located there. She came from Talenburg, she had told Alenor on one of their walks. Her mother was a candle maker there, with a thriving business in the city, if Ilga was to be believed.

"No, I'm quite well," Alenor assured her.

"I'll fetch you some tea once you're settled," Ilga promised, opening the door.

Alenor stepped inside, rather startled to find Kirsh waiting for her. Did he know where his lover had just gone?

"Kirsh!"

"I see you're up and about."

"Barely," she agreed. "Is something wrong?"

Kirsh glanced over her shoulder at Ilga. "Leave us!"

The acolyte bowed hastily and removed herself from the queen's chambers.

"That was a bit harsh," Alenor accused.

"I've neither the time nor the inclination to be polite," he informed her. "Misha has been kidnapped from Tolace by the Baenlanders."

Alenor walked unsteadily to the settee and sat down before she responded. "When did you learn of this?"

"Barely an hour ago."

"Oh, Kirsh! That's dreadful news!"

"Palinov was suggesting that we just leave him there and let him die, thereby robbing the Baenlanders of their prize."

"Your father didn't agree to that, surely?"

"No. But we're going to Mil. That's what I came to tell you. I'm leaving for Tolace in the morning, to see if I can pick up their trail. I don't know when I'll be back."

She nodded slowly, understanding the necessity for such a thing, and not in the least surprised that Antonov was sending Kirsh to do it. Perhaps he had volunteered. Kirsh would do something like that, especially if Misha was involved.

But what had possessed the Baenlanders to do such a thing? Alexin had never even hinted at such a plan. How could they do something like this without consulting her, or at least warning her of their plans? So much for their alliance. *Why do I keep doing these stupid, stupid things?*

"Then I wish you luck," she said to Kirsh, praying no hint of her inner turmoil was visible.

"I'm taking your guard with me."

This time, Alenor was genuinely shocked, and she had no hope of hiding it. *Did he suspect something?*

"Why?"

"For one thing, I'm the Regent of Dhevyn, and it will look better if the world believes that Dhevyn supports Senet in their determination to rescue Misha and wipe out the Baenlanders. The other reason is more personal..."

Oh, Goddess! He knows!

"...although I'd never admit it to my father," he continued, oblivious to her distress. "Your guard is much better trained than his. I want men I can count on. I'd far rather have Alexin watching my back than some Senetian mercenary I don't know."

"I'm sure they'll be a great help to you," she agreed, almost choking on the words.

"Are you all right, Alenor? You've suddenly gone pale."

"I overextended myself with my walk, I fear," she explained, trembling with the strain of keeping her secrets hidden.

"Then I won't keep you any longer," he said, turning for the door.

"If you could send Dorra to me, I would be grateful," she said, certain she did not have the strength to get across the room to her bed. Not that Dorra would be any great comfort, but Alenor knew she needed help.

"I will," he promised. "I hope you've not become too attached to her."

"What do you mean?"

"Father has decided she's no longer required. I believe he's going to allow you to send for someone from Dhevyn to attend you. Perhaps the Lady Jacinta will come. That should please you."

It was almost as shocking as hearing about Misha. Or that Kirsh was planning to rescue him using her guard.

"Why would he suddenly decide to do that?"

"I think Dirk suggested it. Father told me to tell you tonight, in the hope that the prospect of seeing a few familiar faces would alleviate your distress about me going away again. I thought it prudent not to point out that you'd probably welcome it."

"I don't welcome the news that Misha might be in danger, Kirsh. Or that you might place yourself in the same danger trying to rescue him."

"I thought you'd be glad to hear that I'd been killed in battle," he said, a little bitterly. "Or even just that I'd been killed."

"I don't hate you, Kirsh..." she tried to explain.

"But you don't love me anymore, do you?"

"Do you love me?"

When Kirsh did not reply, she looked away. "Then I suppose that makes us even."

The door closing behind Kirsh was his only answer.

Chapter 86

The view from the veranda of Johan's house had always been spectacular, but Tia hardly noticed it as the second sunrise began to wash the red light from the eastern horizon. The delta was quiet, the village below still sleeping; the people garnering their strength for the trying days ahead.

"You're up early."

Tia glanced over her shoulder to find Lexie walking barefoot along the veranda, still in her nightdress.

"So are you."

"Mellie had a restless night," Lexie explained. "She's taking the news about Dirk rather badly."

"So is Eryk," Tia said. "He cornered me down in the longhouse last night. He seems to think it's all my fault. I suppose he doesn't understand what's happening."

"Neither does Mellie, really."

"I wish there was some way we could have kept it from her."

Lexie shrugged as she took the chair beside Tia. "Much as I'd like to, there's no way to protect your children from learning some of the harsher lessons in life. And it's probably not a good idea to try. Have you been to bed at all?"

Tia shook her head. "I couldn't sleep."

Lexie said nothing, waiting for Tia to elaborate. When she showed no inclination to speak further, she placed a comforting hand on Tia's shoulder. "Would you like to talk about it, dear?"

"Not particularly."

"What happened, Tia?" she asked gently.

"I told you what happened yesterday," Tia shrugged. "I told everybody."

"And what about the parts you left out?"

Tia glanced at her foster-mother suspiciously. "How do you know I left anything out?"

"It's a gift that comes with motherhood, I think," she said

with a smile. "This ability to see when someone you love is hurting. Even when they're trying very hard not to let it show."

"Is it that obvious?"

"Not to anybody else," Lexie assured her. "But I've known you since you were two years old, Tia. I've kissed away the pain from your skinned knees and your wounded pride on more than one occasion."

"I wish you could kiss this one away." She dropped her head into her hands for a moment, wishing she could shut out the world for a while. "I feel like such a fraud."

"When have you ever been a fraud?"

"Yesterday, when Dal and Porl and Reithan were all patting me on the back, applauding me for my good sense because I was the only one who didn't trust Dirk Provin."

"Perhaps you should tell me the whole story, Tia. Even the painful bits."

Tia shrugged. "There's not that much more to tell. Dirk and I went to Omaxin, he opened the gate, and then he betrayed us."

"And?" Lexie prompted.

"Do you remember what Johan used to say about happiness?" she asked instead. "He said if you ever experienced a moment of total bliss you should die, right at that moment, because the rest of your life would be downhill from there."

Lexie smiled. "I remember. He nearly frightened Mellie to death with it when she was small. For a while there, every time she laughed at something she'd get very concerned that she might die immediately afterward."

Tia smiled briefly at the memory, and then her smile faded. "That's what it was like, Lexie. Bliss. Sixteen days...count them...sixteen glorious, blissful days, before he turned on me."

Lexie absorbed that for a time before answering. She seemed neither shocked nor surprised by the revelation.

"Do you love Dirk, Tia?"

"I thought I did." She laughed bitterly. "Reithan told me once that I needed to fall in love a few times before I could really understand what it was like."

"And what's your verdict?"

"It's wonderful," she said. "While it lasts. But the part

where he betrays you by handing you over to your worst enemy to be tortured and killed takes the shine off it a bit."

"I imagine it would," Lexie agreed with a faint smile. "Would it help if I tell you that you'll learn to live with it?"

"It would help more if you told me it goes away."

"I don't know that the pain of a first love ever does," Lexie mused. "Not completely."

"Did you know that I'm afraid of the dark?" she asked suddenly, not sure why it was important.

"I didn't think you were afraid of anything, Tia."

"Neither did I, until I stepped into the Labyrinth. But you know what *really* hurts?" she said, her self-pity slowly being replaced by anger. "I never saw it coming. Goddess, Lexie, I went with him to Omaxin to make sure something like this *didn't* happen. I let everyone down."

"Now you're punishing yourself for no good reason," Lexie scolded. "If Reithan or Porl had been worried Dirk would betray them, *they* should have said something or done something to prevent it happening. You can't blame yourself for everyone else's mistakes."

"I don't need to," she said. "Mine was spectacular enough."

Lexie smiled. "I don't mean to sound unsympathetic, darling, but you're not the first woman to fall for the wrong man."

"I want to kill him, Lexie, so badly I can taste it."

"Because he betrayed you—or because he lied to you?"

"Dirk didn't lie to me. I lied to myself. He told me what he was doing, every step of the way. He never once said he loved me, either, but I was too stupid to notice. He even warned me that I shouldn't trust him."

Lexie was silent for a time, and then she looked at Tia thoughtfully. "Tia, are you absolutely certain Dirk *has* betrayed us?"

She glanced at Lexie with a scowl. "No, Lexie, I think he handed me over to the High Priestess out of genuine concern for my welfare, and then he joined the Shadowdancers and decided to tell the Lion of Senet everything he knows about us because he's such a sweetheart."

"I know you're hurting," Lexie said with reproach. "But I don't deserve to be spoken to in that manner."

"I'm sorry," she sighed. "I just can't believe you won't accept the truth about him."

"I can accept the truth, dear. I'm just not entirely convinced I've heard it yet."

"What do you mean?"

"Dirk was here for more than two years, Tia. I don't care how clever he is, nobody can fake sincerity for that long. What I'm hearing just doesn't sit right. If Dirk is really as devious as you claim, why warn you not to trust him? He'd be doing his utmost to assure you of the complete opposite. And why send that message to Reithan? For that matter, why would Kirshov Latanya suddenly decide to let you go?"

"Because at least *he* has a grain of honor left," she suggested sourly.

"You don't think it had anything to do with the fact that Kirshov Latanya and Dirk Provin were once best friends? That perhaps he released you because Dirk asked him to?"

"No, I don't," Tia declared flatly. "I think you're clutching at sunbeams, Lexie. Dirk has betrayed us and there's no nice way of putting it, no favorable light to study it by."

"Perhaps you're right," she conceded. "I've just got a feeling there's more to this than we know."

"Well, as soon as you figure out what sort of brave and noble plan required Dirk Provin to betray all his friends and take a position of power in a religion he knows to be a sham, while ensuring the Lion of Senet has enough information to wipe us all off the face of Ranadon, would you let me know what it is? I'm sure it will be fascinating."

Lexie shook her head sadly. "Don't let bitterness and anger consume you, Tia."

"You gave me that piece of advice once before, Lexie. Do you remember? You told me I should give Dirk the benefit of the doubt. Well, I did what you asked. And I didn't just give him the benefit of the doubt; I gave him everything. Threw myself at him, if you want to know the sordid truth. And guess what? I got screwed—in more ways than one."

"Your language always gets more vulgar when you've been to sea," Lexie scolded.

Tia stared at Lexie in amazement. "You won't accept it at all, will you? You don't want to admit Dirk betrayed us. You think that because he's Johan's son, he must have been born with some inherent streak of nobility that puts him above such a base and despicable act. You're like that with everything! Twenty years in the Baenlands and you don't even want to admit that this is your life now. You're always telling Mellie to mind her manners because she's a princess. You still act as if any day now, we're all going back home, and you'll be a lady and a noblewoman again, with nothing more serious to concern yourself with than next season's wardrobe. What difference does it make, Lexie, if Mellie doesn't act like she was raised at court? She's never going to see the inside of a palace, any more than you will."

"Some habits die hard, Tia," Lexie explained. "Others are so much a part of you that without them, you're not yourself any longer."

Tia sighed heavily, regretting her outburst. "I'm sorry. I don't mean to take it out on you."

"I know you didn't."

"What am I going to do, Lexie?"

"Take one day at a time," Lexie suggested. "Actually, there's not much else you can do. Once you've stopped wallowing in self-pity, things will begin to look up."

"I've always despised people who wallow in self-pity."

"And that's a large part of the problem." Lexie reached over and squeezed her hand with a smile. "You can't alter the direction of the wind, Tia...but you can adjust your sails. You'll get through this and be stronger for it."

"Maybe," she agreed reluctantly. "But right now I have a more pressing problem."

"What's that, dear?"

"How am I going to break this to Neris?"

Chapter 87

If she didn't know better, sometimes Belagren was prepared to believe that there really was a Goddess. The summons she had received from Antonov to attend him the previous night had proved the most fortuitous thing that had happened lately, and she still could not quite believe her luck.

Misha Latanya had been kidnapped—and hopefully killed—by the Baenlanders.

In a thousand years, she could not have thought of a more fitting way to dispose of the elder prince. It left her totally blameless, totally free of guilt. She even spared the poor young man a moment's sympathy, thinking it was such an unfortunate fate to befall someone whose greatest sin was getting in her way.

That the young woman who had apparently kidnapped Misha from the Hospice fit the description of the recently escaped and still missing Tia Veran, just made it all the more deliciously ironic. The look on Kirshov's face when he had heard the news was priceless. The younger prince obviously blamed himself for his brother's plight. He was, after all, the one responsible for letting her escape.

Dirk Provin's reaction was harder to fathom. He had listened to Barin's report with no visible reaction. That could have been simply because he was hearing it for the second time. Or there might have been a more sinister reason.

The boy was uncomfortably hard to read. She made a mental note to herself to spend more time with him in the future. She did not know Dirk nearly well enough; could not tell when he was lying—or even when he was joking—much of the time. Belagren's strength lay in her ability to read people, and not being able to work out what was going on behind those cold gray eyes was a dangerous inadequacy.

Still, knowing that Misha was out of the way had been the most welcome news she'd had since learning that Dirk Provin

had decided to join her and give her back the Voice of the Goddess.

Antonov was furious, of course. Belagren suspected his
anger was driven as much by the thought that the Baenlanders
had the audacity to kidnap his son as it was by actual fear for the
young man. It was the insult that enraged him, not the act itself.
Deep down, Belagren knew, Antonov Latanya would not
grieve his eldest son long if he found out he was dead. But he
would tear the world apart because someone had the temerity to
take something of his without asking.

Belagren walked to the window of the rooms kept for her
here in the palace, wondering what time it was. The red sun
was still shining, and there was no hint yet of the second sun rising, but it felt close to morning. She was tired, but although she
had not slept yet, she was too wound up to seek her bed.

What a strange few months it's been, she mused.

After years of worrying, everything was finally falling into
place. They were through that damn Labyrinth, and Rudi had
sent her a letter last week assuring her that the first section of
the wall they had been assiduously copying down was almost
complete. As soon as he had arranged for the notes to be copied
a second time—she was not foolish enough to leave the only
copy in Dirk's hands—he would dispatch them to Avacas, and
Dirk could finally get to work on them.

Better yet, there was an eclipse coming. She still did not
have the details, but that was something she intended to do
something about this morning. Dirk had prevaricated long
enough. She had given him everything he wanted. It was time
for him to give something in return.

In fact, she thought, *the timing couldn't be better for an
eclipse.* Antonov would appreciate a sign from the Goddess
right now. A little taste of the shadows would go a long way to
reminding him who it was who spoke with the Voice of the
Goddess. *And all I need now is for that idiot Paige Halyn to die,
and have Madalan appointed Lady of the Suns, and everything will
be perfect.*

The first thing she intended to have Madalan do in her new
role was disband the last remnants of the Sundancers. While he

496   Jennifer Fallon

was gloating over how he had foiled her ambition, Paige Halyn
had reminded her of a fact she had overlooked in her haste to
secure the position of her Shadowdancers. There were still a lot
of Sundancers out there, and many of them were well-respected
members of the communities they served. They needed to be
taken out and replaced by her people. Within a few years, nobody would even remember what a Sundancer was.

Perhaps I'll make it easier to become a Shadowdancer, she
thought. *I could ease up on the requirements a little, even welcome
some Dhevynians into the fold.*

The experiment with Marqel had not been a complete disaster. In fact, the girl had been positively helpful these past few
weeks. Dirk Provin had asked for her assistance, which had
made Belagren a little suspicious, until she realized how much
he enjoyed tormenting the poor girl. He was exacting his own
revenge on Marqel the Magnificent for accusing him of rape.

That boy had a streak of sadism in him that she had not
previously suspected.

I wonder if he's sleeping with her? she thought. He might be,
these days, just to remind Marqel who was the master and who
was the servant. Or he might not be—smart enough not to give
the young Shadowdancer a chance to use her considerable talents in the bedroom to gain the upper hand.

Kirsh was still besotted by Marqel, but he was being very
cautious while Alenor was ill. Perhaps he even felt a little
guilty? Men were strange like that, sometimes—blaming themselves for things they had nothing to do with, and refusing to
take responsibility for things that were blatantly their fault.

The lingering suspicion that Alenor's miscarriage was not an
accident was fading from everyone's mind, mostly because nobody could think of a plausible reason why the Queen of Dhevyn
would deliberately abort her own child. She was obviously shattered by the loss, as was Kirsh, who had been morose and moody
ever since it happened. Yuri had warned Belagren that Alenor
might not be able to have any other children, but he did not know
for certain, so she was prepared to hope for the best.

All in all, she concluded, things were going quite well.

A knock at her door surprised her at this early hour. She opened the door herself, to find Marqel standing outside.

"Have you any idea of the time, girl?"

"I need to speak to you, my lady."

"And it can't wait until after second sunrise?"

"It's about Dirk."

Belagren stood back and let her enter. She closed the door and then turned to look at Marqel suspiciously.

"What's the matter?"

Marqel looked down, almost embarrassed. "He's been making...advances toward me."

Belagren snorted in exasperation. "So?"

"But I'm with Kirsh..."

"You're *with* whoever I tell you you're with, Marqel. If Dirk Provin wants you, he can have you."

"Kirshov loves me."

"That's his problem. In fact," she added, "if anything, it might even be time for you to move on. This business with Alenor makes it very awkward for Kirsh to be seen as anything other than a doting husband, especially while he and Alenor are still here in Avacas."

"But Dirk Provin? He hates me, my lady," she insisted. "He's only doing this to persecute me. Why do you let him?"

"Dirk Provin can dip you in custard and serve you up at the High Table for dessert, for all I care, Marqel. My only concern is that he gives me what he's promised, and if he wants to amuse himself by tormenting you, then that's a price I'm quite willing to pay."

The young Shadowdancer scowled for a moment and then lowered her eyes submissively. "I'm sorry, my lady. I shouldn't have questioned your wisdom."

"No, you shouldn't have," Belagren agreed grumpily. She had ruined Belagren's good mood with her whining.

"Would you like some tea, my lady?" Marqel offered, no doubt wishing to ingratiate herself back into Belagren's favor.

"Yes, I would," the High Priestess decided.

"I'll make it myself," Marqel offered, with a small curtsy. Belagren stepped away from the door, and Marqel hurried from the room to fetch her tea. The High Priestess wandered back to the window. The first faint hint of yellow was beginning to lighten the red sky in the east.

She smiled to herself, thinking that at least now she knew the answer to the question about Dirk's intentions toward Marqel. He really was a sadistic little bastard, wasn't he? She would have to bear that in mind when dealing with him. Still, she was not worried about Marqel. The girl had been a whore before Belagren took her off the streets of Elcast. She had probably dealt with far worse in her rather sordid career than Dirk Provin's mild attempts to humiliate her. In fact, Marqel was coming along quite nicely, after a few minor hiccups. She might prove very useful in the years to come.

A little while later, the door opened again and Marqel let herself in, awkwardly balancing a tray in one hand. She walked across the room and placed the tray on the desk near the window.

The cup was steaming and smelled faintly of peppermint.

"Will that be all, my lady?"

"Yes, Marqel. You may go."

"Don't let it go cold," Marqel warned.

"I won't."

Marqel curtsied with suitable respect and let herself out. Belagren picked up the cup and sipped the tea appreciatively, turning to watch the second sun rise as she did each morning.

There it was, right on cue. Right where it should be.

Yes, she thought contentedly, taking another sip of Marqel's peppermint tea. *All in all, things are really going rather well.*

Chapter 88

Marqel was waiting for the Lion of Senet as the second sun rose. He always started his day with a prayer to the Goddess, so she waited for him in his private temple in the palace gardens. She and Dirk had spent hours going over what she would say, and how she would say it, although she found herself quite annoyed by his assumption that she was too witless to figure out for herself how this should be handled.

Dirk did, however, know the Lion of Senet far better than she, and she had to admit that he seemed to have thought of everything, so, in the end, she let him instruct her, promising herself that she would do as he asked unless, of course, she came up with a better idea.

As soon as Marqel heard the footsteps on the gravel outside the small temple she fell to her knees in front of the altar and bowed her head in prayer. Her hair was disheveled, and she looked as if she had been up all night (which she had). She let her eyes fill with tears as she waited, kneeling in front of the two beaten gold suns of Ranadon, with her back to the entrance, quietly sobbing. She heard his boots on the polished schist floor. Heard him stop behind her when he realized somebody had invaded his sanctuary.

"This is my private temple," Antonov said.

Marqel did not answer him, nor give any indication that she had heard him speak.

"Did you hear me?"

She looked up slowly, her face streaked with tears, as if she had only just become aware that she was no longer alone. Antonov's face creased with concern when he saw her obvious distress.

"Is something wrong?"

She shook her head wordlessly, too distraught to speak.

"Are you unwell?"

"She...She...spoke to me," Marqel whispered brokenly.

The Lion of Senet walked across the temple and squatted down beside her. "Who spoke to you?" He sounded impatient.

"*She* spoke to me!"

He looked at her for a moment, his irritation slowly replaced by awe. "The *Goddess* spoke to you?"

"She called...to me," Marqel sobbed, with heartbreaking sincerity. "I was sleeping...and the Goddess called me in my dreams. She told me to come here..." With convincing desperation, Marqel clutched at Antonov's arm. "I'm so frightened..."

"There's nothing to be frightened of, child," he said, patting her hand. "If this is true, then you've been greatly honored."

"She ... She told me things ..."

"What did she tell you?"

"She said something about your son ..."

"Kirshov?"

Marqel sniffed, mostly to cover up her smile. Dirk was right. Antonov Latanya could be so predictable at times. She shook her head. "Prince Misha. She said he'd been taken ..."

"Did she say where?"

Marqel shrugged. "I'm not sure. I don't really understand what she told me. It was something to do with sailing. Something about finding a river ... She said it was spoken ..."

"Spoken? You mean the Spakan River?" Antonov sat back on his heels and stared at her. "You expect me to believe that the Goddess told you how to find the entrance to the Spakan River through the delta?"

"I don't know," she sobbed desperately. "I only know that she wanted me to tell you things ... that she said ..." Marqel let her voice trail off, as if she could not bring herself to say the rest of it. This was the part of the plan she had modified to suit herself. She was not going to wait for Dirk's scheme to come to fruition. She wanted to be High Priestess. And she wanted it now.

"She said that Belagren had let her down ... that I was to take her place ..."

Antonov was understandably suspicious. "Did she now?"

"Please help me, your highness," she begged. "I'm not worthy to be chosen by the Goddess ..."

"I wouldn't have thought you were either," he remarked, which was not a good sign. Antonov *had* to believe her, and it was patently obvious that he didn't.

"Can we ask the High Priestess what to do?" she suggested, wiping her tears away with the back of her hand. "I'm sure she'll know ..."

Antonov nodded. "I think that would be a very good idea."

He rose to his feet and walked to the entrance, issued an order to fetch the High Priestess to one of the guards outside, then returned to where Marqel was kneeling on the floor. He held his hand out to her, and when she accepted it, he helped her to her feet.

Marqel did not let go of his hand. She turned it over and kissed the sword calluses on his palm, then looked up at him through lashes glistening with crystal tears. "The Goddess said something else, too..."

"What else did she say?" He still sounded far too skeptical.

"She said...the High Priestess is her voice...and that you are her sword arm."

Antonov nodded. That fitted perfectly with what he believed, so she was on fairly safe ground.

"She said the two should always be as one..."

"The two are as one, Marqel," he reminded her.

She shook her head. "She said that you had wandered from her embrace."

"The Goddess thinks *I* have failed her?" he asked in surprise. "How?"

"I don't know," Marqel replied, deciding a fresh round of tears was in order. She didn't want to cry too much or she would get all blotchy and look as ugly as sin. "I only know she told me your faith needed to be renewed, and that she would send you a sign, so that you'd know I speak the truth. And I *do* speak the truth, your highness," she cried. "I *swear* I do...I don't know why she chose me. I didn't want her to...Do you think the High Priestess will be able to make things right?"

Antonov put a comforting arm around her shoulder, uncertain as to exactly how to deal with her. "I'm sure she will, Marqel."

She turned into his embrace and threw her arms around him. "I'm so scared, your highness," she sobbed into his shoulder.

Antonov hesitated for a moment before he put his arms around her. It didn't matter that he was just trying to comfort her. Marqel was very good at this. She could easily turn the embrace into something far more intimate, anytime she wanted to. She just was not ready yet.

"What did she tell you about the delta?" Antonov asked,

after holding her for a little longer than was appropriate for a man merely trying to comfort a distressed young woman.

Marqel stepped out of his embrace first, so that she would appear the innocent party. She closed her eyes and gave the impression she was concentrating, trying to remember the details.

"She said, 'The way forward is hidden in the shallows. By the long shadows of the second sun, you must sail to the first marker . . . and hold to that course until the way is obscured by the banks of the broken island . . .'" She opened her eyes and looked up at him, uncertainly. "There's more, but it doesn't make much sense to me."

"That's all right, Marqel," he assured her. "Just try to remember everything she told you."

Marqel closed her eyes again. The instructions Dirk had made her memorize were couched in flowery language to make them seem obscure. It would have been much simpler if he had just made her learn "this many degrees to port, that many degrees to starboard," but even Marqel understood how unlikely it was that the Goddess would be so precise.

"'In the lee of the broken island,'" she continued, "'you must turn your back on the second sun . . .'"

"Your highness?"

"What?" Antonov barked, annoyed by the interruption.

Marqel opened her eyes and looked at the guard who had disturbed them. The expression on his face told her everything she needed to know.

"The High Priestess . . ."

"Where is she?" Antonov demanded.

"I think you'd better return to the palace, sire," the guard advised. The man looked as if he wanted to run like a frightened rabbit.

"I sent for the High Priestess. I don't expect to be summoned to attend her."

"I delivered your summons, sire," the guard explained. "But there was some trouble rousing the High Priestess, so I asked one of the servants to wake her."

"And the problem is?" Antonov prompted impatiently.

"She couldn't be roused, your highness."

The Lion of Senet looked stunned for a fraction of a second, before he reacted. "Watch *her*!" he ordered, pointing at Marqel, and then he strode from the temple without another word, heading back to the palace.

Marqel watched him leave, and then she turned to the man assigned to guard her. "Is she dead?" she asked him.

The guard nodded wordlessly.

Marqel smiled. "It must be a sign from the Goddess," she said.

Chapter 89

Dirk waited for the second sunrise in his room, too tense to seek his bed. The thought that all his hopes and aspirations resided in the untrustworthy hands of Marqel the Magnificent made it impossible to sleep.

He was under no illusions about the risk he was taking by involving Marqel. The problem was, he had little choice in the matter. Of all the people he had access to, the most willing to follow him was the one person he was certain was driven solely by greed and ambition. Marqel had no morals that he could find, no qualms about doing anything required to secure her future, up to and including murder.

Her usefulness was the only reason she still lived. Marqel had no inkling of how close he had come to strangling her the other evening, when she so foolishly tried to seduce him again. He still could not quite believe she had done it. Each time he looked at the Shadowdancer, he remembered Alenor, perched on the brink of death because Marqel didn't like the competition from a child that hadn't even been born yet.

Setting her on to Antonov was more than just revenge, Dirk mused, *it was poetic justice.*

Kirsh would be shattered when Marqel spurned him in favor of his father, but it was about time he faced the truth about his lover. He had been spoiled all his life, allowed to believe anything he wanted was there for the taking. Dirk did not mind a bit that the lesson Kirsh was about to learn was probably going to break his heart. He had broken Alenor's heart without giving it a thought. It was time he got a taste of his own medicine.

Dirk glanced down at the gardens. He could just see the path to Antonov's private temple from his room, but there was no sign of either Marqel or Antonov yet.

"Don't you dare be late, Marqel," he muttered under his breath.

He glanced up at the sky, but it was not quite time for the second sun to show itself. He wondered for a moment what Tia was doing. Was she sleeping soundly, safe in Mil? Or was she awake at this early hour, plotting his demise?

Had she really kidnapped Misha?

Dirk had been relieved beyond words to learn that she had escaped from Senet, but it was all he could do not to laugh out loud when Barin Welacin told him what she had done. The thought still brought a smile to his face. Only Tia would do something so unexpected, so impulsive. What had driven her to do such a thing? Revenge, perhaps? And how had she managed to spirit Misha out of the Hospice in Tolace without being noticed? Surely somebody saw something? Why didn't Misha raise the alarm? Kirsh was furious with him, of course assuming that Dirk had somehow known in advance what she intended.

Dirk sighed heavily. Another friendship irreparably damaged; another casualty in his reckless plan. By the time he was done, he would be the loneliest conqueror in the universe.

Dirk made a conscious effort not to count the casualties of what he was doing. It had already cost him the trust and friendship of everyone he knew in Mil. If he was not careful, it might end up costing him his life.

Dirk had tried very hard not to think about the people in Mil these past few weeks. He could guess what they must be thinking, and knew that they probably wanted to kill him. Well, he had nobody but himself to blame for that. He could have told Tia what he was doing. For that matter, he probably should have. But he could not explain it—not to Tia, not to any-body. Even if his plan worked, he doubted anyone would think him a hero. Heroes did noble deeds against incredible odds. They did not manipulate, lie and use people to get their way. A hero's stock in trade was his stout heart and noble cause, not his ability to prey on the fears and weaknesses of his foes.

On the bright side, he told himself wryly, *if this doesn't work, then I'll just go down in history as the worst traitor who ever lived, and nobody will be any the wiser.*

But so much was riding on Marqel, and Dirk didn't trust her. *I'm as crazy as Neris,* he decided. *I was crazy to even listen to Neris.*

He caught sight of a movement on the path to the temple, and was relieved to find Marqel slipping into the temple as he had instructed her to. *Will she get it right? Will she remember what I told her? Will she do it properly?* His uncertainty ate away at his confidence. What had seemed foolproof a few weeks ago now seemed fraught with danger.

He thought about Tia again, deliberately punishing him-self with the memory. *Perhaps I should I have told her.* Maybe, even now, it was not too late. Against his advice, Alexin was still here in Avacas. He could get a message to Mil through the cap-tain, tell them what he was doing, and ask them to believe in him ...

He smiled ruefully. It was far too late for anything so fool-ish. If he was going to take the Baenlanders into his confidence, he should have said something to them back on Grannon Rock. He could have mentioned it back in Mil ...

He knew he had made a mistake sleeping with Tia. How big a mistake hadn't really hit him, until that morning just be-fore Belagren arrived when she asked: "Do you love me, Dirk?" It was at that moment that the full impact of his stupidity came crashing down on him. He didn't love her; he *could not* love anyone until he finished what he had set out to do. It was a humbling moment for Dirk. Until then, he had been thinking himself smarter than everyone else. Tia had brought him plum-meting down to the ground with the realization that, when it came to dealing with women, he was a nineteen-year-old boy with little practical experience and a great deal to learn before he could even begin to understand them.

He wondered what Neris would think about this. In the two years Dirk had stayed in Mil, they had debated countless issues over the chessboard, and none more vigorously than what it would take to bring down the Lion of Senet and the Church of the Suns. Sometimes Tia had interrupted them, but Neris had sent her away with a scowl, telling her that they were busy solving all the world's problems. Tia would then wait outside Neris's cave for him, demanding to know what they were talking about. She was always suspicious, always suspecting Dirk of keeping things from her.

What would you have done if I told you what I knew, Tia? he asked her silently. He smiled, ruefully rubbing the shoulder that was still stiff and sore from her arrow. He knew the answer to that question. He had the scar to prove it.

But what about Neris? Would he understand what was happening? And if he did, would he give the game away? Dirk suspected he would not, simply because he had enjoyed the fact that he was the only one in Mil clever enough to work out what was going on.

Dirk needed the Baenlanders to believe he had betrayed them. The slightest hope that he had not and they would react differently. They might not evacuate Mil. Tia would certainly not have kidnapped Misha Latanya...

Dirk hadn't planned on that happening, but Tia couldn't have done anything to help his cause more if he had actually asked her to do it. It was always going to be a problem making Antonov believe that the Goddess had suddenly decided to show Marqel the way through the delta, but now that Misha had been kidnapped, it made perfect sense. The Goddess would be responding to a specific need, not just acting on a whim.

And now, if only Marqel can deliver the information convincingly...

He looked down at the path again. Antonov, accompanied by a small escort, was striding toward the temple. Dirk's stomach clenched with apprehension. He had no way of knowing if Marqel would do as he had instructed.

He waited, as Antonov disappeared into the temple, unconsciously holding his breath. Was Marqel convincing Antonov she was the Voice of the Goddess—or betraying Dirk as he stood here and waited?

He would not know, he guessed, until Belagren came roaring into his room, ready to murder him, when she realized what he had done.

A piece at a time, Dirk reminded himself. *If you're going to dismantle something, you need to take it apart a piece at a time.*

And the first step was to splinter the unholy alliance between Antonov and Belagren.

After a time, Dirk noticed a guard hurrying away from the temple, heading back toward the palace. *Antonov sending for the High Priestess,* he guessed. *Or sending someone to arrest me.*

He waited awhile longer, heard a ruckus in the hall outside his room, then a short time later watched the guard hurry back to the temple.

Belagren was not with him. Puzzled, he waited for a little longer, and then saw Antonov leave the temple, heading back to the palace at a run. *What have you done, Marqel?* Dirk doubted she had betrayed him. Antonov would dispatch a guard detail to arrest him, not run back to the palace to do it himself. Something else had happened, something Dirk had not anticipated.

And there was nothing he could do but wait...

So he waited. And wondered if he could really get away with it. Dirk's only currency was information. He had no armies at his beck and call, no resources, other than his own intelligence and determination to destroy something he considered inherently evil. That he must become an integral part of that evil in order to destroy it was something he knew he could never make Tia understand. She would rather die than embrace the enemy's cause.

Dirk preferred to live. And if he was going to live, then he wanted to live in a world of his own making.

It really was as simple as that.

CHARACTER LIST

ALENOR D'ORLON—Princess of Dhevyn. Heir to the throne. Rainan's daughter.

ALEXIN SERANOV—Second son of the current Duke of Grannon Rock. Reithan's cousin.

ANALEE LATANYA—Deceased. Princess of Damita. Wife of Antonov. Mother of Misha, Kirshov and Gunta.

ANTONOV LATANYA—The Lion of Senet. Father of Misha, Kirshov and Gunta. Husband of Analee of Damita.

BALONAN—Seneschal of Elcast castle.

BARIN WELACIN—Prefect of Avacas.

BELAGREN—High Priestess of the Shadowdancers.

BLARENOV—Member of the Brotherhood based in Paislee.

BRAHM HALYN—Sundancer living on Elcast. Brother of Paige Halyn, the Lord of the Suns.

CALLA—Mil's blacksmith.

CASPONA TAKARNOV—Shadowdancer in training with Marqel.

CLEGG—Captain of the *Calliope*.

DAL FALSTOV—Captain of the *Orlando*.

DARGIN OTMAR—Master-at-arms in the Queen's Guard.

DERWN HAURITZ—Butcher's apprentice. Son of Hauritz the Butcher.

DIRK PROVIN—Second son of Duke Wallin of Elcast and Princess Morna of Damita.

DROGAN SERANOV—Deceased. Duke of Grannon Rock until the War of Shadows. Killed fighting with Johan against Senet. Father of Reithan. Husband of Lexie.

ELESKA ARROWSMITH—Baenlander. Daughter of Novin Arrowsmith. Mellie Thorn's best friend.

ELLA GEON—Shadowdancer and physician. Expert in herbs and drugs. Tia's mother.

ERYK—Orphan from Elcast.

FARALAN—Daughter of the Duke of Ionan. Married to Rees Provin of Elcast.

FREDRAK D'ORLON—Deceased. Duke of Bryton. Killed in a hunting accident not long after his wife, Rainan Thorn, assumed the throne of Dhevyn. Alenor's father.

FRENA—Servant in Elcast Castle. The baker Welma's daughter.

GAVEN GREYBROOK—Pirate on Johan's ship. Killed in the tidal wave that hit Elcast.

GUNTA LATANYA—Deceased. Youngest son of Antonov Latanya and Analee of Damita. Sacrificed as a baby to ensure the return of the second sun.

HARI—Pirate captured in Paislee. Sacrificed on Elcast during the Landfall Festival.

HAURITZ—Butcher living in Elcast Town.

HELGIN—Physician and tutor at Elcast.

JACINTA D'ORLON—Alenor's cousin. Daughter of the Duke of Bryton and Lady Sofia.

JOHAN THORN—Pirate. Exiled King of Dhevyn.

KALLEEN—Leader of Kalleen's acrobat troupe.

KIRSHOV LATANYA—Second son of the Prince of Senet.

LANATYNE—Member of Kalleen's acrobats.

LANON RILL—Second son of Tovin Rill, Governor of Elcast.

LEXIE SERANOV THORN—Wife of Johan Thorn. First husband was the Duke of Grannon Rock. Mother of Reithan Seranov and Mellie Thorn.

LILA BAYSTOKE—Herb woman from Elcast.

LILE DROGANOV—Pirate based in Mil.

LINEL—Pirate captured in Paislee. Sacrificed on Elcast during the Landfall Festival.

MADALAN TIROV—Shadowdancer and aide to the High Priestess Belagren.

MARQEL—Also known as Marqel the Magnificent. Landfall bastard. Performed as an acrobat in Kalleen's troupe until she was taken into the Shadowdancers.

MASTER KEDRON—Elcast master-at-arms.

MELLIE THORN—Daughter of Johan Thorn and Lexie Seranov.

MISHA LATANYA—Eldest son of Antonov, the Lion of Senet. Also known as the Crippled Prince.

MORNA PROVIN—Duchess of Elcast. Princess of Damita. Daughter of Prince Oscon. Sister of Analee. Married to Wallin Provin. Mother of Rees and Dirk.

MURRY—Member of Mistress Kalleen's acrobats.

NERIS VERAN—Sundancer and mathematical genius. Believed to be dead.

NOVIN ARROWSMITH—Pirate living in Mil.

OLENA BORNE—Shadowdancer attached to Prince Antonov's court.

OSCON—Exiled ruler of Damita. Father of Analee and Morna.

PAIGE HALYN—Lord of the Suns.

PARON SHOEBROOK—Cobbler's son on Elcast.

PELLA—Baker in Mil.

PORL ISINGRIN—Pirate. Captain of the *Makuan*. Based in Mil.

RAINAN D'ORLON—Née Thorn. Queen of Dhevyn. Mother of Alenor. Johan Thorn's younger sister.

REES PROVIN—The Duke of Elcast. Eldest son of Wallin Provin. Dirk's brother.

REZO—Sailor on the *Calliope*.

ROVE ELAN—Lord Marshal of Dhevyn.

REITHAN SERANOV—Son of the late Duke of Grannon Rock and Lexie Seranov. Johan's stepson.

SABAN SERANOV—Duke of Grannon Rock. Father of Alexin and Raban.

SERGEY—Captain of the Avacas Palace Guard in Senet.

SOOTER—Member of Mistress Kalleen's acrobats.

TABOR ISINGRIN—Son of Porl Isingrin.

TIA VERAN—Daughter of Neris Veran and Ella Geon.

TOVIN RILL—Governor of Elcast.

VARIAN—Nurse to the sons of Elcast.

VIDEON LUKANOV—Head of the Brotherhood in Dhevyn.

VONRIL—Juggler. Son of Kalleen.

WALLIN PROVIN—Deceased. Duke of Elcast.

WELMA—The master baker at Elcast Castle.

WILIM—Officer in the Queen's Guard.

YORNE—Apprentice baker. Welma's son.

YURI DARANSKI—Physician in the palace at Avacas.

ABOUT THE AUTHOR

JENNIFER FALLON lives in Alice Springs, works in Melbourne and writes anywhere she can get her hands on a computer. She works in sales, marketing and training in the IT industry and changes jobs so often that even she isn't sure where she works these days.

Read the explosive conclusion to the
Second Sons Trilogy,

LORD OF THE SHADOWS

available June 1, 2004,
wherever Bantam Books are sold.

Darkness threatens Ranadon again in the form of an eclipse.
The Goddess wants to give the people of Ranadon a sign—and
only Dirk Provin can interpret it.

To do so, Dirk has systematically betrayed his one-time allies to
join his most hated enemies. Now, with neither side trusting
him, Dirk sets his own devious plot in motion.

Also living in danger is Senet's Crippled Prince, Misha, who
has found unexpected and tenuous sanctuary among the
Baenlanders of Mil. To secure their trust, he offers them the
one thing they can not refuse. Meanwhile, Alenor, Queen
of Dhevyn, betrayed by her husband, Kirsh, and Tia
Veran, deceived by Dirk, set out for revenge and to finally
free their people at any cost.

As the second sons and the rest of their generation pursue
different paths to survival and freedom, they discover that the
will of the Goddess—and of men—works in mysterious ways.
And as Dirk's old enemies join with new ones, his attempt to
save Ranadon may cost him his friends, his love . . . and his life.